MALAYATOOR RAMAKRISHNAN (1927–1997) started his career as an advocate and worked as a sub-editor in *The Free Press Journal* in Mumbai before joining the Indian Administrative Service (IAS) in 1957. Malayatoor wrote a semi-autobiographical work *Verukal* (Roots), which won him the Kerala Sahitya Akademi award. In 1981, he resigned from the IAS to devote himself to writing. From 1981 to 1997, he wrote his other famous novels including *Yakshi*, *Yanthram*, *Nettoor Mathom* and *Amritham Thedi*, besides short stories and scripts for several films. For some years, he was chairman of the Kerala Lalit Kala Akademi.

PREMA JAYAKUMAR
Born in Kerala, she studied in Kochi and Bangalore. She does translations from Malayalam into English and writes for periodicals. Her translated works include *Yakshi* and *Doorways to Death* (*Mrithiyude Kavadam*) by the same author among many by well-known Malayalam authors. Her works have been published by Penguin and the Sahitya Akademi. She has retold the Ramayana, the Mahabharata and other stories from the Puranas for Mango Books and Real Reads of the UK. Married, with one son, she stays mostly at Kochi, but loves to travel.

Set in the 1970s and 1980s, this novel traces the story of the young uruli thief, Vedaraman. When the head constable takes his fingerprints, he realizes that the boy has six fingers on his left hand. Shamed by his involvement in the theft case and the whispered scandal about him and the maid Kozhukatta Paru who had both breastfed him and slept with him, Vedaraman leaves home and village. Adrift in the wide world, he meets a series of well-wishers who not only help him in deepening his knowledge, but also expose him to the realities of life. He finds that his sixth finger glows by itself and he possesses supernatural powers of predicting future events. Ministers and businessmen are quick to recognize his yogic qualities. Vedaraman becomes Vedanji and then Vedan Baba with a godlike aura, and is installed in an ashram. Amidst this fame and glory, Vedan Baba finds himself a prisoner of a web of machinations. Will he be able to break the shackles and become a free man again?

RATNA TRANSLATION SERIES

THE SIXTH FINGER

A NOVEL

MALAYATOOR RAMAKRISHNAN

TRANSLATED FROM MALAYALAM BY
PREMA JAYAKUMAR

RATNA BOOKS

Originally published in Malayalam by DC Books in July 1994
Original Malayalam copyright © Malayatoor Ramakrishnan 1994

First published in English translation 2017
English translation copyright © Prema Jayakumar 2017

ISBN   978-93-5290-748-9 (POD)

Published by RATNA BOOKS
An imprint of Ratna Sagar P. Ltd.
Virat Bhavan, Mukherjee Nagar Commercial Complex
Delhi 110009, India
www.ratnabooks.in

One

When fifteen-year-old Vedaraman was arrested for stealing an uruli, a bronze vessel, people in the town and the villages that surrounded it were shocked. He was a scion of the Mulamkunnam tharavad. The members of the tharavad were scattered all over. But people had not completely forgotten the old days. They could not forget the old Mulamkunnam Yajamanans or lords who were powerful people. The family had traditions that went back centuries, coloured by history and legend.

The tharavad itself had come to grief years back. The elephant is dead, all that is left is the tooth of the elephant. Mulamkunnam glory was also something like that. But the local people still held on to their memories.

It was the son of that famous tharavad who had stolen the bronze vessel. And not just any uruli, but one belonging to the temple – the property of Lord Narasimha whose temple it was.

The temple had been repaired eighty years ago. That was organized and mostly paid for by the eldest of the Mulamkunnam tharavad – Kelu Menon, otherwise known as Kelu Yajamanan.

And now…

Vedaraman stood with his head bent in the dock. The trial went on. The prosecution witnesses gave their evidence.

Even as he took down the evidence, the Magistrate, Mr Mathews muttered to himself, 'Unbelievable, absolutely unbelievable.'

Even Mathews from Pala had heard about the old glory of the Mulamkunnam house. Mathews did not mean that the evidence given by the witnesses was unbelievable. What he meant was that he could not make himself believe that a youngster from the Mulamkunnam family would do such a thing, and that made the whole incident unbelievable.

Vedaraman was not represented by an advocate. He did not ask any questions of the prosecution witnesses either. In short, there was no cross-examination at all. Magistrate Mathews did ask some questions on behalf of Vedaraman, but the witnesses stood by their evidence.

No one had seen Vedaraman remove the vessel from the temple. The prosecution admitted that. But Krishnan Namboodiri had recognized the vessel as belonging to the temple. The vessel had been recovered from the arrack shop of Vengola Ittaman. It was the accused Vedaraman who had pointed out the vessel to the police. Ittaman said that the vessel had been pledged for fifty rupees. The accused and someone else with him, whose name he did not remember, had spent the money in the arrack shop itself.

Head Constable Thankappan Pillai who laid out the evidence argued with the skill of an experienced public prosecutor: 'Your Honour, the evidence is complete and obvious. If an accused admits the crime and that leads to the recovery of the stolen items, that statement is admissible according to the "Evidence Act", Your Honour.'

The crime was proven.

But, Magistrate Mathews showed compassion. 'Yes, Mr Prosecutor, the crime is proven. Vedaraman is guilty and he is convicted. But I'm not sending him to jail. He is not sentenced. He is a young man. This is his first offence. The court believes that he will not repeat this. If you sentence a young man who has committed his first offence to a jail sentence, someone who has a chance to be a good citizen might become a criminal. That should not happen. Therefore, the court sets Vedaraman free, with a warning.'

Vedaraman who stood in the box, bowed with folded hands before the Magistrate.

❖

Head Constable Thankappan Pillai brought Vedaraman out of the court room to take his fingerprints. That was when Thankappan Pillai realized that Vedaraman had six fingers on his left hand. There were six fingers on the left hand and five on the right.

Thankappan Pillai did not take the impression of the appendage that had attached itself to the left hand and hung there as if it was wondering whether to go away or continue there. As in all other cases, Thankappan Pillai took ten fingerprints.

Vedaraman bowed before Thankappan Pillai. Wasn't he as good a man as the Magistrate, or even better? Vedaraman had not been beaten up in police custody. And when that Constable Moosa had tried to act funny with him, it was Head Constable Thankappan Pillai who had saved him.

Vedaraman came out. The court had a big yard. There were birds in the big trees that spread shade in the yard. Beyond, lay the vendor office where stamp paper was sold and document writers sat.

If he went down the incline, he would reach the main street of the town. He was hungry and did not have any money. What if he went home directly?

What home! What family! His father Sreedhara Menon had not come even once to enquire about this case – he did not try to get him out on bail. Besides, suppose that incident was repeated if he went home? Would Kozhukatta Paru cause mischief?

Vedaraman felt someone touch him. He turned around to look. It was Mukundan, the son of Sanku Warrier who made garlands for the temple. The friend who had sat in Vengola Ittaman's arrack shop and drunk with him.

Where had he been all these days? The ditcher!

No, he would not show his anger. What was the point?!

He was hungry. That was the immediate problem. Would there be money in Mukundan's pocket? If so, they could go to some hotel. The worst hotel would do. He needed to eat something.

Mukundan said with a big smile, 'I'm so relieved.'

'Why relieved?' Vedaraman wrinkled his brow.

'The court set you free. So.'

'Mukundan, I am a thief in the court records! They took my fingerprints as well. They didn't take the print of this sixth one that hangs.'

'What do you plan to do now?' Mukundan asked.

'Plan now? Let's talk of just now. I'm hungry.'

'Come, we'll find a way.'

They walked to the Potty Hotel opposite the cinema theatre.

Good smells rose. The table swayed on its legs. There were benches on either side. The dark boy with a sandalwood mark on his forehead brought dented bell metal tumblers with his dirty fingers dipping into the water they held…He was marking the start to serving the meal.

'The immediate problem has been solved. What do you plan to do now?' Mukundan asked.

As he stuffed himself with rice as fast as he could, Vedaraman replied, 'I don't know. You tell me. You're the respectable person. The police could have caught you as well. Why didn't they come after you?'

'Because you did not give them my name.'

'That's it. I did not betray you. So, you did understand that, did you?' Vedaraman's voice was rising.

'Are you angry with me, Raman?'

'Che!'

'You think I didn't come to enquire after you all these days.'

'My father didn't come! Why would you?'

'Raman, I used to enquire about you every day. How else would I be waiting for you as you came out today?'

Vedaraman bit the piece of mango pickle and put the last ball of rice into his mouth.

Mukundan said, 'Don't forget, I'm your elder brother. I'll

complete eighteen this April.'

They washed their hands.

Vedaraman got out on to the street first, muttering to himself. 'A brother! Crowther!'

Did he have cash? Or would the Tulu Potty harness the Warrier boy who made garlands to his grinding stone to make dough for the next day's idlies?

'Now?' Mukundan asked.

'Now? I don't know!'

'All right, let's walk for the time being.'

'Walk where?' Vedaraman asked.

'There are lots of paths around us, we'll walk down one of them.'

They walked. When they turned a corner they saw the yellow flowers of the Konna tree. Vishu, the Malayalam new year and the birthday in April were getting closer.

They walked further.

Vedaraman realized that they were going towards the arrack shop, Vengola Ittaman's arrack shop.

'Should we, Mukundan?'

'I want some. Not now, but in the evening. We'll get a bottle and go...'

'Money?'

'I have money,' Mukundan said.

'How much money do you have?'

'Why do you want to know?'

They had reached the shop by now. Mukundan bought a bottle of arrack and some crisp eatables.

'Back home, now?' Mukundan asked.

'And do what?'

'Don't you want to see Kozhukatta Paru?'

Vedaraman did not reply.

Mukundan would not let him go. He asked again, 'What's between you and Paru?'

Vedaraman did not reply to that either.

'And between your father and Paru?'

Vedaraman was now angry, 'Don't ask me stupid questions and trouble me, Mukundan.'

'All right, I won't ask you anything. You can tell me when you feel like it.'

After a while, Vedaraman asked, 'Shall we go to Vattolikavu?'

'Why on earth?'

'We can sleep under the trees. Or look at the monkeys.'

They reached the grove of trees at Vattolikavu and lay down under the trees. They did not see any monkeys. After a while, Mukundan got fed up. He touched the bottle and asked, 'Shall we have a go?'

'There's no water.'

'Never mind! Have just a little.'

They drank a little straight from the bottle. Vedaraman felt that his intestines were burning. He opened the bundle of eats and took a bite.

Three or four monkeys jumped down from the trees when they saw something to eat.

'Pha!' Mukundan tried to drive them away.

They did not turn back. They bared their teeth and came towards them as though to attack. Vedaraman threw a piece of the murukku far off. The monkeys ran after it.

Mukundan said, 'Why don't we go now? If we walk fast we can reach the village before dark.'

'And after reaching the village?'

'We'll lie flat on the sand by the river. Drink a little. Have a bath in the river.'

'And then?'

'We'll decide about that then.'

Two

It was dark by the time they reached the village. They saw people on the way, but none of them paid them any attention. They went down the grass-covered incline and reached the sandy banks of the river.

They walked to the edge of the river. Vedaraman recognized Unneera as he came out of the river after bathing his buffaloes.

'Mukundan, let us get out of the way; don't let Unneera see us.'

They walked a short distance on the edge of the river. A crescent moon shone from the sky.

'Shall we sit here?' Vedaraman pointed to the big granite structure some elder of the Mulamkunnam family had built so that people could wash their clothes there.

They sat there and drank.

They would sip a little from the bottle, then dip their hands in the river and drink a mouthful of water. And so, it went.

'Enough,' Vedaraman said.

An old memory rose clearly in his mind. It was an evening like this. He had come here for a bath. A dog that had been beaten to death had got caught in the granite structure. One could not call it a dog, more the skeleton of a dog. The skull was still caught in a knot of a rope. The back was a mass of festering flesh. Vedaraman had kicked that skeleton into the river. A shoal of fish followed it.

He felt like vomiting when he thought of that.

'Enough.'

'What do you mean, enough? A little more...' Mukundan held out the bottle.

'No, I'll throw up if I have any more.'

'Have a little more, Ramankutty. You will need a little strength for when you meet Kozhukatta Paru, wouldn't you?'

'For that, I'll need to go home, don't I?'

Mukundan immediately gave it the worst interpretation. 'Rascal...so, if you do go home...Eh? So, you aren't all that clean. Not white flowers and purity.'

'Don't talk nonsense.'

'Raman, you can tell me if you feel like it. I am born of a good Warrier. So, you can be sure that I do know something of what happened.'

'Stop it, you fool!'

'Don't get mad, Raman. Didn't your father beat you up because you slept with Kozhukatta Paru? Isn't that why you decided to run away? Isn't that why you stole the uruli?'

'Stop it!' Vedaraman grabbed the bottle of arrack and had a small mouthful.

'You are the one who caused the whole problem. I had planned to sell that vessel and catch a train to leave the place. You didn't let me do it, you took me to the arrack shop...'

'Enough! What happened, happened. Nothing much went wrong, did it?'

Vedaraman shouted, 'And you call yourself my elder brother? I was locked up. I had to stay in the sub-jail. I became a thief in the records. I suppose none of these are problems? None of these are things that went wrong? What am I to do now? Where can I go? If my father sees me...'

Mukundan grabbed back the bottle and swallowed a couple of mouthfuls fast. 'Forget about your father! Do you know who really your father is? I know. Or, my father Sanku Warrier knows. If you ask me who my father Sanku Warrier is, I don't know. But your father is not Sreedhara Menon, but a Tamil brahmin, a pattar, who was a singer!'

Mukundan wondered why Vedaraman did not get angry in spite of his talking about the singer pattar a number of times.

'Here!'

'Um?'

'Here, that pattar cast a line at your mother when he came to the temple to pray there. Does any Nair or Menon, one in a lakh of them, have the name Vedaraman? Vedaraman, Vedanarayanan...all these are names that belong to the pattars.'

Vedaraman leaned forward and asked, 'Mukundan, what does it matter to you who my father is?'

Mukundan could not think of an answer immediately.

'Mukundan, my father might be a pattar or a paraya, it could even be that rascal called Sreedhara Menon who beat me up. Forget all that! Let's talk of something else.'

Mukundan sat there, stunned.

'Mukundan, you idiot! Cat got your tongue? Say something.'

'I'll say something. But you won't say anything.'

'What?'

'About Kozhukatta.'

'Oh that! I'll tell you. Kozhukatta came and caught hold of me. My father saw that. He beat me up. Enough?'

'If you ask me if that is enough...If you'd said it a little longer and wider, it would have been fun to hear.'

'Go, get lost. Go make garlands out of flowers.'

'And you...?'

'I'll lie here.'

'Why?'

'Because I feel like it.'

'I'll go!'

'Go, you stupid idiot!'

'And if you feel hungry?'

'I'm not hungry. And...there's plenty of water here to fill my stomach.'

Mukundan got up. 'I'm going.'

'Idiot! Leave that bottle here!'

Vedaraman took another pull at the bottle. And lay flat on his back on the sand.

❖

The crescent moon rose higher. The sky was clear. Vedaraman looked at the stars and emptied the bottle. All sorts of thoughts, wanted and unwanted, entered his mind. Scattered pictures. Dusty memories. One pushed the other aside. A big confusion all together.

Long long ago, that is centuries ago, did this river exist? Did it flow this way? Or was that shore and this shore one at that time?

He started thinking along these lines. Then he thought to himself, need he go back so far? All he needed to know was who the low creature was who started this Mulamkunnam family.

He had heard stories. Those were days when the King of Cochin and the Zamorin of Calicut fought with each other openly and secretly. Rairu reached Cochin ready to become a spy on behalf of the King of Cochin. The King welcomed him and gave him a lot of land free of tax. Actually, the King did not get much benefit out of his association with Rairu. But Rairu became an important figure.

There were bamboo thickets in the land that he had been granted. Rairu cut them down to build his house. One rainy night, he noticed that the soil was disturbed. Rairu, who had set out to remove the undergrowth, spied three copper pots. Rairu had the intelligence to guess that the three copper pots contained gold coins. So, he killed the men with him immediately. It was after that that he built the house. He called it 'Mulamkunnam' after the bamboo or mula.

From then on it was a story of prosperity for Rairu Nair. He became so important in the locality that people started calling him 'Rairu Yajamanan' or lord.

Rairu Yajamanan was a strong man. He kept twenty-five 'capable' women at the same time. Older people still narrate a story that has dark shades of legend around this.

There was a big, thatched cowshed at Mulamkunnam. Rairu

built another long building parallel to this cowshed. This new building was tiled. Except for this difference, this long building was similar to the cowshed. Rairu's twenty-five kept women stayed in this long tiled building.

Rairu Yajamanan was a strong man. He was also unmarried. It would be reasonable if he had two or three women in his house. But twenty-five! That was a little too much. There was criticism in the village. The information reached the Adhikari, head of the local Thana.

The Thana Adhikari was a man to be feared, he could wield the authority of the police as well. He also took an interest in the administration of the village. The Adhikari came for inspection without any warning. He found that the complaints had been true. He gave orders that the women were to be sent away.

'The women are willing. So, where's the crime or sin in it?' Rairu tried arguing.

The Adhikari twirled his moustache and shouted, 'I'll beat everyone up.'

Rairu felt like laughing, 'Beat them? I normally caress them. You can also do the same. I'll get you their permission. And something else. Even the ruler of the kingdom knows that these women are here. It is surprising that you did not know it till now.'

The Adhikari cooled down, compromised with Rairu. From the next day the Adhikari became a frequent visitor to Mulamkunnam. Days and months passed. Rairu felt that this arrangement could not continue. Of the twenty-five women, he himself liked Rugmini and Madhavi the most. The Adhikari also chose them each time he came.

What could he do!

That was when, by a lucky coincidence, an Usika Rawthar landed up there from Tamil Nadu. He was a practitioner of black magic, had commerce with djinns.

Rairu Yajamanan bowed before Usika Rawthar, presented him with two pouches of gold coins, and explained the problem.

Usika Rawthar asked when the Adhikari usually landed up.

Rairu replied, 'He comes during daytime. His wife doesn't allow him to go out at night.'

Rawther gave Rairu a chant to use, as well as a magic wand. Recite the chant, then wave the wand, the women would all become cows. Rairu tried it out. The long tiled shed became a cowshed. At night the cows would regain their normal forms and become women. The Thana Adhikari came on his usual daytime visit and stood there wonderstruck.

'Where are the women?'

'I could not afford to keep them any longer, Adhikari. So, I sent them all away.'

'Is this the truth?'

'I swear on the goddess at Chottanikkara.'

The saddened Adhikari took a transfer to a distant place in Talappalli Taluk.

And after Rairu...

Raman Menon had been crazy about Kathakali and had dabbled in black magic. The next was Gopi Yajamanan. He used to write love poems in stanza form. That was what he was famous for. The next was Mani Menon who was also known as Garuda Yajamanan. He was renowned for his cure of snake bites. The next was Eachara Menon. This Menon had managed to spend a lot of his family wealth. He had also had to pay a fine for cutting down the royal tree of teak.

And then...?

So many Menons!

Vedaraman rolled in the sand.

Oh yes! There was one more famous Menon. That was Appunni Menon who had migrated to Travancore. Appunni had crossed the river and reached Travancore when the ruler of Travancore had captured Alangad and Paravur. He had heard his mother tell the story.

Mother! His mother who had died long back.

Vedaraman pushed his sixth finger into the sand. Who was his father? Was it the singer Swami or...

He looked across the river. It was very dark. All the trees on the other side had joined together to make a dark fortress. Still, he could recognize some of the bigger palms. Were they glowing? They were growing to the sky. And then, they bent their heads and jumped into the river. Bhlum, bhlum!

Were the palms devils?

It was Kozhukatta Paru who had told him about the devils that jumped into the river. In his sixth year. After his mother died. He wanted breastmilk even in his sixth year. It was the maid Paru who had breastfed him. Kozhukatta Paru. Even when they applied a bitter paste to the breast, he would not let go.

Why was he thinking of all this now? How could he remember all this?

What time was it?

There was a new sound in the river. What was it?

It was Appunni Menon. He was swimming across from the other shore.

Three

There, Appunni Menon was swimming across the river. He had reached Travancore. He had acquired property and wealth. Life went on peacefully and uneventfully. One day, he heard an announcement being drummed at the crossroads.

Dalawa Ramayyan was going to distribute honours to everyone according to the order of the Maharaja. These honours came at a price. For seven hundred and fifty panam, the coin of the realm, you could become a Kaimal. For six hundred panam, you became a Menon. For the title of Panikkar you had to pay only three hundred panam.

The treasury was empty after prolonged hostilities. The Maharaja needed money. This sale of honours was a way of filling the coffers.

Appunni had one of those desires. I am a Menon. But, if the Maharaja said it in so many words, 'Appunni, I declare hereby that you are a Menon,' that would be a good thing. Like underlining a good word.

The day was fixed. Those who wanted the honours stood in a line. One row of those who wanted to be called Kaimal. Another of those who wanted to be called Menon. Another for Panikkars. And so on... and so on...

Dalawa Ramayyan was present. With him was the officer in charge of the treasury. There were sundry officials as well. The treasury officials collected the money under the eyes of the man in charge. Ramayyan was declaring each person Tharakan,

Kaimal, Menon, Panikkar and other names of stature. Appunni was standing in the line of those who wished to become Menons. Why did he get a sudden attack of miserliness? Why did he jump into the row of those who wanted to become Panikkars? Did he wish to save some money?

Ramayyan who saw that jump called out, 'This is Menon Chadi Panikkar or Menon jumped to Panikkar!'

Mulamkunnam tharavad was disgraced by this incident.

It is said that Appunni had to give Ramayyan a full pouch of gold coins to get rid of the honorific 'Chadi Panikkar'.

Vedaraman got up and went knee deep into the water. He was feeling very hungry. What was the point in drinking river water. Vedaraman unlocked his throat and called out, 'Who's left now, stupid ancestors of mine?'

There was an echo from the other bank.

Oh yes! Kelu Menon.

Kelu... Kelu... Kelu...

Hey Kelu, my respected ancestor who got the Narasimha temple renovated! I stole the uruli from that temple. Forget it! I'm actually a good person. Today I became a thief and everyone has disowned me.

Should I carry all the sins of the past ages, respected ancestors? You cut up, divided, fought civil cases and destroyed all the wealth. Finally my father Sreedhara Menon...or rather Sreedhara Menon who is known as my father...what did he get?

He got sixty-eight cents of land. Of that, seven cents were a worked out quarry. And a pond that was full of water snakes.

How many times did my mother bear children?

My eldest brother P.S. Menon or Sankaran is a typist in some company in Bombay. Just after him is P.N. or Narayanan. He ties and unties the red tape on government files in Fort St George in Madras in his job as a peon.

I am a latecomer. A mistake. Even when my mother was alive, my father and Kozhukatta Paru...?

When my mother died, I was breastfed by Paru. So, Paru is also my mother. And then...?

But why did she come and catch hold of me? I'm hungry.

He thought of going to Mukundan's home. He would get something to eat there. But no, they had not parted on the best of terms.

❖

Vedaraman got up. He threw the empty arrack bottle into the river. Bamboo rafts floated down the river. He could hear the song of the man who worked the waterwheel. Was it nearly morning?

The pangs of hunger were so sharp! He would return to his own base. He started walking through the sand. Did he stamp too hard? His foot went into a hole made by the people who dug up river sand. He fell and got up again. Walked again. His legs didn't feel firm. He could faintly see the grassy land that sloped to the river. He went up slowly. If he walked another three hundred or four hundred yards, he would reach Mulamkunnam.

He clambered up the grassy slope and reached level ground. The lane started here; then split into three. Which was his lane? He did not know.

Well, he would walk.

He walked through the first lane. It did not go anywhere. So he turned right and walked. An old woman was sitting and weaving mats with palm fronds.

The old woman looked at Vedaraman and asked, 'Isn't it Ramankutty?'

Her voice sounded familiar. Wasn't it Kochouseph's wife Thressiamma? Vedaraman did not reply. His tongue was in no shape to speak.

Thressiamma, the old woman had given him jaggery and coconut pieces when he had been a child. If this was Thressiamma, this lane was the right one. He only had to walk a little further to reach a broader road. There was a porters' rest there, a porters' rest with Appunni Menon's name carved on it. That was a marker.

If one turned left from there, there would be a broken down culvert. Another fifty yards would get him to his house.

His house! Did he have the right to call it that?

It was getting lighter.

He took the last steps hesitantly. He had been thrown out of the house. What would happen now?

The gatehouse.

Open red hibiscus flowers and the yellow kolambi flowers.

Coconut trees.

He entered the house. Where would he sit? Whom could he call?

Vedaraman stood there, unable to move. He withdrew into the shed where rice was pounded.

He heard a noise then. Paru was moving towards the shed, sweeping the yard. He cleared his throat. Paru lifted her head and looked. She came rushing forward, saying, 'Ramankutty!' She asked, touching him, 'How long have you been here?'

Vedaraman shrugged off her hand and said irritably, 'I'm hungry.'

'There's yesterday's rice.'

'Bring it! I'll eat sitting here.'

'No, come inside.'

'My father?'

'He's in bed.'

'Suppose he gets up and comes…'

'He won't come. Come, Ramankutty!'

Kozhukatta Paru caught him by the hand.

Vedaraman sat on the floor of the kitchen. He looked out through the bars of the window. The aged neem tree was swaying in the breeze. Where was the papaya tree that he had planted next to it? Its stem had started showing girth. The papaya tree was not there.

There had been a bird's nest on the neem tree. He had looked at it the day before his father had thrown him out.

The eggs had hatched. The entrance to the nest was always crowded and active. The little birds greedily opened their beaks. The mother bird would come with something in its beak and feed them. The mother bird had a red crown on her head. The father bird was usually with her, with an even more stylish red crown on his head. The older birds had grey eyes. The eyes were made more beautiful by the black half-circle that surrounded them. Who could have applied black to those eyes?

The nest wasn't there now.

There were just a few hanging tendrils where it had stood. The little birds must have learnt to fly long since. They must have gone in search of the small piece of sky that was theirs.

Paru brought the previous day's rice in an old enamelled metal plate. She also brought crushed chillies and salt with a little coconut oil added in a small piece of plantain leaf.

'What are you looking at?' Paru asked.

'Nothing.'

Paru distended her nostrils and asked, 'Have you been drinking?'

'You're just imagining things.'

When he put the second handful of old rice into his mouth, Vedaraman felt sick. 'Enough. It's this old rice that stinks. Even the monkeys of Vattolikavu won't eat this.' He started getting hiccoughs. Continuously. Paru rubbed his back.

In between the hiccoughs Vedaraman asked, 'Is my father asleep?'

'He's still in bed.'

'In bed? He's up before the birds usually.'

Paru glared at him, 'Do you know what happened that day?'

'What the hell happened?'

Paru touched his cheek with a finger. He struck her hand away and said, 'I'm going, Paru.'

'Where?'

'I don't know that. Ah, I must see my father before that.'

'Don't go see him now, Ramankutty! You can do it later.'

'What's wrong with now?'

'I have to tell you something. Wait till I finish.'

'What's this great thing you have to tell me? I don't want to listen to speeches.'

'Just listen to what I'm saying, Ramankutty!'

'All right, damn it! Tell me.'

'That morning...'

Paru started speaking.

'That morning, I suddenly went crazy. I don't know the rights and wrongs of it. I wanted to feed you again. I came to the south room where you slept and lay close to you. That is when Sreedharan Yajamanan came there. He beat you madly. I screamed. You ran away. Yajamanan pulled me by the hair and roared at me: "You're his second mother, aren't you? You gave him your breast till he was six, didn't you? How could he do bad things with you then?"

'I should have told him that it was me, then. I should have told him the truth then. I should have told him you were innocent. But my tongue would not move, I was so scared.

'It was as though Yajamanan went mad. He rushed outside, with that big stick in his hand. He ran round and round the house. He slashed at your papaya tree. He destroyed the bird's nest.'

'Then what happened?' Vedaraman asked.

'I didn't see him for some time. I was just standing there, struck dumb. Suddenly I heard the kada-kada sound of the drum wheel for drawing up water from the well. When I went and looked near the well, what do you think I saw? Yajamanan was standing there, stark naked. He was pulling up water and pouring the bucketfuls on his head.

'I ran inside and rushed back to the well with two big towels. I wiped Yajamanan's head with one and wrapped the other round him.

'He pulled me with him and came inside. And screamed, "Bring it."

'I brought the can full of arrack and a glass. Yajamanan drank.

He was really drunk. He said he wanted to go to the temple then itself. He was stubborn. I too stubbornly said that he shouldn't go in that condition.

'And then he said, "I want to see Sanku Warrier. I'll go now." He was making an uproar. I tried to stop him. I tried to cool him down by saying that I would ask Sanku Warrier to come here.

'He asked me if I promised. I put my hand in his and promised. That worked. Yajamanan went on drinking. He drank till he lost consciousness. He grabbed me and started biting me. After that he lay flat on his back, unconscious. Actually, he fell.

'I ran to the gatehouse to get hold of Janaki Ammyar from the Thekke Madhom. When I saw her I asked her to tell Sanku Warrier to come here. Warrier came in the evening. By that time Yajamanan was no longer drunk. Do you know what that Warrier said? He said that Mukundan could not be found anywhere. That Achukutty had seen you and Mukundan carry something in a sack.

'It was later that we heard that you had been caught by the police. Krishnan Namboodiri said that you had stolen the uruli from the temple.'

Vedaraman wrinkled his brow, 'Didn't Mukundan say anything?'

'He came here only after five or six days!'

Paru seemed to be listening to something. There were groans from inside. Also a sound like a howling dog. She said, 'I'll just go, check and come back.' Vedaraman followed her, unnoticed.

Four

What he saw from a distance shocked him.

Sreedhara Menon lay, paralysed, on the bed. He was groaning, howling. Paru was rubbing his body.

Vedaraman could not bear to stay there and look. He walked to the veranda in front. What could have happened?

After a little while Paru came in search of him.

'What happened to father?' Vedaraman asked.

'You saw?'

'Um...'

'When he heard that police had caught you...'

Paru described what had happened. Sreedhara Menon had stood there motionless for a while. He then leaned against the wall. He pressed both hands against his forehead. He was sweating all over. He passed urine and stool. And then...he fell as though someone had struck him down.

'I ran to the gatehouse. People came rushing. Janaki Ammyar came and Karunan and Unneera and Kochappu and Thressia and Saidalavi. They lifted him up. What was the use! The entire right side was paralysed. He couldn't speak. Whatever anyone asked him, he would cry. Someone ran to call that cross-eyed Pappi Vaidyan. Vaidyan came, rubbed his body with some oil. Not just that day, we did it for a number of days, medicines, massages, rubbing with cloth, buffalo oil...what use was it!'

Vedaraman listened to the whole thing. He did not feel like saying anything. He got out into the yard and stood there. He wanted to walk, to run. He went into the compound.

So...This was the story. If this had not happened, would his father have come to get him out on bail?

Mukundan must have known that Vedaraman's father had had a stroke and was bedridden. Why didn't he say anything about it?

Instead, he had poked fun at him, hurt him. Those things Mukundan had said on the river bank still pierced his brain like countless needles.

Your father was a brahmin singer...brahmin singer... brahmin singer!

Was that true? The lineage of someone of the higher caste was not bad. But he had to know. Who made me?

He wandered around. Was the Mulamkunnam tharavad just this? Sixty-eight cents. There was the worked out quarry. There was the pond.

Was this a pond or was it just another quarry that had filled with water?

Vedaraman beat a rhythm on his stomach with his palm. Where was his hunger? Where had it hidden itself? There was the last step of the wild pond. Beyond that there was mud and wild undergrowth. And then a rock which looked like a frog that had been cursed to become a stone. The water was full of weeds. Dark green water.

Something moved in the mud among the weeds. Dark spots, one or two yellow streaks. Water snakes. Vedaraman bent, picked up a stone and threw it. The snake went into the water, disappeared.

Vedaraman turned back. He wanted to see his father. Why did he have to see him from a distance? He would go near and see him.

He went and stood before him. Sreedhara Menon looked at his son and wept. His lips moved and the muscles of one cheek moved erratically. No words came out. There was only a groan and a low scream.

Were those eyes trying to say something?

Vedaraman sat on the edge of the cot. He touched his father and whispered, 'I did not do anything wrong that day. You misunderstood what you saw.'

Did his father move his head to let him know that he did not believe him?

'Ramankutty!' He could hear Paru calling him.

She had come close by now. She touched him on the shoulder and said, 'Come away!'

He obeyed her.

She followed him into the outer room.

'You shouldn't have gone to his room.'

'Um?'

'If he gets excited, that tube in the head will burst again. If that happens, he's a goner.'

Vedaraman looked at the ceiling and muttered, 'That's better than lying like this.'

He looked at the iron rings in the ceiling. Those rings had banana bunches during the Onam season and gourds with golden spots during the time of Vishu. This year there wasn't a single gourd there.

After a short silence, Vedaraman asked, as if asking a nonsensical question, 'Do you remember my mother?'

'Of course I do!'

'I don't remember her. Was she beautiful?'

'She looked like the goddess Lakshmi, Mahalakshmi!'

'Paru, it's just as well that my mother died so long ago, isn't it?'

'Why do you say such things?'

'She did not have to see a lot of things... Let that be. I want food. I haven't had any for a long time.'

'I'm cooking. I'll bring you some gruel before that.'

'No, just bring some of that stuff from the can.'

'That's at night.'

'I want a little, now!'

'Not now!'

'All right, then I'll go.'

'Don't get mad, Ramankutty, I'll bring it.'

Vedaraman had a little. When the alcohol entered his empty stomach, he could feel a tingling. It was as though hooks were piercing his temples and the back of his neck.

'Paru, if I ask you something, will you tell me the truth?'

'What is the question?'

'Long ago, that is about sixteen or so years back, did a singer brahmin come here, to worship at the temple?'

'Yes he did.'

'This was before I was born?'

'Yes.'

'How did my mother die?'

'Ramankutty, what is all this? Why all these questions now? You've never asked such things before.'

'How did my mother die? Tell me!'

'Thampuratty lay down saying that she had a chest pain. She did not get up after that.'

'Thampuratty?'

'I always called your mother Thampuratty.'

'Paru, you fed me after my mother died. How did your breasts have milk? Did you have children?'

'I had a small baby when I came here. He died. But my breasts did not dry up.'

'You fed me breastmilk for three years, didn't you?'

'How do you know that?"

'You told me some time back. How can any woman's breasts have milk for so long if she doesn't have babies in between?'

Paru giggled, 'Some women are like that. They don't dry up!'

'What was between my father and yourself?'

'It's something you know.'

'Um, let that be. What did that singer Swami look like?'

'What can I tell you if you ask funny questions like that?'

'All right, I want to lie down for some time.'

'It has gone to your head, I suppose.'

'I'm terribly tired. Call me when the rice is ready.'

Vedaraman lay down on the cement floor. He slept almost immediately, but kept tossing and turning. Dreams hounded him. Magistrate Mathews roared: 'Head Constable Thankappan Pillai! Take a print of his sixth finger!' The monkeys of Vattolikavu were now giants, the size of Hanuman himself. They crowded around and tore open his back. The palms on the other side of the river turned into demons, demons with huge teeth, a single eye on the forehead and spiky hair on their body.

In the midst of all this, his beautiful mother stood, scared. The singer Swami caught hold of his mother and stripped her.

'Amma!' Vedaraman jumped up, screaming.

Paru came running on hearing the scream. 'What happened?'

'Had a nightmare.'

Vedaraman looked at Paru curiously. How come she looked so young? Oh yes, she'd had a bath and dressed up. She was wearing a new red blouse and a clean mundu with a striped border.

'Come Ramankutty, come and eat.'

'Father?'

'I gave him some gruel, poured it into his mouth. He can't swallow anything solid.'

Vedaraman ate well.

'Aren't you eating, Paru?'

'I'll eat.'

She kept trying to find out what had happened to him. 'Did you get food on time in the police station?'

'What police station? I was in a glass palace.'

'Did the policemen beat you?'

'No, they caressed me, fanned me, rubbed sandal paste on me.'

'Why did you steal, Ramankutty?'

'I didn't steal anything. It was that Mukundan.'

'But he came away after a few days.'

'What did he say when he came here?'

'That you were in the lock-up.'

Vedaraman held up his right hand which was covered with rice and said, 'Smart guy! I must see you soon. I must see your father too. And ask a few questions.'

'Don't go and pick a quarrel. That Sanku Warrier is a nasty man.'

'What do you mean by nasty?'

'He caught hold of my blouse once. I chased him away. He started calling me Kozhukatta because he was so angry.'

'Rotten Warrier!'

'Forget it, Ramankutty! This was a long time ago.'

'Enough, no more rice. My stomach is fit to burst.'

Vedaraman went and lay down on the cement floor after eating. He rolled this way and that.

It was late evening by the time he woke up.

There was a terrible stink. He was stinking. He needed to have a bath, wear clean clothes.

He went to the bathroom and poured water over himself.

He went in search of washed clothes. There were some in the wooden box. Some half-sleeved shirts, dhotis with broad borders.

When he reached the gatehouse, he could hear Paru calling. He did not turn to look back. Just walked faster.

There was still a little light.

Lucky! There was no one sitting on the culvert.

Would there be someone in the lane? Would someone look at him and shout 'thief!'?

Vedaraman walked faster when he reached Achukutty's tea shop. He didn't want Achukutty to see him. He wouldn't let him go easily.

But Achukutty had already seen him. 'Ramankutty, come here and mark your attendance.'

Vedaraman hesitated for a moment. It would be better to go into the tea shop. Or Achukutty would be angry with him. That was the way he was.

He went inside and stood there without speaking.

Achukutty was unusually friendly, 'I know what happened. You don't need to tell me anything. I too saw you and Mukundan carry the uruli away in a sack. You got caught. Mukundan got away scot-free. Don't worry about all that. Have a cup of tea and a vada!'

'I'll have it on my way back, Achuettan.'

'As you like. You are going to the temple, are you? Go! But the idol isn't there. People don't care about that. That Krishnan Namboodiri and his younger brother Sakran Namboodiri sold the idol long back. What is there is a duplicate.'

'I'll go to the temple and come back, Achuettan.'

'All right.'

There were some people playing cards on the platform around the peepal tree. Vedaraman stood for a while and watched them. And then he took a round of the outer wall of the temple.

He wasn't in a hurry to see Lord Narasimha in the temple.

He wanted to see Mukundan.

And Sanku Warrier.

Five

Koman Nair sat in a shed made of woven palm fronds, next to the outer building of the temple. Behind him was the wooden board with the list of offerings that could be made to the deity. He raised the wick of the lamp. The dark was getting denser.

Today's income was poor. Altogether there were only seven archanas, four offerings of silver replicas of body parts, one sandal decoration, and eleven fireworks. That was all.

The Namboodiri who was in charge of the temple did not pay him any salary. The agreement was that Koman Nair would get ten per cent of the collection from the offerings at the temple. He would get some money only during the Sabarimala season. Once that season started there would be a flow of devotees from nearby places.

When a shadow moved beyond the outer wall, Koman Nair asked, 'Who's that?'

'It's me, Ramankutty!'

'Who? Vedaraman?'

'Yes.'

'Come up. I'm not a policeman!' Koman Nair said with a sarcastic laugh.

Vedaraman went up to him.

'Ramankutty, go in and bow before the Lord. Ask for Narasimhamoorthy's pardon. Pray that he shows you the right path from now on.' Koman Nair cleared the phlegm from his throat and asked, 'Why are you staring at me like that?'

'Why can't I look at you?' Vedaraman was not in a conciliatory mood.

'Keep looking, your eyes will burst.'

'And who'll make them burst? You?'

'Not me. But, Narasimhamoorthy. When you robbed the uruli from the temple, whom did the god punish? Your father. But he's kept your share for you.'

Vedaraman said in a tone of irritation, 'Okay, if that's so, you can tell your god when you sit here and scratch your itches and write the receipts for the offerings that the rest of the punishment should be given to Sanku Warrier's son.'

'Why do you say that?'

'Mukundan and I stole the uruli together. I've already taken my punishment...in the lock-up and the sub-jail.'

Koman Nair showed great surprise. 'Oh Lord! When Achukutty said something of that sort that day, I didn't believe him. You know, about Mukundan.'

'Uncle, if I had told the police about him, they would have arrested him as well.'

'Ramankutty! You're an innocent soul. It was Krishnan Namboodiri who made the complaint to the police. That Sanku Warrier must have managed to influence Namboodiri. That's why Mukundan got away with it. Ah, Krishnan Namboodiri showed his gratitude to that rascal Warrier.'

'Gratitude?'

'That's right. Sanku Warrier has all the proof and all the documents.'

'What proof?'

'You are a fool. You know nothing about things here. And besides, you are an unlucky sort of chap. What is the reason? It's your sixth finger.'

'Uncle, I don't understand what you're saying. It's not clear at all,' Vedaraman complained.

'A lot of people who live in this place of ours are useless, real low-class. Devils, most of them. Is there anybody about whom you can say: "He is a good man?" Maybe one person – our Gandhi Vikraman Pillai. Let that be. Look at my problems. I've been sitting here and writing receipts and my back is gone. My knees are frozen into wood. I pour kerosene into this lamp and sit and wait here for devotees. What for? Why do I do it? Do I get any salary? Nothing! Earlier I used to get some rice. This rascal Sanku stopped that. Our Krishnan Namboodiri is just Sanku's dog!'

'Uncle, I don't understand anything.'

Koman Nair smiled and winked, 'I'll explain everything. You do something. Go to Achukutty's shop and buy something to eat. I'll wait for you near the big balance scale where the devotees are weighed.'

Vedaraman rushed to the tea shop.

Koman Nair put out the kerosene lamp.

When Vedaraman came back with vadas and banana fries wrapped in a piece of newspaper, Koman Nair was sitting on the ground near the big balance.

Koman Nair spoke as though he had just woken up from some memories, 'Ah, you've come! Just look to your left. Do you see that big laterite stone? Behind that, there is something on the ground. Bring that here.'

Vedaraman searched and found it. Koman Nair became more animated when he got the bottle of arrack. Glug, glug, glug, glum!

That was the end of the arrack. Koman Nair's hands now fell on the vadas and the banana fries. Vedaraman reminded him, 'Uncle, you were saying...'

'Yes, I'll tell you. I'll tell you. I'll go home only after I tell you everything. The whole thing's shaking. I'm not talking about myself, I'm talking about the temple. Not from the intoxication of devotion, but from the intoxication of partition! Krishnan Namboodiri and Sakran Namboodiri are at odds with each other. The fight started long before you were born. Some day they'll go to court. The whole thing will cause a stink. It'll make them stink. If it reaches the court, who'll win? The person who has the documents. The documents are all palm leaf ones. Where are the palm leaf bundles? That is, the documents? They're all with that rascal Sanku Warrier. That's how Sanku makes Krishnan Namboodiri dance to his tune! Never mind. Why should I say anything now?'

'You must tell me, Uncle.'

'Do you know the story of the Brahmarakshas?'

'The Brahmarakshas?'

'Ah! That was the beginning of it! Krishnan Namboodiri built a platform under the coral stalk tree overnight. In the middle of it, there was a hollow. He put a black oval stone in that hollow and started worshipping it. That was the beginning of the Brahmarakshas! Do you know who the Brahmarakshas was? It was a singer Swami.'

Vedaraman's hair was standing on end. He asked, 'A singer Swami?'

'Yes. He was a great singer. He'd come to this temple to worship here for a few weeks. He was very good-looking. One had to wash one's eyes before looking at him. He used to stay at your place. He was teaching your mother Radhamani Thampuratty music. What happened after that? We don't know. But one morning the Bhagavatar, the singer Swami, was lying flat on his back in the temple pond, dead. You know our Vikraman Pillai, our Gandhi Vikraman. He's the one who made the arrangements for the cremation and everything. And then the fun started.'

'What started?'

'Music would start at midnight. All sorts of ragas. I don't know their names and all that – they said words like thodi and kalyani and hamsadhwani...Something like that.'

'Is all this hearsay, Uncle?'

'No, I've heard it myself. At least I felt I was hearing music. Lots of people have heard it. Krishnan Namboodiri also heard it. Namboodiri went and saw the Palachottil Kaniyar, the astrologer. The Kaniyar said that Krishnaswami Bhagavatar had become a Brahmarakshas and that an idol had to be dedicated to him.

Krishnan Namboodiri obeyed him. Sakran Namboodiri did not like this at all. Sakran went around saying that it was not right to place the idol of a Brahmarakshas in the temple premises. He arranged for some thugs to break up the platform. Do you know what they did? They pissed all around the platform, broke it up and levelled the ground. They dug out the black oval stone and threw it into the stream. Oh god! No one would believe the things that happened that night...'

Koman Nair paused.

'What happened?'

'God! When I think of what happened, even now I feel cold with fear. There were terrible screams, drum beats from the sky, music in between...There was loud laughter and roars. That night six women in this place had miscarriage and lost their babies. Your mother too died that night. Ah, my throat is parched from so much talking. Now...Let's try our luck, right?'

'What is it, Uncle?'

'If I'm lucky, if I have any throat-luck at all, there will be some "other one" at Achukutty's shop.'

'Let me go and check...'

'You have money?'

'I'll say I'll pay later.'

Vedaraman returned in minutes with the bottle of arrack.

Koman Nair had a good measure.

'Uncle, the rest of the story...?'

'There isn't much more. Krishnan Namboodiri gave a petition against Sakran at the outpost. The policemen at the outpost had a good time for many days. Finally, everything was forgotten. But the fight between Krishnan Namboodiri and Sakran Namboodiri started that day. There's sure to be a case about the partition. Sakran is an innocent soul, even if he is foolhardy.'

'Who'll win the partition case?'

'Didn't I tell you? Krishnan Namboodiri, of course. If Sakran is to win he should be able to snatch away the documents that are with Sanku Warrier.'

'What if Sanku Warrior himself is snatched away?'

'Ramankutty, what are you saying?'

'Uncle, I want to see him. Just now. Give me the bottle. Let me get some courage,' Vedaraman snatched at the arrack bottle.

'Look here!' Koman Nair protested. Vedaraman grabbed the bottle and swallowed a mouthful. It burnt his mouth and throat.

'I didn't know you had started. To start drinking at this young age...'

'I've left enough for you, Uncle.'

'Oh! Very kind of you.'

'Uncle, I have one question.'

'What is it?'

'Who's your father?'

'How dare you?

'I asked just to know.'

'All right. Long ago, an elephant laid an egg here. I was hatched from that. Okay, who's your father?'

'That's what I need to find out. Let me go and see Sanku Warrior.'

Vedaraman got up.

As he walked away from the temple, Vedaraman started feeling uncertain about what he was about to do. Sanku Warrior was one of the respected people of the village. He was over sixty. He might not be a good man. Still, no one had faced him and called him names so far. No one had fought openly with him. How would he be able to face up to him? How could he start speaking to him?

Vedaraman walked through the raised path in the field. He could see the light from far. At the most, he would have to go another two hundred yards.

He had now crossed the fields and had reached firm ground.

He could see Sanku Warrior from a distance. Light spilled out through the wooden bars. A table lamp was burning in the front room. Sanku Warrior was leaning forward with his elbow on the table.

Taking a few steps forward, Vedaraman called out to attract Sanku Warrier's attention, 'Mukundan!'

Sanku Warrier's voice sounded from inside. 'Mukundan's not here. Who's that?'

'I don't mind if it's Mukundan's father!'

Sanku Warrier came out.

'It's Ramankutty.'

'Why are you here at this time…?'

'You old rascal!'

Sanku Warrier looked around. And then asked, 'What did you call me, you useless fellow?'

'You old rascal.'

'You're drunk!'

'What does it matter to you if I drink, you old fool?'

Sanku Warrier realized that things were not all right. This chap had come here to create a noise and to insult him. When did he get out of jail? Or did he break out of jail? There shouldn't be any shouting and yelling. If his wife Ammu Warrasiar woke up and came out because of the noise, he would lose face. And then he would have to try and hit this boy to save face. It was all dangerous!

As a tactic, Sanku Warrier pretended a fondness he did not feel, caught Vedaraman by both hands and spoke softly. 'Ramankutty, what happened to you? What do you want? Tell me frankly and we'll try to get it done.'

'I want to know something.'

'What is it that you want to know?'

'Who's my father?'

Sanku Warrier pulled back his hands. What was this boy asking? Shameless fellow!

'I'm asking you, who's my father?'

'Did you come all the way here to find out this?'

'Or it might be for something else. You stupid Warrier, did you say that my father was a singer Swami who came from somewhere?'

Sanku Warrier stayed quiet for a while. Then he said very seriously, 'Ramankutty, you lose nothing by speaking to me, so much elder to you, with some respect. Hnh, it's not you speaking now, it's what's inside you. I'll forgive you because of that. I'll answer your question now. I did not say such a scandalous thing, and I'll never say such a thing.'

On hearing this, Vedaraman cooled down a little. 'Mukundan told me you'd said this. That is why I...'

'Never mind! Let Mukundan come here. I'll tackle him. I'll explain something so that you'll feel better about it. Sreedharan Yajamanan is your father. It is true that Krishna Swami Bhagavatar came here to the temple. It is also true that he taught your mother Radhamani Thampuratty music. But Krishna Swami was an "Ammaswami".'

'What do you mean, "Ammaswami"?'

'I mean that he was not a proper man. I've seen him with my own eyes. There used to be a small crocodile in the temple pond. Once the Bhagavatar and I were bathing at the same time. The crocodile caught hold of one end of the Bhagavatar's mundu. He let go of the mundu and rushed for dear life. That's when I saw and realized. Is there anything more you want to know? Do you have any doubts left?'

Vedaraman felt like a fool. His eyes filled with tears. He touched Sanku Warrier's feet and said, 'Please forgive me. I said a lot of things I shouldn't have.'

'Get up, Ramankutty! It wasn't you who spoke, it was the other fellow. Don't kill yourself like this. You must stop this habit. I have no grudge against you. You are young. You must correct your mistakes now. You must keep to the straight path from now on.'

Six

As he walked back through the path in the fields, Vedaraman was thinking. Straight path! And where was this straight path? Would Sanku Warrier advise Mukundan to walk the straight path?

He circled around the temple and reached the lane. Achukutty was about to shut his tea shop.

'See you, Achuettan.'

'Ramankutty, you needn't pay me for the vada and the banana fries. But, who'll pay me for the other thing?'

'Koman Nair will give you the money. Or, I'll pay.'

'How will you pay anything? Um, never mind. You go now.'

'Achuettan, you needn't make me feel small. Here, look at this!' Vedaraman showed the ring that he wore on the finger of his left hand.

'Um, go now!' Achukutty laughed.

Vedaraman walked to his house.

As soon as he entered through the gatehouse and reached the yard, he saw Kozhukatta Paru. She said coyly, 'Do you know how long I've been waiting? My feet are swollen from standing here.'

'Who asked you to wait?'

'No one has to say it. You wait if you like someone.'

'All right!' Vedaraman sat on the veranda.

'Look here, I've prepared chicken for you. Shall I bring it now?'

'Later. I'm not hungry. The other thing's there, isn't it?'

'Ramankutty, this is getting too much.'

'Just do what I tell you to do.'

Paru came closer and said flirtatiously, 'Okay, Kochejamanan, small Yajamanan.'

'What's that smell?'

'Look,' Paru exhibited the jasmine flowers in her hair.

'Bring the stuff.'

Paru went inside and brought the arrack, a glass and some water. She said, 'Sreedharan Yajamanan is not asleep yet.'

'Did you give him food?'

'Um, I poured gruel into his mouth slowly.'

'Paru, I'm feeling bad about a lot of things today.'

'What things?' Paru poured out some of the arrack.

Vedaraman raised his glass and said, 'When I think of these things, my brain gets addled.'

When he drank the whole glass at one go, Paru said, 'Go slow, Ramankutty! If you drink it all of a sudden like this...'

'Everything that happens should happen suddenly. Or it will never happen. Um, pour me a little more. You are the one who taught me the taste of this.'

Paru sat touching him and poured out the arrack.

'Do you remember Paru, you used to bathe me when I was young. How old was I then? Seven or eight...'

'You used to go around in a loin cloth.'

'You'd take out all my stuff and...I'd better not say it.'

Paru rubbed his back and said, 'Say it, Ramankutty.'

When everything was over, Vedaraman felt disgusted with himself. Why had he exposed himself to an attack from this aged woman?

Why was it that his doubts would not rest in spite of Sanku Warrier saying that Krishna Swami Bhagavatar had not been a proper man and had been an 'Ammaswami'? Why had he asked Paru who his father was? Why had he trembled when she said that Sreedhara Menon was not his father? She cleverly evaded all his questions after that. She said, 'I'll tell you. There's the whole night before us. I'll tell you everything when we sleep in the outer room.'

Finally, he'd had to sleep with her.

Paru was not there in the room. Where had she gone? Had she gone to stand guard over Sreedhara Menon? What time was it? He could hear cats fighting in the attic. Were they cats or pole cats? He remembered something that Mukundan had told him long ago. When cats screeched and fought at night, they were trying to make kittens.

Did Paru scream when she conquered him?

Vedaraman turned to one side. He smelled his body. It had the smell of something rotten. No, this was the smell of faded jasmine flowers.

A dirty smell...

Whose smell? Paru's? Didn't he also smell dirty?

It was the first time that his body had united with the body of a woman. Could he say that he didn't enjoy sleeping with Paru at all? Was he putting all the blame on Paru to whitewash himself? If Sreedhara Menon had not come that early morning when Paru was trying to breastfeed him? Wouldn't what happened this night have happened then?

It was stinking. The stink of arrack and rotting jasmine flowers. He could get up. And go to the bathroom. Why didn't he pour a few pots of water over his head and clean himself up? No. The chadu, the drum wheel, would make a 'kada-kada' noise. It might wake Sreedhara Menon up. Whether he was his father or not, he was a man who was ill, who was paralysed. Let him not get agitated. Let the rest of the blood vessels in his head not burst. When he felt a yawn coming on, Vedaraman held his left hand before his mouth. The sixth finger dangled.

That accursed sixth finger.

What did this malformation that was the sixth finger denote? Did it predict bad luck? Or did it mean future prosperity? Cherian

Munshi who taught Malayalam at the school in Kottoor Kavala said that it pointed to future prosperity. Munshi sir with his thick glasses. The glasses would slip down the bridge of the nose every now and then. Cherian Munshi would look over the glasses at the students. He looked like an owl then.

When Cherian Munshi said that the sixth finger was a pointer to future prosperity, Mukundan who was elder to Vedaraman by a couple of years, but studied in the same class because he had failed in two classes, stood up and asked, 'How is that, sir? If he had four hands he could have become a god. How can this sixth finger which has crept in like a bad omen do him any good?'

Cherian Munshi caught hold of Mukundan's ear. He also gave him a thump on the head and said, 'You Warrier boy! Won't this sixth digit, which neither you nor I nor any other boy in this school has, prove more definitive than ordinary palmistry?'

Though he had not understood the meaning of the term 'definitive' then, he had caught the meaning of 'digit'.

Vedaraman looked carefully at his sixth finger. This chap who had crept in unasked was a dirty fellow. Though he was a part of the body, there was no strong connection. Could this fellow who stood there dangling be a warning of future destruction? Cherian Munshi was not an astrologer or a prophet.

Whatever that was, it was important now. It was evidence, evidence of his birth.

Vedaraman struggled to remember everything that Paru had said, to sort it all out and organize it. Okay, before I was born, a singer Swami came here – Krishna Swami Bhagavatar.

Had Paru been here when the singer Swami came here? Were his elder brothers Sankaran who typed in Bombay and Narayanan who was a peon in Madras here those days? How old were they? Never mind, there was no point in losing his way going so deeply into things.

All right. The Bhagavatar came here, taught his mother music.

His mother looked like a goddess, like Mahalakshmi – that was what Paru used to say. He couldn't remember his mother.

But, the face of goddess Lakshmi was before him. She stood on a lotus on the wall in the inner hall, captive in the dull gilded frame and glass. She wore a crimson sari with a broad golden border. She had broad hips. Though the body was fairly plump, not a petal of the lotus was even bent, folded. Was the lotus stronger than Lakshmi? Or was it that since Lakshmi was considered fickle, even her broad frame did not give her body weight?

His mother... Mahalakshmi. When he taught her music, would the Bhagavatar have beaten time on his mother's curved hips?

His mind was wandering into forbidden territory.

Did Kozhukatta Paru make up the story? Paru, who had earlier said that Radhamani Thampuratty died of a heart attack, had changed the story today.

When his mother became pregnant, Sreedhara Menon had become suspicious.

When his mother delivered a boy, Sreedhara Menon completely ignored her. It was Krishna Swami Bhagavatar who sat with the mother and child. It was the Bhagavatar who had given him gold and vayampu ceremonially. Though there was no ceremony as such, Bhagavatar had put him on his lap, given him these and said, 'This boy is Raman... Vedaraman.'

Sreedhara Menon started yelling at his mother and calling her names. Accusations flowed like a waterfall. Yajamanan left his bedroom and started sleeping with Paru. Krishna Swami Bhagavatar fell into the temple pond and died. Became a Brahmarakshas. The night that Sakran Namboodiri got rid of the Brahmarakshas, when Radhamani Thampuratty wept as though her heart would break, Yajamanan kicked her to death.

When she narrated the story, Paru was hugging him close.

He had protested panting, 'Anyone can make up stories. Who saw anything? Did anyone see my mother and the Bhagavatar sleeping together?'

Paru had laughed, 'Who's seen us sleep together? But there was one thing. There is evidence for what I said.'

'What evidence?'

'This sixth finger.'

'Eh?'

'Ramankutty, the Bhagavatar too had six fingers. It is a copy. When two people very much in love sleep together and produce a child there will be resemblances. You inherited the sixth finger of that great singer. That was why Yajamanan became suspicious. If you hadn't had this sixth finger, Yajamanan would not have killed Thampuratty. You would not have been suckled by me.'

Vedaraman turned this way and that. He felt that someone was coming close to him. Who was caressing him? Who was calling him, 'child'?

A very thin form. Very fair. Big eyes.

Vedaraman jumped up, shouting, 'Amma.'

He got out of the room, went to the bathroom and poured a lot of water over his head. At least, let the outside get clean.

How could he continue to stay in this house? It was a jail.

Kozhukatta Paru was the Constable Moosa in female guise.

Seven

Breakfast was gruel and a curry made of tapioca. When Paru went to attend to Sreedhara Menon, Vedaraman served himself and ate. He decided to wander around the compound. Just as he got out of the house, he heard Mukundan's voice.

He was calling, 'Ramankutty!'

Vedaraman went to the gatehouse.

'I hear you came to visit my father last night.'

'It wasn't anything special.'

'Would anyone go around asking who his father is at your age?'

Vedaraman kept silent.

'I said all that about the singer Swami as a joke. How can you be such a simpleton? Che...'

'Forget it, Mukundan.'

'Let's go for a walk.'

'I'm not coming.'

'You're going to just sit here?'

'Maybe.'

'Ramankutty, what are you planning to do now?'

'I don't know.'

'It'll be Vishu soon and then the month of Edavam. The school will reopen. Don't we have to go to school?'

'School! My school life is over. I won't be promoted. And the other boys and Munshi sir will call me "thief". I'm not going to school.'

'You come out of this house! Come with me. We'll walk with our heads held high. No one will call you a thief! You'll see.'

Vedaraman walked with Mukundan. They reached the culvert.

Mullan Sasi, Moideen and Divakaran, who were more or less the same age as them, were sitting on the culvert. When Vedaraman and Mukundan approached them, Mullan said, 'There comes the uruli thief!'

Moideen put his finger to his lips and said, 'Shsh!'

Mukundan asked, 'So what's the programme for the morning?'

Mullan Sasi said, 'The programme's taking place in my stomach. A whole chenda concert. I'm terribly hungry.'

Mukundan laughed at him. 'Doesn't the Ayini tree in Thekkedath Kuttiyamma's house have any fruits at all?'

That was an old story. Mullan had stolen fruits from Kuttiyamma's Ayini tree to eat.

Vedaraman's face flushed. Was Mukundan playing a dirty trick? Was he hinting about the uruli theft?

Vedaraman stood straight, 'Anyone who's hungry, come with me.'

Mukundan tried to whisper caution, 'What is this, Ramankutty?'

Vedaraman ignored that and told everyone, 'Come, come with me to Achukutty's tea shop.'

Vedaraman walked in front. The group, including Mukundan, followed him. When all of them entered the tea shop together, Achukutty's eyes bulged out of their sockets.

He asked, 'Ramankutty, what is this, a whole platoon of you...?'

Vedaraman said, 'Don't worry. This will take care of Koman Nair's money, and what we're going to eat here. There will be some leftover as well.'

He pulled the ring off the finger of his left hand and gave it to Achukutty. Everyone other than Vedaraman had their fill.

Vedaraman went outside the tea shop and stood there. There was a bullock cart near the platform of the peepal tree. A man was coming out of the temple.

He had seen him from a distance – Gandhi Vikraman Pillai.

He had sandal paste on his forehead and temple flowers behind his ear. His white beard flew in the wind.

Vedaraman stood to one side.

Vikraman Pillai got into the bullock cart.

He could easily have bought a car if he wanted. He was driving a bullock cart. Since it had a covering, it was a vehicle for human beings now. If it didn't, it would be for carting things.

The bullock cart departed, throwing up dust.

Days passed.

Vedaraman was seriously disturbed. There was danger in the house. Kozhukatta Paru approached him whenever she got the chance, like a demoness who had tasted blood. She came even in the daytime.

He could escape in the daytime. He could run away to the compound, to the pond. It was difficult to escape her at night. He could evade her eyes and quickly get into the outer room and bolt the door. But what was the use? The demoness would come and knock on the door. When she realized that he would not open the door, she would come to the window. The window could not be shut properly. One of the shutters did not have a hook, and so stayed open. It was lucky that the iron bars still held. Or she would have come in through them. As it was, she would stand in the 'small veranda' outside the window and throw pebbles at him and plead, 'Please open, Ramankutty.'

Suppose, as in the old legend, Usika Rawthar had given Paru a magic wand and a chant to use? What would have happened? He must have thought about it. That must have been why he had that nightmare.

Paru stood on the small veranda and recited the chant. She waved the magic wand. He, Vedaraman, became a small colourful bird in her palm. She pointed the magic wand at the neem tree. A golden cage appeared on the neem tree. Paru said, 'Little bird, little bird, sit in the cage' and put him in the cage and shut the door. Late at night, she poured a little gruel into

Sreedhara Menon's mouth, changed into the mundu with its border of golden lace, wore jasmine in her hair and went to the neem tree. When she sang, 'Come little bird, come little bird!' the golden cage opened by itself. She picked up the bird in one hand and walked to the outer room. She took off her blouse and pressed the bird between her breasts. Then the bird changed into Vedaraman. When he woke up covered in sweat, he was all alone in the outer room.

How could he escape?

The school would reopen in a few days. Mukundan would pass the exam and sit in the next class. What about himself? Would he be promoted? Or would he be detained because of lack of attendance? Not only that, he had not written the final examination. Would he have to sit in the same class as last year?

The uruli thief would have to stay back in the ninth. Vedaraman felt that it would be better to leave the place. That feeling expanded like a balloon. And then burst. He knew he should leave. But where could he go? He was groping in the dark. Where was the light? Who would show him the way? Who would give him some advice? There were a few people who still had affection for him, though he had become a thief. Kochappu, Thressia, Janaki Ammyar, Saidalavi, Charankutty who plied the ferry...

But none of them would understand his dilemma. They would not be able to give him any advice. They looked neither this way nor that, just went ahead with the lives allotted to them, content to do so. So...

To whom could he turn?

There was an important person, someone who counted. Gandhi Vikraman Pillai...

Suppose he went and met him? What reason could he give him for wanting to meet him? Who was Vikraman Pillai? Who was he, this poor Vedaraman?

He had heard about Vikraman Pillai even when he was a child.

He was a congressman, a freedom fighter. In the days when the rich and important people of the village and the nearby town had supported the Dewan's rule and the 'Union Jack' that flew in Delhi, it had been this lion-like man who had raised the roar of 'Quit India' in this remote area. He had been beaten with lathis, suffered incarceration, suffered torture.

When his health was completely ruined the authorities had released him on parole.

That was when he had done some great things. Vikraman Pillai was one of the biggest landlords in the place. No one had even heard about the 'Bhoodan Movement' in those days. Vikraman Pillai had given away some eighty pieces of fifty cents each to the harijans of the area.

Though the ruler had granted entry into the temple to people of the lower caste, Krishnan Namboodiri had not allowed them into the temple of Narasimha. His argument was that this was a private temple. Vikraman Pillai had gathered a group of lower caste pulayas and parayas and led them into the temple. It had created quite a stir. An even more important achievement had been the establishment of the school at Kottoor Kavala. If Vikraman Pillai had not established that temple of learning he, Vedaraman, and a number of other boys in the area would not have learnt to read and write.

A good man, a big man.

In spite of all this, there were people in the area who laughed at him. Even today they continued to laugh at him.

One of the most important among them had been Sreedhara Menon. He used to make fun of him right up to the time when he fell ill. The cloth merchant Melath Padmasanan would give him company.

After swallowing small measures of arrack they would sit near the thulasi thara, the small platform with the sacred basil. Yajamanan sat in the rosewood easy chair with its long arms on which you could place your legs. The body of the chair was woven cane. Behind his head was a small pillow. Yajamanan sat with his legs extended. It was only half sitting. It could become half sleeping in the same posture. The humble Melath Padmasanan sat in an ordinary wooden chair.

In the background hovered Kozhukatta Paru.

The routine always began thus. Paru brought tapioca and fish curry.

'Padmasanan!'

The scene continued.

'Hey, Melath Padmasanan! Why did this Gandhi Vikraman give away land to the pulayas and parayas? Just to become a big man, right? Was that land worth anything?'

'It's just rocks, Yajamanan!'

'That's right! What'll you get if you plant paddy there? The paddy'll fry to puffed rice. Why did he take all those lower castes to the temple?'

'Just to become someone big here.'

'That's right, Padman, just to get cheap applause.'

'Yajamanan, why can't this man live well like us? We'd have taken care of him.'

'Padmasanan, I'd have made him the Karayogam president. He doesn't want all that. He has to become a big leader. That's why he uses that bullock cart. What? People must say that he lives in poverty, that he's Gandhi. Paru, what are you gaping at? Pour some more. Ah Padmasanan! When did a few people get some money here?'

'In the war.'

'When levy and ration came!'

'That's right, Yajamanan!'

'And what happened one of those days? What happened was that our Gandhi Vikraman came out of jail on parole, right?'

What happened was something that the village remembered even now. Other landowners were hiding their paddy. They bribed the government officials and gave paddy on levy for name's sake. The rest they sold on the black market. What

Vikraman Pillai did was to open out his granary to the govern-ment and set a condition. 'I'm going to distribute this paddy to the poor of this village even as you sit here, at a price lower than the government price.' The Tahsildar pointed out that that was against the rules.

Vikraman Pillai's reply was that he did not have much respect for such rules.

The distribution of paddy took place as he had desired. Some youngsters helped him enthusiastically. 'Commu kids!' some people whispered.

The conversation near the thulasi thara continued.

'What happened that night, Padmasanan?'

'Gandhi's wife jumped into the well, didn't she Yajamanan? She wanted money.'

'You, Asanan! Is wanting money such a bad thing?'

Yajamanan laughed long and loud and then asked again, 'And what did Gandhi Vikraman do when his wife jumped into the well? You tell me...'

'Jumped in with her.'

'And then?'

'Neighbours sent down a sling and pulled the two of them up. You, Paru, why are you standing there as if you've swallowed a stake? Is it over?'

Paru poured more.

'You, Padmasanan, what'll you do if I throw a question at you now?'

'I'll throw back an answer, Yajamanan.'

'Good for you! Who destroyed your shop in the war years?'

'Vikraman Gandhi! I worked hard, bribed and flattered people and got some mill saris on "quota". All of them lay there in the godown and were eaten by cockroaches.'

'You hadn't thought that Gandhi Vikraman could make saris, did you?'

'I didn't, Yajamanan. How could I know in advance that he would make a cooperative society, teach all the stupid people around how to dip coarse cloth in dyes and colours and make saris and sell them at a cheap rate? How could I?'

Vedaraman had seen many such scenes.

Another evening. They were sitting as usual.

Sreedhara Menon asked Padmasanan, 'Look here, the Mulamkunnam family is slightly down just now. I know. You needn't flatter me. Tell me the truth! Even today who is more respected and valued in this place? Is it me or is it Gandhi Vikraman?'

Padmasanan said, 'What sort of question is this, Yajamanan? Who else but you is respected here? There is one thing, though, a small thing.'

'What is it?'

'Vikraman Pillai has done one good thing!'

'And what is that?'

'Our Gandhi started that school in Kottoor Kavala. Our children learn their alphabet because of that.'

'Are you making fun of me? Didn't anyone study in this place till he started that school? Is this stupid school of Gandhi's half as good as the school run by the priest on the other side of the river?'

'That's true, Yajamanan!'

'Look here, you fellow! Why did we get freedom?'

'Because of the Congress and Satyagraha and...'

'Pha! Nonsense! The white men got fed up. And they left. That was all. You think Gandhi Vikraman brought a cart load of freedom in his bullock cart?'

'No, no.'

'And then when our very own Gandhi stood for election, who won? Abkari Malasseri's son, Lazar!'

'That's true. That boy Lazar gave a knockout blow to our bullock Gandhi. That was when his wife jumped into the well again.'

'Padmasanan, it is now thirty years since we got freedom. Has this Vikraman Pillai won even one election?'

'But Yajamanan, he stood for election only once.'

Sreedhara Menon laughed as though he had heard a great joke. 'You said it, fellow. Um, let's stop these Vikramadityan stories. Pour some more, Paru.'

The scene continued.

Loudly.

Eight

Cherian Munshi was equally crazy about two things – the Malayalam language and agriculture. He stayed in the compound of Geevarghese, who was a trader in hill produce – on a sort of unclear lease agreement.

Geevarghese had let Munshi have forty cents of land. When they had met several years ago, when Cherian Munshi had first come as the Malayalam teacher at the school at Kottoor Kavala, Geevarghese had told him something like this, 'Munshi sir, if you are interested in taking a spade to the land and cultivating something there, come with me. I'll let you have forty cents of land to use. There is a small house there. You give me some three or four rupees as rent for the house. Finally it will come to you. Along the way, my children can learn enough Malayalam to write the accounts of dried ginger and pepper!'

These were the terms. This was an arrangement that gave pleasure to both of them. Munshi sir, who was a bachelor, was extremely happy. How long ago had it been? It must have been some thirty years ago. Munshi sir had no problem spending time – in the school, cultivating the land, and then his secret hobby of writing poetry. When all these combined, he was happy, contented. 'Mishiha Charitam' or 'The Story of Christ' in four-lined stanzas was progressing apace.

Cherian Munshi was digging the land with a spade on this holiday. Rivulets of sweat poured over his nearly bald head, naked chest and the tummy that jutted out before him.

He finished preparing the beds of a couple of coconut trees and had started putting ash on the yams to be planted when he heard a movement among the nutmeg trees. The spotted koel was trying to pick out the covering of the nut in the nutmegs that had opened out. Munshi spoke to the koel as though he was speaking to the students in the class, 'Why are you alone? What happened to the black koel who's usually with you? Shall I write a poem about you? I'll think about it. But cultivation is more important than poetry. You want to fly away by yourself or you want me to throw stones at you?'

Geevarghese, who had come up to the fence by this time, saw Vedaraman.

'Who are you?'

'I came to see Munshi sir.'

On hearing voices, Munshi turned around to look and asked loudly, 'Ramankutty, uruli thief, what are you doing here?'

Vedaraman hung his head.

'Who's this, Munshi sir?' Geevarghese asked.

'He's my student, Geevarghese! He's Ramankutty from Mulamkunnam.'

Geevarghese opened his eyes wide and said, 'Of the Mulamkunnam family? Then this boy and I are connected.'

'How's that?'

'You know, Munshi sir, all this land you see around you was acquired by my great grandfather in a court auction. All of this once belonged to the Mulamkunnam family.'

'That's a connection all right. But my connection is different. The relationship between a teacher and his student, right Ramankutty? Never mind. What made you come now?'

Vedaraman stammered, 'I want to study.'

'So, you've acquired some sense, is it, uruli thief?'

Geevarghese asked, 'Why do you keep calling him that?'

'Because he stole the uruli from the temple!'

'Really!' Geevarghese stared at Vedaraman.

Vedaraman felt sorry he had come here at all. Munshi sir

hated him. Why was he announcing the story of the uruli theft even to people who did not know about it?

His eyes grew wet. Vedaraman spoke in a broken voice, 'I made a mistake. You don't have to keep saying it. Even the Magistrate, Mr Mathews, said that the first mistake should be forgiven.'

Munshi sir felt bad. He hugged Vedaraman and said, 'Did I hurt you, Ramankutty? Don't be so sensitive.'

Geevarghese touched Vedaraman on the shoulder and said, 'Never mind, Ramankutty! Anybody can make a mistake. I too did steal when I was young. From my mother's clothes box. I searched it and took everything I found – notes and coins, and got twenty-five rupees. That was a big sum then! And I ran away. Do you know where I reached? Bombay! When the money got over I came back like a wet hen, ticketless on the train.'

Geevarghese laughed aloud at the thought of such foolishness. Munshi sir laughed with him. 'Geevarghese, even I didn't know you had a history like this. And what happened after that?'

'What could happen? The river continued to flow. My father tied me to this land. I became a farmer. Then a trader in hill produce, I'm a respectable person now, wouldn't you say, Munshi sir?'

Munshi sir said, 'Ramankutty will also become a respectable person, I'm sure. What do you want now? You want to study, right? That's good. But, you've lost a year.'

'That's a big punishment, sir. I was in jail at the time of the annual examinations. I don't care if I can't study, I won't go back to the old class again. Sir, just set me a tough examination now. I'll pass it.' Vedaraman was very upset.

'You want me to hold an examination for you now? There's no way to do this, there are no rules for that,' Munshi sir said.

Geevarghese intervened at this, 'There'll be some way, sir. There's someone above to show us the way.'

Munshi sir took Geevarghese's towel and wiped the sweat from his big tummy and said, 'You're right, Geevarghese, there's someone above. We'll pray to Him. I have an idea. Suppose we take this guy to Vikraman Pillai. He is a big-hearted man. This fellow has a whole lot of problems. Sreedharan Yajamanan is down with a stroke. There are some other small problems too. It's difficult for him to stay at home. Isn't that right, Ramankutty? That's what Mukundan told me.'

'Which Mukundan?' Geevarghese enquired.

'That Warrier's son. Another student of mine.'

'Let's get to the point. Get this fellow to the next class somehow, sir. There's nothing in the rules against that, is there?'

'There's nothing in the rules against that. His marks in the examinations before that were good. If Vikraman Pillai just suggests it, Headmaster Swami will promote him. Did you notice something, Geevarghese?'

'What?'

'Ramankutty, show him your left hand!'

'Look at that. He has six fingers on this hand!' Geevarghese touched the sixth finger.

'That's luck. This sixth finger will save him.'

'Which astrologer told you that, sir?'

'Geevarghese, I don't need any astrologer to tell me that. I'm saying it. This sixth finger is lucky!'

Cherian Munshi broke his regular routine of eating, sleeping and writing poetry. He had agreed to help Ramankutty. He had to do it now. When he was told the whole story, Vikraman Pillai would agree, he was sure.

How could he let him know all the facts? One had to get hold of him for some time to narrate everything that happened. That was difficult. Since his wife Kanakamma died, he had withdrawn into himself. Reading, praying, fasting. A routine comprising all this. Though he was fairly old, his body still obeyed him. Might have been the result of yoga. But his mind had shattered into innumerable sharp shards of sorrow.

Would he have withdrawn like this if his wife had not died?

Munshi sir's mind went back in time.

Cherian Munshi had been young then. He had just joined Vikraman Pillai's school as the Malayalam teacher. Vikraman Pillai was a strong-looking man then. He had a huge turned up moustache and wore only the purest white khadi. He looked like a great person. When you saw him you felt both awe and respect. His voice was very deep and heavy. But his words were soft and pure. At that time he used to stay in the big house on Chathankunnu that was about two or three miles away from Kottoor Kavala. Cherian had seen Vikraman Pillai's wife Kanakamma at the house. Did she have any love or respect for him? She might have considered him a madman who forgot all about his house and wandered about trying to improve the world.

One of the first stories he heard on joining work here as the Malayalam teacher had been that of Kanakamma's attempted suicide. She had jumped into the well on the day that Vikraman Pillai had distributed his paddy.

And finally, that same well had been the means to Kanakamma's end.

It had been the day that Vikraman Pillai lost the election to the independent candidate Abkari Lazar. He had expected to win, that was certain. Or would he have invited his workers and friends to Chathankunnu for dinner on the day of the counting?

It took a long time for the counting to be over. Was it 7 o'clock in the night or 8 o'clock by then?

The ballot boxes from Manjali Panchayat were the last to be counted. Till then Vikraman Pillai had maintained a lead of more than nine thousand votes. But when the Manjali boxes were counted, Lazar had won by a majority of five hundred and twenty-eight votes. Vikraman Pillai, who had been present at the counting station, asked for a recount of the votes in that panchayat. It was 9 o'clock by the time the recounting ended. The result was the same – Lazar had won. But after the second counting, his lead had increased to five hundred and forty-two.

Vikraman Pillai returned to Chathankunnu in a taxi. He

was quite calm. Without any sign of agitation, he told everyone gathered there, 'You would have got the news. Right, I lost. That doesn't matter. Let's eat now. Analyses and discussions can wait till tomorrow, don't you think, Cherian?'

Within minutes, they could hear shouts and slogans. It was Lazar's supporters. They were climbing the Chathankunnu raising slogans in his favour. When the slogans started getting smutty, the workers started getting angry. He, Cherian, had jumped up; so had a few others.

Vikraman Pillai roared, 'Sit down, Cherian! Let them shout for some time.'

When the liquor that they had imbibed lost its power, Lazar's people went down the hill.

Vikraman Pillai called out, 'Kanakam, you can serve the food now. We are ready to eat.'

Kanakam did not reply.

Within minutes, the cook Kuttisankaran came crying and conveyed the news.

Everyone ran to the well.

Vikraman Pillai did not move from where he sat.

For the first time in his life, Vikraman Pillai had to seek a favour from the police. To avoid the distress of a post-mortem examination. Perhaps because the local Police Inspector was a good man, or perhaps because, though they had lost locally, the state was going to be ruled by a Congress ministry, the ruling was that it was an accidental death – without a post-mortem.

Did Kanakamma commit suicide because she could not bear the defeat of her husband?

Vikraman Pillai gave up the house on Chathankunnu after his wife's death. He gifted it to the panchayat. It now became a library with a fairly good collection of books.

It was later that he built this small house near the school.

On the day of the house-warming, Cherian and some of the other teachers had said that the house could have been slightly bigger.

When he heard this, Vikraman Pillai said, like someone who had no attachment to anything, 'What for? This is enough for me and Kuttisankaran. Both my children are away. They are not likely to come and stay here.'

Finally, one Sunday, after the Church service, Cherian Munshi went to Vikraman Pillai's house. Vikraman Pillai was at his desk scribbling something, in the room the walls of which held pictures of Gandhiji, Nehru, Vivekananda and Aurobindo.

'What is it, Cherian?' he asked.

Munshi explained the matter. Vikraman Pillai did not refuse the request.

'Forget about the theft case. I know the Mulamkunnam family well. I don't have any animus against Sreedhara Menon. And... you said this boy was intelligent and had scored good marks in the class examinations. I hope he does well. I'll speak to Headmaster Ananthu Iyer.'

Nine

Vedaraman went again to meet Cherian Munshi two days before the school reopened. He was immersed in the writing of Mishiha Charitam. Though Vedaraman stood there, Munshi did not raise his head. He was focused on the paper before him and was cutting out words here and there. He seemed to be rather irritated.

Vedaraman coughed to attract his attention.

Munshi stopped his cutting and correction and looked at him. The thick glasses slid down the bridge of his nose. Looking at Vedaraman who stood anxiously before him, Munshi winked mischievously. He laughed and said, 'Don't worry, Ramankutty. You have received the gift of education. It has worked! Vikraman Pillai agreed. You must go to Headmaster Swami and seek his blessings.'

'Thank you, sir. I'll never forget this help...'

'Forever, right? Good. If you consider it properly, I'm your guarantor. I said that you were a good student, a good boy. To whom? To Vikraman Pillai. See that you stay straight. Be a good student. Don't make me lose face. Ah, go now! Just tell Geevarghese the news too.'

❖

On his way back, Vedaraman thought to himself. He had to concentrate on his studies. He should not enter the dirty gutters he had in earlier days. He should be able to make this a new beginning.

And for that?

For that, he had to cut the threads of old relationships, which meant that he should not go back home. He should not see Kozhukatta Paru.

But how could he not go home? All his clothes were in the wooden box there. If he went there, that demoness might imprison him again.

'No, I won't go home,' Vedaraman said to himself, as if he was taking an oath.

He had to get hold of some new clothes. How could he do that?

He needed to buy textbooks and notebooks for the new class. How?

He needed money. How could he get some? Suppose a miracle occurred and some goddess appeared and gave him a pouch of gold coins. He could buy clothes and books. But his problems did not end there. Where would he stay? Where would he get food?

Thinking of this and that, he walked on until he found himself in the surroundings of the temple.

Achukutty called out from the tea shop, 'Ramankutty, why are you wandering with your eyes fixed on the sky?'

'Oh, nothing.'

'Come and have a cup of tea!'

Vedaraman hesitated. The tea shop was crowded. There were some people who knew him. Vedaraman guessed that the strangers were people who had come from neighbouring places to buy tapioca. The lorry near the peepal tree must be theirs. They were not likely to ask him anything. But would Chellappan who sold curds, and Sainulabdeen who scouted for timber for sawmills, and the dhobi Andy leave him alone? It would be the first time they saw him after he escaped from the court case. They might throw unnecessary questions at him.

'Ramankutty!' Achukutty called again. It was not that call alone which persuaded Vedaraman to enter the tea shop. He had suddenly remembered something. There must be some money belonging to him here. Whatever remained of the price he got for the gold ring. What was left after paying for the tea and other stuff he had bought for everyone that day. Vedaraman took a glass of tea and sat in a corner. Andy and Chellappan and Sainulabdeen did not ask him anything. Lucky! The strangers were discussing the availability of tapioca. They had to finish pulling up the tapioca from the compound of the local Namboodiri family before evening. The boats had to be loaded before 7 o'clock. Things like that.

Achukutty went up to Vedaraman and asked, 'So what's happening?'

'There's a lot to say.'

'Tell me.'

'Let the crowd go. I'll tell you.'

It took almost an hour for the crowd to go away and leave them alone.

'All right! Let's hear what's happening.'

'They're not happenings, but problems.'

'What problems?'

'I've been allowed to go to the next class. That means I can continue to study.'

'That's surely a good thing, Ramankutty.'

'That's true. Ordinarily it would be all good. But my situation is not ordinary.'

'Why Ramankutty?'

'I want to go to school, I'm happy I can go. But I don't want to go home.'

'Why's that, Ramankutty?'

'You want to make me say it all myself, Achuettan? Everyone knows everyone else in this small place. You would have heard something of the situation in my house, I'm sure. I'm not talking just about the stroke that affected Sreedharan Yajamanan.'

Achukutty raised his forefinger to his nose and said, 'I did hear some things. You know that Mukundan, he told me a whole lot of nonsense too.'

'Let's stop this discussion here. You know, this talk of my home and this game of hide and seek. I want to study. How can I do that? I need money for that. Clothes, books, a room to sleep in, food! I'm certain about only one thing. I'm not going back to Mulamkunnam.'

Achukutty went to the boiler in the shop. The water was boiling, making the copper lid jump with a noise.

Achukutty stood there and called out, 'Ramankutty, I'm still single. I need very little money. I don't plan to get married, though I'm twice your age. So, money is not an issue with me. I have to give you back quite a bit of money from that gold ring you gave me that day. And then...A place to stay? You can stay here with me. Clothes! What do you need, how much do you need? You can tell me. I'll get you everything.'

Vedaraman stayed at Achukutty's tea shop for two days. That was when he realized that Achukutty had a lot of hidden qualities.

He had taken care of all of Vedaraman's problems so quickly, arranged for everything. A big package came. Achukutty said, 'Open it and see!'

Vedaraman opened the package. There were eight mundus and eight pieces of cloth to stitch shirts from.

'All this...?' Vedaraman asked in wonder.

'I have a running account in Padmasanan's shop. The tailor Ouseph will come here. We have to get the shirts stitched,' Achukutty said.

Tailor Ouseph came to the tea shop that same day and took Vedaraman's measurements. He told Achukutty, 'I'll send them over tomorrow.'

'Look here, Ouseph, don't increase the charge just because they are needed urgently,' Achukutty joked.

Ouseph laughed aloud.

Ouseph sent over the shirts the very next day. Some of them were a little tight, some were a little loose. But they were shirts!

The school would reopen the next day.

He would go to the temple early in the morning, bow before the idol and pray, recite a hundred and one times: Oh Lord! Please show this uruli thief the right path. And after that? Eat breakfast. And then?

He had to wear the new clothes and get to the school. It was lucky that he had not seen Mukundan these past few days. Even if he saw him in school – he would have to, of course – he would keep his distance. There would be shouts and screams to celebrate the new session of the school. The previous year, he had been one of the smaller leaders of the noise. This year he would not get involved in all that. He would be a disciplined student, earn a good name. He must go and bow before the teachers.

First, he would go to Cherian Munshi.

Then to Headmaster Swami.

Then? He had to go and meet Vikraman Pillai and fall at his feet.

As he thought about his new beginnings, he suddenly felt that he would like to see Koman Nair. Just like that. Would Achukutty misunderstand?

Vedaraman went up to Achukutty, who was scribbling that day's accounts, and said, as if he was seeking permission, 'I was thinking of going to the temple to meet Koman Nair.'

'Go meet him.'

'Will you come?'

'Why do you want me to come, Ramankutty? I have plenty to do here. Um, I know what you want to do. You want to go near the big balance scale and have the other thing, right?'

Vedaraman stood there like a fool. Achukutty raised his voice and continued, 'I might sell the other thing secretly. No, I do sell the other thing secretly. But I don't drink it. I'm not willing to ruin myself by drinking it.'

'Achuettan, you're getting me wrong. I just wanted to go and see Koman Nair, that's all. If you don't think I should, I won't go.'

'If you want to go, go. Why do you need my permission for that?'

❖

Koman Nair appeared from the dark, staggering uncontrollably and reciting Sanskrit slokas.

Achukutty cooled down. Koman Nair appeared now like a joker. He told Vedaraman, 'So you got him here by some telepathy?'

Koman Nair was very drunk. He sat on a bench and asked, 'Achukutty, is it the bench that is swaying, or is it me?'

'How much have you had, old man?'

'Achu, that is an unnecessary question. Well, you can say that five or six huge firecrackers burst inside me, you asuran, demon! Do you know who walked all these paths earlier? The devas. They walked this way to kill the asuras. Do you want to hear the Sanskrit sloka that speaks of this?

'Yes, thank you,' Achukutty said.

Koman Nair stood up, swaying from side to side, and started reciting in his harsh voice, 'Poorvairanugato margo devairasuraghatibhi sadbhischanugata pantha...What comes next, Ramankutty? Sadbhischanugata pantha...Tell me the rest, Achukutty. I've forgotten the rest. I'll say with the astrologer, "sesahm chintyam, the rest is to be thought of later". Look here, the people who built this temple have died; Krishnan Namboodiri will also die. That cheap Warrier who keeps the documents so safely will also die. One day, this world will also end. Do you have any doubt about it?'

Achukutty declared that he had no doubt at all.

'But Achu, this idiot Ramankutty is still full of doubt. Do you know what his doubt is? Who his father was? Was it the singer Swami or Sreedhara Menon who is now flat on his back? I tried to help him solve this doubt. I told him and I say this again: all of us are born from eggs! Eggs or andham. So all of us are andhajas, those born of eggs!'

Achukutty began to fear that Koman Nair would stay there, making speeches, till the day dawned. The next morning there would be a crowd at the tea shop. The tapioca traders breakfasted here. He had to make appam, vegetable curry and egg curry. He had to get up very early, much earlier than usual.

'So, Koman Nair, that is now decided. Everyone is hatched from eggs!' Achukutty tried to rein in Koman Nair.

'That's not all, Achu! There are universal truths aplenty.'

'We'll talk of all this on another day.'

'As you like. I'll go now. Achukutty, is there any of the other thing left?'

'Those tapioca traders finished off all that there was.'

Koman Nair turned to Vedaraman and said, 'Ramankutty! Why haven't you spoken to me at all, not even a word?'

Achukutty said, 'He didn't get a chance, did he?'

'That's true! What with my Sanskrit sloka and its explanation, he was enjoying himself. Ramankutty, there will be some arrack in your home. Go there and get me some.'

'Sorry, Uncle, I've left home for good,' Vedaraman said.

'Why have you left home? What happened?' Koman Nair asked.

'I'll tell you everything, Uncle. Come now.' Vedaraman spoke looking at Achukutty.

Achukutty said, 'That's right Ramankutty. Don't make it late.'

When Ramankutty went out with Koman Nair, Achukutty got back to his accounts with a sense of relief.

Vedaraman got up before dawn and had a bath. He went to the temple and did the sayanapradikshana, or circumambulation of the sanctum sanctorum by rolling on the ground. As he rolled, he prayed: Oh god! Show me the right path. Make something of me.

He wore the new mundu and shirt and went to Achukutty for his blessings, 'Achuettan, put your hand on my head and bless me.'

'All right, I have blessed you.'

That was when he tried to touch Achukutty's feet. Achukutty prevented him and said, 'What madness is this?'

'It isn't madness. I wanted to do it.'

'Um, did you take money for lunch?'

'I don't need any lunch. I've eaten such a lot of appam and curry.'

'All that will be digested in a couple of hours, Ramankutty. Open the drawer and take four rupees. Let today pass like that. I'll arrange something permanent in the meantime. There is a hotel near your school, Bhoothanathavilasam. The owner Nanu is an acquaintance of mine. You can start maintaining an account there!'

Ten

The start of the school session did not bring any of the dangers that Vedaraman had anticipated. None of the other children laughed at him. They did not call him 'uruli thief'.

Mukundan kept his distance. He knew that Vedaraman had started staying at Achukutty's tea shop. But he did not ask him anything about it.

Let Mukundan keep his distance. That was better. His, Vedaraman's, life was taking a new direction. He had started on a new journey.

He had a rich breakfast at Achukutty's tea shop. He kept his books under his arm and walked to the school without glancing this way or that. In the afternoon, he had a lavish lunch at Nanu's hotel. He came back in the evening – alone.

Sometimes he would go to the temple pond and have a bath there in the evening. He would go and bow before the idol of Narasimhamoorthy if he felt like it. This was an opportunity to see Koman Nair as well. And then he would read. When he got fed up with reading, he would help Achukutty to prepare the batter for the next day or to wash dishes – something of the sort.

Vedaraman felt that he was earning a good name in the school. The fact that the Headmaster himself had shown his appreciation of him was not a small thing. It was the Headmaster who took English for the higher classes. One day he said, 'I'm going to give you a special test. All of you must write an essay on the topic "My village". The best essay will get a prize.'

It was Vedaraman who got the prize.

Swami spoke before the whole class: 'Here's Vedaraman's essay. Excellent English. I give him seven out of ten marks, the highest I've ever given anyone. All of you must read what Vedaraman has written.'

And then, he was given the prize. The Headmaster gave him a packet covered by thin yellow paper and tied up with a ribbon and said, 'This is Palgrave's *Golden Treasury*. It is a book of poetry.'

Munshi sir was satisfied. Ananthuswami was a rough sort of person, very stingy with praise. He had praised Ramankutty publicly!

When the meeting was over and the rest of the people departed, Munshi sir called Ramankutty aside and said, 'Ramankutty, all this good fortune is due to your sixth finger! The news will definitely reach Vikraman Pillai.'

'It's all due to your blessings, sir. That's what I think. One wish still remains, sir.'

'And what's this great wish of yours?'

'I haven't been able to see Vikraman Pillai and seek his blessings.'

'Don't be in a hurry. The time will come.'

As the days passed, a big fear that had haunted him melted away. Paru had not come searching for him.

But his relief was premature. One holiday, as he lay on his back on a bench in the tea shop and browsed through the poems of *Golden Treasury,* he heard raised voices outside.

Kozhukatta Paru was dancing like a possessed woman before the tea shop, yelling and calling Achukutty names. An audience of some twenty people had gathered.

'You rascal! You rogue, Achukutty! Have you tied him up here? Ramankutty is my son, I gave him my breast milk.'

'Stop talking nonsense. Yes, you gave him breast milk!' Achukutty's voice rose too.

'You son of a bitch! Are you letting him go or not?'

'Che! Get lost, you whore!'

'Achukutty! You bastard! His father is about to die. If Ramankutty is not there, all his nerves will burst.'

'Even if they burst, you know how to stitch them up, you whore! You hag!'

Kozhukatta Paru stood with her chest stuck out and waggled her hips and asked, 'Am I a hag then, you son of a bitch?!'

Vedaraman who had been lying down and listening to all this came out. When she saw him, Paru untied her hair and started weeping, 'My Ramankutty, you don't know where all I searched for you. I thought you'd stolen again and gone to jail. At last, Mukundan told me where you were. You've become so thin. Come with me. I'll look after you. Come, don't be afraid of anything.'

The audience was really enjoying the show.

Vedaraman spoke in a resounding voice, 'I'm not coming. And you are not to come here again.'

'Ramankutty, you're not saying this! This Achu has given you some potion or something to make you say this. Your father is about to die! Don't forget that.'

'We've spoken a lot about my father, haven't we, Paru? Forget it. I don't have a father or a mother. I was born from an egg! Umm, go away. Go!'

Paru screamed, 'I'll come again, Ramankutty! I'll take you with me. Ramankutty, let me see how long this Achu can keep you here with his potions!'

After telling him this, she turned in the direction of the Narasimha temple and said, 'Oh Lord! Narasimhamoorthy! If it is true that I have given this Ramankutty my breast milk, may lightning strike this Achukutty!'

Paru turned around and rushed away like a wounded tigress.

❖

Vedaraman was very upset. He told Achukutty that night, 'Paru will come again. It will become a daily problem for you.'

'Ramankutty! I let her get away with today's performance. If she comes again, I'll cut off her nose and breasts!'

'Can I say something, Achuettan?'

'What is it?'

'You shouldn't misunderstand. Can I say it?'

'Um … say whatever it is!'

'It is better that I stay somewhere else for a little while.'

'Why? Because you are scared of Paru?'

Vedaraman did not reply.

'Tell me!'

'She'll come again. She'll destroy everything. Things have happened between us.'

'Oh yes, the breastfeeding!'

'Things went beyond that, Achuettan. It is better that I stay somewhere else. I'll come back. You can be sure of that. I'm not an ingrate. I owe you so much. Who has given me the clothes I'm wearing? Who gives me the food I eat?'

Achukutty surrendered. 'Ramankutty what do you want me to do? You want to go away from here, right? Though you are very young, you can think. Do what you want. Just one thing now. You shouldn't have a problem there. Nanu will take care of your needs. I'll arrange everything. You can stay at Nanu's hotel.'

The next day, when he went to school, Vedaraman had a bundle hanging on his shoulder that had his clothes as well as schoolbooks.

He had lunch in Bhoothanathavilasam as usual.

When he went to have tea in the evening, Nanu asked, 'How come you're here for tea? That's not usual.'

'I'm not going today. I'll need food at night too. I might want to sleep here as well.'

'You can sleep here. You can do whatever you like. Just think of it as your own place. Achukutty and I are old friends.'

'I'll come around 7 o'clock, Uncle.'

Vedaraman walked to the school and walked around the compound. He had seen what lay behind the school building earlier. But it was only now that he really paid attention to everything. There was a volleyball court. There were no players then. A little further away was the well. And beyond that, there was a grove of banana trees. Beyond that, the land rose like a hill. At the top of the hill, he could see a house.

As he wandered around lazily there, he saw something move among the banana trees. A middle-aged man, strong of body, carrying two big copper pots, was going towards the well at a fast pace. He drew some water, filled the pots and went away.

Within minutes he was back with empty pots. This time he saw Vedaraman.

'Who are you?' the middle-aged man asked.

'I'm a student in the school.'

'Why are you here at this time?'

'Just like that.'

The middle-aged man started drawing water. Vedaraman asked rather hesitantly, 'Who are you?'

The man stared at Vedaraman as though he did not like the question. Then his expression changed and he said with a smile, 'I'm not a student of the school. My name is Kuttisankaran. Now tell me your name and where you're from.'

'I belong here. I'm Ramankutty from the Mulamkunnam house. My name in the school is Vedaraman.'

'Why are you wandering around here?'

'Just like that.'

'I'll make another two trips...to take water. Leave the place before that. After some time, watchman Pankan Pillai will come. He's an old policeman. He also keeps accounts well. He has the list of not just the benches and desks and library books, but even the pieces of chalk and the pieces of cloth that are used to wipe the blackboards. If anything disappears, he'll catch hold of you.'

Vedaraman stood there, stunned. 'Did anyone tell you I steal things?'

'Why do you ask stupid questions? I'm just warning you that Pankan Pillai will cross-examine you if you stand around here.'

'That's all?'

'Look boy! Shall I start with the cross-examination?'

'What?'

'Why don't you go home? You said you were from here.'

'That's true. But I can't go to the home I have.'

'Why's that?'

'That's a long story.'

'So...where do you sleep?'

'Here and there.'

'Hey Ramankutty! Stay here. I'll be back in a minute.'

'Where are you carting this water?'

'Up. For the Big Man's use.'

'Big Man?'

'Yes. Vikraman Pillai.'

Vedaraman wondered if the opportunity that Munshi sir spoke of was coming closer.

'Uncle, I'll draw the water. I'll also carry it up for you.'

'Yes, yes! And then I'll get a pot belly! My chest will no longer be broad or firm. I'm doing this for my reasons, for exercise.' Kuttisankaran flexed his arms and legs like someone doing exercises. His foot knocked against the pots and they fell and got emptied.

'Shoo!' Kuttisankaran blew and rubbed the leg to ease the pain. Vedaraman started drawing water.

'I'll do it, boy.'

'Never mind, Uncle.'

'Um, all right, do it. You'll get credit for it in the next world. The water is for the Big Man, after all.'

Vedaraman was filling the pots with water when Kuttisankaran noticed his sixth finger.

'Look at that! There is an extra one. I mean, your finger.'

'Do you know Cherian Munshi?'

'What do you think?'

'Munshi sir told me that my sixth finger was lucky.'

'Ramankutty, I'll come in a minute. I'll bring four pots in the next trip. You have to carry up two, agreed?'

'Happily.'

Vedaraman stood and looked on as Kuttisankaran's strong frame climbed the hill.

Dusk was falling.

If he carried the pots up the hill, would he be able to see the Big Man? And what would he do if he saw him? He would fall at his feet, and thank him. And then he would have to go to Nanu's hotel. He would have to sleep there. Or should he curl up somewhere on the school veranda? If Kuttisankaran would introduce him to watchman Pankan Pillai, he could do that. In a way, it would be better to stay on the school veranda. The hotel was always crowded. He wouldn't be able to study there. If he stayed on the school veranda, he could draw water from this well and bathe here. And then, he would be able to study for at least two hours before he went to Bhoothanathavilasam for his breakfast.

It was now dark. He could see a torch flashing among the banana trees. Kuttisankaran was coming down. His walk as he carried four empty pots and the torch reminded one of the tightrope walker's balancing act.

'I'll draw the water,' Vedaraman said.

'All right.'

As Vedaraman drew the water and filled the pots, Kuttisankaran's gaze was fixed on the sixth finger. He had a mad idea. Was the sixth finger glowing?

'Come, let's go,' Kuttisankaran said.

They entered the banana grove. It was pitch dark there. Kuttisankaran flashed the torch every now and then. As they climbed higher the torch fell from Kuttisankaran's hand and rolled down.

'Shoo!' said Kuttisankaran. 'Can't see a thing.'

A few moments passed. How wonderful! There was a little light now. It wasn't intermittent like the flash of a torch. Kuttisankaran realized what it was. Vedaraman's sixth finger was glowing.

How come Ramankutty did not know of this?

Vedaraman said, 'That's lucky, we can see the path with the help of the light from the Big Man's house. Uncle, that torch...'

'I'll search for it tomorrow.'

As they climbed the hill, Vedaraman asked, 'Isn't there a well in the Big Man's house...I mean, bungalow? Why do you have to carry the water from the school well?'

'Oh that? Ramankutty, this bungalow is in three-quarters of an acre of land on top of the hill. The house was built when he lost the election. Three wells were dug then. Two were dug in the usual way we dig wells here. There wasn't even any moisture, though we dug down to eighty feet. And then the Big Man brought engineers from Coimbatore. They came with that machine, what do they call it...yes, rig. They dug to a hundred and twenty feet. Do you know what we got? Just imagine if we made a pudding with charcoal. Something which looked like that.'

'And then?'

'And then the Big Man covered all three with thick concrete slabs. He then told me: "Kuttisankaran, we needn't have done this useless thing. If you can bring up eight or ten pots of water from the school well, that'll be enough for my use."'

They reached the back of that small house, which did not really deserve to be called a bungalow.

There was light inside.

'Big Man?' Vedaraman asked.

'He's either praying or reading. Sometimes he stands on his head, doing yoga...'

'What? I wanted to meet the Big Man.'

'Not now.'

Vedaraman felt dissatisfied. He said, 'All right...I'll go, then.'

Kuttisankaran asked, 'Where are you going, Ramankutty?' He asked the question as he looked at the sixth finger. It was not glowing then.

'To Nanu's hotel! I'll have food there. I'll sleep there after eating. Or, I'll go to the school veranda.'

'Let me tell you something, Ramankutty! You sleep here tonight. I know Nanu well. I'll tell him.'

'But Uncle, my clothes, my books...everything of mine is in Bhoothanathavilasam.'

'I'll get it all for you early in the morning. I have to go to bring water anyway. You stay here tonight.'

'All right, Uncle! But I do have a wish. Will you help me fulfil it?'

'Tell me what it is.'

'Will I be able to see the Big Man in the morning?'

'Agreed!'

'Where is that bullock cart?'

'And how do you know that there is a bullock cart here?'

'The Big Man comes to our temple in that bullock cart.'

'If the bullocks weren't there, I wouldn't have to carry so much water.'

Vedaraman could not help laughing, 'But then what would happen to all that exercise that keeps your tummy under control?'

'Hey! You're a rascal.'

'I was just joking, Uncle.'

Kuttisankaran patted Vedaraman's head and said, 'You sit here. I'll just go and see to the Big Man's needs. I have to give him his food and then take him to his room. I'll come soon. We'll eat in the kitchen after that. There's rice and avial and roasted pappads and curds. Isn't that enough? These are the things that the Big Man likes. Once in a while, because my tongue craves for it, I fry the first incarnation without the Big Man's knowledge. What? Fish, you know.'

Kuttisankaran went inside. Vedaraman wandered around.

Three capped wells.

Vedaraman thought to himself, why should there not be a well that had water in plenty?

A dream-like sequence flashed across his mind.

Kozhukatta Paru!

Her naked breasts!

Eleven

His feet got entangled with something. A small piece of wood. Vedaraman picked it up. It was a twig shaped like the handle of a catapult. It looked like the English letter Y.

As he walked around in the compound where so many wells had been covered up, with his hands on the two branches of the Y, Vedaraman felt that the tip of the twig and his sixth finger were moving. He stopped. His body was tingling. A vibration. Vedaraman knelt in the soil. He drew a circle with his sixth finger. He dug the tip of the twig deep into the soil and drew it through the circumference of the circle. If they dug here...?

As he knelt there, as though in a trance, Kuttisankaran came up.

'Ramankutty!'

Vedaraman woke up with a start.

'Uncle, I have an idea. There is an eternal spring under the soil here. It is clear water. Let us dig here. We'll tell the Big Man.'

'You're mad, really mad. Come, let's eat something.'

'I'll come. But, let's mark the place. I may not be able to find the place again. If it rains, the circle I drew will also disappear. Let's put that big piece of rock there...It'll stay.'

'Crazy fellow!' Kuttisankaran said.

Vedaraman pretended not to hear that, picked up the rock and marked the place with it.

Kuttisankaran saw the glow then – Vedaraman's sixth finger was glowing!

They reached the kitchen. Kuttisankaran had his gaze fixed on the sixth finger. What a wonder! It was not glowing at all.

They ate their food.

Vedaraman asked, 'Has the Big Man gone to bed?'

'Yes, he has.'

'Has he gone to sleep?'

'Ramankutty, the Big Man is not like us. He needs very little sleep. Even if he goes to bed, he lies there and reads. Sometimes he suddenly jumps up and writes – ten, fifteen pages!'

'What does he write about?'

'Who knows! I saw him for the first time in Trichur. Long ago. There was a meeting. It had something to do with united Kerala. It was a big meeting. There were some thirty cooks. I was one of them. I don't know why it happened that way... Fate, I suppose. I was serving him in the pandal...'

Kuttisankaran was elaborating the story...

'As I was serving him, Vikraman Pillai asked, "Where are you from?"

'I told him I was from Ottapalam.

– "When you say Ottapalam, what do you mean?"

– "Kothakurissi."

– "What family do you have there?"

– "No one, sir."

– "No one?"

'I felt shy. How could I tell him about Radha? Radha who had smiled at me and given me hope and then run away with the survey fellow...

– "What work do you do?"

– "I don't have any job."

'When I said that, he made a stern statement: "You can come with me."

'And so, I reached here...the young Kuttisankaran. Shall we sleep now?' Kuttisankaran ended the narration.

Vedaraman asked hesitantly, 'Can I see the Big Man tomorrow morning?'

'I told you I'll see to it. I can take a few liberties with him!'

'Uncle, it is about the new well...'

'We'll tell him. Let's sleep now. We have to get up in the morning and draw water from the well.'

Kuttisankaran switched off the light. The kitchen and the corridor where they had spread their mats to sleep were now dark.

After a little while Kuttisankaran called him, 'Ramankutty!'

The boy was fast asleep.

Kuttisankaran could not sleep. A piercing light was entering his eyes.

He opened his eyes and looked. Ramankutty's sixth finger was glowing.

❖

Kuttisankaran got up very early in the morning. Vedaraman was still sleeping. His hands were folded as though in prayer and resting on his chest. Kuttisankaran looked at his sixth finger. It was not glowing.

This was peculiar! He had seen that glow more than once the previous night. Had it been just a dream? Would anyone have a dream like that?

Kuttisankaran did not wake Vedaraman up. He went to the well to draw water. There was a lot of work in the morning. At least twenty pots of water had to be drawn and the cement tank filled. Everything from the water for the Big Man's bath to drinking water for the bulls had to be provided. Water for use in the kitchen too had to be kept separately.

He had finished two trips to and from the well. Vedaraman was still asleep. Finally, after he had finished getting all the pots, Kuttisankaran looked for Vedaraman. Where was he? He was not in the kitchen or the corridor.

That was when he heard voices from the front of the house. Kuttisankaran went there.

The Big Man was sitting on the easy chair on the veranda. Ramankutty stood humbly before him.

When he saw Kuttisankaran the Big Man said, 'I didn't know that Ramankutty had come here last night. I saw him only a little while ago. I've spoken with him a little. He's the beloved disciple of Cherian Munshi. I remembered that Ananthu Swami had given him a present too. Kuttisankaran, look at this. This is Ramankutty's handwriting. I tried giving him a small piece of dictation...'

Kuttisankaran took the piece of paper that Vikraman Pillai gave him and uttered words of praise, 'Very clear. The writing looks good too. I'm thinking of something, Big Man...'

'And what have you thought, Manikyavachakar?'

He explained to Ramankutty, 'Sometimes I call Kuttisankaran Manikyavachakar. Do you know why? He does not speak much to me. But when he does speak, only manikyams or precious stones fall from his mouth!'

Kuttisankaran spoke to Ramankutty, 'The Big Man is laughing at me. I'm not Manikyavachakar, only a plain vachakar, someone who speaks a lot. He has given me the freedom to talk as much as I want to.'

Vikraman Pillai laughed, 'All right, tell me what you have been thinking.'

'Why don't we keep this Ramankutty here permanently?'

'What for?'

'You sit and write every day. You needn't do that work any longer. You can dictate and Ramankutty can take it down.'

'That is something we can think of, Kuttisankaran! At this age, my hand does not have the speed of my mind. If I can keep Ramankutty here, I shall be able to complete some of my work. At least my work on numerology. Do you understand, Kuttisankaran?'

'A sort of game with numbers, isn't it?'

'Manikyavachakar has understood some of it. At its very lowest level, numerology is astrology, the prediction of the future that any local astrologer can do. But at a deeper level...this is a key, a key to the treasure trove of secrets.' Vikraman Pillai seemed to have embarked on a small speech. He continued, 'What is the real colour of this universe? Its true nature? What is its magic, its mystery? That is the full range of the occult. Let me put it succinctly. One can correctly gauge the fate, character and special characteristics of any man by the study of numbers. I've jotted down a few notes on these things. It is still incomplete. Do you know what I specially noticed when I saw Ramankutty? I saw his sixth finger.'

'Is that good, Big Man?'

'I'm not the person to say that. Let the theories of numerology provide the answer. Can you get me a glass of tea before that? Or let that wait. I'll finish saying this while I am in the mood. Balance, contentment, running a household, loyalty, affection, fame... all these are the effects of the number six.'

'Shall I bring the tea...?'

'That can wait. What is Ramankutty's proper name? Vedaraman. How many letters does the name have? Nine!'

'And what is the effect of nine, Big Man?'

'It is the complete number. So, success. Nine is the biggest number in the series one to nine. It is the number of creation. When the ovum and the sperm meet and nine months and nine days are gone, a child is born. Three into three is nine. Three plus three is six. There are three hundred and sixty degrees in a circle. Those digits too add up to nine. You can multiply any number with nine and nine is born again. Three into nine makes twenty-seven. Add two and seven and you get nine again. Enough... let us stop this craziness for the time being. Bring the tea. Let me get on with my routine.'

Vikraman Pillai got up.

Kuttisankaran and Vedaraman walked to the kitchen.

'Have a glass of tea, Ramankutty. You can have your bath after that. Today's breakfast is puttu and kadala.'

'I'll bathe after going to Nanu's. I didn't go last night. He must be sitting there with his face all swollen with anger.'

'All right. But why don't you stay here permanently?'

'Uncle, the Big Man is like god to me! I got my promotion only because of his good heart. I would need to be very lucky. But I have to think it over. I must ask Achuettan his opinion.'

'Who's this Achuettan?'

Vedaraman told him about his connection with him. He had been his first patron.

'He would want what is best for you. So, he won't stop you from doing something that will help you.'

'Even if Achuettan gives his permission, I can't stay here without telling the Big Man my whole story. I'm not a brave sort of person, but I have to tell him everything. You are good people, so you pretend you don't know anything bad about me. And even if he doesn't know now, he might get to know of it some time. So, it's better to tell the truth now itself. I am a thief, I robbed the temple of its big bronze vessel. I've been to jail. Munshi sir knows everything. But shouldn't the Big Man also know? He won't accept me once he knows the whole story.'

'That's where you are wrong. He will take you in. You don't know his big heart. He's seen a lot of life, suffered a lot. He doesn't look at the status of people and all that.'

'Why would he want to keep me here?'

'It may not be for your sake, but for his own sake.'

Vedaraman drank up the tea and said, 'Let me go, Uncle. I'm all confused.'

'I'll come here this evening, near the well.'

Vikraman Pillai finished his routine of doing yoga, bathing and having breakfast and sat down to read.

He called out as if he had suddenly remembered something, 'Kuttisankaran, tell Ramankutty to come here.'

'He's gone,' Kuttisankaran told him.

'Where did he go?'

'He went to Nanu's hotel.'

'What is he doing there?'

Kuttisankaran became 'vachakar' or narrator. He described

what had happened since he had seen Ramankutty near the
school well. The glow he had seen on the sixth finger...the way
the boy had determined the spot for the well...Everything.

When Kuttisankaran described how Ramankutty had arrived
at the place to dig a well, Vikraman Pillai declared, 'Dowsing!'

'What is that, Big Man?'

'It is knack of finding things buried deep under the soil by
extrasensory perception. It might be treasure that is buried under
the soil, it might be something else. This skill is used usually
to find underground water. When the dowser walks, holding a
twig shaped like a Y, his fingers tingle, there is a vibration. It is
believed that at the spot at which he felt that vibration, there will
be water under the soil. The glow you saw in the sixth finger and
the vibration we just spoke about have nothing to do with each
other. The glow in the finger has to be interpreted in another way.
We have to look for an explanation in the field of celestial, astral
bodies...'

Vikraman Pillai did not go further into an explanation of the
concept of astral bodies.

Kuttisankaran said, 'I'm feeling relieved.'

'About what, I don't understand.'

'When I told you that the boy's sixth finger glowed and all
that, I was scared. You'd think I was going mad. I'm feeling
relieved now.'

Vikraman Pillai said, 'Do you know how many phenomena
exist that are difficult to understand which deserve to be studied
deeply? Anyway, I've decided something. We shall dig a well at
the spot that Ramankutty indicated. If we do get water there,
you will have less work to do. You won't have to climb the hill so
many times. And if he stays here, I'll have less work to do.'

'Don't be sure of that.'

'He must be reluctant to leave his home and come here, I
suppose.'

'It's not that. He doesn't want to go to Mulamkunnam. He's
trying to decide whether to stay at Nanu's hotel or on the veranda

of the school. I saw him when he was trying to make up his mind. About staying here...'

'Um?'

'He's a little scared. He was involved in a theft case. That is a black mark. He thinks it would be wrong to stay here without telling you about it...I think that's the way he feels...'

Vikraman Pillai said, 'I'm becoming more and more impressed by Ramankutty, Kuttisankaran. When Cherian came here to speak about preventing the loss of a year in school, he told me the whole story. Whatever that is, he felt that he should not hide anything from me. That's a good sign! Do something. Tell Cherian Munshi to come here. We'll have lunch together.'

Twelve

Vikraman Pillai spoke to Cherian Munshi about Vedaraman as they had lunch. 'I've seen the boy only for a short while. But he seemed a smart fellow. His handwriting is excellent. Kuttisankaran suggested that he stays here. I too think it is a good idea. He'll be of help to me too. I can dictate some of the things I'm trying to write. Some of my articles that are now incomplete might even get completed. If he is eager to learn, I could give him a sort of general education too. Will Ramankutty stay here? Kuttisankaran was not too sure. His background... that uruli theft... How can he stay here without confessing all that? Ramankutty was feeling doubtful about the whole thing. He did not know that you had told me of the theft case. But he wanted to tell me about it before he came here. Don't you think that is a good sign?'

'I've not told him that I had informed you of the uruli theft.'

'Don't tell him, Cherian! I have no objection to Ramankutty staying here, in fact it would please me. But will that Sreedhara Menon be angry about it? As it is, he counts me as an enemy without any reason.'

'From the old election days, sir?'

'No, no. Much before that! I hear that he's now bedridden...'

Kuttisankaran who was serving the food said, 'Ramankutty won't go back to his house anyway, Big Man.'

'Mukundan also said there were some problems at Mulamkunnam,' Cherian Munshi said.

'Who's Mukundan?'

'Another student at the school. Not that what he said has to be true.'

'When you talk of problems…'

'They're rather indecent stories connected with Sreedhara Menon's misdeeds. It's all hearsay. Is that why Ramankutty does not stay there?'

'Let the reason be anything. Why should we wash dirty linen in public? I'll invite Ramankutty to stay here.'

'That's the goodness of your heart. And the good fortune of his sixth finger.'

'A sixth finger is very lucky according to numerology.'

'The local belief is the same, sir.'

Vedaraman and Kuttisankaran met at the school well in the evening. Kuttisankaran informed Vedaraman that the Big Man had sent for Cherian Munshi and that they'd spent a long time talking.

'I think some sort of decision about you has been taken. You'll be staying with the Big Man from now on. You can take it that he's invited you through me. Or do you want him to invite you himself?'

'The Big Man had spoken about it in the morning itself. What more invitation do I need? I hesitate only because I have other doubts.'

'If it's about the uruli theft, you can forget about it. The Big Man knows about it. He'll not say a word to you about it, I'll guarantee that.'

'Uncle, I'll just go and tell Achuettan about this and come back. I'll come tomorrow itself.'

'It'll be for your good, Ramankutty! It's all the luck brought by your sixth finger.'

'Munshi sir must have said that.'

'Actually, the Big Man told me. When I told him how you had marked the place for the well.'

'He must have thought that the thief Ramankutty is crazy as well.'

'Che! What he said was that he plans to dig a well there.'

By this time, it was getting dark. Kuttisankaran saw it then – the glow of the sixth finger.

'Look, look, there it glows.'

'What?'

'Can't you see the glow of your sixth finger?'

'What are you saying, Uncle?'

Vedaraman went to Achukutty's tea shop that night. When told of the developments, Achukutty said, 'Very good. Stay under the umbrella of Gandhi Vikraman Pillai. It'll bring you success.'

Vedaraman, who started staying with Vikraman Pillai, was entering a new world. The first evening itself, he was taken to the library. The number and variety of books on the shelves bewildered Vedaraman.

'Ramankutty, I don't claim to have read all the books or to have understood even those that I've read completely. I stopped reading for pure pleasure some time back. Now I read and re-read books on Indian philosophy. With that, numerology, parapsychology...And books on the occult. You must read a lot too. Just talent is not enough. You must cultivate the habit of thought. Just reading is the lower most step – the level of tiryaks, the lower beings. You have to enter logical thought, consider matters. Only then can you call yourself human!' Vikraman Pillai spoke at length.

'Sir, Big Man!'

'Oh! You've also started calling me that?'

'I don't deserve your affection or your sympathy. I...I'm a thief...'

'Stop it, Ramankutty! I know everything. What does one do if one steps into shit? Does one cut off that foot? What you must do is to wash it well. You have repented. That makes you clean. My lecture has gone on for too long. This will do for the first day. If

I don't stop now, Manikyavachakar, who is waiting for you, will get angry with me.'

Vikraman Pillai walked to his study. Vedaraman went to the cowshed near the kitchen.

Kuttisankaran was bathing the bullocks.

Kuttisankaran asked, 'What was the big discussion?'

'The Big Man was speaking! Mostly things I didn't understand. He advised me to read. There are so many books there. Don't you read any of the books, Uncle?'

'Who, me? I studied barely up to the fourth standard. What can I read? I read the headlines of the newspapers that come here. And sometimes, *The Story of Madanakamarajan*. It's lying in the store room, with all its pages having come apart. I must have read it a thousand times. I cook, I draw water, I bathe the bullocks – that's about the most I can do.'

They could hear the sound of the radio from inside.

'The Big Man is listening to the local news! Did he tell you about the new well?'

'No.'

'He's placed the first stake this afternoon.'

'Where?'

'The spot you had marked. He said the work would start soon.'

Vedaraman was in a hurry to look at the spot he had marked. A big stake was planted next to the rock he had placed. He saw that the number 'six' was written in white on the tip of it.

'Who wrote this number, Uncle?'

'I did. The Big Man told me to. I wrote the number with lime'.

'The Big Man is full of surprises, Uncle'.

'Do you know what I feel very often? Wonder! Fear! Though I have stayed with him for so long, I haven't been able to understand the Big Man. He was not like this earlier.'

Kuttisankaran started pouring out old stories: 'He was the lion who should have ruled this land. Ramankutty, you were not born at that time. I was only nineteen or twenty when I first saw the Big Man. It was at the Aikyakeralam or United Kerala meeting.

The Big Man was god incarnate to the poor people of this place. His great mind and his granary were always open to others. Why did he start this school here? For the sake of the people here. He doesn't have a selfish bone in him. And what is the school called? Kottoor High School. The school was built completely with his money. Why doesn't he name it Vikraman Pillai High School or something like that? That's his greatness. We finally won independence. The first election was in old Travancore. The Big Man became a candidate only because everyone insisted. There was nobody of his stature in the Congress in this area. He should have been elected unopposed. If he had known that some people objected to his being the candidate and that his own people would betray him, would he have stood for election at all? He found out at the last moment that some traitors had brought in the liquor man Lazar as a candidate against him. It was impossible to withdraw at that time. The Big Man, who had been sure of winning, lost the election. We were at the old house on the day the votes were counted. I had made food for all the workers. The Big Man was not upset though he had lost. He told me to serve everyone food. In between, the supporters of Lazar came and started shouting bad words and creating a noise. That was when his wife Kanakamma jumped into the well. She was everything to him. When he lost his wife the Big Man's nature changed completely. He withdrew from public life. Or he took the first steps towards withdrawal. He started growing a beard. Finally, he gave up everything and came to this hilltop, which did not even have water, and made this small house. Time went by. Travancore became Travancore-Cochin. Then it became Kerala. The Communist ministry came to power. Congressmen got it thrown out. And then they ruled. In all these years, do you think a single leader came this way to see the Big Man? Not at all. He immersed himself in reading. The days passed. That was when that incident occurred...'

Suddenly, Kuttisankaran paused and asked, 'You can still hear the radio, can't you?'

'Yes.'

'Then we can talk for a little while longer.

'When I talk of the incident, I mean the big Congress meeting in Kochi. Pandit Jawaharlal Nehru was coming to Kerala to participate in it. It was a wonder that, after such a long interval, he remembered his old co-worker Vikraman Pillai. A message reached Trivandrum from Delhi – the prime minister wishes to meet his old co-worker Vikraman Pillai at Kochi.

'I heard all these stories, Ramankutty! When the message reached the Congress house in Trivandrum and the chief minister's office, there was a small earthquake there. Why did Jawaharlal want to meet the Big Man whom the rest of the party had forgotten? Perhaps the rulers felt jealous.

'A special messenger came with a copy of the message from Delhi and a letter written in the chief minister's own hand to this hilltop. If that message hadn't come, the Big Man would not have gone to Kochi. Cherian Munshi went with him for company.

'It was a huge meeting. Panditji was on the rostrum. With him were the chief minister and other local leaders. Speeches were being made.

'The Big Man was sitting in the second row of the audience. Munshi sir says Nehru said something angrily to the chief minister. Whatever had happened before that, a police officer came to the Big Man and requested him to come to the stage. The Big Man got up. Jawaharlal jumped down from the stage and led him personally to it. The people were thrilled!

'Jawaharlal led the Big Man to the mike and instructed him to speak. The Big Man said, "What can I say? Whatever I say is likely to displease many people."

' "This is a free country. Every citizen has the right and the duty to speak fearlessly and openly," Jawaharlal roared.

'The Big Man's speech was full of things that would make those who held power angry. Cherian Munshi still remembers each word.

' "Dear prime minister, dear Jawahar, the eternal glory of

India! Fearlessness was the face of our independence. Our style was a simple life. Mahatmaji was our leader and our idol. And today? Thieves and smugglers and cheats and murderers have acquired importance in our politics. Do you not see this? I pray that you live eternally. But no one has eternal life on this earth. Once you are gone, the criminals who hide in the corridors of power will capture the parliament. They will strangle the voice of the people. Fearlessness will disappear even as a word in the dictionary. Demons who have grabbed licences and permits will reduce this land to one of corpses. We paid a heavy price for our freedom – the Partition. Will the new traitors vomit the poison of communalism and pave the way for more partitions?"

'The speech went on like this. There was no one to translate the speech and Panditji would not have followed the Big Man's Malayalam. When the speech ended there was loud applause – from the audience. Only one person clapped from the stage, and that was Jawaharlal.

'Do you know what happened finally? After a month, the local committee of the Congress took disciplinary action. They suspended the Big Man, then expelled him from the party. When that happened the Big Man withdrew completely into himself.'

'Uncle, I think the Big Man has switched off the radio.'

'Oh! Let me go then.'

Vedaraman woke up before sunrise.

In the meantime, Kuttisankaran had already collected the water to be used that day. Vedaraman used the water like a miser. After his bath, he opened his bundle and took out a mundu that was white, even if a little crumpled. It was not yet light then. Someone was coming up the hill. He looked out and saw that it was the boy who brought milk.

Vedaraman made tea.

Kuttisankaran said, 'Very good tea. Has the Big Man got up? You take him his tea today.'

Vikraman Pillai was just finishing his exercises. Vedaraman

brought in his tea. Sipping his tea, Vikraman Pillai said, 'I'm seeing your bare body for the first time. This won't do. You are not healthy enough. Your shoulders and chest aren't broad enough. The body should also grow stronger as the mind grows. From tomorrow, you must start pranayama. And then, in due course, yoga too.'

Vikraman Pillai told him about the benefits of pranayama. It was the control of breath. Breath, air, wind. The movement of a flywheel made a whole machine work. In the same way, you can control all the functions of the body by controlling air, your breath. When you control your breath, your circulation, the impulses in your nerves, everything becomes controlled. You can even control the minute functions of the brain and thus your thoughts.

'I'll come after my bath. You'll take a little dictation then...'

'Yes, Big Man.'

❖

Vikraman Pillai dictated.

'What is the first result of the chanting of Omkara and meditating on its meaning? Have you written?'

'Yes, Big Man!'

'Your mind withdraws from exterior matters. It concentrates on your quest for the atmaswarupa, the real qualities of the soul. Did you write?'

'Yes.'

'Barriers to self-realization like illness, reluctance to do anything, doubt, laziness, greed, illusions, the inability to find one's self, changefulness, all disappear. Did you write?'

'Yes, Big Man.'

'When these barriers disappear, the mind turns inward. Concentration is the result. Listen carefully. Have you written all this?'

'Yes, Big Man.'

'Prachchardanavidharanabhyam vaa pranasya... Do you want me to repeat?'

'No need. You said, "Prachchardanavidharanabyam vaa pranasya," didn't you?'

'Have you finished writing that?'

'I've started writing it.'

'Clever fellow. You heard what I said and repeated it to me. You have an eidetic memory, a memory like a blotting paper.'

The days went by this way.

One day, Vikraman Pillai told him, 'I've decided on one thing, Ramankutty! You have to get away from the kitchen and the corridor. You can sleep in the library from now on. We'll arrange a cot, a small table and chair and a reading lamp. If you keep spending time with Kuttisankaran, you will not go beyond the Madanakamarajan stories. And my plans will not work. You must read and grow.'

Vedaraman stood there with head bent, without saying anything.

'Even if I can't read people's thoughts, I do know what's in your mind. You're scared that Manikyavachakar will be angry with you. But listen to this. He was the one who suggested this. He also told me about the glow he has seen in your sixth finger. I can't see anything. But I can't deny what Kuttisankaran has seen. You can count on one thing though. I've decided to dig a well at the place you've marked. And something else. You have now mastered pranayama. But in yoga, two of your poses are not good enough yet – sirshasana and bhujangasana.'

When he later spoke to Kuttisankaran alone, Vedaraman found out that the work on the well would start next Wednesday.

'That's right. Wednesday! Your routine has to change now. You have to sleep in the library. I'll arrange everything. I'll also keep black coffee for you in a big flask. You can sit and read without sleeping much!' Kuttisankaran pressed Vedaraman's hand.

Thirteen

Workmen came to dig the well. The work progressed very fast. The locals laughed when they heard that another well was being dug. 'They dug so many times! And did they get even a drop of water? There isn't going to be any water on this dry old hill even if Bhagirathan's grandfather performs penance standing on his head!'

Some people said, 'There's plenty of water in the well in the school. All they had to do was to instal a pump set in the well, a booster on the incline and an overhead tank at the house. That would have made sense!'

'You know that boy from Mulamkunnam – they say it's being dug on his advice,' some others commented.

His classmates asked Vedaraman, 'Ramankutty, did you decide on the spot for digging the well?'

Vedaraman gave a noncommittal reply. One day Mukundan got hold of him. 'How deep have they dug the hole; no, I mean the well? When the hole fills with water, we'll celebrate. I'll bring the bottle and the glass. You can just pull up some water from the new well.' Mukundan laughed aloud.

Vedaraman did not reply.

'Hey Raman, why don't you laugh? Isn't my idea a good one?'

'I need to think so too.'

Work progressed. They found moisture at a depth of forty feet. Vedaraman felt a little relieved. When he had carelessly fixed the spot weeks back, in a half-mischievous mood, he had not thought that things would reach this far. The Big Man had started out on this because he trusted him. He prayed with all his heart, 'Oh god! Please let there be water!' But what happened was that they found a block. They found rock when they reached fifty feet.

One of those days, Mukundan called out from the school veranda, 'You ungrateful rascal!'

'Che!' Vedaraman reacted.

'I didn't call you that, your Paru did. Here, take this. It's a letter from Kozhukatta!' Mukundan took out from his pocket a piece of paper folded into four.

Vedaraman read: 'You ungrateful rascal, I'm your mother and your lover. I'll always be both. I'm leaving you alone for now. I'm going my own way. I'll not come in search of you again or trouble you. But remember this! My curse will always follow you. Paru.'

Vedaraman rolled up that piece of paper into a ball. Mukundan said, 'I've been carrying that piece of paper for three days. Ah, I feel as though I've got rid of a weight.'

'You idiot! This was not written by Paru. It's your handwriting. It was written by you.'

'True! What you said is true. But there is a bigger truth. I took down what she said. It's a fact that I've polished up the words a little.'

Vedaraman threw the ball of paper on the ground and stamped on it.

'Ramankutty, whether you stamp on it or grind it, the stain will not go away. Oh yes, I must tell you everything. Kozhukatta has been missing since yesterday. No one knows where she's gone.'

Vedaraman started sweating when he heard this.

He bent and picked up the crumpled piece of paper and read it again. She'd said that she was going her own way. What did she mean by this? He put the piece of paper into his pocket.

He had to go and see Achuettan immediately. He had to find out what had happened. He had not gone to see Achuettan since he had started staying with the Big Man. Achuettan must be offended.

He deposited a postcard every week in the post box outside the school addressed to 'Sri Achukutty, Tea Shop, Near Narasimha Temple, Thottunallur Post.'

'I'm keeping well here. Hope it is the same with you. I'm studying well. Please tell Koman Nair Uncle that I asked after him...' Five or six lines of this sort.

Achuettan had not so far sent a reply. But Vedaraman kept sending postcards to him.

Mukundan went into the classroom. Vedaraman stood on the veranda. It was the Headmaster's English class. He was explaining a poem by Shelley. He would notice that his favourite student was not present. He would wonder what had happened. But Vedaraman did not feel like going into the classroom.

He had to go and see Achuettan. He had to find out what had happened to Paru.

If he walked fast, he could meet Achuettan and come back here before the school got over. This way Kuttisankaran and the Big Man would not know anything.

He walked. Actually, he almost ran. As he approached Kittappu's toddy shop, he saw the SIS Company's bus. It was headed the way he wanted to go. If he could get into it, he could save a two-mile walk. And time.

But he did not have any money. He had to walk.

He passed the tailoring shop and Padmasanan's textile shop. There was the culvert. And the path that turned there – to Achuettan's tea shop. When he saw Vedaraman, Achukutty asked, not hiding his surprise, 'You! What happened suddenly? Don't you have school today?'

'Yes, Achuettan, I do have school today!' His voice broke as he replied.

'Then why are you here?'

Vedaraman's fingers trembled. He took out Paru's crumpled letter and handed it over without any explanation.

Achukutty's eyes opened in surprise. But he did not ask anything. He read through the letter a couple of times.

'The handwriting is Mukundan's!' Vedaraman said.

Achukutty looked around. There weren't many people in the shop. Just as well. He spoke rather loudly, 'The handwriting is not the problem. There is something else. Paru is missing. But why did you come rushing here for that?'

Vedaraman hung his head.

'It's time for lunch. Have you had anything, Ramankutty?'

Achukutty spread some cold stuff from the breakfast on pieces of banana leaf.

He said, 'Paru had come here four or five days ago and started making a noise. A crowd gathered. I tried to get rid of her. She wouldn't go. She was dancing and screaming and jumping around as though she was possessed. She said she'd go and grab you. From where? From Vikraman Pillai's house! I couldn't bear it. I said that I'd break her knees if she tried to do something of that sort. She ran away screaming...And then...We found out only yesterday when Janaki Ammyar told Sanku Warrier the news. That Paru had vanished. Koman Nair and I went to Mulamkunnam. Sreedharan Yajamanan was lying there, groaning. There was no one in the house. I went to the kitchen. It didn't look as though anything had been cooked there. There was a vessel of milk. I boiled it, cooled it and poured some into Yajamanan's mouth. How much do you think I poured? A lot. Most of what I poured was flowing out through the corner of his mouth. By then more people came by. There was a sort of meeting. Yajamanan could not be left alone. Baby came by then. You know, our Kochappu's son. And Unneera. They take turns sitting with him. Janaki Ammyar gives him gruel once a day. And I give him gruel once a day. There's plenty of milk. I don't know how long this arrangement will work. I'm talking of the happenings of the last one, one-and-a-half days. If Paru does not come back...we don't know...Some sort of permanent arrangement will have to be made.'

'Achuettan, where did Paru go?'

'Who knows, Ramankutty!'

Vedaraman did not feel like eating anything. He got up. 'Let me go now, Achuettan.'

'You've just come! Oh, you're mad at me. Look there! All the cards you've sent have been kept together on that hook and preserved carefully. I didn't reply, that's true. I need to be free of all the work here to write a reply, don't I?'

'As if I'd get mad with you! It's not that. I've cut class and come without the Big Man's knowledge. That's why I'm in a hurry to go back.'

'Since you came all the way, go to Mulamkunnam and see Yajamanan.'

Vedaraman stood silent for a while and then said, 'No, not this time. I'll come another time...'

'As you like. But if people say something...you'll have to listen to it.'

It was night. Vedaraman sat in the library with a book open, but could not concentrate on it. When he thought of Paru, he could feel the chill of fear. Would something bad...would she have committed suicide? Though the handwriting in the letter and the words were Mukundan's, the thoughts were hers. Wasn't there a hint that she might commit suicide in that letter? There were whirlpools in the river. Would she have jumped into one of them? With a stone tied around her neck? The picture of the dog's carcass that had got caught in the granite wall of the river came to mind. He felt afraid to sit alone. He could not sleep alone that night in the room. He would get nightmares.

Vedaraman put the book on the table and went out quietly. The Big Man was asleep. No light peeped out through the crack in the door of his bedroom. There was light in the corridor.

Kuttisankaran was about to sleep after finishing all his work. When he saw Vedaraman standing near the door, he asked 'What are you doing here? Finished reading?'

'I can't keep my mind on the book.'

'And why is that?'

'I don't know.'

'You didn't come for lunch today.'

'Went to Nanu's hotel.'

'You don't usually do that.'

'You know that Mukundan. He insisted.'

'Go, and read something.'

'My mind must find a little peace before that, Uncle.'

'What happened to your mind now? Um... I can guess. You're worried about the well, right?'

'Yes, Uncle!'

'That black rock is destroying your sleep. Don't worry. The rock is not a problem at all. We won't even need to blast it with dynamite. If we get four strong men and four iron levers, the rock will melt like butter.'

'Will there be water, Uncle?'

'Without a doubt. Hari's birthday is after two weeks. Before that the earth will let its teats flow.'

'Hari? Who's Hari?'

'The Big Man's son.'

He had not heard about someone like that. When Vedaraman wanted to know more about him, Kuttisankaran became a 'vachakar', a narrator.

'Ramankutty, the Big Man has a son and a daughter. Hari and Rema. Both left Kerala long ago. Hari is in Bombay... in Chembur. He is a big officer in a big company. Always on tour. In the country and outside. In aeroplanes. He doesn't come here at all. He came last when Kanakamma jumped into the well and died. That was when Rema and her husband Surendran also came last. From Delhi. Rema is a newsreader in the radio station there. Surendran was a leftist... intellectual... He works in the university. It's so many years now. None of them has come here since then. Hari hasn't got married. At least he could come once a year. Rema has a daughter – Padmaja. The Big Man yearns so much to see that child. Do you know what he has here? A photo of Padmaja's. The photo of a five-year-old in a little frock. That girl must be twenty-two or something now. When you see the Big Man looking at the old photo...you feel really sad! One day I asked the Big Man openly why his children behaved like this. And do you know what he told me?

"'Times have changed, Kuttisankaran. Relationships are not firm any longer. The time of the joint family is long gone. This is the time for small, isolated families. Values, tradition, duties... there's no point talking about all these. I'm not blaming my children, I'm arguing on their behalf. Geographically also, they're so far. We have to take that into consideration as well. They get a few days as holidays. If they had to come here, they'd have to fly. How much do you think it will cost to reach Kochi from Delhi and Bombay? And to return by flight. In my old age, I should realize that Hari and Rema have their own problems. Don't you think so? I should retreat. My health is still all right. I have enough to live on. Then why should I complain? All of them do love me, I'm sure of that. And you are here like a son to look after me. That's my good fortune. I sit here and wish good fortune to Hari and Rema and Surendran and Padmaja. I last went to the Narasimhamoorthy temple for Rema's birthday. I'll go again for Hari's.'"

As Kuttisankaran gave a detailed description, Vedaraman thought back: it must have been on Rema's birthday that he had seen Vikraman Pillai get into the bullock cart from near the peepal tree to return home. The day he went to Achuettan's tea shop with Mukundan and Mullan Sasi and others.

Kuttisankaran asked, 'Why are you sitting like the crow that swallowed marottikka? Go, go and read something. That's why that room has been arranged for you. Including black coffee!'

'Uncle, I don't think I'll be able to study anything today... So...'

'So what?'

'I'll sleep here with you tonight.'

'Why, so that you can keep me from sleeping also? All right. Just one thing. If the Big Man yells at me, saying that I did not let you study, you have to answer him. Agreed?'

'Agreed.'

'Then come. We'll spread the beds and sleep. Let me put out the light. Don't light your torch in the dark at night.'

'My torch?'

'That sixth finger of yours!'

It wasn't very difficult to remove the rock. When people and iron levers worked together, the rock melted as Kuttisankaran had predicted – melted like butter. The imprisoned springs came out with a vengeance, hissing, foaming, roaring.

The water level rose.

The well, which was barely sixty feet deep, held twenty feet of water now. The people who had gathered to watch clapped their hands. Some of them jumped around.

The Big Man who had been standing and watching the work asked Kuttisankaran, 'Where is Ramankutty?'

'He's in school.'

'Go and get him here. This is his moment.'

Kuttisankaran produced Vedaraman.

Vikraman Pillai embraced Vedaraman. He announced before all of them, 'This is the result of a joint effort. But one person has to be given special credit. Ramankutty! He's the person who identified the spot where the well should be dug. Tomorrow, we'll declare a school holiday. And all the students will be given a grand feast.'

That night the Big Man told Kuttisankaran and Vedaraman, 'I was praying that we would find water before Hari's birthday. Narasimhamoorthy gave me the boon. I must make all the offerings tomorrow itself. Including the ghee lamp before the idol.'

Fourteen

The new well was a big boon for Kuttisankaran. He could sleep now. It was now some time since he saw the sunrise. He felt that he had a lot of spare time. His reading diversified. It went beyond the stories of Madanakamarajan. He started reading Vedaraman's Malayalam texts.

Kuttisankaran was nervous about just one thing. Since he no longer had to climb the hill a number of times, he hardly got any exercise. Would his belly become unruly and jump forward?

He would tell Vedaraman once in a while, 'Hey, your well has made me a lazy man. My body hardly moves. If I develop a big belly...you'll get the punishment.'

Vedaraman would laugh when he heard this. He would say, 'I'll accept the punishment, whatever it is. But you have to take care of my affairs, in return.'

'What affairs do you have, anyway?'

'I'm a famous man now. Suppose people queue up here, saying: Find the place where we should dig a well. I'll have a difficult time.'

'Is that all? I'll get rid of them politely, saying: Let our boy study and grow up and then we'll see.'

'You will?'

'I'll do it.'

Days passed the same way.

Vedaraman fell into a routine. Pranayama, yoga, taking down dictation from the Big Man, Ananthu Swami's classes, reading about Indian philosophy in the evenings, then at night...in the library room...

Books on all sorts of subjects rubbed shoulders on the shelves: books on the occult, magic, spiritualism, astronomy, astrology, stories of civilizations, history, geography, Subhash Bose's 'Indian Struggle', Nehru's 'Glimpses', Marx's 'Capital', the Ramakrishna Mission's publications, 'Selections from Vivekananda', 'The Message of the Upanishads', 'Mahabharatam', 'Gitarahasyam'...

And then of course, poetry, novels, biographies...To begin with, he just stood and looked at the books. Then he started leafing through them. Read bits from some. Finally, some books stuck in his mind – astronomy, astrology, the occult. Astrology – the science of forecasting.

As he asked himself whether the relationship between the overarching sky and the earth did not affect the ancient civilizations deeply, things would appear before him.

Several civilizations of the past appeared before him – Egyptian, Babylonian, Greek, Indian, Chinese, Mayan...As he turned the pages he would find interesting captions like 'The Philosophers' Egg', 'Hermetic Conception', 'Tarot Cards', 'I Ching'...

As the days passed evenly he almost forgot Paru. He also forgot another thing. The weekly postcards that he used to send to Achukutty no longer fell into the post box.

In the last card he had sent...when had he sent it? What had he written in it?

One couldn't blame Achuettan if he were angry and sat with his face all dark with anger. They would see each other some time. He would apologize then. Still, guilt filled his mind.

Am I changing without even being aware of it?

Kuttisankaran kept saying that his sixth finger glowed. He had not seen that glow till now. The Big Man was trying to ignite the fire of wisdom in him. But shouldn't that show in the brain?

Achuettan, please forgive me. I've become forgetful.

In a way forgetfulness is a blessing. I've forgotten Paru. When

I read that letter I'd been scared – whether she would commit suicide. Now, I'm not afraid. I do not think about her at all.

I sit in this library late at night and think of various things. Do these thoughts become magnetic waves and reach Achuettan's tea shop?

Vedaraman got a letter from Achukutty most unexpectedly. It was addressed to 'Sri Ramankutty, The Bhoothanathavilasam Hotel of Sri Nanu Nair, Kottoor Cross Roads.' A boy from the hotel brought the letter to him during the lunch interval.

'Ramankutty, I too found time to write a few lines. I'm writing this to relieve you of one of your anxieties and to give you some mild advice. That day, when you showed me Paru's letter, I too got a little afraid. Here's the good news. Paru is not dead. People have seen her at various places. She's wandering aimlessly. Everything's functioning at Mulamkunnam. Janaki Ammyar takes the gruel to the house in the morning and I take it there at night. Unneera's younger sister goes to the house every day to clean it, heat the water and boil the milk. Baby or Unneera sleep there at night. I too go once in a while. Now for the advice . . . People of the village have started asking why you do not even come to see your father. Come and see him. Koman Nair is keeping well. He gets high every day.'

Vedaraman thought.

My thoughts did reach Achuettan's tea shop in the form of magnetic waves. That's why he wrote this letter. He would go to Mulamkunnam, show his face there and come back. He needn't give the village a subject for scandal.

But he did not go.

I'll go tomorrow . . . I'll go next week . . . Days and weeks passed.

The school session had only a couple of months to go. Vedaraman sat and read, studied hard.

One evening, Headmaster Ananthu Swami called him to the staff room and spoke to him. The words still echoed in his ear,

'Raman, you must pass the examination with the first rank in the state and make us all proud.'

On those nights when he was working hard for the final examinations, he started having a dream. A peculiar dream. He dreamt on more nights than one. The same dream.

He, who had never gone beyond the village, even to the town next to it, would be standing in a huge city. It would be a busy intersection. He would be standing on a crowded footpath. A man with thick joint brows, wearing sunglasses, would come driving by. He would apply the brakes suddenly and stop the car next to the footpath and get out of the car. He would say, 'Hi Ramankutty!'

He would reply, 'But I don't know you.' The man would not say anything further, but stand staring at him for a very long while. He would then start weeping. He would cover his face with both hands. When he turned around, there would be holes in his neck and back. Blood would flow in streams from the holes.

When the dream reached this point, he would wake up.

When the dream was repeated, he would be able to see the man's face better and could remember it.

Thick joint brows.

Dark glasses.

A neatly trimmed moustache.

Sideburns that reached almost to the middle of the cheek.

If he knew how to draw, he could have copied that face on paper with the clarity of a photograph.

He thought of telling Kuttisankaran about the dream.

Later he thought he wouldn't. This was just a crazy dream. Did anyone go around telling people about crazy dreams?

Finally, he stopped having the dream. But it stuck in his mind.

There was a book in the Big Man's Library – 'Encyclopaedia of the Unexplained'. Vedaraman found the pages that dealt with dreams and read them.

The book said: Dreams are a mystery. A commonplace mystery that was familiar to mankind through the ages. Dreams inspired, they showed the way, they made you happy, they sometimes frightened you.

If a man sleeps eight hours every day...

By the time he reaches seventy-five years of age he would have spent twenty-five years in sleep. In this long sleep how long would he have spent dreaming? Maybe seven years.

The explanations went on like that.

It was Sigmund Freud who wrote the classic text on dreams. The first edition came out in 1900. Freud kept revising it till his death. He revised not just the text, but also the ideas and arguments.

The play of the dream takes place in the theatre of sleep. As with proper plays dreams are also divided into scenes. They are in dramatic units. Who are the actors? False images, true images, a stream of them, a series of them.

Even if you discount coincidence and telepathy, some dreams at least are signposts of precognition.

It was 8:30 in the morning. It was not yet time for school. Vedaraman reached early as always. Watchman Thankappan Pillai was there, supervising the work of the sweepers who cleaned the school veranda and the yard. That was when they heard screams and shouts from just outside the gate.

Vedaraman went to the gate.

The screams came from the boys who frequented the market. Some of them were throwing stones. In their midst was a mad woman. She was wearing torn clothes, a torn blouse with gaping holes. Her breasts could be seen. Her forehead was bleeding. One of the stones must have hit her. She was laughing and crying intermittently. She kept scratching her brown dry hair and showing her teeth. She was also trying to push open the gate and enter the school.

She was shouting.

He paid attention. When he realized what she was saying, his blood froze.

'Ramankutty, my Ramankutty!'

It was Paru. She had seen him by then.

She pushed open the gate screaming, 'My Ramankutty!'

The urchins became even more excited by the scene.

Paru caught hold of Vedaraman with both hands and kissed him many times.

The hoots and stone throwing gained force.

'My Ramankutty! My pet!'

Vedaraman shook himself free somehow.

Thankappan Pillai reached the gate; swinging a big stick, he got rid of the urchins.

Paru was still screaming, 'My son, my Ramankutty!'

'Scram! Run!' Thankappan Pillai pushed her out on to the road. She fell flat on her face. The urchins were on the other side of the road. They stood there and shouted bad words at Thankappan Pillai. He got really angry. When he rushed to beat the boys, a lorry came speeding down the road. Thankappan Pillai turned round to pull Paru to one side, but the lorry knocked him away. The rear tyres of the lorry went over Paru. The lorry did not stop. The driver accelerated and sped away. The boys created more noise. People from the shops and the market gathered. The students who had come out from the schoolyard stood there, stunned. Nanu took on the mantle of the leader.

'Thomachan, and you, move Thankappan Pillai to a side. You, Gopalan bring a piece of cloth or sacking and cover the corpse. Keep stones or bricks around the corpse and don't move it till the police come. Look, did anyone note the number of the lorry?'

Some of the people gathered there moved Thankappan Pillai to the veranda of Nanu's hotel. Some others covered Paru's corpse, and made a circle around the body with stones.

Vedaraman sat hunched near the gate, in a half conscious state.

Mukundan landed from somewhere and shook him, saying, 'You accursed fellow, you killed Paru. You killed your mother who gave you breastmilk!'

Vedaraman's tongue did not move. As he sat there hunched, his eyes fell on blood. The blood that had been smeared on his clothes from Paru's forehead.

His head started turning round like a top.

Did he throw up?

Did he fall unconscious?

When he came to, he was lying down on the cot in the library room.

Did he feel cold? Did he have a fever?

His eyes seemed to go round and round. Nothing was in focus. Who was standing in front of him? Was it the Big Man? Or Kuttisankaran?

If only he could reach out and get hold of something.

No, he couldn't. Something was clutching at him. Something was knocking him down.

There was Rairu Nair. The long shed of women. Many Menons. The singer Swami. Magistrate Mathews. The uruli that kept expanding. Oil was boiling in the uruli. Arrack mixed with the oil. The palms on the other side of the river turned into demons. They came and fried him in the oil. Then he started glowing. Not just the sixth finger, but all of him.

Fifteen

He woke up soaked in sweat. It was completely dark. Every now and then a small drop of light appeared. Vedaraman looked around. The drop of light flew closer. It stuck to his sixth finger. Vedaraman shook his hand. The firefly flew away.

He was terribly thirsty. Vedaraman got up from the cot. He searched in the dark. His searching fingers found the flask that was placed on the table. There was hot black coffee in it. Thanks to Kuttisankaran Uncle.

When he'd had two mouthfuls of coffee, he started sweating again. He wiped his back and his chest with the edge of his mundu. When the stickiness of the sweat was removed, he felt better. He started wondering whether he should turn on the reading lamp, whether he should pick up a book and read. He was completely awake anyway. And it didn't seem likely that he would be able to sleep again that night. Finally, he decided not to turn on the lamp. If the light spread, the Big Man or Kuttisankaran might wake up. Suppose they came to this room!

He would just lie on his back. And spin a rope from the husks rotting in his mind. What would the colour of the rope be?

His thoughts moved on various rails.

Who had removed Paru's body? Where did they take it? Did they bury it, or did they cremate it? Was he responsible for Paru's death? She was crazy and came in search of him. She was killed by a lorry, wasn't she? Even if a thousand Mukundans stood and screamed, how could he be a murderer?

That accursed Mukundan! He had injected the poison of doubt in his mind. All those months ago, it had been he, Mukundan, who had told him the story of the singer Swami. Till that moment Sreedhara Menon had been his father. Later, Paru had strengthened the story of the singer. Whatever that was, it was Sreedhara Menon who had brought him up till he was fifteen years old. He was therefore bound to acknowledge Sreedhara Menon at least as a foster father. Achuettan had insisted that he go to Mulamkunnam that day, but he hadn't. That had not been right. It was a big mistake. He should go. As soon as possible.

Vedaraman lay there till dawn thinking of all this. He opened the window and looked out. Kuttisankaran was drawing water from the new well. Vedaraman went out.

When he saw him, Kuttisankaran asked, 'Why are you wandering about outside?'

'My fever's gone, Uncle.'

'Go and lie down! I'll get you tea.'

'There's nothing wrong with me now!'

Kuttisankaran filled the tank with water. He clucked at the bullocks as though he was making conversation with them. Then he touched Vedaraman's forehead.

'Everything's gone wrong. That woman who died under the lorry has created all the problems. Mukundan's been saying all sorts of things. Not just to me, but to everyone...'

Vedaraman's heart sank. What was that accursed guy going around saying? What could he tell Kuttisankaran? He had to say something. It wouldn't be sensible to say nothing. He would tell him some of the truth.

Vedaraman said, 'Mukundan's a gabmouth! He would have said all sorts of dirty things. Paru was like a mother to me. When my mother died, she fed me. Anyone can say anything. They said there was something between my father and her. There were all sorts of scandalous stories. I couldn't bear it any longer. You know what happened after that. Cherian Munshi helped me and I reached here...'

'Enough! Let's not talk too much history. Come and have your tea.'

As they went to the kitchen Vedaraman asked, 'Is the watchman all right?'

'Thankappan Pillai is in the town hospital. He's broken his leg.'

Vedaraman wanted to ask what had happened to Paru's body. But he didn't ask the question.

Vikraman Pillai reached there by that time and scolded him, 'This is great! Ramankutty, I came to the library looking for you and found you missing. When we put you to bed last night, you were unconscious. You also had a very high temperature. And now...'

'The fever's gone, Big Man!'

'Really? If so, good. But you are not a doctor. So I say, you have to lie in bed for a couple of days more.'

Vikraman Pillai then ran his hand over his beard and said with a smile, 'I'd also like to have a cup of tea.'

He sat on the stool in the kitchen.

Vedaraman realized that he was in a good mood and said humbly, 'You shouldn't think I'm being disobedient, but...'

'Say whatever you want to say without so much of circumlocution, Ramankutty!'

'Since I don't have fever now...instead of lying in bed...even if I don't go to school...'

'Kuttisankaran, what does this boy want?'

It was Vedaraman who replied, 'I want to go to the temple of Narasimhamoorthy.'

'That's a good idea.'

'If I could go for two days...'

'Why do you need two days to go to the temple?'

'I would like to go to Mulamkunnam as well.'

'Oh yes! To see your father. You can go. Come back soon. The final exams are fast approaching. Swami says you'll get the first rank in the state.'

❖

Vedaraman went by bus this time. He got out at the crossroads and walked with his cloth bag on his shoulder.

It was evening by then and Achukutty's tea shop was crowded.

'It's you! What's in the bag?'

'Clothes.'

'So, you're planning to stay.'

'I might.'

'I've a lot to tell you. Let the crowd thin a little.'

It was late by the time the crowd thinned. When the last customer had departed, Achukutty said, 'Come, let's go and sit on the platform under the banyan tree.'

When they reached the banyan tree, Vedaraman asked, 'You said you had a lot to say...'

'Mostly about Paru. It's big news here now! Mukundan's there, isn't he, telling stories...'

'I killed her, that's his story, isn't it?'

'Forget it! A mad woman wandered around. She died under a lorry. If she hadn't died then, she would have died some other time and in some other way. Just accept that a devil has gone out of your life. That's all!'

'Achuettan, my heart feels very heavy!'

'Bollocks!'

'She cursed me before she went away. The sentences in that letter... I keep feeling that there'll be even greater problems soon.'

'Did you come all the way here to say this? Stop it now.'

'I came to go to Mulamkunnam. I want to go to the temple too. I want to see Koman Uncle. Swim and bathe in the river.'

'Now, that's sense. Go to the house first.'

'I'll first go and meet Koman Uncle.'

'Do you want to? Isn't it better to go to Mulamkunnam when it's daylight?'

'We'll take Koman Ammaman with us!'

'As you like. But, will your uncle be in his senses?'

Koman Nair was sitting on the grass next to the big balance scale. He was fairly drunk. He was running his fingers over the saffron kurta he was wearing and reciting something. Achukutty and Vedaraman went near him.

'Koodeyalla janikuunna nerathum…one has no companion when one is born…'

Vedaraman touched Koman Nair, 'We are here, Uncle.'

'Oh! Ramankutty! The one born from an egg!'

'Get up now, let's go to Mulamkunnam,' Achukutty said.

'To see the man who is called your father?'

Vedaraman squatted near Koman Nair and tried to pull him up, 'Come now.'

'I'll come! Look there's a full incarnation under the stone. Pick him up. Then, pick me up.'

They walked to Mulamkunnam.

Koman Nair asked, 'How's your education progressing, Raman?'

'It's going on.'

Achukutty said, 'That's one side. But the problem is the weight on his mind.'

Koman Nair lifted both hands to the sky and said, 'Haraharo hara! Weight! The weight of Kozhukatta! Tell her to get lost, Raman!'

Unneera asked from the veranda, 'Master…'

'They've come to see Yajamanan,' Achukutty explained.

'How is he, Unneera?' Vedaraman enquired.

'He just lies like that.'

They went inside. Sreedhara Menon was lying with his eyes shut. They crowded around the cot.

'Don't wake him up,' Achukutty whispered.

Koman Nair nudged Vedaraman, 'Give that thing to me.'

Vedaraman handed over the bottle to him. As he moved to the kitchen, Koman Nair winked at Unneera, 'Glass and water…'

Having swallowed a mouthful, Koman Nair let out a long sigh

and said, 'Unneera, I'm seeing Yajamanan after a long while. He's become very thin. Does he have sores in his back? Do you turn him this side and that? If you don't do that, the skin will become loose in the back and the bums. And there will be sores. You wouldn't have turned him. Why should you? You have no responsibility towards him. Neither has Ramankutty. Yajamanan is not his father! Even if she was a whore, Paru did look after him properly.'

When they heard groans and noises, Unneera ran from the kitchen to the bedroom. Koman Nair followed him holding on to the bottle.

Sreedhara Menon had his eyes open. His chest was rising and falling. As he looked in turn at Vedaraman who sat at his feet and Achukutty who stood near him, tears flowed from his eyes.

Koman Nair said loudly, 'Still Achukutty, imagine Yajamanan reaching this pass! Who's there to look after him? Do they turn him every now and then? I wonder if there are sores already!'

Achukutty whispered in Vedaraman's ear, 'This Koman Nair has become a nuisance…'

'Achu, why are you chewing Ramankutty's ear? I'm speaking from experience. My uncle, Manikandan Nair, who used to stay in Chovvara, lay in bed for months and months like this. But he had people to look after him. They put him on banana leaves spread on reed mats. They would turn him around many times each day. So, there were no sores on him. What about the situation here? You can find out only if you lift him up and look.'

'Leave him alone. Don't lift and pull and trouble him.'

'Don't give me orders, Achu! I'm older in age and experience.'

Koman Nair was about to turn it into an argument.

'Shall we go to the river to bathe?' Vedaraman asked.

'Raman, you're trying to evade the issue. Yajamanan, these people say they want to bathe at this time of the day. You'll not get me to do something like that. I bathed in the temple pond with green gram powder and rubbing roots. Why would I need to bathe a second time today? You think there's that much dirt in Koman's mind and body?' Koman Nair held forth, drinking directly from the bottle.

Vedaraman moved away. He walked to the veranda. Achukutty accompanied him.

'Achuettan, I'm sorry. We should not have brought Koman Ammaman along.'

'Well, what's the point... Let's go and have a bath. Do you have a torch?'

'There'll be some palm leaf torches in the pounding shed.'

'We must get back before it is really dark. Before Koman Nair's games get even worse...'

They walked to the river.

Koman Nair rubbed his hands over Sreedhara Menon's limbs.

'You want a little, Yajamanan? You'll breathe easier. Unneera, just hold on to Yajamanan's chin. Lift him a little. Ah! See, he's opened his mouth. Let's pour in a little.'

'Should you, master?'

'Of course I should. I have given this at Chovvara.'

Koman Nair poured the arrack into Sreedhara Menon's mouth, which had been forced open by pressure on both cheeks. A sound 'bglum' came from the throat.

'It's gone down, Unneera. Hold on to the chin without letting it slant. We'll give him one more shot.'

Koman Nair poured more arrack into the mouth.

'Are you feeling better, Yajamanan?' Koman Nair asked.

The corners of Sreedhara Menon's lips moved.

'He's trying to smile, Unneera!'

Sreedhara Menon's forehead was covered with sweat. One palm moved slowly. Koman Nair caught hold of it.

'Unneera, did you see the hand move? Did it move till now? That means my treatment is beginning to work. Do you know how this Yajamanan used to live? He used to have at least two bottles every day. Even when he was bedridden, Paru used to give him some every day. Since she has gone, nobody would have given him any. That's why his condition has worsened.'

Koman Nair held up the bottle. The level had gone down. He asked, 'Unneera, how much is there now in this?'

'Hundred and fifty ml.'

'This is all for Yajamanan. You lift his chin up!'

Koman Nair poured all the arrack that was left into the mouth that was held open. A terrible groan rose from Sreedhara Menon's throat. One leg trembled.

'Look at that, Unneera, he's beginning to move.'

Sreedhara Menon stiffened and fell sideways. He rolled off the bed.

Koman Nair stood there, stunned. He murmured to himself, 'Oh god! Is he gone?'

'What?'

'Nothing! Lift him up. Put him down on the bed as he was.'

Unneera picked up Yajamanan and put him on the bed.

'When they come back from their bath, I'll go with them. You must look after Yajamanan properly.'

Unneera was now afraid. Yajamanan was not moving at all. 'Something's wrong...'

'Nothing's wrong! Yajamanan is in a deep sleep.'

Koman Nair paced the room. He stood leaning against the wall, pulling at the edges of his saffron kurta. His pocket felt heavy. He searched in the pocket. He had filled the flat bottle in the evening. He finished it in two swallows. He walked to the kitchen, staggering. He had to drink water. Would his worry abate however much water he drank? Narasimhamoorthy! Will people say that I killed Yajamanan? What people? Only Unneera has seen that I gave Yajamanan arrack.

Koman Nair threw away the empty bottle and walkted to Yajamanan's bed. Unneera, who had been squatting near the bed, jumped up.

'Master, just touch the bottom of Yajamanan's feet. It's terribly cold.'

'What does it matter if the feet are cold?'

'When I put a thread against his nose and looked...'

'And looked...Tell me whatever it is, you rascal.'

'He's not breathing, master.'

'You mean, he's dead?'

'Master, if you hadn't poured that arrack into his mouth...'

'Pha! Rascal. You think people die if they have a mouthful of arrack? If you drink for a long time you might get liver problem. Even then you don't always die. You son of a bitch! Did I pour anything into Yajamanan's mouth?'

'No.'

'Pha! I did. But if you hadn't held his chin up, I couldn't have poured it, could I? So, if Yajamanan died of drinking arrack, you are the first accused in a murder case.'

'Oh no, master.'

'You are the son of that Konthi who lives on Krishnan Namboodiri's land, aren't you?'

'Yes, master.'

'Till what class did you study?'

'I haven't studied.'

'You have studied. To wash the bums of buffaloes. Suppose Yajamanan has passed over...'

'What does that mean?'

'I mean, if he has died. Who killed him?'

'Master, none of us killed him.

'Say that once more.'

'None of us killed him.'

'Don't say another word to anyone. Do you understand, you rascal?!'

Sixteen

Koman Nair stood near the gatehouse, leaning against a coconut tree, waiting for Achukutty and Ramankutty.

When he saw them approaching, he spoke loudly, 'Come fast! The lord's ways are really mysterious!'

'What happened, Koman Nair?'

'The Yajamanan passed away! He was waiting for Ramankutty to come... it looks like that.'

As they walked together towards the house, Koman Nair continued, 'Ramankutty, you came. Yajamanan saw you. He must have thought there was no point in lying around like that. That's all. The will of god.'

'How did he die, Uncle?'

'What can I say? I was sitting on the veranda with the "other one" for company. Unneera came running. He said Yajamanan had fallen from the cot. I ran to the room. Unneera and I picked him up and put him on the bed. After a while I felt scared. His hands and feet were cold. We tried putting a thread near his nose. The thread did not move. I put my ear to his chest. There was no beat there. Then... I covered him with a sheet.'

Vedaraman ran to the inner room. Achukutty and Koman Nair rushed here and there.

'If you look at it, it's just as well, isn't it Achukutty?'

'Now...?'

'Now? We must inform the people of the village. Do all the ceremonies properly. What else, Achukutty?'

Vedaraman stood near Sreedhara Menon's cot, hands folded together and head bent.

Koman Nair said, 'Achu and I'll do whatever is necessary. You don't worry. Your brothers are in Madras and Bombay. Do you have their addresses? They can reach here at least for the later ceremonies.'

'I don't have their addresses.'

'Then forget it. It's not as if they come and see him. They have forgotten home. You don't worry. Achu and I'll be with you for everything. Just remember one thing – the ceremonies have to be according to the old status of the Mulamkunnam family.'

Sreedhara Menon was cremated. It was only then that Vedaraman sent a man to inform Vikraman Pillai and Kuttisankaran of his death.

The messenger came back with a small bundle. Vikraman Pillai had sent money – five thousand rupees.

The Big Man did not come for the ceremony of collecting the ashes. Kuttisankaran came. There were also some neighbours.

The Big Man had wanted to come, said Kuttisankaran. But two days back, his son had come from Bombay. The Big Man became young again in the excitement of seeing Hari. He said that Vedaraman need return only after all the ceremonies were over.

The feast on the sixteenth day was a grand one. The people of the village cooperated whole-heartedly. Even Krishnan Namboodiri and Sakran Namboodiri marked their attendance. Sanku Warrier and Mukundan joined in serving the guests as if it was their own function. Achukutty worked very hard. Cherian Munshi, Headmaster Swami, Kuttisankaran, Nanu and the textile shop owner Padmasanan were some of the first to eat. Koman Nair rushed around slightly high.

That evening, Achukutty and Vedaraman sat on the veranda of Mulamkunnam and talked aimlessly.

'Ramankutty, shall we place an advertisement in the newspapers?

Your brothers might get to know of it if we do so.'

'That's something we can think of. Anyway, I don't want these sixty-eight cents. There is a curse upon this land, Achuettan! I keep expecting fresh disasters...'

'Talk of something good, Ramankutty!'

'Good and bad! I don't know. I'll tell you one thing though... If we had not gone to bathe that evening, leaving Koman Nair alone in the house, Yajamanan might have lived for some more time.'

'I don't understand.'

'Achuettan, I questioned Unneera rather closely. That's when I found out that Koman Uncle had forced all that arrack down Yajamanan's throat! That was the reason he died. Never mind... If I tell you something, will you get angry?'

'You tell me whatever it is.'

'I want to drink today.'

'Must you, Ramankutty?'

'Yes. Just this once.'

'If you insist, I'll get you some. But, I'll have to go myself.'

'We'll send Unneera.'

'That won't do. I must go myself.'

Achukutty went to the tea shop. Vedaraman walked around in the compound. He reached the weed-covered pond. He picked up stones and started throwing them.

The first stone for the water snake that was hiding somewhere.

The second one for his brother in Bombay.

The third one for the peon brother in Fort St George.

The fourth for Paru.

Paru, this fourth stone is a magical one. Do you know why I throw this? So that your curse does not work!

Now, I must throw one stone for myself.

He stood there for a long while, as if rooted to the ground. It was getting dark.

When he heard Achukutty call out, he realized where he was and started walking back to the house.

'Why did you go to that corner of the compound in the dark?'

'Oh, just like that!'

'Here's the poison! I thought, now that you are under Vikraman Pillai, you would have stopped all this.'

'Actually I haven't had any all these months. Today, suddenly, I felt the need. Achuettan, tomorrow I'll return to Kottoor Kavala.'

'Shouldn't you have a look at the expenses for the feast served on the sixteenth day and all that?'

'You look at it, Achuettan.'

❖

Vedaraman had breakfast at Achukutty's tea shop and set out for Kottoor Kavala. He did not get a bus that day. He walked all the way.

When he reached the house, he moved towards the back in search of Kuttisankaran. He heard someone call out from the front veranda.

'Hi, Ramankutty!'

Vedaraman turned around and looked.

A young man was coming towards him. Dressed in trousers. He had thick brows, a trimmed moustache, long sideburns and a mole on the left side of the forehead.

He asked, 'Why are you staring at me?'

'How did you recognize me?'

'That's funny! Do you know who I am?'

'The Big Man's son?'

'Yes. Kuttisankaran must have told you, right?'

'Yes.'

'Ramankutty, I've heard a lot about you. My father's very fond of you. Once he starts talking about you, he doesn't stop. I heard something about your wonderful gifts as well. I'll be here for a few more days. What I mean is, we'll have time…to talk about your magical powers.'

Hari drew out a pair of dark glasses from his hip pocket. He commented, 'It's terribly bright. Is it because we are on top of a hill?'

When he put on the dark glasses, the picture of the man

he had seen in his dream was complete. Vedaraman started sweating.

The big city. The intersection of the roads. He is standing on the footpath. Hari comes driving. The car brakes suddenly near him... 'Hi Ramankutty! Why are you sweating like this?'

'It is very hot. And the sun is very bright.'

'Go in and have something. Kuttisankaran...'

Kuttisankaran came running up. 'Come Ramankutty!'

'I've eaten already. I don't want anything now.'

Vikraman Pillai came by then.

'Ramankutty, I should have come and shared your grief. I didn't. Pure selfishness. I lost myself in my happiness even when you were grieving. When Hari came I forgot everything else. Hari, have you met Ramankutty yet?'

'Yes. That is, we've made a start. I must get to know him better.'

Vikraman Pillai opened his eyes wide. Looking at Hari proudly, he became eloquent. 'Ramankutty, Hari is coming here after years. His coming is an unexpected bonus to me. That's why I didn't feel like leaving him alone and coming to Mulamkunnam. Look Hari, you may think you are an important person. How long do you plan to stay here? I'm telling you, if you don't stay for at least ten days this time, I'll forget all my principles of non-violence and box your ears hard. Ramankutty, don't think I'm boasting. Hari, this son of mine is the chief of R&D in Dinsha Polymers. Haven't you heard of Dinsha, Ramankutty? It's a huge company. The annual turnover is something like six hundred crores. But you know, a thoroughly high-handed management. They don't give him any leave.'

He stopped for a moment and then asked proudly, 'Hari, you said you'd got an award recently. What was it?'

Hari said as if it was nothing to talk about, 'Ramankutty the name of the award is "Breakpol". It's nothing much. Fifty thousand dollars and a gold medal. A tiny change in the process of polymer technology. This was a small recognition for my contribution in finding it. My aim is the Golden Leaf. That's really something! What happens in basic molecular structure, when the particles lose their way and come up against each other? Like a vehicular accident at a traffic intersection! Do you understand my language? My research is moving in those directions. When I find the answer, there will be holes in the present accepted theories and the formulae based on those. And the present technology will bleed to death. If I can find this, who will I be? I'll be world famous! And the Golden Leaf Award will be mine!'

Vikraman Pillai asked, with pride evident in every word, 'Did you understand anything of what he said, Ramankutty? I must say I didn't.'

Vedaraman did not say anything. Sweat flowed in rivulets down his back. His shirt stuck to his body. Hari's words were reinforcing that terrible nightmare.

Hari laughed, 'I think Ramankutty has got something of an idea.'

'I didn't understand anything.'

Hari asked, 'And what did you understand, Kuttisankaran?'

'I understood that you are going to get some very big award.'

'Correct!'

Kuttisankaran said, 'What does it matter to the Big Man if you get a very big award? He wants only one award. He wants his children to come here once in a while. That's all.'

'Hari, this desire to see children is the weakness of every aged parent. I've often spoken about it to Kuttisankaran. That's why he's taken up cudgels on my behalf.'

'It's not that I don't want to. I don't get leave. Once you reach the top management, you have to suffer some of these problems.' Hari explained his position.

As the conversation continued, Vedaraman asked the Big Man, 'May I go to school now?'

'Ramankutty, hasn't the school closed for the study holidays?'

'Study leave starts tomorrow, Big Man.'

There were few students at school. The Headmaster addressed

the students of the School Final class, 'Use the study leave effectively. I expect the pass percentage to be better than in the previous years. This school year has been comparatively peaceful. To revise each subject properly...'

Vedaraman felt that the Headmaster's speech was not entering his head. What was the time? Someone was shaking him – the Headmaster.

'What happened? Slept off?'

'I'm sorry, sir.'

'Never mind, you must be tired. Go and take rest.'

That entire day Vedaraman was like someone who had lost his balance. When Hari suggested that they eat lunch together, he said, 'I'll eat later, with Kuttisankaran...'

Hearing him, the Big Man asked, 'And if Kuttisankaran is also eating with us?

Ramankutty could not think of an answer to that.

The Big Man was acting as if he had suddenly become a young man. He said mischievously, 'If this old man wishes that the four of us sit together and peck at something, Ramankutty, will you desert the party? Will you become a rebel?'

'I'm sorry, sir.'

'If so, come on. Kuttisankaran, let us start.'

Vikraman Pillai kept talking as they ate.

'Hari, this Ramankutty will be the topper in the school final examinations. Will you take him to Bombay with you? Don't worry about the money. Which is the best college there? Put him into that college. He should grow there.

'Hari, all these ties here...the school, my bullocks...If all these things didn't exist, I would also have come with you...for a short holiday.

'Kuttisankaran, there was an old broken carrom board here. Find it. Let's play carrom in the evening.

'Hari, before you go, before you are once again under the yoke of the company, you must go to the temple of the

Narasimhamoorthy. Don't be lazy about it.

'Ramankutty, why are you staring at my Hari like this? We've all nearly finished. Only you are...'

The Big Man went to bed.

'Shall I also go to bed?' Hari asked in general.

As they walked to the library, Hari said, 'I've grabbed your place. You'll have to sleep on the floor till I go away.'

'That's no problem.'

'Do you sleep in the afternoon? A siesta?'

'No.'

'Oh I forgot. You are a student.'

When they met in the corridor next to the kitchen, Vedaraman told Kuttisankaran, 'I'm feeling very scared.'

'Scared?'

'Something terrible is going to happen.'

'What nonsense is this?'

'All right, then I won't tell you.'

'No, no, tell me.'

'How old is Hari sir?'

'He may be forty or forty-five.'

'Has anyone examined his horoscope?'

'Horoscope? I don't think he has even the basic chart. The Big Man did not believe in anything of that sort earlier!'

'Uncle, I'm feeling very worried.'

'Stop going round and round. What is the problem?'

'I've seen Hari sir long ago. In a dream.'

When Vedaraman told him the whole dream, Kuttisankaran asked anxiously, 'Should we tell the Big Man about this?'

'No need. I told you just to unburden myself. No one else need to know. We'll hope that my dream does not come true.'

Seventeen

It was midnight.

Hari leaned against the pillows and lit a cigar. He looked with interest at Vedaraman who was lying on a mattress on the ground.

He asked, 'Not sleepy, Ramankutty?'

'No, Hariettan.'

'My coming at this time is a nuisance to you, isn't it? You need to study. Now that I have occupied this room...Your exam preparations have gone for a toss.'

'I am prepared, Hariettan! Even if the exams take place this minute, I'll be able to write them. I'll get a rank too.'

'Good for you! I really admire you.'

'Don't make fun of me, Hariettan.'

'Ramankutty, I was telling the truth. My father has spoken so much about you. Not just my father, Kuttisankaran too. They say you have strange powers.'

'I don't have any powers.'

'Don't be so humble! My father complains about my not coming here, doesn't he?'

'He's sad about it.'

'That's because he doesn't understand the nature of my work. I have to get leave, don't I? It's not easy to get away from Bombay. Ramankutty, I've the utmost love and respect for my father. More respect than love, I suppose. I do not smoke in front of him. Besides smoking, I would also wish that he did not know of my other bad habit – occasional drinking. If you don't object, I plan to have a little now.'

'Who am I to object, Hariettan?'

'I'd told Kuttisankaran to keep a glass and some water here.'

'They're here.'

'If you don't mind, my briefcase is in that corner, will you bring me the bottle from that?'

When Vedaraman took out the whisky bottle from the brief case, he saw some other things there. Under a small towel, there was a pistol. Air tickets and different currencies peeped out from various pockets of the briefcase.

As he drank, Hari asked, 'You identified the spot for the well here, didn't you?'

'Yes.'

'Do you know how many times my father spoke about it? He says you have the power of "dowsing". The ability to find anything hidden in the earth. Is that true?'

Vedaraman did not reply.

Hari laughed, 'You don't know, do you? Never mind. As long as other people know about your ability. Come with me! Why should you search for worthless water under the earth. You could find oil. In the Bombay High and other places on the shores of the Arabian Sea. You could help the ONGC. Do you know what the ONGC is?'

'No.'

'Oil and Natural Gas Commission! I have influence there. I can get you a job there. Just think of it! Think of what you could get. A whole lot of money. A Padma Shri at the very least...'

As he continued to drink, Hari muttered, 'The possibilities are immense!'

Suddenly he said, as if he was coming up with a serious proposition, 'Or, we could find gold.'

'Gold?'

'That's right, gold! We cover the coast from Goa to Bombay. In a motor launch. We take a couple of expert divers with us.

At the bottom of the sea lie the gold bars and gold biscuits that smugglers throw away when pursued by the Customs people. Our divers search in the areas pointed out by you. What do you think of the idea?'

'Will you get angry if I say what I think?'

'Say whatever it is.'

'Hariettan, your imagination is taking wings.'

'Ramankutty, I'm not a storyteller. I'm speaking of things that are possible.'

'I'm thinking of something else.'

'And what's that?'

'You said you were in search of another type of gold – the Gold Leaf Award. That's a better idea. You keep pursuing that.'

Hari had in the meantime finished the bottle. He said, 'Well said, Ramankutty! I'm going to sleep. Are you planning to read for some time?'

'No, I'll also sleep.'

Vedaraman switched off the light.

His mind was still caught in the thorns of that old dream.

Dinsha Polymers...

There might be an institution like that. But why did Hariettan, who was doing research there, carry a pistol in his briefcase?

Vedaraman went to sleep. He had that dream again. The busy intersection. Footpath. Hari who came driving by. That call, 'Hi Ramankutty!' There was Hari covering his face and weeping. He turned around. The holes in the back with blood gushing from them. Golden coins floated in the blood.

'Don't go, Hariettan, don't go to Bombay, Hariettan! Don't go!' Vedaraman cried out in his sleep.

Hari woke up with the noise and looked at Vedaraman. He was still crying out, 'Don't go, don't go to Bombay, Hariettan!'

Hari shook Vedaraman awake. He noticed that Vedaraman's sixth finger was glowing.

'What is it, Ramankutty, did you have a nightmare? You were screaming.'

Vedaraman got up. He was sweating all over.

Hari switched on the lamp. He looked at Vedaraman's sixth finger. No, it was not glowing now.

'Do you know what you screamed out?'

'No.'

'That I shouldn't go. That I shouldn't go to Bombay! What is the matter?'

'I had a nightmare.'

'Get up. Go and wash your face. It's almost morning.'

Hari got out of the room first. The sky was just getting a tinge of red. Kuttisankaran usually gave the bullocks their cotton seed and coconut cake at this time.

Hari went to the cowshed.

'Kuttisankaran!'

'You have woken up so early?' Kuttisankaran asked.

'I had to wake up. I was woken up. Ramankutty had a bad dream and screamed. He said I shouldn't go to Bombay. What's wrong with him? Is he mad or something?'

Kuttisankaran did not say anything in reply but stood looking at the sky.

'Now why are you standing there like a pillar without saying anything?'

'What can I say? For some time Ramankutty has been having a nightmare.'

'What nightmare?'

'My loyalty is to the Big Man and this family. So, I'll tell you the dream. But don't let Ramankutty know that I told you this...'

After this preface, Kuttisankaran told Hari everything.

'But that's incredible! That he saw me in a dream even before he saw me for the first time!'

'Not just once, Hari sir, he had the same dream a number of times. There isn't any danger in Bombay, is there?'

Hari said dismissively, 'What danger? As if danger exists only in Bombay. Anyone who works is always in danger wherever he is.'

Vedaraman reached there just then.

'Have you got over the hangover from the bad dream, Ramankutty?' Hari teased him.

'I'll make some tea,' Kuttisankaran changed the track of the conversation. 'Tea ... breakfast ... Let things proceed quietly. The Big Man would also be around.'

After breakfast, Hari asked, 'Can I get a taxi here – to go up to Kochi and come back?'

'There's Korulla's taxi that's usually parked near Nanu's hotel,' Kuttisankaran told him.

'Why do you need to go to Kochi, Hari?' Vikraman Pillai asked.

'I've to make a couple of STD calls to Bombay. Some fax messages have to be sent. I've to get my return ticket confirmed.'

'When do you have to go?' Vikraman Pillai asked.

'Next Wednesday.'

Vikraman Pillai counted, 'Today's Friday. Leaving that out, there are just four days more.'

❖

After Hari left for Kochi, Vedaraman revealed his fears to Kuttisankaran. Why should Hari, who was doing research in a company called Dinsha Polymers, carry a pistol? Was he hiding something?

'A gun?'

'Yes, a pistol.'

Vedaraman explained how he had found it. Why had Hari spoken about gold and smugglers after he had had a couple of drinks? Could even the story that he had a job in Dinsha Polymers be a false one?

'Ramankutty, what are you saying?'

'I have this feeling that Hariettan is in great danger, something bad is going to happen to him.'

'When you say that I too start getting afraid.'

'My premonitions need not come true, we can pray that they don't.'

'You do have some special gifts. That's what makes me afraid. Shall we tell the Big Man all this?'

'No, no. He'll just worry unnecessarily. He won't be able to prevent Hariettan from going back, anyway. No need, Uncle. Just my stupid imagination.'

Hari returned from Kochi at about 1 o'clock in the night. The Big Man was fast asleep. Vedaraman was reading in the library.

When he heard the raised voices of Hari and Kuttisankaran, though the words were not clear, he stopped reading and got up.

They were coming in, Hari was drunk and Kuttisankaran was supporting him as he walked.

There was a plastic bag dangling from Hari's hand. As they entered the library, Vedaraman moved back a few steps to let them in.

'Ramankutty, you clever fellow. You managed to study for some time when I went away, right?' Hari spoke as he staggered towards the cot. He sat on the cot, rather fell on it.

'Kuttisankaran Uncle, just catch this!' Kuttisankaran managed with difficulty to catch the plastic bag thrown at him.

'Take out the guy inside!'

There was a full bottle of whisky inside.

'Enough for today, Hari sir!'

'What is it, Uncle?'

'Enough, son.'

'No need for son or sir. You can call me Hari. Or, Hari Nair. That's what they call me in Bombay!'

'Enough, Hari!'

'I decide whether it is enough or not enough! Cut his throat!'

'Eh!'

'Open the bottle!' Hari ordered glancing at Kuttisankaran and Vedaraman in turn.

When they stood without moving he said, 'All right, no need for you to do it. I'll do the throat-cutting!'

Kuttisankaran said, 'I'll save you the trouble. I'll pour some out for you. If you could speak quietly that would be good. We don't need to wake up the Big Man.'

'Great!' said Hari.

After drinking a large portion of the bottle, Hari sat and laughed. He said, 'Sit here both of you! Sit with me on the cot. I don't have much time left. I'll say what I need to say in the time left.'

Vedaraman and Kuttisankaran looked at each other.

Hari laughed aloud. 'What I mean when I say that I don't have much time left is simple. I'm returning tomorrow. To Bombay! I've told the taxi chap to come in the morning. I should not have come here. This is a pedestrian, provincial hellhole. Does my sister Rema come here from Delhi? Does her husband... that stupid Surendran come here? Do they send their daughter Padmaja here? But this stupid Hari Nair came. To see his father!'

Hari drank again.

'I don't know when I'll be able to see my father again. I do have respect for him. But Hari Nair will tell the truth. Is there another stupid idiot on this earth like my father? He went to jail! He has made sacrifices! And what did he get for that? The people who rule the land, the businessmen, the intellectuals, the opinion makers – aren't all of them criminals? This father of mine who runs a school did not learn this basic lesson. Who is god to the man who succeeds these days? It is the devil!'

Hari kept on talking in this vein and preventing Vedaraman and Kuttisankaran from sleeping.

When he had finished all the liquor in the bottle, Hari said, 'Uncle, I'm going to take a short nap. Tomorrow is Saturday, right? I'll be going. Make my father understand, please.'

Kuttisankaran took tea to the Big Man when he got up in the morning.

The Big Man asked, 'Didn't Hari get back from Kochi last night?'

'He came. But he was very late.'

'Oh, I didn't hear him come. Call him.'

'He's sleeping, Big Man. Also...'

'What also?'

'He's returning today, to Bombay.'

'He'd said he'd be here till Wednesday.'

'There's some urgent work at the company.'

'I see.'

Vikraman Pillai went to the library. Hari was snoring on the cot. Vedaraman who had been sleeping on the floor heard the Big Man's footfall and jumped up.

'Ramankutty, don't tell me you are also sleeping late.'

Vikraman Pillai saw the empty liquor bottle under the cot, but pretended he had not.

'Hariettan came very late. And then we sat talking for a long while, Big Man!'

Vikraman Pillai went back to the veranda and lay down on the easy chair. He decided against his usual practice of pranayama and yoga for that day.

'Kuttisankaran, when does he have to leave?'

'I don't know. But Korulla's taxi will come.'

'I don't think he'll get up if you don't wake him up.'

'I'll go and wake him up.'

Kuttisankaran went in and pulled Hari up from bed.

'Here's your tea. Come soon. The Big Man's waiting for you.'

'Did you tell father that I'm going today?'

'Yes.'

'What did he say?'

'He didn't say anything.'

As they sat at breakfast, the Big Man asked, 'Hari, are you going back today? Kuttisankaran said so. What happened suddenly?'

'Some problems at the company. I found out about it when I rang up yesterday. MD wanted me there at once.'

'No chance of staying till Wednesday?'

'No chance, father. I have to go today.'

'You haven't gone to the Narasimha temple. Finish that job. Kuttisankaran said that you've asked for the taxi. When will it come?'

'At 9:30.'

'So, you can go to the temple. There's still time.'

'I'll go next time I come, father! The flight is at eleven-thirty. If I go to the temple, I'm likely to get delayed and miss the flight.'

Vikraman Pillai did not say anything further.

Eighteen

Hari went back. Vikraman Pillai turned silent and stayed away from everything for a few days.

The study leave got over. Vedaraman wrote the examinations, fairly well. He felt that he might be among the first ten students. Headmaster Ananthu Swami and Cherian Munshi enquired, 'You will be the first in the state, won't you?'

'That is too much to expect, sir. If I'm lucky I'll be among the first ten,' Vedaraman said with humility.

The Big Man would ask every day when Vedaraman came after writing the exam, 'Did you write well, Ramankutty?' He asked the same question on the day the exams ended too. The Big Man did not ask about the rank he expected or anything of that sort. He just said, 'You are brilliant. And hard working. You'll succeed in life.'

Days passed.

Life went on as before. Pranayama, yoga, taking dictation from the Big Man, reading widely from the library... and so on.

Kuttisankaran and Vedaraman had forgotten that terrible dream and even Hari to a certain extent.

Vedaraman went to Mulamkunnam for a short visit with the Big Man's permission. Just being away from books put Vedaraman into a holiday mood. He stayed with Achukutty, bathed in the river, visited the temple, met with acquaintances including Koman Nair. All this made him happy.

One morning Mukundan came running to Achukutty's tea shop, holding aloft that day's newspaper.

He pointed to a page and told Vedaraman, 'Ramankutty, look at this photo! Read the news. Look who's lying dead there!'

Vedaraman's eyes fell not on the news, but on the photograph printed with it. A car with bullet holes. It had climbed onto the footpath from the road. Hari's head and half his body were hanging out from the open door.

Vedaraman was shattered. He read the news.

It was like a horror story.

It was late at night. The signal lights in midtown Bombay, on the Mahim causeway, had just turned green.

A white Premier Padmini 118NE came by.

When the signal turned green, the car accelerated. There was a passenger beside the driver. It was not known whether he was aware that he was being followed by enemies. Whatever it was, the driver was watching the rearview mirror. There were two cars behind them. Though they were keeping a distance, their speed was such that they could catch up any moment.

The Premier Padmini reached the Bandra Telephone Exchange Road.

The cars that were following closed the distance suddenly. In a split second, they blocked the path of the Premier Padmini. There were six men in the two cars. They fired continuously.

Did they use sten guns or Kalashnikovs?

Hari Nair died.

Tracing the background of the incident, the newspaper narrated a story from Bombay's underworld. A history that started with Haji Mastan and Yusuf Patel and their quick and terrible rise to power. It soon became a story of magic and wonder. The djinns of politics and the good-looking devils of the Bombay film industry were characters in the story.

Many names were scattered in the body of the news.

Dawood Ibrahim.

Arun Gawli.

Their gang wars.

The Malayali connection.

Chembur Rajan.

When Chembur Rajan died in a shootout, Rajendra Nikhalji a.k.a. Chotta Rajan rose to replace him.

The newspaper report ended with hints that it could have been Chotta Rajan's gang that had killed Hari Nair, who was a rising star of Bombay's underworld.

Vedaraman dropped the newspaper.

Achukutty had not understood anything, he asked, 'Who died?'

Mukundan said, 'Vikraman Pillai sir's son, Hari. He had come here recently.'

❖

Hari's death completely shattered Vikraman Pillai. He wondered what sin from a previous birth could have made him suffer such sorrow. Why had Hari tricked him all these years? Why had he cooked up the façade of the 'company executive'? Had he come here to hide from the guns of the rivals? If he had not gone back...

He displayed a strength that he did not feel when people came to condole. But his mind was in pieces.

His ways changed, he stopped following a routine. He gave up pranayama, yoga, reading and writing. He was even reluctant to eat. When Kuttisankaran tried to persuade him to eat, he said, 'Isn't what I've had so far enough? Why should I strengthen my body further? It is time to follow the ancient practice of prayopavesa, starving oneself to death.'

Weeks passed. The results of the school final examinations were declared on a day when the monsoon rain was pouring down. Vedaraman secured the third rank in the state.

Vikraman Pillai was happy when he heard that. He told Vedaraman and Kuttisankaran, 'Don't worry about not getting the first rank, Ramankutty. Even if you didn't stand first, you did get a decent third rank. There won't be much difference between the first and the third. So, what should he do now, Kuttisankaran?'

'You must guide him,' Kuttisankaran said.

As he spoke, caressing his beard, Vikraman Pillai's voice grew deeper, 'I'm a person who's failed at everything. How can I guide anyone? Ah, let him join college, Kuttisankaran! Ramankutty has some unusual gifts. He'll find his own way at the proper time.'

Vikraman Pillai thought over the direction of his own life on nights when he could not sleep. What now? There was nothing in particular that he wanted to do. There was nothing he wanted to achieve. Even the peace of mind that an old man was entitled to was now denied to him. However much time passed, he would not be able to recover from the blow that Hari's terrible death had dealt him. People were not commenting aloud. But they must be talking among themselves. 'The son of the ture Gandhian Vikaraman Pillai was a member of the underworld in Bombay. People found out only when he was killed.'

He was not needed here to keep the school running. Then why linger here?

Should he go in search of his daughter?

No, that wouldn't work. Those links had been snapped long ago. It would be impossible to mend them again. Anyway, the solitude and peace that he wished for would not be available in Delhi.

He would leave everything and become a wanderer. Become a pilgrim. He would visit temples, go right up to the Himalayas. If he wandered aimlessly, he might find an aim. Did he have time enough to see the whole of this sacred land? He would try. Finally, when he reached some confluence of rivers, or a tall peak or a beautiful valley, his body would tire. He could then spread darbha grass and lie on it; and think of the creator.

Vikraman Pillai took some decisions.

He would entrust the school to the Nair Service Society (NSS). They would keep it running, make it grow. He would gift this house to Kuttisankaran. There was about one-and-a-half lakh rupees in the bank. He would keep some of it for his travelling expenses. The rest could be divided between Kuttisankaran and Ramankutty.

Ramankutty could join the Maharaja's College. His old friend and co-worker in the Theosophical Movement, Madhavan Nair, could be requested to be Ramankutty's local guardian.

He informed Kuttisankaran and Vedaraman of his decision. Though they pleaded with him not to leave, Vikraman Pillai was adamant.

Before he set out on his travels, Vikraman Pillai handed over the ownership of the school to the NSS. He got a gift deed registered, giving the house to Kuttisankaran. He took the money he needed in the form of currency notes and traveller's cheques. He divided what was left into two and opened accounts in the names of Kuttisankaran and Vedaraman.

The letter to Madhavan Nair asking him to be Vedaraman's protector and guardian was a fairly long one. He handed it over to Vedaraman, saying, 'Here Ramankutty, take this. May it be the passport to your future.'

He informed only two others that he was leaving the village – Headmaster Swami and Cherian Munshi.

After fixing the date of his departure he called Kuttisankaran and Vedaraman and blessed them. He said, 'Ramankutty! All the books in this library are now yours. And Kuttisankaran...take care of the bullocks. They should not reach a slaughter house.'

Korulla's taxi came.

The Big Man got into the taxi, carrying a small suitcase.

Both Kuttisankaran and Vedaraman felt that the house had lost its light when the Big Man went away. It was Kuttisankaran who found it more difficult to pass the time. Vedaraman sat in the library and read something or the other.

The night was cold. It was pouring.

Vedaraman lay in the library in a state between sleep and wakefulness.

He felt that the big toe on his right leg was throbbing. Needles of cold were coursing from that toe to the rest of the body. The left leg was also now in the same state. Suddenly the cold left his legs. Now it was as if there were coal burners between his feet. The burning heat reached the knees. The heat crossed the knees and suddenly pierced his brain like a bolt of lightning.

Vedaraman looked at the ceiling.

Two long legs came down from the heights. He could see the hair on those legs in the glow of his sixth finger. The legs were placed on either side as the being stood astride his body. He could see a part of the thighs now. And now there were two long hands.

Hands carrying a length of chain.

The chain jingled... Softly at first, and then loudly.

Vedaraman asked, 'Have you come to imprison me?'

The other replied, 'No! To set you free. To detach your dream self from the material body!'

The chain became a garland of flowers now.

The legs that stood astride him became the smooth thighs of a woman.

Music flowed in from somewhere.

A soft voice like the rustling of silk said, 'Wake up!'

Vedaraman woke up; he was now detached from his body. As he looked down, he saw a motionless body, lying on the cot. It was his body. Was it his soul that now watched, detached from that body with its bones and flesh and skin? Was it a dream body? A body made of energy? The astral body of which he had read in one of the books in the library.

He was now weightless.

He rose higher. He pierced through the ceiling and the roof, the rain and the dark sky. Was it the stars that he saw around him? Meteors flashed by. The planets spun among the wild paths of the meteors. Perfumed clouds covered him. As he rose higher and higher through them, he felt afraid. He could hear terrible roars. Corpses danced. Peculiar beings with huge misshapen heads and pointed teeth and short vulture legs stood around and shouted and screamed. Afraid, he rose higher. He had now reached a beautiful yard. All the noises had ended. It was all peace. Peace.

There was a walkway in the middle of the yard. Pillars encrusted with jewels bordered it.

He was walking. Young and beautiful girls who had just crossed into adulthood appeared from behind the pillars. They surrounded him and drew him forward. Their voices were sweet. Their laughter was like the scattering of glass beads.

He passed through curtains of coloured mist. There was a beautiful bedroom beyond them. On the silken bed a dark beauty wearing a mask awaited him.

The little beauties said in one voice, 'Mother, we bring the treasure you had sought before you. Please permit us to go back into the pillars and infuse youth and lust there!'

The dark beauty made a hissing sound. The little beauties vanished.

The dark beauty removed her mask and danced like a serpent who had heard the flute of the snake charmer. Drums sounded. The beat of demonic instruments filled the place.

He heard someone call, 'Ramankutty!'

The dark beauty was Kozhukatta Paru. She came forward, completely naked. When she came close to him, she shed the dark skin, became a golden beauty.

'Ramankutty! Do you remember my curse?'

He could not reply.

'Will you drink at my breast?'

He did not reply to that either.

Paru embraced him. Her shape changed then. She became an anthill. A strong wind blew. The anthill broke up and scattered. There were so many motes of dust. As they rose like a tornado, he could hear the curse from among them.

'Ramankutty, you shall never know what love is, you shall never experience it. You shall never have young bodies. You were born to embrace anthills!'

He fell down.

To the floor of the library.

Nineteen

Vedaraman went to the Narasimha temple with Kuttisankaran before he left for college. They met Koman Nair at Achukutty's tea shop. He said, 'Bow before the lord with all your heart. I'll pay for the offering. Study and become a big man.'

It was Koman Nair who fixed the date and time of his departure for Kochi.

Vedaraman packed his suitcase. There was nothing much to pack. Just four or five shirts and mundus.

'Aren't you taking the books?' Kuttisankaran asked.

'How can I take this whole library? I'll take a few books the next time I come. I've to find a place to stay first of all.'

'Did you take the letter for Madhavan Nair sir?'

'Yes.'

'And money?'

'I've taken a thousand rupees from the bank.'

'Will that be enough?'

'I can come and take more when it gets over. It is not all that far.'

'Madhavan Nair sir is an important person. You must obey him implicitly.'

When he reached Madhavan Nair's bungalow, which was next to the Durbar Hall, Vedaraman said to himself: he is an important person, and very rich.

His name was engraved on the brass plate embedded in the gate post. Below that was the name 'Eastern Star'.

He entered. The lawn looked like green velvet. There were beautiful flowerbeds. The water that scattered from the sprinklers had a thousand pieces of rainbow in them. There was a garden lamp and a garden umbrella in the lawn, with cane chairs beneath.

A young man came running from the outhouse. He was wearing a white uniform and there was a piece of plastic on the breast pocket with a name – Balu.

'What's it?'

'I have come to see Madhavan Nair sir.'

'Where are you from?' Balu took out a small scribbling pad and a ball pen from the lower pocket of his uniform.

'I'll write it.' Vedaraman took the pad extended by Balu and wrote – Vedaraman, c/o Sri Vikraman Pillai, Kottoor Kavala.

Balu took the chit into the bungalow. Within minutes he came out and said, 'Come with me.'

Madhavan Nair was sitting at a big table in the study and giving dictation to the stenographer. When Vedaraman entered the room, he said, 'Mani, that's about all. You may go.'

The stenographer left the room.

Madhavan Nair turned to Vedaraman and said, 'Sit! What can I do for you?'

Vedaraman handed over the letter from the Big Man.

As he read it Madhavan Nair murmured to himself a couple of times, 'Interesting!' When he finished reading, he said, 'Vikraman Pillai is like a guru to me. So, Vedaraman, your interests are mine now. I'll arrange everything. You have a rank, so admission is not a problem. But why the hostel? You can stay with me. Vikraman Pillai has appointed me your local guardian!'

'If I stay here…'

'Um, if you do?'

'It'll be a problem for you.'

Madhavan Nair laughed, 'I'm your local guardian. So, you have to do things as I tell you to. Vedan, are you willing to obey me?'

The voice had a resonance to it, the eyes were commanding.

Thick brows and hair that was starting to go grey. Vedaraman looked at him for a little while and said, 'Yes, sir!'

'Well then. That's like a good boy!' Madhavan Nair got up and came up to Vedaraman. He put his hand on Vedaraman's shoulder and said, 'Come Vedan, we'll sit on that sofa.'

Sitting on the sofa, Madhavan Nair said, 'My friends tell me I have this weakness – that I talk too much. That's true. But I don't count it a weakness, I claim it as a strength. Why are you standing there like that, Vedan? Come and sit down here near me, boy.'

Madhavan Nair pressed the buzzer on the small table near the sofa.

A liveried servant appeared.

'Vedan, I like to have an aperitif before lunch. You don't mind, do you? Tony, I'll have my usual. Get a soft drink for Vedan.'

Tony went inside.

'Vedan, how's Vikraman Pillai?'

Vedaraman told him about Hari's death and the Big Man's departure from the village.

'How tragic! Ah, he's written that you have some unusual gifts. Interesting! What sort of gifts do you have? You don't have to tell me now. I won't rush you.'

As he got to his third gimlet, Madhavan Nair exclaimed, 'I who speak too much usually, sometimes don't speak at all. You may find it unusual. But liquor makes me silent very often, Vedan!'

After keeping quiet for some time, Madhavan Nair said, 'This house is an empty one. Totally so. Move in. Where's your luggage?'

Vedaraman mentioned the name of a hotel.

'Haven't heard of it. Anyway, collect it after lunch. You can take my car.'

'I'll take an auto, sir.'

'As you please. Finish your drink! Fresh lime, is it?'

When Vedaraman lifted the glass to show him, Madhavan Nair saw the sixth finger.

'One too many!'

❖

As he went to the hotel to pick up his luggage, Vedaraman thought of many things. Wasn't Madhavan Nair's behaviour unusual? He spoke such a lot to a stranger like himself, without caring about the difference in age. It could be because he was a simple person. Or, had it been an effort to impress him? But what for? What had this important person to gain from impressing him? He could decide not to return to Madhavan Nair's bungalow. Since he had the third rank, he would get admission in any college in the city. If he did not get a room in the college hostel, he could continue in this third-rate hotel. Or he could shift to a better one.

But how could he go against the Big Man's wishes? He had entrusted Madhavan Nair with Vedaraman's guardianship. Madhavan Nair had taken up the responsibility with pleasure. If he did not go back, that would be extremely ill-mannered.

Vedaraman reached the bungalow in the evening by auto. Balu came running out from the outhouse and took the iron trunk.

Madhavan Nair and a couple of friends sat around a card table in the light of the garden lamp in the lawn.

'Is that Vedan? Come, join us,' Madhavan Nair called out.

Vedraman walked to the group. There were four chairs around the card table. Madhavan Nair gestured to him to sit on the empty chair and asked, 'Vedan, do you play bridge?'

Vedaraman did not sit down. He said humbly, 'No, sir. I don't know any card games.'

Madhavan Nair spoke to his friends, 'It looks as if Chackochan has ditched us. So...let's play cut throat.'

'Right!' the friends agreed.

'Vedan, you just relax. We'll break up at about eight, eight-thirty.'

'Who's the boy?' One of the friends asked.

'He's a protégé of my guru Mr Vikraman Pillai. He came today. I'm his local guardian from now on. All right, shall we begin?'

'Begin what?'

'Cut throat! Or whisky, if you wish!' Madhavan Nair laughed.

It was 9 o'clock when the card game ended and the friends departed.

Madhavan Nair reached the sitting room of the bungalow. 'Vedan!'

There was no reply in spite of his calling out a number of times.

'Tony!'

Tony arrived.

'Go and find out where Vedan is.'

Tony brought Vedaraman from the outhouse.

'Were you sitting in the outhouse all this time?' Madhavan Nair asked.

'Yes, sir. I'll stay there.'

'Vedan, that's for me, your local guardian, to decide. Why should you curl up in the outhouse when this whole bungalow is empty. Where is your luggage?'

'In the outhouse, sir.'

'Go and get it!'

Vedaraman went to pick up his luggage.

'Tony, which is Vedan's room?'

'I've prepared the downstairs bedroom, sir!'

'Fine! Get me a drink, Tony. Also some cigarettes.'

Vedaraman came in carrying his trunk.

Madhavan Nair said, 'Sit down! Feel free. Are you hungry? Tony will serve you dinner. I'll join you after a drink.'

'I'm not hungry, sir. I'll wait for you.'

'That's better.'

When he saw Vedaraman's box, Madhavan Nair started laughing, 'An iron trunk? This won't do. You are joining college, and this is a city!'

Vedaraman thought to himself. Did Madhavan Nair mean: You country bumpkin, you have to acquire some urban polish!

Twenty

Vedaraman was taken aback when he reached the bedroom. Soft foam bed, pillows with blue pillowcases, gleaming white sheets, a lamp that brought the daylight into the room, and a painting on the wall. There was a reading lamp near the bed. There were English magazines on a side table. There was also cool water in a glass jug.

Vedaraman could not sleep. He felt that he was not entitled to sleep here. He switched on the reading lamp and flipped through the pages of one of the magazines. There was nothing in it that could hold his attention. He switched off the lamp and lay in bed, twisting and turning.

No, he could not sleep.

He got up from the bed and lay down on the carpet in savasana. When did he sleep?

A clock struck five somewhere. He got up then. He rose from the carpet and wandered round the bedroom. That was when he realized that the room had a door that led out. When he opened that door he saw a sit-out. A number of pots holding roses were placed between the parapet of the sit-out and the wall of the compound. A rose creeper grew from a corner, beating them all in glory. The white flowers of the creeper were so beautiful in the spreading light of the morning!

He heard a knock on the door. When he opened the door, he saw Tony with a coffee tray.

Tony withdrew. Vedaraman entered the bathroom. The

hot and cold taps and the commode were all new to him. After brushing his teeth Vedaraman looked at the coffee tray. Everything was placed on it separately – decoction, milk, sugar cubes in a small bowl. He mixed everything and had a cup of coffee.

He sat on the carpet in padmasana and started pranayama.

❖

As Madhavan Nair strolled in the lawn in his dressing gown, Tony came and placed the coffee tray on the table near the garden lamp.

'Is Vedan awake, Tony?'

'Yes, sir.'

Madhavan Nair had his coffee; he then walked to Vedaraman's bedroom. He looked in through the door that was not fully shut. When he saw that Vedaraman was in the classic pose of sirshasana, he turned and walked away.

When they met at breakfast, he asked Vedaraman, 'You do yoga regularly?'

'Yes, sir.'

'I looked in. You didn't hear me. In earlier times, when I was involved with the Theosophical Movement, I was also a yoga enthusiast. Now, the only thing that reminds me of Theosophy is the name of this bungalow.'

'Eastern Star?'

'That's right. Have you heard of The Order of the Star in the East? The set-up created by Annie Besant and others to make Jiddu Krishnamurti the guru of the world. It's a long story. Let's finish breakfast. Vedan, be ready by 11 o'clock. We are going out. Till then I'll get on with my routine. From shaving to getting through the paperwork.'

Vedaraman went back to the bedroom and opened the trunk. He took out paper and pen and wrote brief letters to Achukutty and Kuttisankaran. He did not have post covers. He had to buy some.

When it was nearly eleven, Tony knocked on the door, 'Master is calling you.'

Vedaraman looked at himself. He was in the mundu and shirt

that he had worn after his bath. That would do.

Madhavan Nair had said they were 'going out'. Where were they going? What for? Vedaraman came out.

A big car waited in the porch. Next to that stood the chauffer.

Madhavan Nair came out of the study in a blue safari suit. Mani, the stenographer followed him.

'Vedan, come, get in,' Madhavan Nair called out to him.

As the car moved, Vedaraman asked, 'Where are we going, sir?'

'Just a shopping trip.'

Madhavan Nair took Vedaraman to a couple of big textile shops, a shopping mall and a shoe mart. He bought him ready-made clothes that fitted him, shoes, a suitcase, and an expensive watch. As he bought each thing, Vedaraman tried to protest saying, 'No need for all this, sir.' Or 'This is too much, sir.' Each time Madhavan Nair said, 'Shut up!'

'Sir, I'm feeling bad about it.'

'What for?'

'I just came here yesterday and you're doing all this for me...'

'For you? Don't be silly! And don't be embarrassed by all this. I do all this because I wish to. When you stay with me... Well, there has to be some style, some class. Do you understand? Vikraman Pillai has made me your local guardian. Don't forget that.'

Vedaraman could not say anything after that. He tried to add up the thousands of rupees that Madhavan Nair had spent on him. They had been greeted with respect at all the shops they visited. He did not pay cash anywhere either.

Balu opened the gate.

'Did anyone come, Balu?'

'No, sir.'

As he got out of the car, Madhavan Nair told the driver, 'You can go now, Bakkar. Come at six in the evening, all right?'

'Yes, sir.'

'Tony, take all this to Vedan's room. And fix me a drink.'

As he had his usual aperitif, Madhavan Nair said, 'Vedan, you must understand me properly. Do you know what lies behind each of my actions?'

'Your good heart!'

'Wrong! Only pure selfishness. Utter selfishness. I do whatever gives me pleasure. Do you understand?'

'Sir, you spent so much money on me today, I don't know how much.'

'Neither do I. I did not pay cash, you see. I just signed, that's all. Who invented this credit card? Whoever, he deserves congratulations. Sign away and relax! Ah, you must understand another personality trait of mine. I speak openly – to anyone! Someone of my age and someone of your age are equal in my eyes. Hey, you're just sitting there. Have something…'

'I don't want anything, sir.'

'Some chilled beer?'

'No, sir.'

'Vedan I'm going to ask you a straight question. You must answer truthfully. Have you ever drunk liquor?'

Vedaraman hung his head and said, 'Yes, I have.'

'Fine! I'll give you a beer. A foreign brand – Orange Boom.'

The beer came. Vedaraman hesitated.

'What is it, Vedan?'

'I don't want this, sir.'

'I dislike false morality and hypocrisy, Vedan. Are you worried about the difference in our ages? Just because you don't take this, will that make you more respectful towards me? Be a man, I say!' Madhavan Nair poured the beer for Vedan.

As Vedaraman picked up the glass, Madhavan Nair said, 'You are honest. If you had told me that you had never drunk before, I would have started disliking you. Because honest Mr Vikraman Pillai gave me your background in full in the letter – including the uruli incident. Why do you change colour? Correcting your mistakes is the beginning of growth. The step towards goodness. Goodness! If we start searching for a proper definition of that… Hey Tony! Bring the bottle, I'll fix myself another one.'

Vedaraman could not relax.

Madhavan Nair continued, 'Yesterday, I declared that liquor renders me silent. But today, I plan to talk. You are young. Lookswise, though, you are an adult. Strong, young horse. Idealism fills your brain and your sinews, isn't that so? But you must realize something. This is the age of criminals. People who stick to the straight and narrow path will be left behind. An excellent example is Vikraman Pillai.'

Madhavan Nair's conversation was developing into a little speech, 'History is a subject that I find interesting. Vedan, what is history? It is the story of criminals. The story of murderers and looters. From the Roman Empire to the Soviet Union, the basic story is that. We did have a Mahatma Gandhi. But did that change things here? We shot the Mahatma. Because he was so inconvenient! Who rules us now? A set of criminals! I had foreseen that this would happen. But the innocent Mr Vikraman Pillai did not see this. And so he withdrew from the public domain...He was made to withdraw. Do you think I have criminal instincts? Anyway I did anticipate the shape of things to come. I entered the field of business and became a wealthy man. I can now make the world listen to me. I meet the world on my own terms. Is there any political party or party man who does not come here to greet me and take money from me? Every bastard comes. And I play my part. I'm an important person today. I enjoy myself. But I'm not a pure hedonist. This man that enjoys life so much is also a man who cries in secret. That is a different story. Ah! What were we saying. I sit behind the scenes and exercise my power. Am I cruel man? A heartless man? Not at all. I help people as much as I can. I give money to charities. I am a criminal in one sense. But Vedan, I do not use any illegal means to rise in business. But then...the law is like rubber, it's elastic. Sometime, on another occasion, I'll show you the way...'

❖

At lunch, Madhavan Nair said, 'We're going to Willingdon Island in the evening. Around six-thirty. There's a party there.'

It was very late when the party got over.

Madhavan Nair was not quite steady on his feet when they got into the car. He caught hold of Vedaraman's hand and asked, 'Vedan, did you enjoy the party?'

'Yes, sir,' Vedaraman replied. What else could he say?

He was a helpless piece of straw caught among the seniors.

Was it enough to say just 'seniors'? They were the leaders of society – the crème de la crème. There was no subject that was not discussed there.

Business. Current politics. The problems and convolutions in institutions of the establishment ranging from the high court to the collectorate. The new methods of money laundering. The share market. Insider trading...

Madhavan Nair had introduced him right at the beginning, 'This is Vedan, my nephew.'

'Madhavan Nair, was it wise of you to bring your nephew to this company of bandicoots? We may corrupt him.'

And so he had sat among the seniors, not saying much, sipping a mug of beer.

Nobody paid much attention to him. That was just as well.

The new trousers and shirt felt uncomfortable. The shoes bit his toes. The cut of the trousers was tight around his crotch.

Balu opened the gate.

The garden lamp in the lawn was spreading light.

Madhavan Nair moved towards the chairs. He asked, 'Shall we sit here for some time?'

'Sure.'

'Are you sleepy?'

Madhavan Nair called Tony, 'Tony, you can tell Bakkar to go. And get me some liquor.'

As he was sipping his liquor, the garden lamp went off suddenly.

'Damn it!' Madhavan Nair cursed.

The next moment he said in an awed voice, 'What's this? Fantastic!'

Vedaraman's sixth finger was glowing.

Madhavan Nair asked, 'What's this? Does that finger glow like this always?'

'I don't know, sir.'

'So, you don't see its glow?'

'I don't know about any glow or light, sir. Sometimes it feels as though fireflies are entering my finger.'

'This is a gift, Vedan. Highly marketable. This is a key to open great doorways. If Surekha comes to know of this...'

'Surekha?'

'My niece. When I read Vikraman Pillai's letter I didn't pay much heed. Now I'm convinced. He speaks in the letter of your identifying the spot for the well. Was there anything else that was extraordinary?'

Vedaraman explained in brief about his dreams before Hari's death.

'And then?'

'Then...then...I sometimes feel that my heartbeat and the pulse rate at my wrist are not alike. That the pulse rate at the right wrist and the left are different.'

'What do you mean when you say sometimes?'

'When I do pranayama, concentrating on numbers.'

'Have you got it tested?'

'What sir?'

'Has any doctor checked your pulse rate when this happens?'

'No.'

They saw Tony approaching with a lighted candle and a torch.

'There's light here, Tony!'

Tony did not understand what Madhavan Nair was saying.

The next moment the garden lamp came on again. The lights in the bungalow also came on. Madhavan Nair looked at Vedaraman's sixth finger.

The finger was not glowing now.

Twenty-one

Vedaraman went to his bedroom. As he was about to lie down, he saw, between the magazines on the side table, the letters he had written to Achukutty and Kuttisankaran.

He would post them tomorrow.

Or he wouldn't. He would go back to the village after joining college and meet Achukutty, Kuttisankaran and Koman Nair in person. There was too much to tell them about this new world where he had landed to do it justice in a letter, however long.

Also, he had to bring at least some of the rare books from the Big Man's library.

Vedaraman lay in bed thinking of Madhavan Nair. What were his businesses? Was there a hint among his words that he had not made his fortune by honest means? What did he mean by saying that the glow of his sixth finger was 'highly marketable'?

He grew close to Madhavan Nair in the days that followed. It was Nair's behaviour that led to it. He was open in his conversation with Vedaraman.

'Don't call me "sir". I'm your uncle,' he had said. Hadn't he accepted him without holding back anything when he had said that?

Madhavan Nair allowed him to be in the study; dictated letters to his stenographer Mani in his presence. He instructed Vedaraman to call his business friends and to take incoming calls. He would tell him every now and then, 'Vedan, this is a kind of training. You may get involved in the intricacies of my business without much delay.'

Or, 'Even if I'm not here for some time, Vedan, you must be able to manage. You know, some correspondence, routine work, that kind of thing.'

The interview card from the college arrived and Vedaraman joined.

He liked the atmosphere of the college. He was really a country boy. But he was wearing the smart clothes that Madhavan Nair had bought him. If style started with clothes, he would be able to go further. This was the world of the handsome and the beautiful, of fun and laughter and small love affairs. He would be able to cope with this world.

Madhavan Nair asked him one day, 'Vedan would you like to have a two-wheeler?'

'No, Uncle. It's only walking distance.'

'I say, did your sixth finger get noticed?'

'It did, Uncle. It's also given me a nickname – SF for sixth finger.'

Madhavan Nair laughed, 'No! It's a flaming finger. FF for short!'

After a couple of weeks, Madhavan Nair spoke to Vedan as if he was issuing a proclamation, 'Vedan, why do you always curl up in that stupid bedroom? That room is only for sleeping. Is sleep enough? Don't you want to study? Don't you want to fight? Dream big even when you are awake? Stand on your head? Do whatever you want to do, whenever you want to, wherever you want to? Isn't there enough space here for all that? Who stands in your way? Balu? Bakkar? Tony? The sweeper? The other servants? All of them are answerable to you. You are my nephew, damn it! The whole place is yours.'

Everyone heard the proclamation. They seemed to have absorbed it well. Balu, Tony, Bakkar and the other servants showed him great respect now.

Life here had taken on a rhythm too. Pranayama, yoga, time spent in the study with uncle and then to college.

In the evening, uncle and his friends would play bridge while he watched. On some evenings, he would go for parties with uncle.

One evening at bridge, as he watched, Madhavan Nair lost a rubber. They had been playing for big stakes – thousand rupees per point. Madhavan Nair lost more than a lakh-and-a-half.

Vedaraman lay in bed... He felt very guilty. It had been so many days since he had come. Even now the letters he had written to Achukutty and Kuttisankaran sat within the leaves of the magazines. He did not go to the village either. Had he detached his umbilical cord from his own soil in this atmosphere of luxury and pleasure?

He picked up the letters and tore them up. Either he should go to the village or he should write more detailed letters to them again. His silence must have hurt Kuttisankaran and Achukutty. That was for sure.

Someone was knocking on the door.

He heard Madhavan Nair's voice, 'Open up, Vedan.'

He opened the door.

Had Madhavan Nair had more to drink? His words were not clear. Placing his hand on Vedaraman's shoulder, he said, 'You know, Vedan, I'm a gambler! I'm not talking of the card games. I'm speaking of the gambling instinct that is rooted in my psyche. I don't care if I lose five or six lakhs in one sitting in a card game. A gambler gets his thrills from losing in a card game too. Yes, I'm a gambler. I'm a sort of semi-criminal. I'm used to juggling with crores. You only know that I'm a businessman, right? You'll understand slowly. Why am I saying all this to you now? I don't really know. But I have a gut feeling that you are going to play a big role in my scheme of things.'

Were Madhavan Nair's legs rather unsteady?

'Sit down, Uncle,' Vedaraman said.

'I'll sit down. I'll even lie down. If necessary I'll stay motionless too. But is it time for that? No, Vedan. If the health of the A.M. Chinnappa group of companies improves, if the control of their flagship company Bengal Bay Fertilizer Complex lands in my hands... Well, is there any reason for me to be the setting sun? I might perhaps become the rising sun? Surekha says it will be in my hands in time. She's smart, my Surekha... my niece. You don't understand a word of what I'm saying, do you? Perhaps it is better that you do not understand too much just now. Look, open that back door. Let's sit in the sit-out.'

Vedaraman led Madhavan Nair to the sit-out.

'Vedan, look at those rose plants. My pet roses. I've grown them in pots. Just beyond them, take a look at that white climbing rose that came from somewhere and pushed itself forward. Look boy, people who push themselves forward will always win. Only they win!

'Uncle, isn't it time to sleep? It's quite late.'

'I'll go to bed. But there's one condition.'

'What's that?'

'I want to see the glow of your sixth finger.'

'Will the glow come if I want it to?'

'Of course it will. You must understand something. Learn this first lesson. Have faith in yourself. Say goodbye to doubts. Now, do it.'

Madhavan Nair switched off the lights.

Vedaraman's sixth finger started glowing.

'You see, Vedan?'

'No.'

'Look again!'

'I see now. I'm seeing it.'

'You are different, Vedan! Let the time come. Let me talk it over with Surekha. You'll become a new Jiddu Krishnamurti. A new baba!'

As they were having breakfast the next morning, Madhavan Nair asked, 'What is it Vedan? It looks as though you wanted to tell me something and then stopped?'

Vedaraman spoke hesitantly, 'I want to go to the village – for a couple of days.'

'Must you?'

'Vikraman Pillai sir has given me a lot of books. Rare books, some of them. I want to bring some here. They'll be destroyed by termites if they are left there.'

'All right, go and get them. When do you want to go?'

'Today and tomorrow are holidays. If I go today, I could return the day after tomorrow.'

'All right. You can take Bakkar and go.'

'I won't take the car, Uncle. I'll go by bus.'

'As you like.'

Vedaraman felt that he should take something for Achukutty, Kuttisankaran and Koman Nair.

What could he buy, shirts? But suppose the measurement was not correct?

He could buy mundus for all of them. Two bottles of whisky for Koman Nair.

He packed six double dhotis with gold borders and the bottles of whisky and reached the bus stand.

He caught a bus that stopped at the town near his village. The town where the court and the police station were.

People there were unlikely to remember the uruli theft case. The only people who were likely to remember, Magistrate Mathews, head constable Thankappan Pillai who was a good man and that dirty Moosa, would have been swept away somewhere by the winds of transfers. Anyway, was he, Vedaraman, so important, that people would keep him in their memory for long years? Who would remember him? There were plenty of other things for people to remember.

Vedaraman took a taxi from there.

The taxi stopped at Kottoor Kavala.

He told the taxi driver, 'Please wait for a little while. I'll come soon,' and climbed the hill with one of the bundles.

Kuttisankaran was beside himself with joy.

He hugged Vedaraman and said, 'I was really angry when I did not get a letter from you. But now that's all gone.'

'I'm really sorry. I thought I'd come and tell you everything in person. I have to go tomorrow. Shall we go to Mulamkunnam? The taxi is waiting.'

Kuttisankaran stepped back a couple of steps and looked at Vedaraman intently, 'You have changed a lot, Raman. Your shirt's shining. There is a difference in the way you look and talk too. You came by taxi, did you? Your comforts are increasing. But don't let that change you too much.'

'Uncle, are you getting angry again? There is no direct bus from Kochi to this place. So, I came to the town and took a taxi from there.'

'What's in the bundle?'

'There'll be something in it. Come, let's go to Mulamkunnam.'

'What's your hurry?'

'I have to go back tomorrow.'

'All right. Let me see to the bullocks and then we'll go.'

They got into the taxi and reached Achukutty's tea shop.

Koman Nair too landed up.

Old scenes were repeated.

In his bedroom, Madhavan Nair was lazily turning over the papers in the file containing the horoscope of the Bengal Bay Company.

Three factors had led to the growth of the Chinnappa Group – the chairman's hard work, his innate talent for business and the favourable political climate. What did Chinnappa have to start with?

He had an agency business. He was an agent for various things. The main thing was Australian wool. As time passed, three textile mills became Chinnappa's own. All three were rather weak, 'sick units' as they were called. The powerful in the Tamil Nadu were Chinnappa's friends, nanpars or trusted folk. And so, the Industrial Development Corporation gave Chinnappa money in plenty. Chinnappa used a portion of the money he got to start a moped factory. Some of the money found its way back to the pockets of his political friends. Like the waters of the Kaveri that went into the Koovam stream. One of those days a licence to start a small scale fertilizer factory fell into Chinnappa's lap from the heights of Fort St George. From 'small' it morphed into 'large', thanks to a collaboration from Italy. When the Bengal Bay Fertilizer Complex was established as the flagship company, Chinnappa had this desire to make cars in his moped factory. The papers moved in Indraprastha to support this desire. Though Hindustan Motors and Premier tried to block the move, Chinnappa's Mercury Automobiles got clearance.

The capital was raised: Six crore rupees was invested by the Chinnappa group. Thirty-two crore was given interest-free by the government out of the rehabilitation package. Fifty crore was to be given by the State Industrial Development Corporation as a loan at six per cent interest.

With this capital, they could bring out the prototype of the Mercury. Once that was done, the banks would help out.

A clean operation.

A start was made. That was when the ministry changed. The new rulers removed Chinnappa from the chairmanship of Mercury Automobiles.

The rule was that only sick textile mills were to be helped from the rehabilitation package. So what the earlier government had done was corruption. Did anyone have a doubt?

The new government cleverly tethered Chinnappa. Chinnappa was exercising executive powers as the chairman of the Bengal Bay Company. That was not right.

'From now on, Mr Chinnappa, you will be just a figurehead, a decorative piece. Also, the board has to be reconstituted. The number of government nominees on the board has to be increased.'

Madhavan Nair turned the pages of the file again.

There was a newspaper cutting from a press interview.

Anand Ghosh, the star reporter of the magazine *Business Intelligence* was the interviewer.

Question: Mr Chinnappa, how do you react to the recent developments in the Bengal Bay Company?

Answer: There's nothing to worry about.

Question: What was the reason for your removal from the post of chairman of the Bengal Bay Company?

Answer: But I haven't been removed. I continue to be the chairman of the company.

Question: A figurehead?

Answer: [*Laughing*] Why? Is my figure so bad?

Question: Is the present chief minister your enemy?

Answer: All chief ministers are my friends.

Question: Can you still claim that the Bengal Bay Company is the flagship of your group? It is effectively under government control, isn't it?

Answer: The government? Where is the government control? You mean agencies of the government. Institutions like the Industrial Development Corporation and so on. Did any of these agencies do anything for us when we were facing a crisis? We continued to run on the energy we generated ourselves.

Question: The government is planning to induct a new finance director in your board. Why are you opposed to the proposal?

Answer: What has gone wrong now? Why do we need a new finance director? He will only destabilize us. The Central government is also of this opinion. Why does the state government have doubts about our integrity? I don't understand.

Question: If there is a change in the ministry?

Answer: Ministries come and go. We are not interested in all that.

Madhavan Nair set aside the file and called out to Tony, 'Whisky'.

As he sipped the whisky, he thought to himself. He wanted to take control of the Chinnappa group. He was preparing the weapons for that. But it was not time yet; this was the wrong time. Let the Chinnappa group continue like this for a while. Or things would get into a mess. Wouldn't he be able to sort everything out with Surekha's help? Surekha who was Chinnappa's special private secretary and playmate and PRO and everything! His niece Surekha.

The fact that she was Chinnappa's playmate did not make him jealous. Chinnappa was seventy-five, after all.

Surekha – his niece. That was what he told the world. Niece... darling...lover.

She must be fast asleep in the luxury flat next to the Adyar Gate Hotel.

Madhavan Nair made an STD call to Madras.

The phone rang for a minute.

Then came a voice, 'Yaru? Who's it?'

'Isn't Surekha there?'

'No, sir.' It was the Tamilian maid. Madhavan Nair placed the receiver back on the telephone and picked up the glass of whisky again.

Twenty-two

When Madhavan Nair rang up from Kochi, Surekha was lying on a bed in the five-star hotel at Adyar. The sheets of the double bed were crumpled. A smell of male cologne lingered. The smell of a minister from the Centre.

He had left the room only minutes ago. He was a good-looking man and pleasantly spoken too.

But today, he did not have pleasant words to say when she asked him about Chinnappa.

'Why are you so bothered about Chinnappa?' The Central minister had asked.

'He's my boss, after all!'

'What does it matter to you even if he gets into trouble? Why should you curl up in this corner of the country? Come to Delhi.'

'That's something to be thought of. But if it's not a big state secret why can't you tell me? What's going to happen to Chinnappa?'

The minister was willing to say some things about politicians and businessmen in general.

'You know, Surekha, politicians and businessmen are complementary factors in a country. Businessmen give us funds during elections. We have to give something in return, don't we? When we come to power, we too give them gifts. Sometimes we have to go a little out of the way to make those gifts – a licence, a letter of intent, or an approval for a collaboration. If the help received earlier was a "special" one, a "tip-off" on policy changes

– leaking information, I mean. Hey businessman, the tax on polyester pellets is going to be increased manifold in the next budget. So import now if you want to make money. Or perhaps the defence ministry plans to buy fifty helicopters. France, Sweden and the UK are in the field. France has the advantage. Come and become a middleman in the deal. Or there is information like there will be an announcement of the rupee being devalued on such and such date.'

'Will you stop mouthing these generalities and answer my question? What is going to happen to Chinnappa?'

'But Surekha, that's exactly what I'm coming to. Chinnappa forgot the ground rules of the game. You won't like what I'm going to say, but let me say it all the same. Is Chinnappa an industrialist of the first rank in India? He's just a small fry! Even the top ten worship at the feet of politicians. Since they know that the rulers and leaders in politics change every now and then, they do not make enemies in the political class. They don't get identified too closely with any one group either. Chinnappa earned a lot of bad publicity. He was labelled the lackey of the earlier ministry. That label is still visible on his forehead like a patch of leprosy. Now that the rulers have changed and the climate has changed, what is the point in moaning?'

'And so, now...?'

'What now? He may not be able to continue even as the figurehead chairman. Is he in station?'

'No, he's in London. He gets back on Wednesday.'

'Everything might seem the same this time. The company's money will flow. There will be a red carpet and garlands of roses. But the next time? Or the time after that? There won't be a red carpet or rose garlands at the airport. Instead, there might be manacles. Surekha, the state government is thinking of slapping a case against Chinnappa.'

'A case? You mean...'

'A criminal case. Chinnappa has set up a distillery at the cost of two-and-a-half crore. That was set up with no regard for law, just using his influence in the previous ministry. A big question is – where did this money come from? Was it siphoned from the first instalment of the rehabilitation package? The Enforcement Directorate believes that it is even more than two-and-a-half crore. How did Chinnappa start distribution of liquor on a large scale even before he started the distillery?'

'You shock me!'

'There's more. How come you don't know any of this? You are his PRO. Has Chinnappa secretly taken over the Kovai Distillery and MacKinnon Distillery that had been shut down? How much did he pay for those? Enforcement is really going into it deeply. Does Chinnappa own a company called "Taste Tickler" in London? Does that company run a restaurant chain? Does Chinnappa's nephew Murugappan manage that company? Is bran oil manufactured from the bran of soya and rice exported to this benami company at under-invoiced prices? Is the "balance fund" so obtained being used to import stuff into India using the same technique of under-invoicing? So...'

'FERA violations?'

'Not just FERA. Violations of Customs rules and regulations. And then all those ordinary laws we have – cheating, criminal conspiracy and many more like that...'

The sheets were all crumpled. Even the orchids in the flower vase were faded and shrunken. Surekha turned and twisted in the bed. What was the time? It was just 11 o'clock. The night was still young.

Surekha came down into the bar. As she sipped her drink she felt like talking to Madhavan Nair.

The operator connected her to Kochi.

'It's me Surekha!'

'Where from, sweetheart?'

'From Adyar.'

'I had called you a little earlier. Didn't get you.'

'I've just got back, Uncle.'

'I want to see you.'

'When?'

'As soon as possible.'

Madhavan Nair started speaking at length. His voice was not steady at all. Surekha realized that there was no point in talking to him that night. He'd just say this and that, try to draw glowing pictures of the future, describe the white climbing rose, declare that only people with push succeeded in life...

'Uncle!'

'What is it, Sura?'

'I'm sleepy.'

'Okay, go to sleep.'

Surekha placed her palm against the telephone and kissed it loudly.

'Did you get my kiss, Uncle?'

'Yes, I did, darling. Give me one more.'

Surekha wondered: was everyone using her? Or was she using everyone? It was difficult to find an answer.

Why do I trouble myself with all these questions? Why do I open the black jars of memory and let out old devils?

There, there was that huge railway junction. Was it Podanur? Or Jolarpet? Whichever it was.

She was sitting on the lap of Grandpa Stanley in the railway quarters. Grandfather was all hunched and old. Next to him was his sister Margarita Aunty. She was fat. She could see the frilled dress she was wearing more clearly than her face. A dress with blue polka dots.

In earlier days, Grandpa Stanley was supposed to have had a good physique. He was over six feet, they said. He had been employed in the Indian Railways. An important person in the local Anglo-Indian community. The trains ran only if Grandpa waved the flag.

Her father Anthony came in. He too was employed by the railways. Grandpa complained that he was not doing his job properly. He spent a lot of time dressing up and loafing around, playing the harmonica, and drinking and dancing. He was quite willing to work at his job in the railways if he had time to spare after all this. How could he ever prosper this way?

'Anthony! You'll never amount to anything!' Grandpa Stanley cursed his son.

'Don't talk nonsense, Stan!' That was Margarita.

Anthony laughed sarcastically, put the harmonica to his lips and played a tune.

Where was her mother? Her mother Stella?

Surekha looked intently into the cocktail glass. Could she see her mother's face there? Could she hear her mother's voice?

Her mother was calling her from a distant, distant place – 'Irene! Irene!'

The scene changed.

Margarita Aunty was surrounded by the neighbours. Margarita was swaying and dancing. Her hands were raised. She was saying something.

Margarita Aunty could speak to the dead.

One day, Aunty told her, 'Irene, I spoke to your mother.'

'What did my mother say, Aunty?'

'She said a lot of loving words, Irene. And then she cried a lot.'

'Where is my mother, Aunty?'

'Far away, beyond the clouds.'

'Is she dead?'

'I don't know. I know that she's not here, but she is somewhere else.'

'Why did my mother leave me and go away, Aunty?'

How old had she been then? She had got the answer to that question only years later. She had been fifteen then. She remembered how old she had been because of the birthday celebrations. The house was decorated with streamers and balloons of different colours. All the friends and acquaintances in the Railway Colony had come. She had blown the candles out and cut the cake. Grandpa Stanley was wandering around excitedly.

Anthony was playing the harmonica. Margarita Aunty came up to her and put a silver bracelet on her left wrist. She whispered, 'Irene! This belonged to your mother.'

That night as she slept, Margarita Aunty came and shook her awake, 'Irene!'

'What is it, Aunty?'

'Have you heard of psychometry?'

'No.'

'It's a kind of measurement, Irene. Taking the measure of a soul. Some people can tell you a lot about people who have passed away by touching something that they used to wear. I can do it. Please let me touch that bracelet. I feel like saying some things about your mother. Let me shut my eyes and meditate on her. There's Stella, so beautiful with her blue eyes. She was the prettiest of the girls in this area. There's Dotty, who's a nurse in the Railway Dispensary. She has light, colourless eyes and pimples on her face. This stupid Anthony gets close to her. One night, a night when it rained heavily, Stella sat and waited for Anthony. He didn't come. He was with Dotty. I see another man. A man with a scarred face and long sideburns. Was he another of Dotty's lovers? He gets into a fight with Anthony. People crowd around. What do I see now? Anthony has been stabbed. Who carried him here? And then…police case, investigation, questioning…And then…'

Margarita Aunty started crying inconsolably.

'Irene, I did not see it that day. But today, now, I see it. Stella's dead body on the railway tracks. Her head and body are detached and lie in two pieces.'

Surekha ran down to the bar again and had another drink.

Grandpa Stanley died. Margarita Aunty too died. Anthony left her behind and vanished somewhere.

She was all alone in this world. Irene, a.k.a. Surekha. Director Philips of Salem Modern Studio had renamed her Surekha. He had given her bit roles in Tamil movies; promised to make a star of her.

Finally, she had reached Madras. She had been twenty-five then. She had become the model for an advertising company. At the same time, she also became a 'not-so-cheap' call girl.

Call girl...party girl...

Time passed. She met and got acquainted with Chinnappa at a party. A drunk Chinnappa placed his hand on her thighs and cracked a really poor joke – I like this place a lot, this thighland!

The relationship continued. It grew, encompassed a lot. She became one of Chinnappa's private secretaries. The PRO of his companies.

Madhavan Nair had helped Chinnappa when he set out. He was the director of some of Chinnappa's companies. Chinnappa's 'frontman' in some of his companies. Chinnappa used Madhavan Nair. Now Madhavan Nair was trying to use Chinnappa. Did Uncle believe that he could use the now-broken Chinnappa's back as a stepping stone? Chinnappa's very existence was in danger. Wasn't that what the Central minister had said?

What would happen to Chinnappa?

At the final count, who would have used whom?

She did not know.

But she did have to sleep at least a little.

Should she crumple up the sheets and throw them in a corner? The smell of the cologne was bringing on nausea.

Twenty-three

Vedaraman returned with a bundle of books from Kottoor
Kavala and set up a small library in the room next to his
bedroom. Madhavan Nair went through the books casually and
commented, 'Esoteric stuff! But there's nothing here about the
Theosophical Movement.'

He became loquacious about the Theosophical Society,
'Vedan, have you heard of a great lady called Helena Petrovna
Blavatsky? She was born in Ukraine in 1831. In her eighteenth
year, Nikifor Blavatsky, who was Vice Governor of the Eriwan
region, married Helena. And she became Madame Blavatsky. But
that marriage did not last long. Madame's life after separation
from her husband is the stuff of legends. She wandered around
the world and reached America – Vermont, to be exact. There
she met Colonel Olcott. Colonel Olcott was very interested in
extrasensory experiences, the occult I mean. He believed that he
had extraordinary powers. He found out that Madame Blavatsky
also had such powers. They teamed up, lived in the same
apartment and started a movement called the "Miracle Club". It
was this which later developed into the Theosophical Movement.
Theosophy means "knowledge of god". I'm summarizing, Vedan.
The Colonel and Madame reached India. They got involved with
the Arya Samaj. Adyar became the centre of their operations.
They spoke about the "Masters" who controlled the world at all
times. Where were the gurus or the masters? Were they in Tibet?
On the peaks of the Himalayas? The ideas propagated by the

Colonel and Madame Blavatsky attracted a lot of people. It was at this time that Annie Besant also reached Adyar. After the death of Blavatsky and Olcott, Annie Besant became the chief of the movement. A priest called Charles Leadbetter became her right-hand man. He was a homosexual. This Leadbetter found Jiddu Krishnamurti – on the beach at Adyar. Krishnamurti was the son of an employee at the Theosophical Society's headquarters. Leadbetter and Annie Besant declared that Krishnamurti was the master and guru who would lead the world. They formed an organization called "The Order of the Star in the East" in 1911, with Krishnamurti as the leader and head of the Order.

'Murti's father filed a case asking for the release of his son from the custody of Leadbetter and Annie Besant. The case went up to the Privy Council, but the final decision was in favour of the Theosophical Society. "The Order of the Star" grew, became highly successful internationally. Do you know what happened finally? In 1929, Krishnamurti disbanded the Order. He declared that he did not possess any extraordinary power and that all religions were false. What Vedan, have I bored you?'

'No, Uncle.'

'Vikraman Pillai and I had links with the Theosophical Movement for a long time. Annie Besant had been a part of our freedom movement too. Well, Vedan, each age waits for a particular preceptor, a guru; it tries to find him. The market for bhakti, for devoutness, is huge. I've often felt that the hotel business and the spirituality business are very similar. Five-star hotels...five-star spiritual trips! Both groups put up interesting packages to attract attention and business. After a while, people get fed up with what is available. Then new packaging is required, new brand names. New mantras! Empty thrones await new gurus in the heights of the spiritual business. If you ask me, don't we have innumerable gurus, babas – well, yes we do. But are they enough to satisfy everyone, to give everyone the nectar of bliss? The market is so huge, and people have different tastes. People want new thrills, new highs. New products take birth according to the needs of the market – including babas. Most are purely seasonal products. Even if they are fast moving during their time. Very few last. Vedan, you could also become a guru. The market might find you acceptable.'

❖

A month passed. Vedaraman went to the village again. He felt that the hours he spent with Kuttisankaran and Achukutty and Koman Nair were not as enjoyable as they used to be. Was there a sense of distance in the atmosphere, unacknowledged by everyone? Nobody said anything unpleasant. But he felt that he was no longer the old Vedaraman to these people. They considered him a stranger who was now travelling on a path unknown to them.

'Will you come to the village again?' Was there a hint of blame in Achukutty's question?

'Of course, I will!'

Kuttisankaran then said, 'You might come, once or twice. You'll not come after that. It's not your fault. When you grow in the world you've reached, things will change even without your noticing. When you study in the college and go further, your views will change.'

Vedaraman showed his hurt, 'How have I changed? I haven't changed at all. I've just gone. And you talk about change. I won't change in any way.'

'You're angry now. Did anyone say anything to criticize you?'

Koman Nair intervened, 'You know, this fellow, this Ramankutty... Isn't he an andaja, born of an egg? So, he will grow wings. One day, he'll fly away. He'll rise on his wings. That's the way of the world.'

'You'll come here before you fly away, won't you?' Kuttisankaran asked.

'I'm not flying and I'm not going anywhere right now. Satisfied?' Vedaraman yelled.

'We were just joking, Raman!' Koman Nair said.

❖

Madhavan Nair had changed. But what was the change? Vedaraman could not put his finger on it.

Everything went on as usual. There wasn't an iota of difference in the routine. Uncle worked in the study every morning as he always did. On many evenings the members of the high society of the city came to play cards. There were large parties every now and then.

He was sleeping very late at nights. Was he drinking a lot after dinner? But then, could you call that a new habit? He would often come into the room saying, 'I'm not feeling sleepy, Vedan.' And then would sit and talk about some business matters. Most of it was about a man called Chinnappa.

What were the knots in the business just now?

Vedaraman gathered up the courage to ask once.

Madhavan Nair did not hesitate to answer. He started explaining, 'I told you about Chinnappa in Madras once, didn't I?'

'Bengal Bay Company is the Chinnappa Group's flagship company. I helped in setting it up. Now, with the change in the ministry, Chinnappa has become a nobody. The new government is harassing the man, hunting him down. In effect, the company has been taken over by the government. A majority of the directors are government nominees. My niece Surekha says there is likely to be a move for a criminal prosecution of Chinnappa. If that happens, the hands of law may stretch right up to Kochi – I mean, towards me. I was the frontman for a number of Chinnappa's deals. I found out about the extent of the problem only recently. Honestly, I'm scared!'

Madhavan Nair continued, 'The Chinnappa Group and the Alliance Group from Bombay had entered into a secret agreement. They wanted to take over the Torson and Marbro company, which has a turnover of a thousand crore annually. It is the biggest engineering company in India. The Chinnappa group is small fry compared to the Alliance Group. But at that time Chinnappa had immense political power. Ramesh Nimbani, with the support of Unit Trust, LIC and General Insurance

Corporation and I, as the Chinnappa Group's representative, got into the board of T&M. The Bank of Golconda helped us achieve this. To be able to do this, they created a subsidiary called "BOG Fiscal Services". A company called "Krishna Investments" was created simultaneously by Alliance and Chinnappa. It was Krishna Investments that retained the shares of T&M bought secretly. You must understand that Ramesh Nimbani and I entered the board of T&M before the shares were transferred in the names of Alliance and Chinnappa. It was not a strictly legal move, as you must realize.

'Did I say that the shares had been bought secretly? Actually, it was not all that much of a secret. Shares were bought from LIC and the Unit Trust of India. Shares worth twenty-seven crore were bought in the name of BOG Fiscal Services. The Fiscal Services then obtained twenty-four crore of credit from the Golconda Bank. Also, a call deposit of thirty crore came from a stock broker called Kanak Desai. Kanak Desai gets thirty crore from the satellite companies of the Alliance and Chinnappa groups. Do you understand the game, Vedan?'

'Um,' Vedaraman grunted though he had not actually understood anything.

'When all this was happening, Vedan, a national daily raised the sword against the Alliance and Chinnappa groups. There was a rush of public interest petitions in the courts.

'Unexpectedly, the Central ministry changed. There was also a change in the government in Tamil Nadu. Now, Chinnappa and I and Ramesh Nimbani are in a dangerous situation. The chairman of the Golconda Bank has been removed from his post by the government, and then he was reappointed. So, he will reveal everything to remain in their good books. Nimbani will be able to influence the political circuit even under the new circumstances. So, he might escape. Only Chinnappa and I will end up ruined!'

Vedaraman lifted his right hand and pressed the palm against his forehead. He bent his head. His whole body trembled.

Madhavan Nair asked anxiously, 'What is it, Vedan? What's wrong with you?'

Vedan lifted his head and looked up. He raised his arms high. He looked as if he was about to have a fit.

He started speaking. His voice was different as if he was speaking in a dream.

'What...what did you say?'

The sixth finger was glowing now.

'Uncle, there might be an arrest at any moment. But don't worry, nothing's going to happen. You must take anticipatory bail...anticipatory bail!'

The arms came down. The glow of the sixth finger was gone. Vedaraman fell down as though he had been cut down by someone.

Madhavan Nair lifted him up. He was burning with fever. He rang up the Medical Trust Hospital and the doctor came without delay. When he examined Vedan, his eyes opened wide in disbelief. The pulse rate was what surprised him.

The pulse rate at the right wrist was eighteen while that of the left was twenty-six. The heartbeat was ninety-two.

'Doctor, you look worried?'

'Nothing, Mr Nair! His pulse rate is rather erratic. I'll look at it a little later.'

When the doctor checked again, everything was normal. The rate at which the heart and the two wrists pulsed was the same.

'Nothing to worry about, Mr Nair! We'll give him some paracetamol. Let him take rest. The fever will go.'

Twenty-four

Surekha telephoned from Madras, 'Uncle, things are getting into a mess. You must take anticipatory bail immediately. Chinnappa has already done so.'

'I'll take anticipatory bail tomorrow itself.'

'Will you get bail there for a crime that is registered here?'

'I'll get advice on that.'

'Uncle, the matter's urgent. There's no time to be lost. Don't take any risks. Come to Madras tomorrow, apply for bail here.'

'All right. I'll reach there by tomorrow afternoon. Will you be at the airport?'

'Certainly.' She put down the receiver after the usual kiss.

Madhavan Nair called Tony and arranged for two tickets on the Madras flight the next day through Jupiter Travels.

Surekha was a sensible girl. There might be problems taking anticipatory bail here. Anyway, there'd be a lot of noise about it. Taking bail in Madras would be no problem. Chinnappa's lawyer could also be entrusted with the task.

Chinnappa was a giant among industrialists. Before him he, Madhavan Nair, was just nobody. Should he ring up Chinnappa and inform him that he was reaching Madras the next day? No, he might not like it. When trouble started Chinnappa had warned him, 'Nair, don't ring me up directly. Our telephones might be tapped. Let's play it safe.'

Madhavan Nair went to Vedaraman's room.

Vedaraman was writing something busily.

'What are you so busy with?'

'Oh, nothing much.' Vedaraman set aside the papers and stood up.

'Did I disturb you?'

'Not at all, Uncle.'

'Vedan, when you got a fever that day, you'd told me something, do you remember? It was about taking anticipatory bail.'

'I don't remember, Uncle.'

'Well, you did.'

'Anticipatory bail? Why?'

'I'll tell you all that later. You haven't flown till now, have you? I mean you wouldn't have travelled by air. Tomorrow, we fly – to Madras.'

'Why Uncle? Why do you want me?'

'For company. Also, I want you to meet my business friends in Madras. You can meet Surekha, my niece. I told you earlier, didn't I, that you must get involved. You should be able to manage my affairs in my absence.'

Madhavan Nair could not sleep though it was very late at night. He was thinking of what needed to be done at Madras. Anticipatory bail, of course. Then? How should he use Vedan? Chinnappa must get a good impression of him. He should be convinced of Vedan's powers. If Chinnappa who donated money to temples, who prostrated himself before any so-called sanyasi, could be convinced of Vedan's powers, his own ambitions might find fruition even under the present difficult circumstances. Vedan was a marvel. It was he who had first mentioned anticipatory bail. He does not remember saying it. But what did it matter if Vedan did not remember. He, Madhavan Nair, could remember. From the beginning – he did not wish to remember about that beginning – but when a lot of liquor went in, the scattered shards of that old time pierced his brain.

Today, he was an important person in the local society. Someone who stayed in the big bungalow 'Eastern Star'. Before getting to know Vikraman Pillai, before getting involved in the Theosophical movement and the freedom struggle, where had he been?

FMS…

Rubber plantations.

He was young and adventurous when he worked as an accountant in the rubber planation. He had fallen in love with a yellow girl, with big slanting eyes. He, Madhavan Nair, was known as 'M. Nair' then.

He left the rubber plantation and wandered around.

The next stage – M. Nair was now the postmaster at a place called Sarawak.

The yellow girl was still with him.

While working as a postmaster, he had this sudden urge to make a lot of money quickly. He dug into the savings bank fund of the post office. This went on for three or four years. As he reassured himself that everything was safe, the District Postal Superintendent came on inspection. He was Chinese. There was no reason for him to suspect anything. He had entertained the Superintendent royally too. He had even lent him the yellow girl for a night. And yet the Chinese Superintendent had found the discrepancy. One couldn't blame him. Actually Madhavan felt grateful to him. The Superintendent had said, 'Tomorrow I'll write my inspection report. I'll not be able to hide this big swindle. Nair, run, leave the country. If you stay here, you're sure to get seven years' hard labour. Run. I'll take care of your girl.'

Madhavan Nair drank some more.

Tomorrow, Madras…

Surekha, Chinnappa, anticipatory bail…

His brain was working on overdrive. Was he thinking like a political analyst, like a financial expert?

Industry. Business.

After independence, in the first three decades, hadn't 'business' been a bad word in the socialist lexicon of the country? A dirty word! There was a caricature definition of the businessman. A villainous character who stood surrounded by fraudsters and black marketeers. But the picture changed in the 1980s. The unsavoury businessman turned into a 'matinee idol' and appeared glamorously on the front pages of the national dailies. The dark cellars of industry and business were lit up by the glow of a new respectability. The economy had a healthy growth rate, from a measly three per cent to a whopping seven per cent. The stock market had the strength of a giant awoken. The ordinary man was chasing blue chip shares. A new word entered the vocabulary – 'mega issue'!

The Indian middle class was raising its head. Where had poverty gone? Shares, marble bathrooms, tiles, micro-ovens, designer clothes...For the first time, in the market place, in the hurly-burly of business, there was public and intense competition. The government's socialist policies took a backstep.

There was thrust and parry in the arena of competition, manoeuvres and contra-manoeuvres. The old emperors of the industry who had worn their crowns of tradition proudly now became skeletons. The upstarts and the rebels crowed over their victories. When the newcomers received support from the highest echelons of the rulers, they became the heads of huge projects!

Great times!

Wasn't that the reason our group was even formed, Surekha? Alliance and Bengal Bay. Madhavan Nair and Chinnappa. Synthetic yarn, petrochemicals, engineering, manufacturing a new car...

Madhavan Nair filled his glass again. His thoughts wandered over many different tracks.

Where had he lost his way? And now it had become imperative to take anticipatory bail.

None of these were problems that occurred because of his mistakes. Time rushed in this land and stories changed quickly!

Why did Nimbani and Leslie Kapadia get into a fight? And that raised such waves, set loose so many storms. That one incident was enough to prove the dirty nexus between the government and big business. In this sacred land called Bharat, whatever field you looked at, you could see the play of mafia power.

The old business aristocracy had deteriorated so much.

Firla, Gody, Sreejith, Mangania...

When Firla died, the six branches of the family divided up the empire, in a fairly gentlemanly way, without a drawn-out fight or unpleasantness.

The story of the Gody group was different. There was a big fight there, cheating and betrayal. Finally they required the services of a mediator to settle everything. The mediator had not been an ordinary man. It was the prime minister of the country.

The story of the Sreejith group was not too different either.

When the old business aristocracy lost power, new pirates entered the arena, under a non-resident label.

Durai Raj Kaul – he had great political clout. This giant would have swallowed ACM and Discourt. But the high court caught him by the neck – in a decision that the newspapers called a 'landmark judgment'.

Chinnappa was not a Nimbani or a Kapadia, or a Mangani... he was not a giant in the national arena. But for him, for Madhavan Nair, he was a giant. Chinnappa played some games. He had lent his support for those games.

As time passed... Madhavan Nair felt guilty. As time passed, his greed grew. The dirty worm that slept in his mind became a serpent and lifted its hood. He made plans to throw Chinnappa down and take over the control of the company. He was sure he would have Surekha's help.

And now, he needed an anticipatory bail.

He wondered whether he should laugh or cry.

He did not feel sleepy. Should he take some sedative? No, the pills and alcohol might disagree with each other and tomorrow's trip would have to be cancelled.

Madhavan Nair went out of the house and wandered around in the lawn. He reached the back of the bungalow. He looked at the climber rose that grew among the potted plants. Would it not push forward further?

Only the 'one with push' would succeed. But this was not the occasion to push against Chinnappa. He would stand by him. After all, Chinnappa had helped him all this while. He shouldn't betray him now. He could try to influence him. That should be the game. Though Chinnappa was a hard-boiled businessman, he was also highly superstitious.

Vedan's powers might help in influencing Chinnappa.

But what was the point?

If things did not work out?

Meenambakkam.

When she saw Vedaraman with Madhavan Nair, Surekha asked, 'And this is?'

Madhavan Nair introduced them, 'This is Vedan! I'll tell you just that, for now. What I mean is that there's a lot to say about him. Vedan, this is Surekha, my niece.'

'Hi Vedan!' Surekha ran her eyes over Vedaraman.

She drove them from the airport. They reached the flat at Adyar.

When Surekha suggested going to Hotel Adyar Gate for lunch, Madhavan Nair demurred. He said, 'My dear Sura! I'm too tired. I did not sleep at all last night. Just get something made here. And before that, get me a drink.'

'Gimlet?'

'Right! Vedan can do with a beer. What about you?'

'I'll have a Bloody Mary.'

Surekha instructed the servant Subbamma. And served the drinks like a good hostess.

Surekha sat next to Vedaraman. She said, 'Vedan, you can relax. Uncle and I are going to talk about some boring things.'

As Vedaraman raised his glass to his lips, Surekha saw the sixth finger. Madhavan Nair noticed her gaze lingering over it.

'Sura, this is the famous sixth finger. I'll speak in detail about it later. Let's get on with our conversation. What are the boring things you spoke of?'

Twenty-five

'Uncle, I've made all the arrangements for an anticipatory bail. Advocate Ananthasivam will come here tomorrow morning.'

'Good work, Sura!'

'What good work? I now feel that this anticipatory bail is the least of our problems.'

'What do you mean?'

'Uncle, things are in a mess. I didn't want to talk about everything over the telephone.'

'Tell me! All the bad news.'

'We've seen only the tip of the iceberg.'

'Don't beat around the bush, Sura! What's the scenario?'

Surekha started throwing questions at him.

Uncle, had Unit Trust invested in the Bengal Bay Company?

Is Unit Trust the biggest institutional shareholder in the company?

Did BIFR have any suspicions?

Who are the real players in this drama? Unit Trust? BIFR? SBI? IDBI?

Madhavan Nair's face darkened, 'Sura, you can't keep shooting questions at me like this? You shock me! Anyway, tell me all the stinking news.'

'Uncle, Chinnappa and Murugappan from London made the group "sick" – or that is the prima facie case. At the first estimate, the loss is somewhere around a hundred and ten crore. The present liabilities are something like two hundred crore.

The annual liability on account of interest alone comes to about twenty-six crore.'

'My god!'

'That's not the end of it. You know that MD whom the government imposed on us?'

'Gopikrishnan IAS…'

'That's right, Gopikrishnan. He's found other anomalies – some secret deals that Chinnappa made, the nexus between the Hong Kong Bank and City Bank. Even if you ignore all this, the question remains: how did twelve crore end up in the account of Murugappan's London-based Food Chain?'

'Sura, is there anything more?'

'Well yes, there is. The latest one. Chinnappa, who had been favoured out of the way by the earlier regime, had received twenty-five acres of land in Thiruvanmiyur. Land that might soon become prime property for development. The market value was seventy-five lakh. Chinnappa paid a mere one lakh. The real problem is that this land had been earmarked for the Civil Supplies Corporation's use. When the new government came, the Revenue Department raised this issue. The Housing Department also joined hands with the Revenue Department. Their finding was different. This land had been earmarked for housing development for the middle-income group. Anyway, the relevant files are all missing.'

'Then, what's…'

'Does the fact that the files are missing save Chinnappa completely? Chinnappa had built factory sheds in these twenty-five acres of land. Last week the police came into the picture, they pulled down the sheds, burnt them. The land is now under police protection. There is a new case against Chinnappa on this matter.'

Vedaraman sat and listened. But his mind was not on the discussion. It was going down other paths.

This Surekha appeared to be an Anglo-Indian. She was beautiful, and was definitely not a Malayali. How could an Anglo-

Indian woman be Madhavan Nair's niece? What was their real connection? Surekha must have come to Kochi. So, Tony and Bakkar and Balu would have seen her. They too might have had the doubts that he, Vedaraman, now had. But they would not have asked any questions, they would not even have muttered among themselves. Madhavan Nair was a rich man and a good paymaster. The salary they got was probably not just for the work they did, but for not speaking about what went on in the household.

'Are you bored, Vedan?' Surekha asked.

'Not at all,' Vedan responded.

'Then why are you looking so sleepy? Leave that beer. I shall get you gin.'

Vedaraman was feeling queasy. Had the drink gone to his head? This queasiness had started in Kochi. When the aircraft took off, he had felt that his intestines had reached his mouth. He had thrown up. If Madhavan Nair had not opened the bag in time the seat before them and the carpet of the aircraft would have been soiled. He had thrown up a second time before the airhostess when he had tried to eat something off the snack tray provided.

He could hear the dialogue continue, but not very clearly.

What were they saying?

'Sura, Vedan is a marvel, a small prophet. He told me about the need for anticipatory bail even before you rang me up.'

'Uncle, isn't he really handsome? The only drawback is that sixth finger.'

'Sura, don't be stupid! It is that sixth finger that makes him a marvel.'

'Vedan is falling asleep, Uncle.'

Madhavan Nair woke Vedaraman up, 'Vedan, come let's have lunch.'

Vedaraman muttered, 'I don't want anything. I'll sleep for some time, Uncle.'

❖

How long ago had that been?

How many days had it been?

Vedaraman woke up with a start.

This bedroom was full of the smell of perfume. When had he reached here? What was the nightmare that he had just woken from? When he woke up suddenly, bits of the nightmare were still sticking to his brain, in dark colours. Now, they had vanished. Was it night or day? The hands of the watch stood hugging each other.

Who was piercing his temples with needles?

Vedaraman pushed back the curtains of the bedroom. It was broad daylight.

His throat was parched. He needed to drink something. He saw that there was food on the side table, cold food – a breakfast tray, a coffee pot and a cup. Who had come and placed all this? When he poured coffee into the cup, he saw a white layer on top. He drank a mouthful of coffee. And felt like throwing up. He ran to the bathroom and vomited. He felt ashamed of himself.

He had downed arrack mixed with river water on so many evenings, meditating on his ancestors in the Mulamkunnam family. He had not even had a hiccough then. And now...

The pain in his temples seemed to have drums for accompaniment.

Vedaraman got out of the room and wandered around. Where was everyone? There was absolutely no noise.

Vedaraman picked up a sheet of notepaper and a pen from the drawing room. Am I mad? Why do I feel like writing something now? I'm trying to sort and arrange the feelings in my mind. So, I could not be mad.

Returning to the bedroom, Vedaraman started writing: I am a thief, an uruli thief. Something has hold over me. It is not madness. So, what is it? Is it some extraordinary power? I identified the spot for the well, that is true. Is it such a great thing to do? Do people believe that I have some sort of magical medicine paste that shows me things, that I can see anything on earth? Aren't the people who believe all this the real madmen?

Uncle had said right from the beginning, 'Vedan, you should not fall prey to doubts. You should believe in yourself. You are highly marketable.'

What did Uncle mean by that? Did he mean that I, the uruli thief, would become a highly valued commodity in the market of bhakti?

Aren't we all thieves, Uncle? Isn't this world under the control of thieves? So, I'll come with you, I don't mind. Who said that this sixth finger of mine was a dirty thing? This extra finger is a bore, it is unneeded. But it was Kuttisankaran who said that this finger glowed. I had protested then. I'd said that he was imagining things, that perhaps fireflies had got stuck to the finger. But from now on, I'm going to believe. Yes, my sixth finger can glow. Still, I do have a small doubt, a grain of doubt. Why does the sixth finger not glow always? At the very minimum, it should glow at least when I want it to. It should obey my orders. But it does not obey; it glows only when it feels like it. Is the sixth finger being recalcitrant? Does it have its own will? That cannot be allowed. This finger is a part of me. I shall tame it, make it obey me – through intense meditation. The sixth finger is only a bulb. The battery and the switch are my mind.

'Vedan!'

Vedaraman lifted his head when he heard the call. Madhavan Nair and Surekha stood before him. He set aside the paper and pen.

'Well Vedan, busy writing?' Madhavan Nair asked.

'Oh, it's nothing. You got anticipatory bail, did you, Uncle? But there's a hidden catch in it. Your lawyer was not a good one. You got only a conditional bail, and only you. You are the third accused. The first accused Chinnappa and the second accused Murugappan who stays in London have got unconditional anticipatory bail! Only you have been asked to report to the court every month, right?'

'That's right.'

Surekha's eyes widened in wonder. How did Vedan get to know all this?

'What Sura, surprised? I told you Vedan is a wonder boy.'

'Can't you get another lawyer, Uncle? Get him to file an amendment petition. That condition will be removed.'

The days have lost their order.

I, Vedaraman, sit in the bedroom with the door shut. I'm going to meditate. I must bring my sixth finger under my full control. I want to change my pulse rate at will. I feel that something that is not myself is living in me. Why do I hear disembodied voices sometimes? Are they just illusions created by the mind? Or am I going beyond rational thought and reaching the level of extrasensory knowledge? Yogis say that the mind is the master. Yes, the mind is all-pervading. Then, does only the impact of the senses of the body cause reactions in the mind? Can't the mind grasp realities other than through the perceptions of the senses? The kundalini had to be awoken by pranayama, raised through the sushumna, crossing the swadhishtana and other circles and reaching the sahasrarapadma.

Dreams, imagination...these were the fruits of the unconscious working of the kundalini.

It is said that the kundalini awakes at least once for every man. That means any man can attain self-realization and extrasensory knowledge if he wants to. But how many births does it take? How many yugas, kalpas? He had to meditate, quicken this mental evolution.

How many days had passed? Vedaraman wondered. Or had not even one day passed?

He was sitting on the floor, concentrating on a small circle drawn on the wall.

A picture grew clear in his mind.

It was a huge bungalow. A beautiful bathroom with marble tiles. A middle-aged man lost his footing and fell. A man with a grey moustache. His face was full of pock marks. He had not seen that man before, but he felt that this was Chinnappa. Vedaraman jumped up and reached the drawing room. There was no one there. The feeble light of a night lamp showed from the kitchen. It was night. He stood on the balcony and looked at the street. The street lamps were shining. There was hardly any traffic. He returned to the drawing room and called out aloud, 'Uncle! Sura!'

There was no reply. Everyone must be asleep.

He was terribly hungry and thirsty.

He walked to the pantry and opened the refrigerator. There were vegetables, butter, cheese, eggs, dosa batter and half a bottle of brandy in it. He ate two or three tomatoes and a couple of raw eggs. He also drank a little brandy directly from the bottle.

He staggered back to the bedroom and lay on his back on the bed. Images danced before his eyes. Long sharp nails rose from cactus plants. The nails scratched and dragged at his closing eyes and eyelids. The nails withdrew. Shadows started dancing. They grew thicker. They became bodies of men and women. The 'capable' women of the cowsheds at Mulamkunnam. Rairu and the Adhikari...the policeman Moosa...Kozhukatta Paru...

Who kissed him?

He opened his eyes. It was daytime. Surekha stood before him.

Surekha said, 'Vedan, you're stinking.'

'The smell of brandy?'

'No, your whole body is stinking. Come, I'll bathe you.'

'No, Aunty, I'll bathe by myself.'

Surekha laughed, 'Aunty? Call me Sura, you shy virgin!'

Twenty-six

Vedaraman was disturbed. His mind was racing like a maddened horse. He could not control it. When had he lost the reins? Did he ever have the reins to lose them?

All the hard-won order was lost.

Why had Madhavan Nair brought him here? How many days had passed since they came here? When would they return to Kochi? Didn't he have to study? Many such questions.

Whom could he ask?

At Kochi, he had maintained a slight distance from Madhavan Nair. Since they had come here, had he been talking nonsense? Had he taken unwarranted liberties with Uncle? Why did Surekha keep tickling him and touching him? Which night had she come to his bed? He had got excited then and had had to struggle hard to regain control. He had shut his eyes, meditating on Kozhukatta Paru and the anthills. Only then had he been able to control his imprudence.

Someone was asking: Vedan why are you sitting there with the door shut?

Why do you hide in your hole?

Why don't you eat something? Are you ill? Shall we call the doctor?

Vedaraman rubbed his eyes, held his palm hard against his forehead and muttered, 'I'm all right!'

All the images scattered and then gained focus again. This was the breakfast table.

He was sitting at the table with Madhavan Nair and Surekha.

'Eat something. Don't just pick at the food.'

'We have to go to meet Chinnappa. The appointment is at 11 o'clock,' Madhavan Nair said.

'Hey, Mr Handsome! Boss is in an almighty hurry to see you. Uncle has told him so much about you,' Surekha pinched his thigh as she said this.

What could Uncle have told Chinnappa? The story of the glowing sixth finger? Was Chinnappa in a hurry because he wanted to see the glow of that finger?

Chinnappa...the towering figure of the industry...a tough guy. He might laugh when he saw the sixth finger glow, 'Oh! Just a parlour trick!'

Vedaraman's head felt heavy. A face grew clear before his eyes, a face full of pock marks.

'What happened, Vedan? Why are you silent?' Madhavan Nair asked.

Nothing, Uncle. Just a feeling...that I've seen Chinnappa. Am I talking nonsense, Uncle? Perhaps I am. But I have to say this. Chinnappa has had a fall...He fell in the bathroom.'

'Vedan, this is absurd!'

Surekha drove to Poes Garden. The car stopped before the gate. The security guard in the pillar box recognized Surekha and saluted her. When the car moved to the portico the guard picked up the telephone in the pillar box.

Rangarajan who received the call came to the portico – a tall, fair, middle-aged man, wearing thick glasses.

'Hello, Rangan,' Surekha said. 'Meet Mr Vedaraman. Vedan, this is Rangarajan, the Boss's PA.'

'Rangan, is Chinnappa sir in a good mood?' Madhavan Nair asked.

'He had been, Nair sir. Till he slipped and fell in the bathroom.'

Madhavan Nair looked at Surekha, a reproachful look. They could have rung up from the flat. If he had heard that Vedan had predicted the fall, Chinnappa would have been impressed, wouldn't he?

Rangarajan was explaining what had happened, 'Boss was dictating to the stenographer. I was there too. Suddenly, he started belching. He rushed to the bathroom, massaging his stomach. In his hurry, he tripped over the mat there...'

❖

They walked through the carpeted corridors, through the centrally air-conditioned coolness.

Vedaraman looked around.

There were paintings on the walls, sculptures in marble and metal in the corners, chandeliers hanging from the ceiling.

There was not just wealth here, there was an aesthetic sense too.

How long had they been walking? Vedaraman felt that Chinnappa was a minor deity. How long would they have to walk to reach his presence?

The large drawing room of the bungalow appeared before him. Chinnappa sat in a high-backed chair, clad in a kurta and a lace-dhoti. His left leg was kept raised on a footstool with a foam rubber top. All around were shining leather sofas. Near Chinnappa, on a low table stood a whisky bottle, ice bucket, soda and glasses.

Vedaraman looked at Chinnappa carefully. Medium complexion, greying moustache, a round face full of pock marks. His eyes had the power of command. Was he rather short? Perhaps that was only because of the high back of the chair.

Chinnappa welcomed everyone with a general 'hello'. He asked only about Vedaraman, 'Nair, this must be your wonder boy? What shall I call him?'

'Vedan.'

'Ah, Rangarajan must have told you. I fell. I'm lucky I did not break any bones. But you know this fellow, my phlebitis...' Chinnappa rolled up the lace-dhoti till his knee and said, 'He got bruised on the floor. I'm in terrible pain. That's why I'm drinking at this time of the day.'

Chinnappa picked up the whisky glass again.

Vedaraman's eyes lingered on Chinnappa's left leg. The veins stood out. The leg was swollen here and there. There were bubble-like eruptions too. Was one of them burst and oozing?

After a few minutes, Vedaraman was restless. Chinnappa was not even looking at him. He was ignoring the others too. He had forgotten the existence of everyone other than Madhavan Nair.

He had placed him next to himself and was speaking to him, 'Nair, this is not a good day. My fall…then there is all the confusion regarding the Thiruvanmiyur case. My prestige is at stake in that case. I'll explain everything. Come, join me!'

Madhavan Nair too picked up a glass. Chinnappa continued to speak to him.

Surekha nudged Vedaraman and asked, 'Shall we sit a little to the side? Their discussion is sure to bore you.'

Rangarajan and Surekha and Vedaraman formed another group.

'Rangan, I don't know whether you'll believe me if I say something.'

'Tell me, madam.'

'Vedan had predicted that Boss would slip and fall in the bathroom. If only we had thought to let you know…'

'Even if you had let us know, Boss would have fallen. I'm a philosopher, madam. What has to happen will happen. Vedan, do you know, I was part of the personal staff of the President, Dr Radhakrishnan. Such a great person! Let that be, Vedan, how did you know that the Boss would fall?'

'I just felt that, Rangan sir.'

'That is intuition. Let me ask you something. How old are you?'

'About seventeen.'

'I thought you must be twenty at least. You are big for your age. He has a muscular body, right madam? Do you read a lot, Vedan?'

'Quite a bit.'

'Rangan, is the cross-examination likely to last long?' Surekha asked.

'Madam, we have nothing else to do. The Boss and Nair sir are busy with their business discussion. The lubricant is flowing freely. They'll continue till lunch time. Now, Vedan...about reading – there's no point in reading a lot. The quantity of reading does not really matter, it is the quality that counts.'

Surekha caressed Vedaraman and said, 'My poor dear! It looks as though Rangan is determined to kill you.'

Rangarajan wandered to new topics. The idea of god in the six streams of philosophy – Sankhya, Yoga, Nyaya, Vaisheshika, Purvamimamsa and Utharamimamsa; the stand taken by Patanjali, the author of *Yogasutra*...The visible world, which man has created.

It was past midnight and Surekha was getting bored. She wondered whether to go to the anteroom and wet her throat.

When she suggested it, Rangarajan agreed whole-heartedly, 'Grand idea, madam! We shall have some gangajal.'

Rangarajan went to the drawing room in response to a call and came back to the anteroom. 'Madam, they're waiting for us.'

In the drawing room, Chinnappa and Madhavan Nair continued their conversation, 'Nair, that plot in Thiruvanmiyur. I see that as the biggest problem before us.'

'But Boss, isn't that the smallest problem?'

'From the angle of my personal prestige, Thiruvanmiyur is the number one problem.'

Surekha interrupted them, 'Boss, we'll come a little later. After you finish your discussion.'

'It's over, right Nair? Somehow that Thiruvanmiyur issue keeps coming up. To hell with it! Come Vedan. Did you get bored waiting? I've heard a lot about your special gifts. Yes, you predicted that I would fall, didn't you? That's what Nair said.'

Vedan sat near Chinnappa. Surekha and Rangarajan stood behind him.

'Vedan, Nair spoke of your sixth finger too. Does it glow?'

'Sometimes, right Vedan?' Madhavan Nair was leaving a loophole. Suppose it did not glow now?

Vedaraman started meditating. Within moments the sixth finger started glowing.

'Amazing!' Chinnappa said.

'Fantastic!' Rangarajan's eyes opened wide.

Vedaraman looked at the ceiling. His whole body quivered. His voice broke, 'I can do it...I can...I can cure this disease.'

Vedaraman repeated this many times. His body was covered with sweat. He leaned back into the chair as though he had lost all his strength.

Surekha who was standing behind him murmured, 'Why did you stop Vedan? Say everything. All that you feel...'

'Get me a drink,' Vedan's voice was weak.

'What is it, Sura?' Madhavan Nair asked.

'Vedan wants a drink.'

Drinking the whisky poured by Surekha in one gulp, Vedaraman sat up straight. He said in a firm voice, 'I'll cure you of this disease...'

Chinnappa looked wonderingly at all of them in turn. And then laughed out aloud, 'You mean to say that you can cure my phlebitis? Surely, Vedan, you are joking. Expert doctors in Chennai and London have given up on it. Even surgery can give me only temporary relief.'

'I'll cure you of it, Chinnappa sir! Without surgery, and permanently!'

'Have you cured such a disease before?'

'No, I've not cured any disease so far. But I can cure this, if you have faith in me.'

Chinnappa looked at Madhavan Nair and smiled, 'Nair, we have had faith in so many things, haven't we? There was a time when we believed in theosophy, the masters of Tibet, Krishnamurti. And today? We have faith in all the gurus. We give offerings to all the temples. We might buy any share in the market, right? Who knows which will appreciate? Vedan, I'm willing to try anything. Even the medicines offered by roadside quacks.'

Madhavan Nair said, 'Vedan, go ahead! Cure the Boss of this disease! Let me get some credit for it too.'

'Sorry, Uncle. Chinnappa sir does not have faith in me. So, I'll not try to treat him.'

Chinnappa asked, 'Have you taken offence already, Vedan? Don't take a hasty decision like that. Tell me what your plan for the treatment is.'

'Uncle, shall I show all of you a parlour trick?'

'What trick?'

'A trick connected to Chinnappa sir's illness.'

Nobody knew what was on Vedaraman's mind.

Vedaraman leaned forward and asked Chinnappa, 'How's the pain in the leg now?'

'I don't have any pain at the moment. Thanks to this excellent whisky.' Chinnappa said.

'And now?' Vedaraman's sixth finger glowed.

Chinnappa's body contorted in pain.

Vedaraman withdrew the glow.

'And now?'

'No pain… Ah.'

The sixth finger became aflame again.

'Vedan, stop it!' Chinnappa screamed.

Vedaraman shook his left hand. The sixth finger which had lost its glow hung there as if it was broken.

'Nair, Vedan was manipulating me.'

'That's true, Chinnappa sir! My treatment will also be a kind of manipulation.'

'Agreed! Please cure me of this, Vedan. Promise me. On a drink.'

Chinnappa poured out whisky for Vedan. Vedan drank some and started talking, unaware of his surroundings.

'Who am I to say that you should have faith in me? I'm a nobody. But all of you shall have faith in me. You'll acquire that by experience. I heard that day about the land in Thiruvanmiyur.

I heard about it today too. All the problems about that land will be over soon. The land will be yours soon. The police will withdraw from there. You might even get compensation. The hearing on the criminal case has been suspended. The lost files have reached the court in response to the civil suit filed by you. Even your advocate is not yet aware of that. The ruling of the civil court will be favourable. It is the beginning of good times, Chinnappa!'

It was night.

Vedaraman opened his eyes. He was in a bedroom. Surekha was there too. But it was not the bedroom of the Adyar flat.

'Sura, where am I?'

'We're in Chinnappa's bungalow.'

'What's the time?'

'It's quite late.' She ran her hands over Vedan's body and said, 'What Rangan said is true. Your body is really muscular.'

'Um.'

'Don't you want to sleep, Vedan?'

'I don't think I'll get sleep.'

'Of course you'll sleep. I'll sleep with you.'

'No.'

'Why? Don't you like me?'

'I didn't say that. I don't like cheating.'

'What do you mean?'

'You're Uncle's bedmate, aren't you?'

'So what? Do you think you're a bigger person than Krishnamurti?'

'What?'

'Rajagopal was Jiddu's guardian. Rosalind, a white woman, was Rajagopal's wife. The preceptor of the world, Krishnamurti, was her lover. For many years.' Surekha held him close and said, 'There's no reason for you to feel any prick of conscience.'

Madhavan Nair, Surekha and Vedaraman returned to Adyar. The

second day after they returned, the judgment on the civil case was received. The lawyer gave a summary of the judgment over the telephone. Chinnappa was delighted. Vedaraman's prediction had come true. He was regaining his prestige. The twenty-five acres in Thiruvanmiyur was his permanently, according to the judgment.

The advocate explained that there was criticism of the government in the judgment. How did the rumour that relevant files were missing spread? Hadn't there been an attempt to hide the relevant facts? The files revealed that the title to the land had been received by Chinnappa earlier. The land had been paid for. The government's argument that the present market price was much higher than the price paid by Chinnappa was not a valid one. The file of the Revenue Department was examined by the Civil Supplies Secretary and the Housing Secretary before the title was handed over. Neither of them had noted any objections on it. Therefore, the government had no right to argue that the land was required for public purpose now and should be repossessed. Chinnappa had built sheds on the land. It was the right of the property owner to do so. The government had pulled down the shed. They had exceeded their authority and it was evident that there were malafide intentions. The circumstances of the case were such that Chinnappa could even ask for compensation. He had not done so, so far. And so the court was not giving any directions in that matter.

Chinnappa rang up the Adyar flat. All of them should come to Poes Garden – to celebrate!

They reached the bungalow at Poes Garden. Chinnappa greeted Vedaraman with respect. Surekha, Madhavan Nair and Rangarajan were stunned to see a meek and biddable boss, who was otherwise known for his temper, heartlessness and a lack of conscience.

Chinnappa's voice was apologetic when he spoke. 'Vedan, who won the Thiruvanmiyur case? Was it my advocate, was it his legal skill? Definitely not. Vedan predicted, matters occurred according to the prediction. That was all. It was all your blessing, Vedan. That is something I'm sure of. All the papers will report the case in detail. It's my prestige that has been salvaged, right Nair? Sorry, Vedan. When we saw each other for the first time, I was a little arrogant. Or should we say, distant. I was not ready to believe. Please forget all that. I have a hundred per cent trust in you. Total faith. I know now that Vedan will be able to cure me of this phlebitis.'

When Vedaraman stood silent, Madhavan Nair said, 'You can do it, Vedan!'

Curing diseases. It was a completely unfamiliar field. He had no knowledge or experience. What could he do now? Vedaraman chased away the doubts that invaded his mind and said, 'All right, Chinnappa sir. I'll start the treatment.'

'When will you start it?' Chinnappa asked anxiously.

'From tomorrow.'

'Fine. Let Vedan stay here, Nair.'

Chinnappa got into the details, 'Let Vedan stay here so that the treatment can continue uninterrupted. Let Surekha stay here to give him company. Nair, you can stay here too. Or do you want to go to Kochi? You decide. Before that the petition to remove that condition in the anticipatory bail has to be filed. What's your doubt, Vedan? That you'll not be able to go to college? That's only a minor problem. Nair, speak to the college principal. The issue of shortage of attendance is easily solved, isn't it?'

Madhavan Nair said, 'Oh yes, that's easily done. Let the treatment begin, that's the important thing. I'll meet the advocate tomorrow. And get the amendment petition filed. Then I'll go to Kochi. And once the old ban is lifted, I'll ring up every day, Boss!'

Chinnappa laughed, 'It won't matter even if they tap our phones, Nair. The conversation will be about phlebitis, won't it?'

Twenty-seven

Chinnappa's phlebitis was cured in two weeks.

First, the thickening of the veins vanished. Then the bubble-like protrusions cleared. Finally, the skin below the knees fell off like the scales of a snake. The skin looked raw and red. It started darkening slowly. Chinnappa was now able to bend and straighten his left leg without pain.

How could he express his gratitude to Vedaraman? Chinnappa did not know. Respect bordering on worship grew in his mind. He forgot the difference in ages and his own position and started calling him Vedanji.

Vedanji! This is a real miracle.

Vedanji, my old verve and optimism are rising like a tide.

Surekha, Rangan, I've changed totally, haven't I? Nothing can trouble us anymore. Vedanji is with us! Why has Nair not returned? Rangan, call Kochi again.

How did Chinnappa get cured? Vedan did not know how to explain it. Anyway, no one here wanted an explanation. All of them believed in his supernatural powers.

He was the only one with doubts. What had he done? What was the treatment?

Late night. All the people working in the bungalow are asleep. Chinnappa lies in bed, twisting and turning, groaning. He is drunk.

He, Vedaraman, starts meditating. Surekha stands behind him. Her breasts are pressed against his back. That distracts him.

Still, after a while the sixth finger starts glowing. He rubs Chinnappa's left leg with the glowing finger. Chinnappa's groans stop. He falls asleep.

Thirteen nights passed like that.

On all the nights, when the treatment was over, when he stopped rubbing Chinnappa's leg, when Chinnappa fell into a deep sleep, Surekha captured him. She seemed crazy. But why should he call her terrible? He had enjoyed her embraces. His manhood had awoken many times locked in her arms.

Madhavan Nair returned from Kochi.

When they met alone, without any of the others present, Chinnappa spoke at length, 'Nair, good times are starting. Not just for me, but for all of us. Vedanji's presence will open new paths for us. Let's leave aside the matter of the Thiruvanmiyur case. How did my illness vanish? Wasn't that a miracle? I am deeply indebted to you. If not for you, would I have met Vedanji? Matters will sort themselves out. Do you want to know what I plan to do then? Was I a complete pauper when I started out, just a low-class man? No, that is not true. But my beginnings were modest. The agency for the Australian wool was the beginning. I grew from there. You could say that the circumstances were favourable. But is that all? Wasn't it I who created those circumstances? Then and now I do not think of morality, I only think of profits and losses. I have acquired a lot of wealth. As for the present trouble, that doesn't matter. In between I had pulled back, withdrawn into a shell. A complete social withdrawal. I stopped going to the clubs, did not renew my political connections, refused all honours. I even refused to become the president of the Indian Commercial Federation. I was in the grip of a terrible sense of failure. That darkness is now at an end. From now on, it will be all light, light alone. Vedanji has assured me.'

Chinnappa's words fell like nectar on Madhavan Nair's ears.

Soon after Vedan came to the 'Eastern Star' with Vikraman

Pillai's letter, within a few days, he had felt for no particular reason that this boy would be the cause of his prosperity.

Then, there had been not even a hint of logic in that feeling.

But today...now...

Everything was in focus. The shapes were defined clearly.

Why should he push himself in? Why should he cheat and betray? Why become the thorny climber rose?

His desires would be fulfilled without any effort on his part. Chinnappa had already offered him the post of MD of Bengal Bay on a golden platter.

Madhavan Nair asked once more to make things clearer in his own mind, 'What did Vedan, sorry, Vedanji, say exactly?'

'I told you. He assured me that all my troubles would be over within months.'

'Did Vedanji speak in a trance-like state, as though his body and his soul were detached from each other? As though he was possessed?'

'What do you mean?'

'After a couple of drinks, in a sort of half-awake state! Let me tell you from my experience. It is in that state that Vedanji's powers really awaken. Shall we try out an experiment?'

'An experiment?'

'A simple one! Let's call Vedanji and Surekha. Let's sit in a circle. On drinks, let's ask him specific questions – about the future. If he does say something, it would be of help, wouldn't it?'

'Nair, what are you saying? Don't you have faith in Vedanji? Why do you want to do this now, this test?'

'Boss, I do have faith in Vedanji. That's why I suggested this.'

'All right, Nair, as you wish. After all, you brought Vedanji here.'

They gathered in the drawing room. At the centre was Vedan. Chinnappa, Madhavan Nair and Surekha had their gazes fixed on him. Vedaraman sat in silence with his head bent. He was buried in the valmika, the anthill, of silence. How could they entice him to the path of speech?

Madhavan Nair nudged Surekha and asked in a quiet voice, 'How many has Vedanji had?'

'Three.'

'Give him one more... a stiff one.'

When Surekha held out the drink to him, Vedaraman lifted his head and murmured, 'If I have another I'll be drunk. Should I have this?'

'You can hold it, my pet.'

Vedaraman accepted the glass and drank what was in it in one gulp as if he was just performing a duty. He got up and started pacing the room like a caged animal.

The sixth finger started glowing.

Chinnappa asked in a voice filled with devotion, 'Vedanji, why do you not say anything?'

Vedan did not reply. He suddenly lay on his back on the carpet.

His head was beginning to feel heavy. Who was clawing at his insides? Were they the monkeys of Vattolikavu?

Something was opening and shutting. Bhlum – bhlum – blum – blum! The palm trees were changing into demons. They were jumping into the river.

He shut his eyes tight. The dance of the silver dots started.

Where did the sound of the conch come from? With that, the sound of cymbals.

His ears became an asylum for the sound of instruments.

His sixth finger was glowing. So many arm-like torches held high... Kochappu, Thressiamma, Saidali, Cherian Munshi, Kuttisankaran, Koman Nair, Achukutty, Janaki Ammyar who stayed in the next house, Mukundan, that old Warrier, those useless Namboodiris...

He started speaking...

But the sound came from miles and miles away.

'...I have thought of some things. I have seen some things. A man is coming here. He's a strong man. He was a strong man, he will be strong again. He'll reign again, reign over the country. And because of that Chinnappa's fortunes will look up. These good times will serve as a huge umbrella. Anyone who can stand in its shade will prove lucky. The strong man will come soon. A man with joined brows, wearing a kurta and a shawl. His spectacles are as thick as the bottoms of a soda bottle. Get ready to welcome him. Within months he will be the uncrowned king of the land. It will not be easy to go near him then.'

The voice lost its resonance. When it ended feebly, Vedaraman was very tired.

Surekha touched him and asked, 'What is it?'

'I want to lie down...to sleep.'

Surekha helped him rise. That was when Rangarajan came rushing in. He announced, panting, 'Boss, Arunagiri sir is coming here. He's already started. I just received the message.'

Chinnappa jumped up. He spoke without hiding his awe and wonder, 'Nair, what Vedanji predicted, happens. This is something that I did not expect at all. Come, let's receive him. Surekha, all of you, go inside.'

Arunagiri had been the darling of the people when he was ruling. There was no another leader in Tamil Nadu who could stand shoulder to shoulder with him in 'Medai pechu' or speeches. His speeches inspired fervour and enthusiasm among the people. He did not lose power because he lost majority in the Assembly. The political heavyweights in Indraprastha were waiting for an opportunity to sideline Arunagiri who was a severe critic of the Central government. When the occasion arose, the weapons came out. Arunagiri was dismissed at a time when his party was entitled to rule for another one year.

Tamil Nadu came under President's rule.

The Central government used the media intelligently to highlight the corruption of the Arunagiri regime. Arunagiri's image took a beating. In the elections that followed a few months later, the Centre used all its weapons. While it was not wiped out, Arunagiri's party lost. The Centre saw to it that a coalition was somehow formed and that coalition sat on the throne of Fort St George.

Arunagiri did not remain quiet. He continued to battle. He mercilessly criticized the undemocratic actions of the Central government. He did retain a great part of his glamour in his role as the leader of the opposition. His terrific skills in public relations and his showmanship made this crafty opponent a permanent headache for the ruling party.

Chinnappa's heart was beating faster as he stood outside waiting for Arunagiri.

His personal equation with Arunagiri was strong. He was one of the few privileged persons who had the freedom to call him 'Aruna'. Still, he was a little worried. He had not visited Arunagiri as often as he used to, after he lost power. It was true that he continued to make large donations as he had always done. But so many people continued to supply Arunagiri with funds. Arunagiri was an absolute realist. Still, he was a person who could get emotional before people he was close to. It may have been good acting. Who knew! Would he be upset about the fact that Chinnappa had not visited him frequently? Only time would tell. Why was he coming here? It was extraordinary behaviour on his part. He could have sent word to ask Chinnappa to go over to meet him.

A Mercedes drove in and stopped at the portico. The driver opened the door. Arunagiri got out smiling and said, 'Vanakkam'. Chinnappa and Madhavan Nair folded their hands in response.

The car was not sporting the party flag. Arunagiri had come without his security men and hangers on.

Arunagiri said, 'Chinnappa, this is a private visit. You could even say it is a secret visit.'

'Aruna, if I tell you that this visit makes me blessed...'

'I shall believe you. But why do you want to say that? Don't be formal. Who's this with you?'

'A friend – Mr Madhavan Nair. You met him a year or year-and-a-half ago.'

'Oh yes!' Arunagiri shook Madhavan Nair's hand.

As they walked into the bungalow, Arunagiri asked, 'Chinnappa, is your leg less troublesome? You walk better.'

Chinnappa smiled, 'Nair fixed up a treatment. It was successful.'

They reached the drawing room.

Arunagiri did not waste time in small talk. He got straight to the point.

After congratulating Chinnappa on his recovery, he started speaking. 'The victory in the Thiruvanmiyur case is not yours alone, it's mine too. If you look at it politically, it's mine alone. Enemies had painted that land deal as an example of extreme corruption. And now what's happened? The court has ruled that it was all above board. All the newspapers wrote articles favouring my stand in it. The editorials praising me have my supporters thrilled. This is the beginning of my new aswamedha, the journey of conquest. Nachimuthu, who's ruling Tamil Nadu for the time being with the support of the Centre – a wooden horse at best – will fall within the year. Perhaps even before that. Do you know a number of senior officers in the state are against Nachimuthu? After the judgment in the Thiruvanmiyur case, a number of them had come to meet me. Even Guhan, the chief secretary. I know what's on their minds. After all, I have dealt with them before; I've controlled them. I have used them, made them do things they shouldn't have done – but very cleverly. So they did not raise their heads; they stayed quiet. Nachimuthu also played my game; he continues to play that game. All chief ministers try to reduce the civil service officers to eunuchs. There's nothing wrong with that. But you should move wisely. That's where Nachimuthu erred.

'He promised chief secretary Guhan, who's almost at the retirement age, that he would extend his tenure. And who did that upset? It upset Gopikrishnan, the present MD of Bengal Bay. It is Gopikrishnan who should have become the chief secretary after Guhan according to seniority.

'And what do you think happened finally? Nachimuthu decided that Guhan's tenure need not be extended. But also that Gopikrishnan should not become the chief secretary. What do you think caused this rethinking? There was pressure – from Nachimuthu's party – to offer the post to Rajendran, who returns from deputation to the Centre. To accommodate him, Gopikrishnan had to be sidelined. There are moves to shift Gopikrishnan to the Centre on deputation. Do you understand the situation, Chinnappa?'

'Yes, Aruna.'

Arunagiri continued, 'Gopikrishnan is now a sworn enemy of Nachimuthu. So I called him and spoke to him. During my rule, he had been the finance commissioner and planning secretary. He's a capable man. Gopikrishnan treated me as if I was still the chief minister. He's taken some decisions – at least some of which will be favourable to us. Do you know what the most important one is? He's filed some of the questionable instructions given in writing by Nachimuthu regarding the running of Bengal Bay. He's willing to hand over that secret file to me. He's planning to go on leave immediately. It is unlikely that someone else will be posted to Bengal Bay now. What do you think we should do now?'

Chinnappa said, 'We must collect that secret file immediately.'

'What do you say, Mr Nair?'

'I'm of the same opinion.'

Arunagiri outlined his plan, 'There's something else that needs to be done. Chinnappa should get out of this shell of his. You must go to the company office regularly. Gopikrishnan is not going to wait for sanction, but proceed on leave immediately. Before that, he'll give you a note.'

'What note?'

'A note requesting the chairman to look after the duties of the MD for the time being. It is stretching procedural propriety a little, but you do become the chairman and managing director. He'll also hand over the secret file to you. You must call a Board meeting and get a ratification of the decision. Let the secret file continue to be secret. There'll be opportunities to use that file. An important fact is that Delhi is not going to be able to carry Nachimuthu for long. The conflict between the Centre and the state on the Sri Lankan issue is getting worse and worse. Intelligence agencies have sent reports indicting Nachimuthu. Nachimuthu will be ousted.'

'And the new chief minister is sitting before us,' Madhavan Nair said.

Arunagiri enjoyed the flattery in the comment, 'Thanks, Mr Nair. We'll suppose that election work has started already. What do you say, Chinnappa?'

'I'll alert Murugappan. Fund collection…?'

'Money is not an issue, Chinnappa.'

'Everything will work out. As Vedanji predicted, you'll be the uncrowned king within months.'

'Vedanji?' Arunagiri asked.

Madhavan Nair narrated what had happened.

When he heard about the supernatural powers that Vedan exhibited, Arunagiri asked cynically, 'You and Chinnappa believe that these are all miracles, don't you?'

'Yes, we do.'

'It could just be a coincidence, couldn't it?'

'Not possible!' Chinnappa intervened.

'The glow of the sixth finger might be a peculiarity that can be explained by science.'

'Aruna, I'm not interested in a debate. You don't have to believe, if you don't want to.'

'Don't take offence, Chinnappa.'

'What offence? One knows only on experiencing. They say that a miracle is an event that creates faith.'

'A definition! Anyway, since I've heard so much about him I'd like to see this miracle boy. When can I meet him?'

'Vedanji is here. But I think he's sleeping.'

'If that's so, don't disturb him, Chinnappa.'

'Let me go and see,' Madhavan Nair stood up.

Vedaraman was lying flat on his back in the bed. When he saw Madhavan Nair enter the room, he muttered, 'The powerful man wants to see me, is it? He wants to test me. I'm not willing to be tested. Tell him something. Victory is assured. But he should pay special attention to Coimbatore. Or he'll have problems.'

'Coimbatore? What's happening in Coimbatore?' Madhavan Nair asked.

'He knows that,' Vedaraman did not say anything further.

Madhavan Nair returned to the drawing room and said, 'He's resting... so...'

'That's all right. I'll meet him on another occasion,' Arunagiri said.

'Also, Vedanji said something.' And Madhavan Nair quoted what Vedaraman had said.

Arunagiri was struck dumb with wonder. He said, 'Chinnappa, your Vedanji is not to be trifled with. How did he know about the Coimbatore problem?'

'What's the problem?' Chinnappa asked.

'At present, there's no problem. The problem is only going to start. I'll tell you since it's between us. It's something that's not known even at the highest levels of the party. Veerachami is building a group against me. Who built him up into a leader in Kovai? I did. And now... All right, I won't postpone things. I'll take care of him. Since Vedanji said so!'

'So, Aruna, you too have faith!'

Twenty-eight

Within weeks, there were changes in the bureaucracy as Arunagiri had predicted. Guhan retired. Rajendran, who had returned from Delhi, sat in the chief secretary's chair.

When he received the order for the deputation from the Central ministry, Gopikrishnan took leave. As he handed over charge to Chinnappa, he said, 'Everything will work out, Mr Chinnappa! I'm taking leave just to express my protest. A civil servant can protest only in this fashion! I know they'll ask me to cancel my leave. I also know that I'll be dragged to Indraprastha. I have two years of service left. Things could change radically within that period. We might have an opportunity to work together under changed circumstances. Let's see. Anyway, let this file remain in your personal custody.'

So, the secret file found its place in a locker in Chinnappa's bungalow. In the meantime, Veerachami from Coimbatore was sacked from the party by Arunagiri for indiscipline. The action garnered headlines in newspapers for three or four days.

It was then that the idea of establishing an ashram came up.

Arunagiri called Chinnappa to the party headquarters and said, 'So, Chinnappa, my chariot has started rolling, has it?'

'Everything is happening as we had discussed; it's a good beginning.'

Arunagiri asked with a mischievous smile, 'What would you say if I declare that I've started believing in god and spiritual gurus?'

'I'd probably laugh aloud.'

'Naturally! Atheism is the backbone of the party's philosophy. But times are changing. My people have started going to Tirupati and Sabarimala for darshan.'

'There's no harm in that, is there?'

'Chinnappa, not just that there's no harm, good comes out of it. In today's world, it is good for a politician to have the backing of saints and human gods.'

'That's true, Aruna.'

'So let's also get a small god of our own.'

'You mean…'

'I was thinking of your Vedanji. Why don't we make him a divinity? A new Baba?'

'Are you planning to use Vedanji as an instrument?'

'Instrument? That's not a very pleasant word.'

'Aruna, in my eyes Vedanji is already a divine person. I fully believe that we won the Thiruvanmiyur case and my disease got cured only because of Vedanji's blessings.'

'That's right!'

'Aruna, do you also believe that?'

'My belief is beside the point. Will the people believe? That's the point. They'll believe. Even you believe. So need we doubt that the ordinary man will? A divine person who has the power to bless and to punish… a yogi… a baba. Call him what you will. We shall establish an ashram and install Vedanji in it. What do you say? How do you react to the idea?'

When Chinnappa remained silent, Arunagiri continued, 'Vedanji hinted that there might be trouble in Coimbatore. I immediately got rid of Veerachami. What does that mean? It means that I too have some faith in him. I'm ready to admit that Vedanji has some unusual powers. I have not seen him. Maybe, if I had seen him, I would also have fallen for that charisma. There's no point in our continuing this discussion now. I just want to know if you agree with me in principle.'

'Why do you want to make Vedanji into a Baba? Why make

this private limited company of devotion public?'

'It's not to get more votes. I foresee that when the time comes, Vedan Baba will be able to influence the leaders from Delhi. That's the reason. The top political brass in Delhi don't sleep peacefully unless they've touched some divine person's feet every day. The President and the prime minister go in search of the heads of various religious institutions; they bow before bearded sages and wait with bent heads to receive their feet on their heads as blessing. Chinnappa, let's not keep Vedanji as our private property. Let's make him the resident deity of Tamil Nadu. Don't we have to get rid of Nachimuthu? Shouldn't I be the ruler of Tamil Nadu? Don't the cases against your companies have to be dropped? Shouldn't the enterprises that you started in the earlier period of my rule flourish and flower again?'

'Yes, all that should happen.'

'So...you agree?'

'I agree. Let me consult my friend Madhavan Nair also. He's Vedanji's guardian.'

'Consult any Nair or Namboodiri you want to. But remember that you're the boss and the decision should be yours. And you have decided, haven't you?'

Chinnappa surrendered, 'Yes, I have.'

Doubts started growing in Vedaraman's mind. How long were they to stay in this bungalow at Poes Garden? What was his future? Was he just a puppet who hung from strings in other people's hands? They sought meaning in each word he uttered, believed that anything he said was a prophecy. They stand in awe and devotion before the glow of the sixth finger. When these things happened, when everyone deferred to him, shouldn't he become stronger? Shouldn't he be the master?

But he would go back to the old times and become weak. The collapse of the Mulamkunnam family...the theft of the uruli... his doubts about his paternity...the curse uttered by Kozhukatta Paru.

Kuttisankaran, Achukutty and Koman Nair had become pale shadows – in such a short time. He himself had become the bird in the golden cage. Kozhukatta Paru had reincarnated herself as Surekha.

Surekha – Kankali, the goddess of the cremation grounds. Kamarupini, one who could take any form.

She says that his muscles have the strength of steel. She runs her finger under his nose and says: there is soft hair growing here. It looks so good!

Was he drinking too much? Was it intoxication that made him say the kinds of things he said, prophecy like the oracle in a temple? Was he just a fake coin that people accepted because they did not pay sufficient attention?

He had not seen the city at all since he had arrived here. Why the city, he hadn't even seen the whole of this bungalow. Who all lived here? Didn't Chinnappa have a family? Wife, children, grandchildren...where were all of them? There had to be a battalion of servants here. But he had not seen any of them. Were the jailers Chinnappa, Rangarajan, Uncle and Surekha being careful that he did not see anyone?

He could hear the ding-dong sound of the clock. Was the sound trying to tell him something?

Ding-dong, Vedan!

Take a piece of paper, Vedan!

Vedan obeyed.

Many things that happen are beyond the control or will of human beings. Death, diseases, tornadoes, floods, drought, sunrise, sunset, growth, destruction, the good, the bad...

What was behind all this?

There was a power that made all this happen.

No, not one, but two...god who made the good things happen. And devil who initiated the bad things...'

Ding-dong, Vedan!

Did you write, Vedan?

Ding-dong. The rest later. Vedan, you should not doubt.

Continue to show your miracles! Haven't you read that miracles are credentials of divine mission?

Vedan lifted his head. It was Surekha.

When he saw her, he said, 'Ding-dong bell!'

'Nursery rhymes?' Surekha asked.

'You won't understand even if I explain. It was between me and a clock...All that can wait. Everyone's waiting for me, right? What do they want? My opinion? Approval? Let's go.'

Paying no attention to Chinnappa and Madhavan Nair who waited in the drawing room, Vedaraman paced like a tiger. He paused before a glass case that stood in the corner of the room. A decorative clock brought from abroad rested in the case. He had not noticed it before. Under the face of the clock, within an arch decorated with shining stones, stood a young white man and a young woman, ready to dance. His one hand encircled her waist and the other held her hand. She had one hand on his shoulder.

There were only moments before the hands of the clock united at the number twelve. Vedaraman waited. When the hands met at the top, they could all hear the sound ding-dong. The man and woman danced twelve times in rhythm with the ring.

Keeping his gaze fixed on the clock, Vedaraman spoke in a resounding voice, 'It's about the ashram, isn't it? It was I who put this idea into the mind of the man who's going to rule. Thiruvanmiyur is the symbol of a victory. Let my ashram rise there. It should be beautiful. You are businessmen. Let me put it in your language. You must launch me as a new product. With terrific publicity and first-class packaging. The man who'll come shortly from the West will advise you. He will not be alone. There'll be a white beauty with him!'

Murugappan had earned a name for himself in Madras society before the age of thirty: 'Philanderer!'

Murugappan was not particularly good-looking. Of medium complexion and height, with a slightly flaring nose, he looked ordinary. But he had a sort of compactness that was attractive.

He was also good at talking. Always well-dressed, he was a constant presence in theatres and concert halls. Women fell for him in droves and often behaved in ways that were not suited to their position in society. Murugappan knew that he had done nothing to deserve his sobriquet. He had never attacked and conquered anyone. He had only yielded to the requests of others. This pose – that of an innocent – served as protective armour. Even Chinnappa did not criticize him or try to control him. In spite of the fact that he was playing with Chinnappa's money.

Murugappan was a manufacturer of ready-made garments. Chinnappa had financed Murugappan to start the unit. Charity was not a strong part of Chinnappa's make-up. And he would not have helped another young man like this. But Murugappan was not any young man. Chinnappa could not consider Manonmani's brother an outsider.

Chinnappa had married a woman from a famous family in Chettinad. Seventeen-year-old Kannamma was beautiful. Chinnappa, who had thought that he would lead a happy life, found that he was mistaken. Kannamma developed a rare disease – she would bleed almost non-stop. Chinnappa realized that it would be impossible to have sexual relations with her, but even in his despair he did not lose his sense of reality. He behaved in such a manner that neither her family nor their circle of friends had any suspicion. Her treatment continued. Chinnappa explained to anyone who asked that the treatment was for anaemia and irregular menstruations.

Chinnappa would go out with Kannamma. They would go to the Marina beach in the evening, they would go to see plays. The world believed that they led a very happy life. Kannamma did not recover from the condition in spite of protracted and expensive treatment. But Chinnappa did not fall prey to easy liaisons in spite of being a normal young man in good health. A sort of undefined and perhaps unreal sense of morality held him back from illicit relationships with other women. He felt that to go to another woman would be cheating Kannamma, and this kept him on the straight and narrow. This is how things were till he saw Manonmani.

He saw her for the first time at a music concert. She sat in the first row in the audience. Her beauty captivated him. He approached her through his acquaintance, the secretary of the Music Society. He soon became a constant visitor to her house. Her brother Murugappan did not raise any objections. After a while Kannamma started having suspicions. Chinnappa did not deny anything but told her the truth. Her reaction surprised him. She said, 'Bring her here as your second wife. I have no objection.'

So Chinnappa married Manonmani. Kannamma treated her like a much loved younger sister.

Chinnappa's business grew. He made political connections. Murugappan's garment unit flourished under his patronage.

Life flowed smoothly and successfully. Then fate dealt a cruel blow. Chinnappa and his wives went to Ooty for a short holiday and had an accident on their way back. Kannamma died on the spot. Chinnappa received minor injuries. Manonmani had head injuries and lay in a coma for six weeks. She opened her eyes just before she died and looked at Murugappan and Chinnappa who stood near her. She made a feeble attempt to place Murugappan's hand in Chinnappa's.

And then... her neck twisted. Manonmani became still.

Chinnappa worked harder than ever to get over his sorrows. He got involved in the Theosophical Movement to gain peace of mind.

As years passed, the old political connections turned out to be useful. When Arunagiri became the chief minister he helped Chinnappa. In a short while, Chinnappa became the head of a huge business empire.

He did not forget Murugappan. When his business abroad needed someone to be there to keep an eye on it, he did not have to search long for the man.

Murugappan made a number of friends in London – both in

the Indian society there and in the Indian High Commission.

Everyone accepted Murugappan as an important man – the boss of the famous Kasi Food Chain; the owner of the Taste Tickler Restaurants. Tabloids described him as the holder of 'Aladdin's magic lamp'. He was the first Asian to own a residence in the exclusive WASP area – a penthouse. He also had a countryhouse with all the frills thirty miles away.

Besides all this, his 'Latin look' was so enticing. The charm of that slightly flaring nose! Such a combination!

It was usual for Murugappan to be surrounded by women all the time. Murugappan had decided very early in life that he would not get permanently involved with any woman. All his affairs would be temporary ones.

One could stay with someone only until one got fed up. That might happen sometimes in a night. Sometimes it might take a week. At best, a month. Then the parting had to come. There should be no tears and recriminations when that moment came.

Provide for the girls well. Break up without tears. These were Murugappan's articles of faith and he lived according to them.

Once or twice in a year, Murugappan would come to Madras to visit his 'cousin'. His acquaintances thought Chinnappa was Murugappan's older cousin.

Whenever he came to Madras, he did not forget to visit Arunagiri. Wouldn't the future flaunt the colours of the rainbow?

His faith was justified when Arunagiri became the chief minister. But it all ended suddenly. What they had built proved to be a house of cards!

Everything was frozen.

Criminal cases... bad publicity in the media... total disaster!

None of this made Murugappan change his lifestyle.

The only difference was that a new beauty entered his life around that time – Nina Hyde.

Twenty-nine

Nina Hyde – thirty years old, a divorcee, and a copywriter in an advertising agency. She looked like a model. Her stories about her background and her family were very interesting. Her father had been an ICS officer in India. Her grandfather had been a judge in Burma at the end of the nineteenth century.

Nina did not go away. She often landed at his apartment in London and stayed over. She even reached the countryhouse over the weekend.

Going steady, Mark? Acquaintances asked Murugappan.

Murugappan a.k.a. Mark was having to think about this relationship. He'd thought it was just a casual affair. Was it becoming a noose around his neck?

Nina remembered that Murugappan had gone to Madras recently. Why was he going again in such a hurry? There was unlikely to be any terrible problem to be solved urgently there.

Lying naked on the bed, Nina asked, 'Mark, why do you have to go now?'

'Business, my dear.'

'How long will you be there?'

'I don't really know.'

'Shall I come with you, Mark?'

'This is a business trip. You'll be bored stiff.'

'But...we can combine business with pleasure. Extend the trip from Madras to Singapore, then Kuala Lumpur, Hong Kong, Tokyo...'

Murugappan grunted. There was no point in arguing with Nina. She'd become even more stubborn. And then she'd have to be taken along anyway. Would he be able to colour this trip with the shades of a holiday? He might not be able to take Nina around even Madras. The only consolation was that Surekha was there. She might agree to becoming Nina's guide and friend.

Chinnappa had rung up many times this week. He insisted that Murugappan had to reach Madras immediately, but had not explained why it was so essential. Politics...business...several other problems...So the explanation meandered. All covered and wrapped.

Were the court cases getting hotter? Had they reached the stage of trial?

'Hey Mark?'

'Tell me, sweetheart.'

'We're flying together.'

'As you say, Nina.'

As he surrendered before her, Murugappan was very nervous. His big cousin Chinnappa did not know of this entanglement – this tie named Nina. He had to be careful. He would not land up at Poes Garden with her when he reached Madras.

Murugappan and Nina Hyde reached Madras and checked into the Taj Coromandel. Murugappan needed only a bath and a change of clothes to feel refreshed.

'I'll go out for a while and be back soon, sweetheart.'

'Where to, Mark?'

'To meet that cousin of mine, Chinnappa.'

'Shall I come with you?'

'No need to do that. I'll get back soon. I'll be here for dinner.'

'Mark, I'll be bored sitting here all alone.'

Murugappan hid his irritation and cooed, 'I'll call the bar. Have a drink and relax. I'll be back within no time.'

As soon as he saw Murugappan, Chinnappa said, 'I was waiting for you. Where is the white woman you brought with you?'

Murugappan could not hide his surprise as he looked at Chinnappa, Madhavan Nair and Surekha who were in the room. 'Annan, how did you know that Nina was with me?'

'I knew. Why didn't you bring her here? Where have you parked her?'

'At the Taj. I didn't know how you'd take it if I brought her here.'

'You heard what the crook said, Nair? Murugan, let go of the hotel room. Nina..., that's her name? She can stay here. She'll have Surekha for company.' And then, Chinnappa spoke as though to himself, 'What Vedanji said turned out to be true again.'

'Vedanji?' Murugappan asked.

Chinnappa rolled up the dhoti he was wearing to his knees and said, 'Look!'

'Your phlebitis...'

'Is cured. Do you know who cured it? Vedanji!'

Chinnappa waxed eloquent. How did the phlebitis vanish? How did they emerge victorious from the Thiruvanmiyur case? They did not have to worry about the future. The Bengal Bay Company set-up was about to change. Nachimuthu's end was near. Arunagiri's victory in the next election was an assured thing. They had to start collecting funds for the election immediately. Vedanji's ashram at Thiruvanmiyur had to come up soon. This was Arunagiri's desire too.

Murugappan's eyes started popping out of their sockets. Why did the self-declared atheist Arunagiri wish to establish an ashram? What was the connection between his coming to power and the ashram?

Chinnappa said, 'Once the ashram is built, the north wind will start blowing in our favour.'

'Murugappan, miracles will always influence society, especially the pillars of the society,' Madhavan Nair said.

'Surekha, call Vedanji...No, rather, take Murugappan to Vedanji.'

'Annan, you mean, Vedanji's here?'

'Go...Go and meet him. And then rush to the Taj. You

shouldn't have left her alone. Come tomorrow and bring her along. Come for breakfast. We must meet Arunagiri too.'

'Right, Annan!'

Arunagiri was very cheerful when Chinnappa, Madhavan Nair and Murugappan met him. His special messenger had returned from Delhi with good news.

The prime minister was upset with Nachimuthu. When a controversial bill was put to vote, the MPs from Nachimuthu's party were absent. Reporters had asked their parliamentary party leader about this unusual absence. He trotted out the river water issue, implying that the absence was a protest.

'Protest by the Tamil Nadu government', screamed the headlines the next day.

There were waves of displeasure in the prime minister's office. The prime minister summoned Nachimuthu to New Delhi, spoke harshly to him. The papers wrote about the Delhi trip as well.

Nachimuthu announced that he had gone to Delhi for discussions with the Planning Commission. That excuse was widely seen as specious.

'Chinnappa, things are moving in our favour ... I believe that. You have told Murugappan all the news, haven't you?'

'Yes, Aruna.'

'I've understood the scenario, sir!' Murugappan said.

'That's good, Murugappan. You have been assigned a special duty.'

'Overseas fund collection, sir?'

'That's unimportant. Money is not really an issue. I plan to give permission for three new medical colleges as soon as I come to power. Then there's the leasing and licensing of around fifty granite quarries. I also have plans to hand over the running of the state lottery to a private agency. Let me tell you what I want you to concentrate on – overseas propaganda!'

'I don't understand, sir.'

Arunagiri looked at Chinnappa and asked, 'Didn't you tell him about the ashram?'

'Of course.'

'Murugappan met Vedanji as well,' Madhavan Nair said.

'I've not had an opportunity to do so, so far. My laziness. Okay Murugappan, what do you think of Vedanji?'

'He's got divinity in him.'

'Murugappan, the ashram will be built within no time. It must become famous in other countries too, without any delay. You have to do whatever is necessary for that.'

'What should I do, sir?'

'A lot can be done. Branches of the ashram can be established in England and America. Groups of Vedanji's devotees can be formed. You have to transform Vedanji into a cult figure. This has been done before, can be done again! Many Indian gurus have been celebrated in the West... are still celebrated.'

'Sir, with your help...'

'That goes without saying. My help is always available. But you have to remember this! I'm a politician, and that means a tightrope walker. I may have to blow hot and cold. I'll be with you in the open for now. But at any moment, I may perform a vanishing trick. You remember what I said that day, Chinnappa, my movement started out from the platform of atheism. Rama was not our ideal, Ravana was. But today, our people wear ashes and sandal paste on their foreheads. They get crushed in stampedes at temple ponds and rivers as they try to bathe at the auspicious moment. Let all that go on. Do I object? Not at all. Does the party object? No, because I am the party. But there's one thing – the leader cannot reject the basic tenet of the party. This is just theatre. I know what is required for survival. I know the magic formula for that. That's politics. This ashram is now necessary for me. Call it anything you like – cynicism, tactic, trick, anything you please. But this is necessary – this ashram.'

Chinnappa was disturbed, 'Aruna, do you mean to say that you don't have faith in Vedanji?'

Arunagiri smiled, 'Chinnappa you asked me something like this earlier too. I thought I'd made everything clear then. I'll tell you once more. What does it matter if I believe in Vedanji's powers or not? That's immaterial. But there's one thing. I do respect your faith. What did I do when Vedanji hinted about Veerachami in Coimbatore? You know that. So, effectively, I'm also a believer. The President and the prime minister are believers. They are worshippers at the feet of the seers at Kanchi, Sringeri, Puri and other holy places. Before the time for Nachimuthu's dismissal comes, before we receive the President's approval for that, let us also show that we have a famous guru with us. Call him Guru, Balaguru, Balababa, whatever. You do understand my point, don't you, Chinnappa?'

Chinnappa nodded.

❖

Nina and Murugappan started staying at Chinnappa's bungalow. Nina's behaviour endeared her to everyone there. Though Surekha was jealous of her youth and beauty, she hid it well and behaved as a friend.

Nina was full of questions – about India, about Indian gods, about the caste system...about everything.

'Nina, our Pandit will answer these better than me,' Surekha would evade the questions.

Rangarajan was the 'Pandit'.

Rangan was happy to provide answers to Nina's questions. He soon became an admirer of Nina's.

He told Surekha, 'Madam, Nina knows a lot. She's read a lot of books on India, especially about Indian history. After all, her father had been in the ICS. Nina has great faith in and devotion to Vedanji. She calls him a living god.'

There were a number of discussions during those days, and decisions were taken too.

Murugappan's voice was heard above the others, and it was very assured. More than anyone else, he seemed to have understood the aims and plans of Arunagiri.

Thirty

Murugappan spread out the architect's plan, the elevation sketch and the pith model on the table and started talking.

'Have a good look! This is not the master plan, only the core of it. I mean, a detailed plan is under preparation for the utilization of the full extent of the land available. This pith model, if you see, is roughly the visualization of the final shape. The staff quarters that will be needed in the future, the pilgrims' cottages, prayer hall, meditation centres, canteens, cultural complex…and much more! Let us begin with the construction of the ashram building. What do you think?'

'That's right.' 'Fine.' Various voices of approval rose.

'Shouldn't we seek Vedanji's approval?' Nina asked.

'Right you are,' Surekha responded.

Surekha took the elevation sketch and the pith model to Vedaraman's bedroom.

'Look!'

'I like it, Sura. I just have one suggestion. If the front had the look of a temple gopuram, wouldn't it be more impressive?'

Surekha came back to the others and conveyed the comment.

'Great! Why didn't any of us have this idea?' Nina clapped her hands and asked.

Chinnappa said, 'Murugan, see to it that the change is incorporated.'

'Right, Annan!'

Rangarajan turned to another track at this juncture, 'We know who Vedanji is. Now, Tamil Nadu has to know. Then, the whole of India and then the western countries. How do we go about ensuring that this happens? Literature about Vedanji should be prepared – an attractive package! Who is Vedanji? Where did he come from? What were the miracles that occurred first? A book detailing all this should be prepared.'

Great idea! Everybody agreed. When a new product is launched, all the techniques of marketing should be utilized. We are introducing Vedanji as a world guru. The ashram should grow. The new movement should acquire international relevance. Therefore, there should be first-class publicity material on Vedanji.

'I'll write the book,' Nina volunteered.

'Have you written any book before this, Nina?' Madhavan Nair enquired.

'Mark, you answer that question,' Nina looked smilingly at Murugappan.

Murugappan said, 'Nina has not written any book. But she can write. She's the star copywriter of Ajax Advertising.'

'So…that's settled,' Chinnappa said.

'Boss, the book should be published in England or America. Only a western publication will get noticed immediately.' This was Rangarajan's opinion.

We have to prepare an outline first. Let's have a sub-committee level brainstorming session for that. Nina, Uncle and I'll participate.'

The three of them sat together. Madhavan Nair detailed all the facts that he knew.

Vedanji…Vedaraman. He was born in an illustrious family in a small village on the banks of the river Periyar seventeen or eighteen years ago. He grew up as an ordinary village boy. He completed his education under the guardianship of the old freedom fighter and well-known social worker Vikraman Pillai. It became evident at that time that Vedaraman had extraordinary powers. He marked spots for wells that were always full, where there had been no water at all. He predicted a number of events that proved true. He had the ability to control the rate of his breathing and could vary his heartbeat and pulse rate at will. He succeeded where expert doctors failed and cured diseases including Chinnappa's phlebitis. Vedanji's sixth finger had a wonderful glow at times...

'The whole thing's as dry as dust! This won't do. The book must have a romantic flavour. Surekha, will it be possible for me to interview Vedanji? Some frills, a little attractive padding. I can do it. Can we get hold of a tape recorder?' Nina asked.

'I'll tell Rangarajan to get one.'

It was night time. Vedaraman was sitting back in an easy chair, in a half conscious state and was gazing at the ceiling when Nina and Surekha entered the room. On a side table near him rested a glass and a bottle of whisky.

'Sura!,' Vedan moved his eyes from the ceiling. 'Who's with you? Oh, Murugappan's girlfriend, right? It wouldn't be proper for me to act as though I'm the host. I'm a prisoner here. You are the hostess, Sura. Fix her a drink... and one for yourself.'

Surekha obeyed.

'Vedanji, why did you say you are a prisoner here?'

'How long has it been since I came to Madras? Have I seen anything other than your flat at Adyar, this room and the dining and sitting rooms of this house? I feel that I am in a jail. And you are my jailer.'

'Nina, listen to him tease me!'

Nina switched on the tape recorder and asked, 'Vedanji, does this feeling that you are a prisoner depress you?'

'Not at all. When I like my jailer, even imprisonment can be sweet. Is it such a big thing to see Madras city? I could fly away from here without anyone being any wiser. There's no need for me to do that. I can see everything with my inner eye. Why should I wander around outside?' Vedanji lifted his glowing sixth finger as he asked this.

'Vedanji, Nina is here to interview you. I'll go away and let you get on with it.' Surekha said.

'Please stay,' Nina requested her.

'Nina, if the interview is to work, you need privacy. I'll come after an hour or so.'

After Surekha left the room, Vedaraman asked Nina, 'Why don't we change your name? Why "Hyde"? Why not "Seek"? To seek...to search...'

'All right, I shall seek. Seek and you shall find...this is what all religions and all gurus have said. What do you seek, Vedanji?'

'Just now what I seek is a drink. You shall find it for me.'

'Vedanji, your sense of humour is great.' Nina poured out the liquor into Vedan's glass. She pulled out a pack of cigarettes from her handbag and asked, 'May I smoke, Vedanji?'

'Oh yes!'

'One for you?'

'I don't smoke. Earlier, I used to have a beedi once in a while. Anyway, since you offer it, I'll have a cigarette.'

She lit his cigarette for him.

'Now for the interview. The tape is running.'

'Why do you want this interview?'

'I'm going to write a book about you. So you must tell me everything...your entire story.'

Vedaraman emptied his glass, pulled hard on the cigarette and started speaking, 'Seventeen or eighteen years ago, or was it a hundred years ago...a golden casket floated to the shore of the Poorna river. When a strong wind blew across the shore the lid of the casket blew away. There was a child in the casket. Doves flew in from somewhere. The wind quietened down and the doves asked the baby, "Are you well?"

'The baby's reply floated back like a song, "I'm well, I'm well, I'm well..."

'The doves told him, "You were hatched out of the egg laid by our queen. Therefore, you shall be known as the 'Andayoni' or 'One born of an egg'. The power of the creator dwells in you. Do not go in search of your father or your mother. Such a search will only bring sorrow."

'A golden serpent came there at this time. When the serpent hissed, the doves flew away. The serpent spread its hood over the casket and shaded it from the sun. The child played in the casket. The left hand of the child had six fingers on it. Days and nights passed. The serpent continued to shelter the casket under its hood. One night the Poorna overflowed. The golden serpent shed its skin and became a black serpent. The black serpent bit the sixth finger of the child. A flame rose from the sixth finger. The light from that flame rose and spread in all the fourteen worlds...Bhuloka, Bhuvarloka, Suvarloka, Maharloka, Janarloka, Tapoloka, Satyaloka, Patala, Rasatala, Mahatala, Talatala, Sutala, Vitala, Atala...the entire universe.'

Vedaraman's head was not steady on his neck by this time. He started repeating the words in no particular order – Vitala, Atala, Sutala, Vitala...

He suddenly put his head on Nina's lap. He mutttered, 'My head feels light. My body also feels weightless. A floating sensation.'

'It could be because you smoked the cigarette. You are not used to it.'

'What cigarette is this Nina Seek?'

'Grass...marijuana.'

'Nina, who am I?'

'Guru...No. You are the "living god".'

Surekha, who came back to the room after about an hour, stood there stunned.

Vedaraman lay on the bed with his eyes shut. On him lay a half-naked Nina.

Surekha withdrew. Without making any noise.

❖

Reports against Nachimuthu started appearing in newspapers.

The Centre is displeased with Nachimuthu. Tamil Tigers were gathering strength in Tamil Nadu. Nachimuthu was not willing to control them. The Tigers shot down fourteen people they considered enemies in the Zacharia colony in broad daylight. The Tamil Nadu government had been aware of the movements of the Tigers months before this happened.

The Eelam Tigers were landing on the shores by means of fibreglass boats fitted with Yamaha engines. Were the police pickets in Pillayar Thadal, Vedaranyam, Muthupettai, Athiramapattinam and Rameswaram asleep all the while? Didn't the tigers have bomb factories in Ranipettai, Coimbatore and Salem?

Why does Nachimuthu continue to support Durai, the panchayat minister? Durai had a criminal record. Who had kidnapped the businessman Ibrahim Sait from Pondy Bazar in broad daylight? Weren't they the supporters of Durai?

Ibrahim Sait had been found with his hands and legs tied on the platform of the Central Station after three days.

The case was investigated by Superintendent Mishra, an honest police officer from Bihar. The newspapers accused Nachimuthu of interfering when the investigation reached the bungalow where Durai stayed.

Mishra was transferred suddenly. Then he was suspended. The accusation was that years back Mishra had falsified his TA bill for a small amount.

Mishra's successor saw to it that the kidnapping case was forgotten.

A Tamil weekly, which was renowned for its exposes, asked, 'What happened to the thirty-five-year-old housewife who had come to the circuit house to present a petition to the revenue minister?'

Arunagiri's self-confidence mounted. It would not be long before the north wind started blowing favourably. He spoke to Chinnappa about his calculations.

Chinnappa spoke with the certainty of the believer, 'What Vedanji said will not be in vain. You haven't met Vedanji yet. I'll arrange a dinner at my place before Murugappan returns to

London. You must definitely come, Aruna. It'll be a chance for you to meet Vedanji.'

❖

Vedaraman was in good form. His behaviour surprised everyone.

Madhavan Nair, Chinnappa, Murugappan, Surekha and even Nina behaved as humble followers before Arunagiri, who was a political leader and an ex-chief minister. Vedan acted as though they were equals.

Was Arunagiri rather displeased to begin with? Within minutes though, he became a victim of Vedan's charisma.

Vedan started speaking to no one in particular.

'I'm not myself now. I'm someone else, someone whom even I don't know. A great power...a great mind...a mind that is capable of denying even god, is here now. I'm going to bless the owner of that mind now.'

Vedaraman stood before Arunagiri. He took out a pen from Arunagiri's pocket without asking for his permission.

Rubbing that pen, Vedan announced, 'This is September. In January, perhaps even before Christmas, today's king-player will be ousted. There will be an election in June. After that, it will be this pen that will sign on government orders!'

Vedaraman seemed to have become weak suddenly. His body trembled and he fell on the carpet. As Madhavan Nair and Murugappan lifted Vedaraman, his sixth finger could be seen glowing.

Though he had understood what Vedanji said, Arunagiri asked Chinnappa, 'What did Vedanji say about my pen?'

'That you'll be chief minister in June, Aruna. What else?'

'Chinnappa, if this works...'

'It will, definitely.'

'Work on the ashram must be over by Christmas.'

'It shall be.'

Thirty-one

Surekha looked at the mirror. Was her beauty fading? Were there thin lines under the eyes? When she brought her eyebrows together were there small furrows on her forehead?

No, her shape was still perfect. Her breasts didn't need the help of a wired bra to stay up. There wasn't even the hint of excess fat anywhere on her body. But she had to be careful. It had been months since Chinnappa came to her. The old man wasn't really up to it, but he would touch her often, put his arm around her waist and hold her close. Forget Chinnappa's neglect, what had happened to Madhavan Nair? It was as if he had become detached from this world. He did not joke, did not try to make love to her. Perhaps uncle suspected that she and Vedan were sleeping together.

Had even Vedan lost interest in her? He had got caught in Nina's clutches. Nina was good-looking, much younger than herself. How could she compete with her? Anyway, Nina was in far-off England for the time being. She could leave that worry aside. The ashram would come up soon. Vedanji would become famous.

'Vedanji . . . Vedanji . . .' Surekha repeated the name to herself many times.

It sounded awful. To her, this boy was 'darling' and 'my pet'. At a pinch she could call him Vedan. But she had to call him Vedanji in the presence of others. He was a 'living god' after all. At the very least, a demi-god.

All right, my darling, I shall call you Vedanji. Once the ashram is established and you reign there as a demi-god, who'll take care of you, look after you? Me, of course.

❖

No one was appointed to fill the vacancy left by Gopikrishnan in Bengal Bay Company. Under normal circumstances, the Company's board would seek the opinion of the government before appointing a replacement.

Chinnappa had an idea. Why not just ignore the government? The company was a self-governing unit and according to the law, the company could ignore the suggestions of the government. The only thing was that the people who were at the top needed a strong backbone.

Earlier, under unusual circumstances, the government had intervened in the functioning of the company and had appointed bureaucrats to the board. Though Gopikrishnan had left, there were other government appointees on the board. The number of such directors was not mentioned anywhere in the memorandum and articles. These were the facts. So, why should someone not be appointed without the approval of the government?

Once it was done, the government might suddenly open its eyes. They could then say, 'Sir, this is *fait accompli*.' If they stood firm on that, the government would hesitate to intervene. It would not be able to dismiss the newly inducted director.

Chinnappa instructed the company secretary to call a board meeting. At the meeting, Chinnappa introduced the matter of the induction of a new director as an item outside the agenda. He also mentioned Madhavan Nair's name. A business magnate with the experience of Mr Madhavan Nair would be an asset to the board.

No one objected. And Madhavan Nair became a member of the board of Bengal Bay Company.

Madhavan Nair was very pleased. His aims were being accomplished. Chinnappa was keeping his word. Was this due to Vedaraman's blessings?

When Madhavan Nair thanked him at the bungalow, Chinnappa patted him on the shoulder and laughed aloud. 'Nair, what is this? Why do you thank me? This is only the first step. You know what the next step is – you take over as the managing director.'

'Don't be in a hurry, Boss!'

'Nair, leave it to me.'

Chinnappa's calculations had been accurate. No questions were raised by the Department of Industries about the appointment of the new director.

❖

Arunagiri went secretly to Delhi in October. He stayed in a suite at Hotel Maurya that Maniappan, one of his followers, had booked in his own name. Maniappan had called Gopikrishnan to the hotel. Gopikrishnan was respectful towards Arunagiri. He informed Arunagiri that the prime minister was displeased with the state of affairs in Tamil Nadu.

Arunagiri asked, 'Wouldn't it be a good idea for me to meet the PM?'

'Yes, sir. But it might be difficult to get an appointment.'

'You'll be able to manage it, won't you? You must have friends in the PMO.'

'I do. But there is a problem. The PMO does not have its earlier power. The power centre is now a group of the prime minister's cronies. You can meet the PM only if one of them can manage it. I'll try, though.'

'If you try, it'll work, Gopikrishnan!'

'Sir, I can't assure you that I'll be able to manage it. Even chief ministers of the ruling party have stayed for five or ten days in the capital and have gone away without meeting the PM.'

Arunagiri stayed quietly in the hotel for two days. On the third day he got a message from Gopikrishnan: An appointment with the prime minister had been fixed for that afternoon, at 3 p.m.

The meeting lasted only ten minutes.

The prime minister was pleasant. After discussing a number

of live issues that were relevant to Tamil Nadu, he said, 'Arunagiriji, sometimes we do regret what we did earlier, right? When political decisions go bad on us? Well... I wish to see you once more before the winter session of Parliament begins. I'll let you know when.'

Even after he reached Madras, the prime minister's words echoed in Arunagiri's ears. What had he meant?

This prime minister had dismissed his government even when he had a clear majority in the legislative assembly. He had also dismissed the assembly. Was he hinting that he regretted having done so? That action had been taken against the advice of the governor. The governor who had invited the PM's displeasure had been removed almost immediately.

Executive powers were vested in the President of the Indian Union. The Constitution held that there should be a council of ministers to help the President, and that the President should act according to the advice of the ministry. The prime minister advised, the President put his signature, and he had been thrown out. Did the prime minister's conscience trouble him now? Had there been a hint that Nachimuthu would be thrown out after the winter session of Parliament? Even if the prime minister decided to do it, would the President okay it? It was to be supposed that he would. Only two presidents had held their own against the prime ministers of the time – one was Rajan Babu and the other S. Radhakrishnan. President Rajendra Prasad and Jawaharlal had fought over the Hindu Code Bill. In 1962, President Radhakrishnan had managed the ouster of the then defence minister, V.K. Krishna Menon – against the wishes of Nehru.

But the present President was no Rajendra Prasad or Radhakrishnan!

Why should he think so far ahead just now?

If Nachimuthu were dismissed and the assembly were not dissolved, things would become a mess. There would be ample scope for horse-trading. The Congress might try to form a government with the help of his party. Some of the MLAs, at least of Nachimuthu's party, would be willing to join this coalition. Could this be what the prime minister wanted? If so, the PM might be willing to make him, Arunagiri, the chief minister to ensure the success of the coalition.

That should not happen.

His return to Fort St George had to be with the blessings of the Tamil people, keeping his identity intact. There had to be a mid-term election to ensure that. The victory should be his, only his.

He would keep his trust in Vedanji's prediction.

Work on the ashram should start soon...immediately.

'Nair, I'll see that you're the MD at the next board meeting.' Chinnappa told Madhavan Nair.

'Shall I go to Kochi before that, Boss? I need to wind up matters there.'

'That's a good idea,' Chinnappa agreed.

If someone had said that he did not have much of a business at Kochi, Madhavan Nair would have been insulted; he would have lost his temper.

But that was the truth.

There wasn't much to do in Kochi as the representative of the Chinnappa group – a little liaison work, something to do to show that he was doing things there, to keep up an image – that was all.

If he gave up his establishment in Kochi, what he would lose would be his private business. It was a dangerous business... illegal business – mainly the export of snake skins, under the guise of cashew export.

If he could manage to export snake skins five times a year to Singapore, his profits were huge. If the Kochi customs caught him at it, he would have to go to jail. So far, luck had favoured him. Some ten or twelve agents brought snake skins to his godown in Willingdon Island. There was a big board in front of the godown – 'Simple Cashews'.

The snake skins that were brought there had to be packed. They were placed at the bottom of the crates and covered with layers of cashew. This packing and the export formalities that followed had to be done under his direct supervision.

It was a dangerous business, like lighting a cigarette in an ordnance factory.

So far everything had gone smoothly. Enough. He did not want that tension anymore. At this moment, when everything was moving in his favour, he should not take any risk.

When he heard that Madhavan Nair was going to Kochi, Vedaraman stubbornly insisted that he would also go. 'I'm coming. I want to go to the village, visit my old friends.'

Madhavan Nair sought Chinnappa's and Surekha's opinions.

'Obey Vedanji!' Chinnappa said.

Surekha asked, 'Shall I also come with you?'

Madhavan Nair stopped her, 'No need. We'll be back in a few days.'

Madhavan Nair and Vedan reached Kochi. The very next day, Vedan went to his village in Madhavan Nair's car.

When he reached Kottoor Junction, he saw Nanu by the roadside. He told the driver, 'Bakkar, please stop the car.'

Vedaraman got out of the car. When he waved, Nanu approached him hesitantly.

'Ramankutty! You've changed a lot. You are at Ernakulam now, aren't you? Was there anything special, to come here now…'

'I wanted to go to the temple of Narasimhamoorthy. I also wanted to see everyone.'

They could hear the noise made by the children in the school. It was 4 o'clock. The school was giving over.

'What are you looking at?' Nanu asked.

'It's my old school. Never mind, Nanuettan. I want to go there, to see Kuttisankaran.'

'Oh, don't you know? Kuttisankaran has left the place. He's gone to Kothakurissi.'

Vedaraman stood there for a while without saying anything; he then got into the car. When they reached Padmasanan's textile shop, Vedan told Bakkar, 'To the left.'

The car stopped next to the peepal tree. Vedan saw that Achukutty had lowered the reed screens of the tea shop and was about to step out.

'Achuettan!'

'You, Ramankutty! Whose car is this? I suppose you plan to go back immediately.'

'I need to go only tomorrow.'

'So kind of you. Send the car away. You can go after three or four days.'

'I have to go tomorrow. Madhavan Nair sir will wait for me. This is his car.'

'As you please.'

'I heard that Kuttisankaran Uncle has left the place?'

'Yes. He's gone. To Kothakurissi...How did you know?'

'Nanu told me when I was coming here.'

'What does it matter to you who goes and who stays? You have cut all connection with us, haven't you? You don't even have the time to write a letter, do you? You have changed completely, Ramankutty?'

'Are you angry with me, Achuettan?'

'Take it that I am.'

'Achuettan, I might be at fault. But don't judge me before you've heard my side of things. I've been in Madras for the past few weeks. With Madhavan Nair sir. We are going back there.'

'To Madras?'

'Yes, sir says that I should study there. His business has shifted to Madras.'

'So...you've come to say a final goodbye, is it?'

'Don't be angry, Achuettan. It's not as if I can't come here from Madras.'

'All right, I won't argue with you. I've got you for today – so far, so good. What do you want to do? Tell me.'

'Let's take Koman Nair and go to Mulamkunnam. I want to bathe and swim in the river too.'

Unneera came running when he heard the noise. He joined his hands together, bowed low and asked, 'When did you come, Thampuran?'

'I've just come. Unneera, we're going to have a bath. Make something for all of us to eat. You must make tapioca curry anyway. Let the car stay here. Bakkar, why don't you come? You can have a swim.'

'I'll stay here,' Bakkar said.

'Unneera, take care of Bakkar.'

'I'll take care of him, Thampuran.'

'Bakkar, take out that cane basket from the boot.'

Achukutty and Vedaraman swam in the river. Koman Nair sat on the sand and started drinking. He liked the cane basket. Each item had its own compartment.

As Vedaraman and Achukutty swam and played around in the water, Koman Nair looked at the stars that were coming out and spoke loudly, 'The idiots in this place never understand, however much I tell them, that this Koman has no dirt either inside him or on his body. Therefore, I shall not bathe!'

When Vedaraman and Achukutty reached the shore, Koman Nair continued, 'This basket is really good. Look at the order of the compartments. The bottle goes into this, glass in this small one. The soda is nearly over. Never mind. The river still flows! Hey boy! Raman! Aren't you having a little? Or have you given up this good habit?'

'I'll have a little, Uncle.'

Koman Nair hugged Vedaraman.

'So you haven't stopped. That means you haven't really changed...'

Koman Nair shut his eyes and started weeping, 'But Ramankutty, you have changed in other ways. Did you send us a letter? Did you come here once in a while at least? Forget us. You forgot even that poor Kuttisankaran. He was so upset when he left, right Achukutty?'

Achukutty said, 'Ramankutty, Kuttisankaran came to see us before he left. He wept a lot. Mainly because of the bullocks. He'd just sold them when he came here. He kept asking whether the people who had bought them would send them to the slaughter house.'

'Do you know his address in Kothakurissi?'

'He'd said he'd write after he reached. But there's been no letter.'

Koman Nair said, 'Ramankutty, he said he'd go to Kothakurissi and get married. He said this in secret. That would be good. What are you looking at? Take it.'

Vedaraman picked up a glass. 'Achuettan, I want to go to the temple tomorrow.'

Koman Nair laughed, 'Why do you want to go there, Raman? There's only a stone there. The idol's power has been taken to the civil court by the two Namboodiris. What I'd said then has come true. What is happening, Raman? I keep drinking and talking. You don't say anything about what's happening to you.'

Vedaraman lay flat on his back. It was good to feel the slightly rough grains of sand on his wet back.

'There's nothing to say, Uncle!'

Darkness was spreading. The palm trees were turning into demons.

Vedaraman looked at the sky and wondered: Shall I ever come here again? I, who am about to become a god?

He wouldn't tell them all those stories. His bank account here had some money. He didn't need it any longer. Before he left the place, he must put that money into Achukutty's account. A small portion could go to Unneera as well. Let Unneera continue to enjoy anything that could be got from this sixty-eight cents of land.

He would lie on this sandy shore for some more time.

As he lay there, Vedaraman suddenly thought of Mukundan

and asked Achukutty, 'Do you see Mukundan these days?'

'You'll have to go to Viyyur if you want to see him.'

'Viyyur?'

'Ramankutty, he's in jail. During the last temple festival, he snatched a woman's gold chain…'

Thirty-two

Madhavan Nair and Vedaraman returned to Madras. Work on the ashram started. Bhoomipuja was performed at the site at Thiruvanmiyur. The heart of the ashram had to be completed before December. That was what everyone wished.

Murugappan and Nina stayed in constant touch. There were frequent telephone calls. Murugappan spoke to Chinnappa, Nina to Vedanji. Nina did not forget to send long letters to Vedanji every week either. To begin with, those letters excited Surekha's jealousy. When Vedaraman passed on some of those letters to her to read, she felt better. They were not love letters. They were all about the book.

Dear Vedanji, the writing's going on well. I've already completed five chapters. They have the glow of legend. I've let my imagination fly…

Vedanji, I've got the outline of the book in my mind. As soon as I complete it, I'll send you the typescript. You must show it to Surekha. It will need some polishing. Surekha would be able to help me. Rangarajan must also help with the editing.

Dear Vedanji, the book has to come out by December. I've found publishers – Rex and Stout. It's a well-known publishing house. The contract has been signed. Five thousand hardbound copies. Twenty-five thousand paperbacks. We have to bear the cost of printing the first edition. Do you feel that is a humiliating condition? Never mind. It is the usual practice in the publishing trade. Just think of it in those terms. Murugappan will give them the money. I'll reach there in the beginning of December – if all goes well.

Though Surekha's jealousy vanished, she was worried about the future.

Within months, and if Arunagiri took a real interest, within weeks, the ashram would be a reality. It would become Vedan's permanent place of residence. The ashram would come into being with huge publicity. Devotees would come pouring in. That rush would continue; it would become daily routine. When Arunagiri took up the sceptre of power again, money would flow in like many Kaveris. Without much delay, the dream of the architect, shown on paper, would become a reality.

An auditorium, staff quarters, pilgrim cottages, meditation groves, a Sanskrit school, Tamil research centre, music hall, a stage for dances... everything.

People in search of good fortune would hover like flies around a honey pot. They would try to take control of the ashram and make Vedan their puppet. So many dangers lurked around.

So there had to be someone to take care of Vedan, to see that he did not wander from the right path. Who else could it be, but she, Surekha?

She must forget her past. She had to wash herself clean of her past life's sins. She could not continue to be the playmate of Chinnappa and Madhavan Nair and that Central minister who smelled of eau de cologne. She had to give up her job as PRO in Chinnappa's company as well. She would stay with Vedan in the ashram and the world would see her in this new incarnation.

She would no longer be Surekha, but Yogini Amma, Yogini Mata, the Yogini Mother.

When Vedan Baba became a god, when Vedanism became the new world religion, she had to be there to keep everything running.

Vedan, my pet, I shall keep you safe under my wings.

I shall be Meera to your Krishna, Shirin to your Farhad, Laila to your Majnu.

How many roles will I have to act out? Administrator, financial controller, Yogini Mata, the mother of the divine god. And then... Didn't she have another role? An important role? That of the secret lover?

My little pet, do you think I don't see the dark bees gather under your nose. Vedan, your thick black moustache makes you look even more handsome.

❖

Though he was busy with other matters, Arunagiri kept himself posted on the progress of the ashram.

He told Chinnappa when they met at the party headquarters, 'Chinnappa, the inauguration of the ashram should take place immediately. Tell that contractor to hurry up.'

Chinnappa reassured him, 'It shall be done, Aruna! As long as I have your support, I'm sure it will be done on time.'

'Don't call it support. Call it my selfishness. As the days pass, I have this feeling that my rise and Vedanji's future are entangled...'

Chinnappa replied with a mildly sarcastic laugh, 'So, Aruna, you have become a believer too...'

'Hey, Chinnu!'

That 'Chinnu' touched Chinnappa. Arunagiri called him like that on rare occasions when he had given his ego a holiday.

Chinnappa said softly, 'Don't misunderstand me! I was not mocking you. I was just trying to reiterate that Vedanji does have supernatural powers.'

'I know, Chinnu!'

Arunagiri was satisfied with the way things were moving. He shared his news with Chinnappa, 'Chinnu, I recently got a secret message from Gopikrishnan. You know he is our contact at the PMO. A lobby favouring me has taken shape in Delhi. I too have noticed the news in the national press and their assessment of the political climate. Bad times have started for Nachimuthu. Recently he stayed for a week in Delhi to meet the prime minister but could not manage it.'

Arunagiri quoted the headlines in the newspapers. The *Indian Express* had said, 'PM cold shoulders Nachimuthu'. The *Times* had been briefer, 'PM nasty to Nachi'.

'Chinnu, my self-confidence is growing. The prime minister had hinted that he wanted to see me before the winter session of Parliament. I'm sure he was not just being polite.'

An extraordinary board meeting of the Bengal Bay Company was convened by Chinnappa. No particular agenda had been laid down for the meeting. Madhavan Nair wondered why Chinnappa had taken this step.

Chinnappa wrapped all the sharp weapons he had acquired over the years of board room battles in soft silk and began, 'Gentlemen, I'm not speaking of new things. These are matters all of you are aware of. Still, I explain again – only because it is my duty as chairman to lay out all the facts. For some time now, our company has been facing crisis after crisis. You know that the company is basically a sound one. Still, these crises have kept coming up – not once, but many times. How did this happen? Why did it happen? The government appointees on the board may find it difficult to acknowledge the truth of my findings at least in public, but still...'

One of the government appointees intervened, 'Objection, chairman. Why do you beat around the bush like this? All of us know that it is dirty political intervention that has brought the company to this state.'

Chinnappa smiled, 'Thank you, Mr Ambrose. I have tried to resist the unnecessary interference of politicians as best I could. Some of the power centres imagined that they could hold me back by making me just a figurehead chairman. Did it work? Of course not! When Mr Gopikrishnan resigned, I had to take up the duties of managing director as well. A new load...and at my age. The government is like an ocean. Losses are not a problem for them. Just a little drop in that ocean. But think of the ordinary shareholder. A good citizen, hardworking, someone who saves.

The small amounts that these small men invest are the real strength, the eternal lamps of industry. How can we forget them? Gentlemen, it looks as though I've wandered far from the point I want to make. I gave way to emotion. Forgive me!'

Chinnappa stopped for a moment and then continued, 'I was able to induct Mr Madhavan Nair into the board with all your support. I consider that it was a step in the right direction for the progress of the company.'

Someone thumped the table in support of the statement.

Chinnappa stood up straighter and told the company secretary, 'George, please circulate those papers.'

The Secretary distributed the 'note' that rested in beautiful folders.

'Gentlemen, what you have before you is a synopsis of the study made by Mr Madhavan Nair about the present state of the company.'

Madhavan Nair was stunned; he hadn't done any study!

'There is also a forecast about the results of this financial year. Mr Nair believes that we should be able to declare a dividend of at least fifteen per cent. Do you find it excessive self-confidence?'

Flipping through the pages, some of the directors said, more or less in unison, 'This is quite a realistic forecast!'

'If so, gentlemen, I have a suggestion. Please remember that I am old and my health isn't too good. It would be a great relief to me if Mr Madhavan Nair became the managing director.'

Madhavan Nair kept silent. The other directors thumped the table to show their agreement. The meeting ended.

Madhavan Nair was looking for words to express his gratitude when he and Chinnappa were left alone in the room. He said, 'Boss, what magic is this? My study! I was stunned. Your stage management was something to watch. Thank you, Boss!'

'Nair, express your gratitude to Vedanji! All this is due to his blessings.'

When informed of Madhavan Nair's appointment as the managing director, Arunagiri said, 'Very good, Chinnappa!'

He also gave a suggestion. It was not proper for Madhavan Nair to continue to stay as a guest at Poes Garden after becoming the MD. Nair must have another residential address that was suitable for the managing director of the company.

Chinnappa too agreed.

He would continue to pull strings and rule over the company. But to the outside world, the MD must appear to be independent. So, Nair should not continue to stay in this bungalow. Surekha's Adyar flat was not a suitable address for the MD of Bengal Bay Company. For the time being, let Madhavan Nair shift to a suite in a luxury hotel. The only condition was that Vedanji should continue here, with him. Let Surekha also stay to keep Vedanji company.

Madhavan Nair did not have to stay long in the hotel. Rangarajan soon found an excellent bungalow at Guruswami Road.

❖

As the political climate became cloudy, Nachimuthu added to his troubles by giving an exclusive interview to a popular English weekly. His tongue wagged without control. He said that the Tamilians would not put up with the overlordship of the northerners for long, and that the embers of the Dravida movement lay under the ashes of patience in the minds of the people of Tamil Nadu.

There was no direct reaction from New Delhi. But something that spoke volumes and was stronger than any direct reaction happened. The prime minister cancelled a long-planned visit to Madras. And rubbing salt in the wound, he decided on the spur of the moment to visit Bangalore.

A message came secretly to Arunagiri via a messenger.

The prime minister reaches Bangalore on the evening of the 27th. The programme has not been officially announced. Ostensibly, the purpose of his visit is a trip to Puttaparthi. He'll be staying at the Raj Bhavan. The occasion will arise at a dinner at the Raj Bhavan. Prepare for a trip to Bangalore immediately.

On the 27th, you must organize a Tamil cultural event there. That shall be the cover for your Bangalore visit.

Arunagiri's joy knew no bounds. This was only the 24th. There was time to arrange everything. Arunagiri rang up Mahabala Rao, the chief minister of Karnataka. He wanted to participate in the Tamil Cultural Fest on the 27th. He would like him, Rao, to preside over a session. Rao, who was an old friend, agreed happily.

Arunagiri then sent some junior leaders of his party to Bangalore. He already had a huge following in Bangalore. They had to be alerted. Full page advertisements had to appear in the major Kannada newspapers and the *Deccan Herald* on the 27th...

Kalai Kuberar Arunagiri, ex-chief minister of Tamil Nadu speaks on the topic 'Bharatiyar, Bharatidasan and the Unity of India'.

The chief minister of Karnataka, Thiru. Mahabala Rao will preside over the function.

Arches and huge cut-outs of Arunagiri rose in the city on the 27th.

In the evening, the ground overflowed with people. Arunagiri and Mahabala Rao, the chief minister of Karnataka, occupied the dais with other dignitaries. It took an hour just to get over the ritual of garlanding.

The magic of Arunagiri's oratory captured the audience. The audience clapped and roared, 'Long live Arunagiri!' The atmosphere was one of hysteria. Even Mahabala Rao clapped frequently.

When the uproar had died down a little, Mahabala Rao asked, 'Arunagiriji, where are you staying?'

'Windsor Manor.'

'That is an insult to me. You could have stayed with me. Or at the Raj Bhavan...'

Arunagiri spoke in the language of the erstwhile revolutionary, 'Raoji, I'm outside the charmed circle of power these days. I came into public life fighting every inch. Just like you. I don't need to tell you. Don't you think it is better that I keep a low profile just now? I can always smash my way in. And then I can show my power. If you scratch my skin you'll find...though my politics is different, I'm of the same breed as Gandhiji and Kamaraj. I belong in huts, to floors plastered with cowdung. I came from there, rose from there. But my people will not let me be. I have a lot of followers in Karnataka too. They're the ones who chose Windsor Manor for me.'

Mahabala Rao winked, 'Anyway, we are getting together tonight. Dinner at the Raj Bhavan. You know the invitation is not from me. It is from the Emperor of the North.'

'I know, Raoji.'

There was a cultural programme before dinner at the Raj Bhavan. It was held on the vast lawns.

As the programme went on, the prime minister looked at the men sitting on either side of him – Mahabala Rao and Arunagiri.

Arunagiri was happy. The prime minister had broken protocol to seat him next to himself.

The programme ended and everyone got up.

The prime minister took Arunagiri's hand and walked a few steps apart, 'The weather in the South will change after the winter session. Before that, my political secretary will come and meet you. He'll brief you. Arunagiriji, be ready!'

When the Governor and the Karnataka chief minister caught up with him, the prime minister set aside his usual seriousness and spoke lightly. He patted the Governor on the shoulder and said, 'Ramanji, I'm in a good mood today. And that means I'm very hungry.'

Governor Raman Khanna looked at Mahabala Rao and smiled.

Mahabala Rao said in a mischievous tone, 'The cooks in the Raj Bhavan are very good.'

The prime minister caressed his paunch and laughed aloud. 'I sincerely believe so. Arunagiriji, the cooking at the Madras Raj

Bhavan is also excellent, isn't it? I have an idea. Let us all get together at the Madras Raj Bhavan after the winter session of Parliament. I must get excellent South Indian food then. Do you agree, Arunagiriji?'

'But sir, shouldn't you be asking the Madras Governor or Nachimuthu this question?' Arunagiri asked, looking intently at the prime minister.

The prime minister laughed aloud, 'Arunagiriji, you have a tremendous sense of humour!'

Thirty-three

Chinnappa and Madhavan Nair went to the party headquarters to meet Arunagiri on his return from Bangalore. Nair spread out the newspapers with reports on the visit.

Arunagiri was very pleased and said, 'I didn't know there was so much coverage.'

'Did you see the angle of the news, Boss?' Madhavan Nair asked Chinnappa.

'What angle?' Arunagiri asked.

It was Chinnappa who replied, 'Aruna, that Raj Bhavan dinner is the main focus of all the reports. Why did the prime minister go against protocol and seat the Opposition leader of Tamil Nadu next to him? Has a new relationship developed between the prime minister and Arunagiri? All the papers ask these questions in one voice.'

Arunagiri laughed aloud, 'Chinnu, it is all due to Vedanji. Our victory chariot has started rolling, it's gathering speed. Every step has to be taken with care now. Let me tell you something.'

Chinnappa and Madhavan Nair leaned forward.

'Chinnu, we are together in everything – one team. But our activities must be channelled in two different directions from now on. The construction of the ashram, at least the heart of it, must be completed immediately. That is your duty, yours and Nair's. That and the presentation of Vedanji as the new godman. You are in sole charge. By you, I mean you, Madhavan Nair and Murugappan. I have to devote all my time to the political arena now. Don't you think it's time I did that? The ranks have to be mobilized. If the bhootas don't do their part, where will I, the Bhootanatha, be?'

Arunagiri paused for a moment and asked suddenly, 'Chinnu, where is that secret file? The one Gopikrishnan gave you?'

'It is resting in the cellar room of my bungalow. In a locker that only I have the key to. Why did you ask?'

'Gopikrishnan had rung up yesterday from Delhi. He said now might be the best time to use that file. What is in that file? Both of you go through the file carefully. And then brief me...in person.'

'All right, Aruna.'

Arunagiri tapped the table with his fingers rhythmically and asked, 'That book about Vedanji in English. How far has it come? The one that white woman is writing...'

'How do you...?'

'How do I know about it, you're asking? You can't become a leader without knowing everything. Chinnu, you're becoming forgetful.'

'Aruna, I must have told you myself.'

'Let that be! It's good that an English edition is coming out in London. But that won't do us any good immediately. A book about Vedanji must come out in Tamil. It must be done without delay. At least a lakh copies. Who'll write it? Is your Rangarajan any good? If so, let him write it. If not, I'll entrust the work to Minnal Babu of the Agastyar Press.'

'Rangan can write. It's an advantage that he knows Vedanji personally.'

'Okay, Chinnu. We'll ask Minnal Babu to edit what he writes and give it shape. Shall we break for now?' Arunagiri stood up.

Chinnappa was in the very heaven of delight as they said goodbye. Arunagiri had called him Chinnu so many times. He had used the informal 'you' throughout the conversation.

❖

Vedaraman's mind was being tossed by waves of uncertainty.

He would stand before the full-length mirror and caress the moustache that was growing. Then he would go and lie down flat on his back on the bed. He would get up suddenly and start writing small notes.

What is this world? What was its origin? How does it survive? Who am I? What is my relationship with this world?

Is there a god who created this world and who keeps it like this? Does the soul have rebirth? How can I, who doesn't even know who his father is, say I'm wise? Why should I become a guru in this land where there are so many teachers and sages? Isn't the glow of my sixth finger dirty? I stand tall on the platform of that idiotic glow. Or rather, I'm being installed. I'm the prisoner of hypocrisy. Perhaps, I'm the greatest hypocrite.

Achukutty, Koman Nair, Unneera, Kuttisankaran Uncle who went to Kothakurissi in search of a new life, Big Man who brought the light of knowledge to my mind…

After crumpling up and throwing away the papers he had written on, Vedan would start meditating.

Often, Surekha would enter his room then.

She would stand and gaze at him. Didn't that moustache make him even better looking? It made him look very masculine. She would walk up to him and touch him. He would not appear to have noticed her at all. He would not respond if she called him.

When things continued to be this way, Surekha was disturbed. She felt weak. What had happened to Vedan? Why had he changed like this? Whom could she ask? Who was there to whom she could speak freely?

Finally she expressed her doubts to Rangan, 'Rangan, I'm feeling very disturbed.'

Rangan tried to pacify her, 'Madam, perhaps these are only symptoms of the journey to self-realization.'

'Rangan!' Surekha's eyes were moist.

'Madam!'

'I haven't talked about this sorrow of mine to Boss or Uncle so far. Rangan, shall we get together for a discussion?'

'A discussion? On what?'

'About the changes in Vedanji.'

'Madam, I have a sort of answer in this small brain of mine. Will you get angry if I tell you?'

'Never.'

'Madam, the problem is that you're jealous. You want to keep Vedanji, who is about to become guru to the world, to yourself. Isn't that right? That's not possible.'

'Are you saying that I'm at fault, Rangan? Whether he's the preceptor of the world or a living god, I'll have a special relationship with him. What's wrong with that?'

'There's nothing wrong with that. That is what you want. But if Vedanji has different ideas…?'

'Are you speaking of Nina Hyde?'

Rangarajan could not help laughing out aloud. 'I had not thought of the white woman at all. It looks as though my guess was right, though. The problem is jealousy.'

Surekha's face flushed. Her eyes flamed. The next moment, she sat on the sofa nearby as if she had lost all strength. She covered her face and started weeping.

Rangarajan was in a quandary. He felt rather bad about what he had said. He should not have been quite so frank. He said, 'Madam, don't be so upset. Matters will sort themselves out. Vedanji is in some confusion – about the different strands of Hindu philosophy. He doesn't know which he should adopt – Dehatmavada or Advaita. These things trouble him. I'm trying to help as much as I can.'

Rangarajan himself was not sure exactly what he was saying. He had just said whatever had come to his mind.

Anyway, Surekha seemed to have regained her equanimity for the time being. So much the better.

❖

Chinnappa looked at the peculiar face of the clock in the drawing room. It was 6:45. In another fifteen minutes the handsome young man and the pretty young girl in the clock would start dancing. They would twirl seven times.

Chinnappa rang up Madhavan Nair at his Guruswami Road residence, 'You must come at once.'

The dance in the clock was over by the time Madhavan Nair arrived.

As soon as he came, Chinnappa said, 'I somehow managed to get rid of Rangarajan. Vedanji and Surekha are discussing something behind closed doors. They're not likely to come here. You would have understood why I asked you to come.'

'To examine the file?'

'Exactly!'

Chinnappa and Madhavan Nair went to the cellar room. When he took out the secret file from the locker, Chinnappa's hands were trembling.

What were the secrets hidden in this file?

They examined the file carefully.

It was very dusty. The papers were all of different sizes. Some were of the foolscap size. Others were only as large as a medium-size letter pad. There were pieces of paper that were only as large as postcards. There were holes in many of the papers from attacks by silver fish.

The file contained illegal orders given by Nachimuthu. Some of the papers were signed by Nachimuthu himself. A number of papers were signed by officers, most of them senior IAS officers. They had all written the escape clause: 'As instructed by the chief minister...'

If they fell into the hands of the Accountant General they would be enough to create a number of audit enquiries. There would be controversies when audit comments were discussed in the Public Accounts Committee. There would be a stink. That was all. Nachimuthu had done only what any chief minister would have done. Tomorrow, when Arunagiri became the chief minister, he might do worse things. He had done such things earlier too. The only thing was Arunagiri would not commit the blunder of signing the papers himself.

In short, the papers were not enough to bring down a political foe.

Why had Gopikrishnan handed it over as though it was a matchless weapon? Secret file indeed. He must be a fool to think that.

When Chinnappa said this, Madhavan Nair again looked through the papers with all the cunning he had exhibited in the times of snake skin export.

He found a sharp knife. Thirty-eight lakh rupees had been diverted from the accounts of Bengal Bay Company through various channels and sent to an account in Pondicherry. The record said that this account was in the name of a 'V.M.'. There was a note signed by Nachimuthu like a black mushroom among these papers.

It said, 'Proper and timely measures should be taken to recover the temporary loan given to V.M. under special circumstances.'

A bell rang in Chinnappa's head at the sight of these papers.

V.M.?

V.M.? V.M.? Who was this V.M.?

He suddenly realized who it was. V.M. was Vasanthamalli.

She was the granddaughter of Kokila, who had been the uncrowned queen of the Tamil stage. Vasanthamalli had been the light of Kodambakkam. Nachimuthu managed to capture her as she sparkled on the Tamil film firmament. He bought a chinna veedu or small house in Pondicherry and installed her there. She did not act in films after that. Nachimuthu did not permit her to.

After narrating the story, Chinnappa said, 'Nair, you know that most of the leaders in Tamil Nadu have such "small houses". That does not create any scandal. It won't work here. Tamilians will in all probability be disappointed if their particular leader did not have such an arrangement. In short, Nair, this file is a damp squib. Thoroughly useless!'

'But Boss, that thirty-eight lakh...'

'How do we prove that definitely? One can create a noise. Call for an enquiry. Do you think Gopikrishnan will admit to this in open court? The opposing side will tear him to bits. If a crime had been committed, he would be branded as a party to it. Would he be ready to destroy his own career like that? No. He'll certainly back out.'

'Boss, shall we ask Arunagiri for his opinion?'

'Oh yes! He had asked us to meet him and give him the gist of it in person.'

When he heard about the file, Arunagiri said, 'Forget about this file. I'll play the political game. You get the ashram ready as soon as possible.'

Thirty-four

It was November.

The main building of the ashram complex was ready. It was a huge building. From a distance it reminded the viewer of the gopuras of the Meenakshi temple at Madurai. The architect had used marble and pink sandstone from Rajasthan and unpolished granite artistically. The walls were lined with carved rosewood panels with slivers of Belgian glass reflecting the light from the chandeliers. Beautiful woollen carpets lined the floor. Antique furniture, which was not shadowed by the least bit of modern vulgarity, was placed tastefully in the rooms. Extra care was taken with the construction of Vedanji's bedroom and the prayer hall. The floor of the bedroom had alternating strips of sandalwood and ivory. The walls of the attached bathroom had glazed tiles and golden aluminium sheets vying for attention. The bed had two dancing peacocks on the headboard and the footboard. Blue gems glittered in the carved feathers. The three-foot high platform in the prayer hall was in the shape of an open lotus. When Vedanji sat there, the devotees could sit on the floor in front of him. There was place for a hundred and fifty people in the hall. There was a mike placed on the platform. And speakers all over the compound of the ashram. Thus the devotees who could not gain entry into the prayer hall could also take part in the prayers. The meditation centre was beyond the prayer hall. This room would be a part of the area set apart for Vedanji's exclusive use. The other bedrooms were beyond the meditation centre. The dining hall and the kitchen lay in the building behind this structure.

The architect spoke to Chinnappa and Madhavan Nair, who had gone there to take a look at the building, 'This site is twenty-five acres. So far we have used only about an acre of land for the building, car park and a small garden. We have to enclose the whole twenty-five acres with a wall. We can convert two acres into a small meditation grove. And ... if there is no problem about the funds, we could go ahead with the rest of the construction ...'

'Funds are not a problem. You go ahead. Make it fast, though!' Chinnappa said.

Surekha and Rangarajan also came to see the ashram. When they left the ashram, Surekha asked Chinnappa, 'Shouldn't we show the place to Vedanji?'

'You ask Vedanji about it.'

When Surekha asked Vedanji about it, he did not seem particularly interested. He said, 'Why should I see it now?'

Chinnappa went to see Arunagiri and held forth on the beauties of the ashram, 'Aruna, you should see it!'

'You saw it, Chinnu! That is enough for the moment. It would be better for me to stay in the background for a while.'

In the meantime, Rangarajan had written a book in Tamil about Vedanji. The book was full of stories of miracles performed by Vedanji and declared that he was the incarnation for whom this century had been waiting.

Surekha read the manuscript carefully. She congratulated Rangarajan, 'It is really impressive!'

'Madam, should we show this to Vedanji? If you could read it out to him ...'

'Sorry, Rangan! I can't do that. Vedan still behaves as though he is not involved.'

'Isn't that just the way you feel, madam?'

'Perhaps. If it all turns out to be just a misunderstanding on my part, I shall be the happiest person around.'

'I want some advice from you.'

'What is it?'

'Boss says that I should show this manuscript to Minnal Babu who writes in *Agastyar*. Do you think I should? Suppose he corrects it and makes a mess of it?'

'Rangan, I think you should do what Boss says. We can always accept any good suggestion that Babu gives and ignore the rest. Anyway, we must get it printed at the Agastyar Press. They do a very good job there.'

'They had better! The print order is for one lakh copies.'

Three or four days later, Nina Hyde rang up Surekha from London. She had finished writing the book. Could she send the typescript to Surekha for her approval?

Surekha said, 'No need to do that Nina. I know that you would have written an excellent book. I can't improve on it. Give the typescript to the publishers. Rex and Stout, isn't it?'

❖

Arunagiri remembered what the prime minister had said at the dinner at the Bangalore Raj Bhavan.

The climate in the South will change totally after the winter session. Before that, my political secretary will come and meet you. He will brief you. Arunagiriji, be ready!

The month of November had come. And three weeks had passed. There was no message from Delhi.

Arunagiri paced the room as though he had been caged. He suddenly thought, why didn't he go and meet Vedanji?

Though he was reluctant to admit it openly, wasn't it a fact that like Chinnappa he too had faith in Vedanji's powers? When he had seen him for the first time in September, Vedanji had declared that he, Arunagiri, would be the next chief minister of Tamil Nadu. He had even announced the exact time when Nachimuthu would be thrown out of power. If he could get a further assurance on the prediction made, then he could wait in peace.

Why not go to Poes Garden?

Would Chinnappa laugh at him? Arunagiri who had been

reluctant to visit the ashram was now seeking Vedanji's blessings. Even if he did not say so openly, Chinnappa's expression would say so. Never mind. He was not an agnostic. He was the person who had first mooted the idea of building an ashram.

His mind cleared of doubts, Arunagiri telephoned Chinnappa, 'Chinnu, I want to come over in the evening. I want to meet Vedanji.'

Arunagiri reached Chinnappa's bungalow without any escort. Chinnappa and Vedanji were sitting in the drawing room. Chinnappa got up when he saw Arunagiri. Vedanji did not move from his seat. Arunagiri stood respectfully before Vedanji. Vedanji lifted his left hand in blessing. The sixth finger glowed.

'Sit down,' Vedanji said.

Chinnappa felt that Arunagiri had given up all pride and ego on this visit. He had sat near Vedanji respectfully.

What should he say...how should he say it...Arunagiri wondered. Finally, he started speaking, 'The ashram building is complete. You would have been told about it.'

'Yes.'

'Did you see it?'

'Did you see it?' Vedanji asked.

'No.'

'I too have not seen it. Why should I see it now? Let the time come,' Vedanji smiled.

When Arunagiri struggled to continue the conversation, Chinnappa intervened, 'Why don't we have a drink now?'

'Chinnu...you know, I don't normally drink.'

Vedanji laughed, 'I insist. Have a drink. I'll join you. I wish to speak to you after that.'

Chinnappa moved towards the sideboard. The drinks were served. Arunagiri and Chinnappa were swirling the liquid in their glasses. In the meantime, Vedanji had poured his third drink.

He shut his eyes and asked, 'Arunagiri, do you have faith in me?'

'Yes, I do. That is why I came today.'

Vedanji opened his eyes and shook his sixth finger. When the finger looked like a flame, he said, 'Why do you carry these doubts with you? Everything will work out as you wish. All the circumstances are in your favour. Oh right! The messenger from the North has not come. Don't worry. The messenger will come within three days. The one who comes will not be the servant of the Northern emperor. He will be your servant. He will bring the message of the emperor.'

Vedanji's eyes closed. As he leaned back in the chair the glow of the sixth finger stopped.

❖

Two days later, as he sat at the party headquarters, Parliament member Maniappan came to meet Arunagiri.

'Maniappan, why are you here? The Parliament is in session...'

'I'll tell you, thalaivar, my leader,' Maniappan was all excited. 'You won't believe me, but it actually happened.'

'Tell me what happened!' Arunagiri was impatient.

'The PM sends for me, an ordinary junior MP. I present myself at the Race Course Road. PM tells me, "I wish to see Arunagiri immediately." I ask him when and where.'

'And what did he say? Speak clearly.'

'The day after tomorrow. At 4:30 p.m.'

'You haven't mentioned this to anyone, have you?'

'Only to Gopikrishnan.'

'That's not a problem, he's our man. But let me warn you... No one else should hear about this.'

Arunagiri reached Delhi. With Maniappan.

When he met the prime minister at the appointed time, he received a very warm welcome.

The prime minister spoke openly, 'Arunagiriji, we had planned a dinner at the Madras Raj Bhavan. That may take place sooner than we expected. Let me ask you something? Could you bring a no-confidence motion against Nachimuthu? My party will abstain. What happens then? What is the pitch? What is the arithmetic? Tell me.'

'Even if your party does not support him sir, he can manage to hold on with a majority of four votes.'

'Just four people! Can't you manage four people?'

'I'll try.'

'Would it be possible to do it without the Centre dismissing Nachimuthu? That is the way I would prefer to do it. If a no-confidence motion is passed, the Centre is on strong ground. Still...if it is impossible to pass the no-confidence motion, we'll use the option of dismissal. You must start an agitation to set the stage for all this. There are plenty of issues, aren't there? The CBI has given a very comprehensive report against Nachimuthu. I have no problems with that report being leaked.'

Arunagiri fired the first salvo of the agitation as soon as he reached Madras.

Tamil Nadu bandh.

Road blockade.

The justification for all this was the allegations that were made against Nachimuthu. Most newspapers, local and national, printed news that favoured the agitation led by Arunagiri.

The agitation turned violent in some places. Buses were burnt. There was stone-pelting and even stabbings. People flowed in huge streams to take part in the great meeting that was called by Arunagiri at the Marina beach. The police tried to block a procession that moved through Anna Salai. When people broke the barricades and moved forward, there was police firing. Eight people died.

Tamil Nadu was in turmoil.

Arunagiri demanded a judicial probe into the police firing. The police officers who were responsible for the killings in Anna Salai should be suspended right away. That was not enough. The state assembly had to meet immediately. The people would not put up with the rule of Nachimuthu any longer.

Arunagiri roared from many platforms, 'Does Nachimuthu have the courage to call the assembly into session immediately? Does he have the guts to face a no-confidence motion?'

Nachimuthu responded: there were no plans for a judicial probe. Why should the police officers who were performing their duty be victimized? Impossible. The assembly would be convened as scheduled earlier. As for the no-confidence motion, he would see to it when it came up.

Another idea occurred to Madhavan Nair during the days of strife. Why not use Vasanthamalli, a character in Gopikrishnan's secret file? It should be possible to cook up a sex scandal connecting her and Nachimuthu. Wouldn't a sex scandal be helpful to Arunagiri at this juncture? Thirty-eight lakh and a chinna veedu or small house may not be much of a sensation. But a proper sex scandal... Surely that would have a different dimension.

How could they do that?

The brain of the snake skin exporter started working. Vasanthamalli had to be brought to Madras. That would be step number one.

Suppose she managed to meet Nachimuthu? Suppose Nachimuthu and Vasantha were caught in a 'compromising position' in the bedroom. Suppose someone managed to photograph them. And the photo came out in the yellow papers?

Oh! It was a very far-fetched idea...

Madhavan Nair exercised his brain. Finally he decided: let the first step be completed. Further plans could be made after that.

Nachimuthu had made Vasanthamalli his mistress when she was shining as a superstar. She had not acted in films after that. Perhaps Nachimuthu forbade her from acting. She probably still desired to return to the silver screen. Why not go to Pondicherry in the guise of a film producer? What was wrong with making an attempt? Even Chinnappa need not know for the time being.

Madhavan Nair set out on his mission.

It was not difficult to locate Vasanthamalli's bungalow. Madhavan Nair got out from his air-conditioned Contessa and asked the chowkidar who stood on the veranda, 'Is Vasanthamalli Amma at home?'

'Who are you, sir?'

'I'm film producer Sivasankaran. Go in and tell her I would like to meet her.'

The chowkidar went in. Vasanthamalli appeared within five minutes. Madhavan Nair was taken aback by her beauty.

She invited him in, 'Good morning, sir. Please come in.'

'Good morning. I'm Sivasankaran, a Malayali film producer.'

They had entered a beautifully appointed drawing room by this time.

Madhavan Nair did not waste any time in getting to the purpose of his visit, 'I'm Sivasankaran. I'm planning a multi-crore project. The film will be made in Tamil first, and then there'll be a remake in Hindi. I want you to act as the heroine in both the films. Though you have been away from the field for some time now, people remember your name and your glamour. They desire to see you again, wait to see you again. Why shouldn't I exploit that situation – to our mutual advantage?'

Vasanthamalli's face glowed. Madhavan Nair was convinced that she was rather innocent. She spoke haltingly, 'Acting is my life, sir! I had to leave the field due to some peculiar circumstances. I'm grateful for your offer. I would like to act in your films, but there are some problems. Will this work? I don't feel very confident.'

Madhavan Nair patted her on her shoulder and consoled her, 'Vasantha, I know everything. The chief minister told you that you must not act...and so you stopped acting. That's what you're saying, isn't it?'

'How do you know all this, sir?'

'Vasantha, it is common knowledge. Let me suggest something. You go to the chief minister and ask him for permission to act in my films. He is a generous man. If I am lucky...yes, I am lucky, Vasanatha, he will give his permission.'

The conversation continued for some time.

Finally, Vasanthamalli said, surprising Madhavan Nair with her naiveté, 'I trust you. I'll come with you. If he does not give his permission, you have to get me back here, without anyone else coming to know of it. If he does permit me to act...Oh my god!, I'll be a star again, won't I?'

It was 5 o'clock in the evening when Madhavan Nair reached the bungalow on Guruswami Road. He was losing confidence in his plan by then.

Vasanthamalli meets with Nachimuthu. She tells him about the film. He either permits her to act again. Or he does not give her permission. Vasanthamalli returns to Pondicherry. It was his responsibility to see that she reached there safely. There was not much chance of a sex scandal. I have been stupid...Madhavan Nair told himself a number of times. How could I get such an idiotic idea!

Another danger occurred to him. If Nachimuthu gave her permission to act in the film, Vasanthamalli would not leave him alone. When she realizes that the film producer named Sivasankaran was actually Madhavan Nair, the managing director of Bengal Bay Company...Oh my god! The scandal will be about me then...And from me, it will spread to Chinnappa and from there to Arunagiri...

What could he do?

Let whatever happen, happen.

What did happen was entirely unexpected. It was like this. At 6 o'clock in the evening, Vasanthamalli got dressed and came to Madhavan Nair. She said that she would meet the chief minister that very evening. She needed a taxi. But before that, would he dial the chief minister's residence for her? She would talk to Vadivelu, the chief minister's PA.

Madhavan Nair tried the general number of the chief minister's residence. It was constantly engaged. Finally, they got through to one Ponnayyan, and through him, to Vadivelu.

Madhavan Nair handed the telephone over to Vasanthamalli and went to the next room to listen in on the parallel telephone. He had to hear what was said.

'Vadivelu, this is me, Vasanthamalli.'

'Where are you speaking from?'

'From here, Madras.'

'When did you come?'

'A little while ago.'

'What's the matter?'

'I need to see him.'

'It's not possible, Vasantha. He's very busy. There are so many visitors... And there's also a press conference.'

'But I have to see him, today itself.'

'Vasantha, don't talk like a child. It is impossible!'

'Who are you to stop me from seeing him?' Vasantha's voice rose.

'Don't you know who I am? Are you trying tricks on me?' Vadivelu's voice was even louder.

Vasanthamalli replaced the receiver on the cradle. She started crying.

Madhavan Nair came back into the room and asked her, 'What's the matter, why are you crying?'

She controlled her tears and said, 'Nothing. Could you do me a favour... get me a taxi.'

Madhavan Nair did not see Vasanthamalli, who departed for the chief minister's house by taxi, ever again.

There was news in the papers the next day.

During the press conference at the chief minister's residence, a young woman broke into the hall. The security staff followed her in and caught hold of her. When some of the newsmen heard her scream and came outside, they saw the young woman lying unconscious on the road outside the gate. She was burnt badly on the neck and face. She was removed immediately to the Apollo Hospital. The doctors there said that someone had poured acid over her.

The papers recovered from the handbag that lay open near where she had fallen showed that the young woman was the film star Vasanthamalli.

Some newspapers had printed two photographs along with

the news – Vasanthamalli's face and the burnt face of the young woman.

The newspapers announced the next day – Vasanthamalli died from burns.

A local newspaper known for sensationalizing news asked: Who killed Vasanthamalli? Why had she come to the chief minister's residence? Why did an old love story end so tragically?

Vasanthamalli's death strengthened the agitation against Nachimuthu. Women's organizations took out processions and held protest meetings.

Silent marches holding up banners said, 'Will the murderer Nachimuthu convene the assembly?'

Finally, the legislative assembly was convened.

Arunagiri moved the no-confidence motion. The prime minister's party abstained from voting. Arunagiri had managed to win over five MLAs earlier. The no-confidence motion was passed by a narrow majority.

Tamil Nadu came under President's rule.

There were murmurs that the action of the President in dissolving the assembly had not been correct. No one really bothered. People were not interested in the arguments of the intellectuals who dissected the Constitution minutely and argued about the finer points.

Thirty-five

Poes Garden.

Arunagiri was in a good mood when he invited Chinnappa, Madhavan Nair and Surekha, who sat before him to express their views.

'So what Vedanji predicted came true. That rascal Nachimuthu is out. We should not delay introducing Vedanji to the world. The ashram must become famous before the elections take place. What are the preliminary steps we need to take immediately? Please say what you feel without hesitation.'

Chinnappa said, 'There's a lot to be done. A trust has to be formed. The ashram has to be controlled by this trust. It's better that we limit the number of members on the board of trustees. All the money we have collected so far for the ashram should be handed over to the trust. I'm making a special contribution to the trust fund – twenty-five lakh rupees. The whole ashram complex should be completed within a year. What else do we have to decide?'

'The structure of the trust. Who should be the chairman?'

'Aruna, if everyone agrees, I shall become the chairman of the trust. I say this in spite of knowing that you are the best qualified for the position. However, you'll be chief minister within six or seven months. It would be difficult to be the chief minister and the head of a religious trust at the same time. One shouldn't give scope for embarrassing situations...'

'Right, Chinnu! You must be the chairman. My place is in the background. I'll be the actor who never appears on the stage. Madhavan Nair and Surekha will be members of the trust. What do you say?'

'Who'll be the secretary and the treasurer?' Chinnappa asked.

'Let Surekha do that,' Madhavan Nair said.

'Fine,' said Arunagiri. 'What other points do we have to discuss?'

'A name...'

'Name? I don't understand, Chinnu.'

'I've thought of something. Why don't we call Vedanji, Vedan Baba? It seems more impressive, don't you think?'

Arunagiri waited for the others to give their opinion.

Surekha said, 'Vedan Baba! It has a nice ring. Shall we wait for Vedanji's approval to take the decision?'

'Right! That's sensible,' Arunagiri agreed.

'The next thing to be decided is Vedan Baba's costume. Every godman needs a uniform – if you'll pardon the expression. Let's hear what Nair thinks about it.'

'Loose kurta, dhoti and a turban. All in saffron.'

'No, that won't do,' Surekha said.

'What's your suggestion?'

'Boss, I've been thinking about this for a while. The colour saffron and kurta and turban are very common. We should have something different. We have to consider Vedan Baba's age and his form. He is young, handsome. There should be a touch of glamour. I've designed a dress for him.'

'Really?' Arunagiri expressed surprise.

'Yes, sir. I've also got Vedan Baba's approval for the dress.'

Chinnappa asked with the enthusiasm of a child, 'What's the design? What colour?'

'White silk upper garment, tight across the chest and loose below the waist. A sort of flowing tunic. Trousers of white silk. A blood red cloth around the waist, and a white silk cap with a red border. In the middle of the cap, there should be a large diamond.'

Chinnappa clapped his hands, 'Sura, that's fantastic! You said you'd already got Vedan Baba's approval. So that's that.'

'Let's take up the most important matter now, Chinnu! When should the inauguration be? That is, when do we instal Vedan Baba in his ashram?'

'Let Vedan Baba decide that.'

'All right! There's only one thing. It must happen before the end of January. Gopikrishnan had called me. The PM is coming in January to meet the Kanchi Swami. The date has not been fixed. I've been thinking. If we could get the prime minister to participate in the inauguration of the ashram…Well, it is just wishful thinking. It need not happen.'

'Of course it will happen. Why should it not? The only thing is that Vedan Baba should think it should happen.'

As the discussion continued in the drawing room of the bungalow, Vedaraman reached there unexpectedly.

Everyone stood up when they saw Vedan.

Vedaraman began with a big smile, 'Product launch, right? Who'd said it earlier – was it Chinnappa, or did I say it myself? That I should be launched as a new product in the market of devotion with great fanfare. Though I didn't listen to your discussion, I know what you said. You have decided that I shall be Vedan Baba. Surekha has told you about my costume. I'd agreed to that earlier. The inauguration will take place in January, on full moon day. Don't worry, the Northern emperor will participate. Arunagiri, you must invite him personally. You seem to have forgotten some things, though.'

'What is it, Baba?' Chinnappa asked.

'Has the book written by Rangan been printed?'

'It shall be done immediately, Baba!'

'That has to be distributed by the beginning of January. Nina's English version should also be ready by then. Something else…Chinnappa, isn't it necessary to compose a few bhajans about me?'

'It shall be done, Baba.'

'The ashram should have its own orchestra.'

'That will be arranged.'

'Murugappan and Nina must be here by the end of December.'

'Yes, Baba!'

Vedan Baba looked at everyone with eyes filled with mercy. Suddenly, he took Surekha's hand and said, 'Sura, I want to do something.'

'What is it, Baba?'

'I want to see my ashram...now. You shall be the guide.'

Surekha was thrilled. She touched Vedan Baba's feet and said, 'I've been blessed, Baba.'

Chinnappa murmured, 'I'll come with you.'

'No, no. I shall not trouble the chairman of the trust just now,' Vedan Baba smiled. 'Only the secretary need come. We need a car.'

'You can take my car, Baba!' Arunagiri said.

'I'll ask for it, Arunagiri when you are chief minister. A taxi would be enough for now.'

The taxi reached Thiruvanmiyur. Surekha showed Vedan Baba every room in the ashram.

'Do you like it Baba?'

'Beautiful. Fantastic!'

Surekha touched Vedan Baba's right hand and then threaded her left through it.

'Come, don't you want to see the Baba's bedroom?'

When he saw the floor laid with strips of sandalwood and ivory and the bed with its dancing peacocks, Vedan Baba pulled Surekha closer and murmured, 'Sura, somehow, I've started feeling nervous.'

'How can you, the Baba, become nervous?'

'Never mind. When I become the Baba and am installed in this building, will all of you be less acessible to me?'

'I shall not, Baba!'

'Do you feel that I've been distant from you in the past few weeks?'

Instead of answering the question, Surekha made Vedan Baba sit on the bed.

'What is it, Sura?'

'Nothing, Baba.'

'Am I Vedan or Baba to you?'

She sighed and stayed quiet.

'What is it, Sura?'

'Now...I too feel as though I've lost my courage.'

'That's good. Tell me, am I Vedan or Baba?'

Surekha cupped Vedaraman's face with her palms and said, 'Vedan, my pet.'

'Sura, you are my mother!'

'No, I'm your lover!' She sat next to Vedan and embraced him.

Arunagiri reached Delhi before Christmas. The prime minister gave him half an hour's time. His attitude was very friendly. 'Arunagiriji, we are crafting a new chapter. Forget the old stories. I am well aware that my party does not have roots in Tamil Nadu and that we'll never be able to rule there by ourselves. I only want a government there that does not fight with the Centre all the time and that is not a threat to the integrity of India. When I decided to support Nachimuthu, that was all I thought of. What to do! He bit the hand that fed him. Let that not happen again!'

'Prime minister, you can trust me one hundred per cent.'

'I know, Arunagiriji. That's why I talk so freely. I do not want the state to continue to be under President's rule. According to intelligence reports, my party will retain its present seats in the assembly. Nachimuthu will face a loss of at least thirty per cent. Even if all this works out, you may not get absolute majority. Still, you will be able to form a ministry. My party will support your ministry.'

'Thank you, prime minister.'

'I'm coming to the South in January. To meet the Kanchi Seer. If possible I shall come to Madras as well.'

When he remembered what Vedan Baba had said, Arunagiri

found the courage to say, 'You must come to Madras. If it is on the full moon day, we shall be blessed.'

'Full moon day? What's special about the full moon day?'

Arunagiri spoke about Vedan Baba with all the enthusiasm of a true devotee. And about the planned inauguration of the ashram on the full moon day.

The prime minister could not help laughing. 'This is wonderful. I thought you were an atheist. When did you start believing in babas?'

'I do have faith. Just that I don't have the courage to make that faith public.'

The prime minister turned serious. 'Why should you be afraid to make your faith public, Arunagiriji? Can you dismiss the soul of India? We have always had faith in gods and gurus. I go to meet the heads of mathas (monasteries) and seers and bow before them. Their blessing is important to me. Columnists and cartoonists make fun of me for this. But I don't care. I would like to know more about Vedan Baba. You said his sixth finger glows. That certainly is a miracle. Let me see. You said full moon day, didn't you? I may be able to make it.'

As soon as he reached Madras, Arunagiri rang up Chinnappa, 'Chinnu, the Delhi emperor has agreed.'

❖

Chinnappa, Madhavan Nair and Surekha were very busy. Everything had to go off well. There should not be any flaws, even in small matters. It was almost confirmed that the prime minister would take part in the inauguration ceremony. There would be massive publicity. There had to be massive publicity. The function should be grand, unforgettable.

Minnal Babu of the Agasthyar Press did not make many changes in the book written by Rangarajan. What he did mainly was to write a foreword in poetic language. The printing was done in two weeks – one lakh copies. They had fixed the price of the book at twenty-five rupees. But the plan was to distribute it free and only in Madras. That would be better for impact.

The bhajans were written by Minnal Babu. He also arranged for a choir and an orchestra for the ashram. Murugappan and Nina reached Poes Garden. Nina had brought a hundred copies of the book published by Rex and Stout. The book was titled, *The Most Perfect Master*.

Nina asked Surekha, 'How has the book come out?'

'The production quality is great.'

Murugappan presented Arunagiri with copies of the book.

Arunagiri instructed Murugappan, 'Two copies should be sent to the prime minister, with my compliments. Two copies should go to Gopikrishnan as well. Oh yes, send the copies for the prime minister to Maniappan. Let him meet the PM and present the copies in person.'

The preparations were in full swing. Surekha and Nina checked and rechecked every small detail. They grew closer in the process.

'Nina, the fact that you're here gives me confidence...'

'Sura, you are the guide and leader. I'm just a foot soldier.'

They formed a mutual admiration society.

Surekha was the one who suggested that Vedan Baba should pose for a photo session. The silk costume and headgear had reached the ashram from Flamingo Outfitters.

'Capital idea!' Nina said. 'Sura, pictures are more important than books and other written things. We must flood the city with posters of Vedan Baba.'

Full moon fell on the 20th of January.

When the 10th passed with no word from Delhi, Arunagiri's blood pressure started rising. Would the prime minister stay away? He had reminded the PMO twice through Maniappan, but had not got a firm and positive reply.

Arunagiri rang up Chinnappa from the party office, 'Chinnu, I'm getting worried.'

'Come and meet Vedan Baba. You'll get peace of mind.'

'I'll come immediately.'

It was noon when Arunagiri reached Poes Garden.

'Where is Vedan Baba?'

'He'll be here soon.'

They waited in the drawing room.

When Vedan Baba entered the room, Arunagiri and Chinnappa stood up with respectful gazes. This was not the Vedanji they'd seen earlier. This was the real Vedan Baba. He was clad in white silk clothes with a red waistband and a turban with a diamond in its centre.

Vedan Baba was not alone. Surekha and Nina accompanied him. Chinnappa touched Vedan Baba's feet. After hesitating for a moment, Arunagiri also did the same.

Vedan Baba laughed, 'Aruna, you're still a doubter, aren't you? You haven't started believing in me yet.'

Arunagiri was rather embarrassed, 'Baba, please don't get me wrong. To begin with, I...No, I don't want to say it. Today, now, I have full faith in you.'

Vedan Baba lifted his hand. The sixth finger was glowing. 'Look Aruna, you always have my blessings. You can be sure of that. The Northern emperor will come to the inauguration ceremony of our ashram. You'll receive the messengers tomorrow evening.'

And that is what happened. The next day Gopikrishnan and Maniappan reached Madras from Delhi. They informed Arunagiri that the prime minister would visit the Kanchi seer and reach Madras on the day of the full moon. The inauguration of the ashram had to be at 4 o'clock in the evening. The prime minister would fly to Delhi at 6 o'clock.

Thirty-six

After Gopikrishnan and Maniappan had come and gone, Arunagiri got an official communication from the PMO. There was also a semi-official letter from the secretary to the prime minister, 'Dear Arunagiriji, please let us have a write-up on Vedan Baba and the ashram.'

Arunagiri rang up the secretary. The write-up would be sent immediately, and also, the books on Vedan Baba. Party MP Maniappan would give them personally to the PMO.

When the Raj Bhavan and the office of the Advisers to the Governor received information on the prime minister's visit, the state government also woke up. The chief secretary came to meet Chinnappa. What should the government do to ensure the success of the function?

Chinnappa said that no particular help was needed. If more buses could run towards Thiruvanmiyur, it would be of help.

The chief secretary said that he would see to it. After discussing a few details about the security arrangements, he departed.

One lakh copies of the Tamil book about Vedan Baba were distributed in the city before the 10th of January. It was Rangarajan who suggested that there should be a press conference. Vedan Baba should also be present.

A press conference was a good idea, but Nina and Surekha were insistent that Vedan Baba should not be present. It was important to preserve the mystique of Vedan Baba. It would be stupid to throw Vedan Baba to the press and make him face their absurd questions. Wouldn't it be better to arrange a release for Nina's book instead? It could be held at Taj Coromandel. The press could be invited. If they asked her questions, that would be all to the good. They could arrange cocktails and dinner after that.

And that is what happened.

Nina, Surekha and Rangarajan organized the book release function. It was Nina who held the stage. Rangarajan distributed the hand-out that Nina had prepared in advance. Nina gave the members of the press autographed copies of the book. She also claimed that Vedan Baba had become a cult figure in England and America.

She answered the questions of the press cleverly.

'Why do you White people run after these babas and godmen?'

'The West is a spiritual desert. It is not surprising that we come here to this sacred land in search of spiritual gangajal.'

'The prime minister is coming to the inauguration of the ashram. Is he a devotee of the Baba?'

'You know better than me that your prime minister is a strong administrator who has no qualms about offering obeisance to spiritual gurus.'

Rangarajan, who was nervous that Nina might lose her footing if the question and answer session went on too long, intervened, 'Now, may I suggest that we adjourn for cocktails?'

One of the reporters asked, 'Doesn't Vedan Baba oppose drinking?'

Nina's reply made everyone laugh. 'Don't measure Vedan Baba with the measuring scales of our lives. These questions occur to us only when we wear materialism and atheism like medals on our chest. Baba is highly evolved. He is a living god. Nothing affects him. We have not enquired whether the Baba drinks alcohol or not. To him, the lava that flows from a volcano, the fuel from an atomic reactor and the highly dangerous dirty water of your Koovam canal are the same. It is all under his control. My dear friend, do you have the courage to pull down your trousers and exhibit your nudity to this gathering? I'm sure you don't. And yet the sanyasis, the naked sages of your land walk everywhere without any kind of covering. How can they do it? They can, because to them, all parts of their body are under their control. I'm not trying to be salacious, just making a point.'

There was loud laughter and clapping from the audience.

As the reporter who had asked the mischievous question stood embarrassed, Nina went up to him and murmured, 'Hey, did I hurt you? Come, let's have a drink.'

It was late when the cocktails and dinner ended.

The major English newspapers carried big headlines on the next day: 'Nina Hyde does a spiritual striptease'; 'Vedan Baba, the new cult figure'.

The arrangements for the inauguration were completed before 18th January. The background of the twelve-foot high stage was a curtain with alternating broad stripes of saffron and gold. Two rows of gilt-covered chairs were lined up on the stage. Four of the chairs in the first row were larger than the others. These were for Vedan Baba, the prime minister, the Governor and Arunagiri. A red carpet with a thick pile was spread on the stage. Twelve mikes were placed above the podium for the speakers. A black and gold platform with six sides extended from a corner of the stage on the support of cantilevers. This was meant for the choir. Just below this, at a lower level, there was the orchestra pit.

The steps that were placed for the VVIPs to climb on the stage had carved statues on either side. The flexible ceiling over the stage had colours reminiscent of Arunagiri's party's colours.

Fifty yards on all sides of the stage were left vacant for security reasons. This area was protected by barricades. There were separate enclosures for men and women.

Chinnappa, Madhavan Nair, Rangarajan, Surekha and Nina walked around, looking at everything and discussing the unsorted issues. Where should the Doordarsan crew be positioned? Would the seating arrangements for the press be sufficient? If garlands of flowers were hung up in the afternoon, would they wilt by the evening? Should there be more first-aid posts? What would happen if a large number of people came much before the meeting started? Shouldn't they be provided with drinking water? Shouldn't some arrangement be made for its distribution?

'Don't worry, Boss. All will be well!' Madhavan Nair told Chinnappa.

'I know, Nair! Why should I worry when Vedan Baba's blessings protect us?'

January 20th came. This was a day when all roads led to Thiruvanmiyur.

People gathered at the meeting place before noon. By 2 o'clock the security personnel started controlling the crowds. By three, the choir had started singing.

Even before that, Vedan Baba had reached the ashram in a car with tinted glasses.

When it was five to four, the motorcade of the prime minister appeared.

The prime minister, the Governor and Arunagiri sat on three of the four big chairs in the first row on the stage. When Vedan Baba, clad in white with the red waistband, white turban with the huge diamond, was led to the stage by Chinnappa, Surekha, Nina and Murugappan, everyone – including the prime minister – stood up and folded their hands.

The meeting started after prayers. Arunagiri delivered the welcome address. He praised the prime minister to the skies, 'India remains united because of great political leaders like our prime ministers and our spiritual preceptors who help us to overcome difficulties. They are part of a long chain. Vedan Baba is the latest link in that chain and its glory. All of us are insignificant before the Baba. What do we know? We know nothing. As for the Baba, he knows everything. I have no doubts at all that his presence in our state will bring prosperity and glory. Vazhga Vedan Baba! Long live Vedan Baba!'

Countless voices echoed, 'Vazhga Vedan Baba!'

The prime minister's inaugural speech went on for more than half an hour. He waxed eloquent on the spiritual tradition of India. 'This sacred land has always been a guide to the rest of the world. Our sages were men of wisdom who knew everything. Nothing that was discovered thereafter is not recorded in the writings of these sages. Nothing that was not already discovered by them will ever be found anywhere. Other countries seek light and energy from this eternal lighthouse. We become conscious of our ancient greatness only when we read books written by outsiders. We have forgotten ourselves.

'We're immersed in darkness, in so deep a sleep that we are not conscious at all. This sad state of things has to change. It will change. What gives us that hope is the emergence of great preceptors in our midst, the new babas. Vedan Baba is a boon given to us. He's our hope and our shelter. I have no doubt that I have this opportunity to inaugurate this ashram due to the good deeds of some past life. I've always been a seeker of truth, a pilgrim in search of light. I hope I have the good fortune to keep coming here and to bow before the sacred feet of Vedan Baba.'

The prime minister suddenly bent down. As though unaware of his surroundings, he fell at Vedan Baba's feet.

'Vedan Baba vazhga!' the people screamed.

Vedan Baba lifted up the prime minister and seated him on the chair.

Vedan Baba moved forward on the stage and blessed the audience with both hands extended. The sixth finger started glowing. Though it was broad daylight, everyone on the stage could see that light clearly.

The prime minister, the Governor, Chinnappa and Arunagiri folded their hands.

Vedan Baba started talking. There was no order in his words. And yet, it thrilled the listeners.

'My dear people, our beloved prime minister rules over the Indian subcontinent. He strives ceaselessly for the welfare of millions of people. I, my dear people, rule over your hearts.

'You must attain your ambitions in this life. And then you must reach the ultimate bliss. It is natural that human beings strive for pleasure. I see nothing wrong in people trying to attain various types of worldly pleasures. But after you have enjoyed those pleasures, you must grow and get detached from them. You must let the curiosity about the nature of the world, the truth of the universe, awaken. Your hearts and souls must seek shelter in the universal soul. Treat pleasure and sorrow, profit and loss, victory and defeat, with equanimity; do what life puts before you as your duty. You will never be a sinner.

'Dedicate all your deeds to me. Fix your mind on me. I am the perfume of the earth and the light in the fire. Know me to be the eternal source of all wonders of the world.'

Suddenly Vedan Baba jumped down the steps that led from the stage and walked towards the people. As he walked between the enclosures that had been made by bamboo barriers, men, women and children extended their hands to touch Vedan Baba. As they rushed forward, the bamboo barriers broke in places. The police rushed to the spot fearing that the crowd would mob Vedan Baba.

He stopped them saying, 'Please stay away. I don't need your help.'

Vedan Baba lifted his hand and showed them the glowing sixth finger. He put his right hand on the head of some of the people; he shook hands with some of them.

Countless throats shouted, 'Vedan Baba vazhga! Vedan Baba vazhga!'

A middle-aged woman, who was carrying her son in her arms, rushed towards the Baba. She put the boy down at the Baba's feet and cried, 'Bhagwan, Baba, give my son legs! He cannot walk!'

What was happening? People tried to move forward to see better.

Vedan Baba bent down. He patted the boy on his head and shoulder and said, 'Get up, my son!'

When the boy who had been left paralysed by polio stood up without anyone's help, the crowd roared.

The Baba gestured to the boy to follow him.

Vedan Baba started walking towards the stage. The boy took a few steps as though he was a little child just learning to walk. His mother walked behind him. When the boy tripped and fell, the mother tried to lift him. The Baba scolded her, 'Don't touch him. He'll walk!'

With great struggle, suffering a lot of pain, the boy somehow stood up again.

'Come, come after me. Be brave!' Vedan Baba encouraged him.

The boy started walking faster.

People clapped.

When they reached the steps to the stage, Baba stopped. When the boy reached him, Baba lifted him up and hugged him. He carried him up the stage and came to the centre of the stage. Everyone there, including the prime minister, stood up.

Vedan Baba placed the boy into the hands of the prime minister and said, 'You are the emperor of India. I've cured one boy afflicted by polio. That's my strength and my power. But you have great strength and power in another way. You must help the children afflicted by polio in Tamil Nadu and all over India.'

The television cameras moved as if they had gone mad. Klieg lights, old mini bruts, other lights – together they spread the light of a thousand festivals.

Vedan Baba lifted his left hand. The light from the sixth finger made every other light pale.

The prime minister reluctantly kissed the boy and announced, 'Vedan Baba's miracle makes me helpless. I promise to obey his words. The people of Tamil Nadu are dear to me. I declare, I swear on this little boy in my arms, a grant of two crore rupees to eliminate this disease from Tamil Nadu. I request the Governor and his advisers, please see that my promise is not caught up in the red tape of archaic rules and regulations.'

The roar that came from the crowd made the acacia trees in Thiruvanmiyur sway. Bhajans rose to the skies.

Thirty-seven

Vedan Baba was bewitchingly good looking as he sat on the peacock bed and smiled. Surekha, Nina, Chinnappa, Madhavan Nair, Murugappan and Rangarajan, who were all sitting on the sandal floor inlaid with ivory, looked at him with devotion.

Was the tableau a little less impressive because Arunagiri was absent? Arunagiri could not linger. The prime minister had changed his programme at the last minute. He decided that he would stay over in Madras. He was staying at the Raj Bhavan tonight. Dinner was to be with Arunagiri. The prime minister was redeeming a promise given earlier.

The ashram was now empty.

Vedan Baba was going to sleep in this ashram for the first time this auspicious night. This was going to be his permanent abode from tonight.

Chinnappa said, 'Baba, happiness and sorrow are coming in waves in this devotee's heart.'

Vedan Baba took off his turban and kept it beside him. Running his hands through his hair, caressing his moustache, he laughed and asked, 'Sura, Nina, tell me. Why does Chinnappa feel like that?'

Surekha said, 'Baba, all of us feel the same. A mixture of happiness and sorrow.'

Baba asked with a laugh, 'Why is it like that? What is the reason? I demand an explanation. Nina, do you get the hang of what we are saying? Rangan, explain to Nina.'

Rangarajan whispered something in Nina's ear. She touched Baba's feet and started talking, 'Baba, I'll reply to your question. You are omniscient. If you, our living god and master insist on testing us, I shall try to answer. Do you know why we are happy? It is because the world at large has accepted you as a living god. You have proved that the sceptre of the ruler is not the last word in power, that the staff of the sage is more powerful. You showed the prime minister that however many crores of rupees the government spends, it may not be sufficient to wipe the tears of one child. Isn't that enough to make us all happy? As for the sorrow – perhaps Surekha can explain that better than me.'

Vedan Baba's sixth finger glowed. He raised his voice and said, 'I, who was born to remove the sorrows of others, will tell you the reason for the sorrow. Till today, I was your private property. From today I've become public property. Isn't that true? You find it difficult to digest that. You will not be able to play with me as your own toy or to pet me as your own from today. That realization is the cause of your sorrow. So, listen. I'm also sad. I'll tell you about my sorrow. From today, I shall be living here. I have been installed here. Can I laugh openly as I used to, in this place? Your arms were the bars that imprisoned me in a cell of love. When I'm released from that imprisonment, even if that release is inevitable, I feel sorrow.'

Baba sat with his head bent as though he was lost in a vortex of sorrow.

When he started speaking again, his face was calm. His words formed into a small speech with a lot of instructions.

'Chinnappa, I know you'll do everything necessary as the chairman of the trust. Still, let me remind you of a few things. The appointment of security staff should not be delayed. The full complement of kitchen staff should also be appointed immediately. The stage on which today's function took place should become a permanent one. I shall stand on that stage and give darshan to the devotees. Only devotees who form the core of the group shall be admitted to the prayer hall. Once I come to this room and lie on this bed, everyone, even you people who sit before me, should come only if I call you. When I am in the meditation centre no one should come there. The ashram complex should be completed before the month of June according to the plans. Remember, June is an important month. That is the month when Arunagiri will come to power. It is the month when good times will start for Chinnappa, Madhavan Nair and Murugappan. All the cases will be withdrawn. Bengal Bay Company will grow as never before and make unexpected gains. Yes, there's something else. The number of devotees who come here will increase day by day. Important people will come from various countries to meet me. We have just two telephone lines here. That will not do. There should be a mini telephone exchange in this complex. There should be all the conveniences of the electronic era.'

'That shall be arranged,' Chinnappa said.

Rangarajan cleared his throat, 'Baba, shall I bring the gangajal?'

'Yes, why not? We can sit together and drink now. But from tomorrow there shall have to be certain controls here. I don't have to tell you about the false sense of morality that our people possess. People who are willing to accept all counterfeit coins of the world may try to denigrate the value of the real coin too. Why should we give them a chance to do so?' Vedan Baba looked at everyone in turn as though he was seeking their opinion.

'Baba, what you said is true,' Murugappan said humbly.

'Sura, Nina, help Rangan!' Baba instructed. The women left with Rangan.

Baba asked Murugappan, 'When do you plan to return?'

'If the Baba permits, I would like to return to London after a couple of days.'

'I give you permission. What about Nina?'

'Nina wants to stay here for some more time.'

'Good. Murugappan, let Nina stay here for the time being. But remember one thing. The field of endeavour for both of you is the West. You and Nina must be the propagators of my divine mission there.'

'Definitely, Baba!' Murugappan said.

Rangan, Surekha and Nina came back in a mini procession. They carried trays with scotch, soda, cut glass goblets and bowls filled with almonds, pistas and cashewnuts.

When Nina and Surekha started pouring out the scotch, Baba got down from the bed and sat on the floor.

'All of you, sit around me. Hold hands and make a magic circle.'

As they sat like that, Baba murmured, 'This is the perfect circle. Hold up your glasses. Let us break the bonds of logic that tie us. Let us allow our minds to be free!'

Everyone started drinking.

The room became the sanctum of some great temple. Baba became a speaking god.

'Let me tell you some things. Nina and Murugappan will be my ambassadors to the western world, especially the countries of Britain and America. Chinnappa, Madhavan Nair, Rangan and Surekha will serve the same role in this sacred land of India. Of these, it will be Surekha and Rangan who will always be with me. Chinnappa and Madhavan Nair have to win great victories in the material world from this June. It would not be right to tie them to my sixth finger though they are also entitled to the glow of it. Surekha and Rangan should be with me at all times like my shadow. I declare Surekha the mother of this ashram. My mother. I call her "Yogini Mata". Does anyone disagree with that? Keep filling my goblet, again and again. I might write a new commentary to Jaimini's sastra with its 2644 sutras. I might change the entire Indian philosophy. Philosophy...points of view...So many different philosophies and points of view about life, god, karma, this visible world. Each religion has its philosophy, its viewpoint. Don't you know this? I know it. I, who knows, ask you this – does anyone have an objection to calling our Surekha, Yogini Mata?'

All of them turned to Surekha and bowing their heads addressed her in one voice, 'Yogini Mata!' Surekha bent her head as if she were in a trance and untied her hair. She started swaying as though she had been possessed.

Vedan Baba lifted his sixth finger. Its glow seemed to rise to the ceiling. Surekha's movements were gaining speed. She was bending more and more towards the floor. Her nose rubbed against the floor inlaid with ivory. Blood started flowing from the tip of the nose. Vedan Baba dipped his forefinger in the blood and wrote on his silk kurta, 'Om!'

'Be still, Yogini Mata!' When the Baba ordered her, Surekha lay face down at full stretch on the floor.

As everyone sat stunned, the smell of sandalwood paste permeated the air.

Baba said, 'Nina, rub Yogini Mata's back and help her up.'
Nina obeyed.

When she sat up, Surekha's eyes seemed to lack life. Had they changed into glass beads?

Baba started speaking again, 'I'm immutable, eternal. I am the mud and the pot. I am the thread and the cloth. You are tied to this earth, I am free. Do you understand the meaning of all this? Who designed my clothes and got them made? It was Yogini Mata. I'm going to design her clothes. She shall wear saffron. There shall be spots of the colour of breastmilk on the chest. Let all that be. I am at the cusp of a great change. I have still not become a poorna avatar, a complete incarnation. You can still disown me. I'm waiting for that. I'm waiting to see which Judas will turn against me. I wait.'

A heavy silence pervaded the room.

'I'm waiting,' the Baba repeated after some moments.

That small assembly folded their hands and called out, 'We are your slaves, Bhagwan, your slaves, we exist only to follow your orders.'

Vedan Baba wept on hearing this. He lifted both hands as though he were blessing them.

'Sura!' the Baba called.

Surekha, the Yogini Mata, responded. She said, 'I'm the mother, Bhagwan. I'm Yashoda. Come Krishna, come and lie on my lap.'

Baba lay like an obedient child in Surekha's lap.

Thirty-eight

Within a few days, life at the ashram falls into a routine. The choir starts singing bhajans before sunrise.

The Yogini Mata rises from her bed in the room next to the Baba's. Nina wakes up in the room next to that. They bathe and dress.

Rangarajan is up before that, and takes a round of the ashram. He is always the first to wake up and get ready.

The Yogini Mata caresses Vedan Baba to wake him up, who lies asleep on his peacock bed. She kisses him on the head. He touches her breasts and compliments her on her beauty.

'Bath?' Yogini Mata asks.

'Please get everything ready. I'll come now.' Bhagwan slips out of the thin top of his sleeping dress and gets half naked.

Once his morning routine is over, Yogini Mata and Nina lead him to the bathing room. Their hands take over his body. The Bhagwan sits with his eyes closed. They bathe him.

After the bath, the Yogini Mata combs the Bhagwan's hair. Nina sprays him with perfume.

Rangarajan enters, 'Baba, it's time for breakfast.'

'Rangan, I'm ready.'

They sit around the dining table – Vedan Baba, Surekha, Rangan and Nina.

There are many things on the breakfast table.

The Baba smiles, 'Rangan, it is difficult to live as a Bhagwan, don't you think?'

Rangan turns to Nina and says, 'Bhagwan can be very humorous.'

'Rangan, I'm serious. It is difficult to be a Bhagwan.'

This makes everyone laugh.

Baba looks at Surekha, 'Yogini Mata!'

'Please call me Sura once in a while.'

'Oh, that's naughty! Bhagwan winks at everyone. He picks up a bunch of grapes and says, 'I remember that Rangan said these were a very special kind of grapes – Anab shahi. All of you open your mouths; I'll give you prasad.'

Surekha, Nina and Rangan open their mouths. The Baba picks grapes from the bunch and puts one into each of their mouths. All of them shut their mouths. Nina opens her mouth again. The Baba pinches her on her cheeks.

Rangan gets up at this point and goes outside to talk to the security chief of the ashram, Major Chandrasenan.

He comes back and says, 'Bhagwan, there's a big crowd outside. About six thousand people. They're waiting for your darshan.'

'Rangan, it's time I put on my costume, right? Sura, Nina, get me ready.'

The women's fingers help him into the costume that he wears when he appears in public. The turban with its diamond. The white silk costume. Bhagwan stands before the seven-foot mirror adjusting the red waistband.

'Sura, Yogini Mata! Anoint my forehead.'

Surekha marks Baba's forehead with a red sindoor mark. Baba gestures Nina to his side. Now he stands in the middle with Surekha on his right and Nina on his left.

'Rangan, now to the duties.'

The Baba stands on the permanent stage. On either side are Rugmini and Satyabhama. Rangan is perhaps Garuda, and behind Garuda is Major Chandrasenan.

Before them are the thousands who have come for darshan. The people call out, 'Jai Baba! Jai Bhagwan!'

The Baba comes down the steps and moves among the people, among the seekers of peace and the seekers of help. His very presence is like a shower of nectar for them. He blesses everyone, touches a few. He tells the old women gathered, 'Mothers, please bless me. I may be Bhagwan, but you are living goddesses to me.'

The Baba lifts up a small child and looks around. He kisses the child. A leper comes through the crowd and reaches the Baba. He touches the edge of Baba's clothing, lifts it to his eyes for a moment. He cries aloud, 'Bhagwan, I'm a sinner! A terrible sinner! Why did this white disease come to me? Why do people run away when I approach them? I have not knowingly committed any sin, then why am I a sinner? Is this because of the sins of some previous birth? Baba, Bhagwan, even you will not touch me.'

The thousands gathered in the ashram yard hold their breath. What will the Baba do now?

Major Chandrasenan and Rangarajan rush to the Baba. He pushes them aside saying, 'Chandru, Rangan, move aside!'

Then he hugs the leper and speaks to him, 'What is your name, my friend?'

'Chami, Bhagwan!'

'Chami, I'm not the saviour, not Jesus Christ. Your disease is on the outside. The great men of this sacred land of ours are diseased inside. Leprosy that affects the skin can be cured, but the one that affects the soul cannot be cured.'

'Enough, Bhagwan! This is a great blessing for me. You've shown me so much mercy. You are the new incarnation of god!'

Many cars come into the compound. Rangan lowers his voice and tells the Baba, 'Bhagwan, we have to go to the prayer hall. A session for the VIPs has been scheduled.'

The Baba looks at the crowd, waves his hands. The sixth finger glows and the Baba holds it up. He hugs Chami once more. Then he goes back to the stage and from there to the prayer hall with Nina and Surekha.

The Baba sits on the lotus mandap. He talks to the important people, the pillars of society seated before him, 'I don't want to talk about bhakti or devotion today. I want to talk about service. I saw a leper today, I felt his sorrow, I held him to myself. I have taken over his disease. Are you shocked? Why? That man called Chami does not hide his leprosy. He does not wear a three-piece suit and gloves to hide his leprosy. You are important people, rich people. None of you has leprosy that can be seen. But what about your inside? My devotees, there is only one method to cleanse ourselves of the diseases and dirt that hide inside us – the worship of the poorest of the poor. Please do not come and worship me. You need not pour gold and currency notes into the treasuries of the ashram. Devote yourselves to the service of the poor.'

The Baba lifts his sixth finger, and the sixth finger glows.

Nina and Surekha sing, 'Lead, kindly light...'

It is afternoon now. The Baba sits in the meditation centre with the door shut. Rangarajan has arranged gangajal there.

After lunch, the Baba speaks to Surekha, Nina and Rangarajan about the problems of the ashram. What has been the progress of the construction activities? Has the architect given final shape to the landscaping plans including the garden and the fountain? Is Major Chandrasenan paying attention to the training of the security staff, their daily drills, etc.? It might be worthwhile to have a small fire-fighting unit as well.

The discussion lengthens.

And then a little rest.

From five in the evening to seven, there are visits from important people by prior appointment. Chinnappa comes every day. Arunagiri would also come now and then. Madhavan Nair always comes with Chinnappa.

Arunagiri asks, 'Baba, the election will take place in June, won't it? You don't think President's rule will be extended?'

'No. We told you long ago. You will be the chief minister of Tamil Nadu by the end of June.'

'Baba, it is March now. Party work and preparations for the

election takes up all my time. That's why I'm unable to come every day.'

'I understand, Arunagiri.'

Chinnappa speaks, 'Bhagwan, if anything has been left undone, if there is any lacuna in our work, if there is anything more to be done, please tell us.'

The Baba laughs, 'My devotees, where does my strength come from? What is the source of my power? Arunagiri knows. He's a leader. When thousands of people come before him with their heads bent, he becomes a leader of stature. When you love me, when you call out, "Victory to the Baba", I become Baba, I become god. I sometimes call myself "I" and sometimes "We". Both denote myself. When you really look at it, it's all madness, isn't it?'

The Baba looks at Surekha and continues, 'Sura, you are the treasurer and secretary, the Yogini Mata of the ashram and much more. There is the quorum to conduct a trust meeting right now. Arunagiri who will rule Tamil Nadu after June is also with us. Though he is not a member of the trust, Aruna should be aware of the state of health of the ashram at all times. I say this so that all of us can hear: What are the details of the assets and liabilities of the ashram?'

Surekha replies, 'The trust has no liabilities. And the assets are increasing. The nucleus was formed by the twenty-five lakh contributed by Chinnappa sir. Then there is the value of this land. There are large amounts contributed by the prime minister from his secret fund through Gopikrishnan and Maniappan. Businessmen have contributed generously. And the ordinary people have contributed small sums in large numbers. It would come close to twenty crore. Besides, we are expecting a large flow of funds from abroad soon. Nina will explain that.'

Nina explains, 'International divine dialling service! Murugappan has almost completed the arrangements. Needy people from all over the world can dial a number at the ashram. They will hear Baba's taped voice giving counsel and consolation.

Advertisements have already appeared in major newspapers in the West.'

'What did you call it?' Arunagiri asks.

'Dial-a-god!'

'Great!'

Weeks pass. Cricketers and filmstars come to bow before the Baba. Judges and diplomats come. Central ministers come. The number of ordinary people who visit the ashram daily is now between twenty and thirty thousand.

The construction of the ashram complex is almost finished. Beautiful landscaping – this land that had only acacia trees now has a wonderful garden. There are fountains, groves...

A Japanese garden with just white sand and pebbles.

One day at dusk, the Baba evaded everyone's eyes and came to the Japanese garden. He meditated. He thought about his fame and the joys and sorrows of life as a Bhagwan.

They came running – Surekha and Nina, and behind them came Rangan and the Major. They spoke individually and as a group, 'We got scared...'

'Why?' the Baba asked.

'When we couldn't find you, Bhagwan...'

'How can you not find the Bhagwan? Whether you can see him or not, the Bhagwan is the Bhagwan, isn't he? I am present in the pillar, the grain of sand and this Japanese garden. Don't ever speak of fear again.'

'Yes, Bhagwan!'

'Please go now. I am going to, or rather, we are going to capture this whole universe in the casket of our heart.'

After sending everyone away, he lay on his back in the sand and looked at the countless stars in the sky. As the thoughts churned in his mind, doubts arose...

'I am still a thief, aren't I? To everyone from the prime minister to the leper Chami, I'm god. The uruli thief has become a god. The butter thief and cowherd Krishna became the charioteer of

Partha and bestowed the wisdom of the Bhagavad Gita upon the world. What do I offer? What do I know? Still, it is pleasant to be acknowledged as a god, isn't it? A great pleasure. How long will this last?'

Vedan Baba shut his eyes.

From where did the roar of the sea come?

Was it the sea or was it the Periyar? What was that sound? Bhlum...bhlum...bhlum!

The demons were jumping into the water.

His ancestors were swimming across the river to reach this shore.

Where did the music come from?

The singer Swami?

His mother who was known as Thampuratty?

There came Kozhukatta Paru.

She had long nails. Twenty long nails in all. She spread apart her legs and jumped across him.

Vedan Baba opened his eyes.

What had actually jumped across his body was a black dog. A female dog or a bitch in other words.

The Baba could not help laughing.

What should he, the living god, do now? He could call Major Chandrasenan. Why only him, he could call all the staff and devotees in the ashram.

He could gather them in the prayer room. He could dress up and sit on the lotus dais.

He could start like this, 'The clear. Is the exact opposite the unclear? The cause is always broader. What about the effect? The effect is never as broad as the cause. Buddhi or intelligence creates the feeling of ahankara or ego. Ego creates the cells and the senses. My devotees, who am I? I am the yogi who practises samyama in the light at the centre of the lotus which is the heart. Nothing blocks my sight. I can see anything that happens, however distant it may be.

'If someone says a lot of stuff like that, everyone would bow before him. "I, the Bhagwan". It is a great thing to live as a Bhagwan. It is a great pleasure.'

Vedan Baba got up.

He put his sixth finger in the sand of the Japanese garden.

He wrote, 'Yes, it is a great pleasure to be the Bhagwan. But actually I am just a thief, aren't I?'

He sat and stared at the lines he had written.

Then he wiped them out with the palm of his right hand.

Thirty-nine

The Baba had entered his bedroom early that night.

It was about midnight. Surekha and Nina, who stayed in the adjacent rooms, were still together. The next day a special bhajan session was to be held in the drawing room. The chief minister of Karnataka, Arunagiri, Chinnappa and Madhavan Nair would be present. They would go only after dinner. Chinnappa had reminded them that since the Karnataka chief minister was coming for the first time, the dinner should be especially good. Surekha and Nina were discussing the menu for the dinner. It was about one when they parted.

They went to their own rooms and went to bed.

As she lay alone in the coolness of the air conditioner, snuggled under the blanket, hugging the satin pillows, Surekha was happy. She was thinking about the working of the ashram.

Everything was working according to plan. The story of growth continued. This was the beginning of May. The bank balance of the trust was over twenty-three crore rupees. Baba poured words of praise about the ability of the Yogini Mata. The assembly elections would take place in June. Arunagiri would come to power. And after that...

Rainbows of contentment spread out in her brain. Surekha pressed her face into the satin pillows and dreamt pleasant dreams.

She woke up suddenly in the early hours. She felt a vague sense of fear. How long was there to go before daylight? She looked at the bedside clock. Yes, it would be morning in about two hours. She got up. Should she knock on Nina's door and wake her up. She did not feel she could go back to sleep. Even after switching on all the lights, that vague fear did not leave her.

Surekha came out of the bedroom.

Nina's room was open. Nina wasn't there. Where had she gone? Was there the sound of laughter from somewhere?

Surekha walked through the corridor.

She saw something. Nina and Vedan Baba were standing just outside the meditation centre, wrapped in an embrace. Nina wore a nightgown that reached her knees. Baba wore just a towel wrapped round his waist. Nina and Baba were talking to each other, laughing aloud.

Surekha felt as if all the strength was draining out of her body. Her legs seemed too weak to support her. She felt she would fall. She leaned against the wall. No, she shouldn't stay here. Baba and Nina should not see her. Surekha went back to her room. When she shut the door and fell on the bed, tears flowed ceaselessly. The satin pillows were soaked. She spoke between her sobs: Baba, are you deserting me?

When the day dawned, Surekha had recovered her equanimity to an extent. She joined Nina in the morning routine of the Baba's bath and dressing. When they sat for breakfast, her mind wavered again. Was Baba neglecting her? Were his jokes directed only at Nina? Did he give Anab shahi grapes only to Nina?

Baba 'appeared' before the public that day too. As he gave darshan to the thousands who had gathered outside, Surekha and Nina accompanied him.

As he waved aside Rangarajan and the Major and wandered into the crowd, Baba invited only Nina to go with him, 'Nina, come with me!'

As Baba and Nina moved among the crowd, Surekha who stood on the stage started trembling. She felt as if she were drained of all strength. If Rangarajan, who stood next to her, had not supported her, she would have fallen.

'What happened, madam? You are trembling and sweating,' Rangarajan said.

'I don't know...I feel rather giddy...' Surekha muttered.

'Come, rest for some time.'

'No, Rangan. I will not move from here without Baba's permission.'

'Madam, come. Rest for a while. I'm telling you, Baba won't misunderstand you. I will explain to the master.'

Rangan clapped his hand and attracted the Major's attention. He told him, 'Major Chandru, I'll come in a moment. It seems that the Yogini Mata is rather unwell. I'll escort her to her room and come back.'

Rangarajan ignored Surekha's protests and took her to her room.

She lay down on the bed.

'Feeling better?' Rangan asked.

'Will you get me a stiff brandy, Rangan?'

'Yes, of course. It'll do you good.'

When she swallowed the brandy, Surekha started sweating all over. Rangan was flustered when he touched her hands and feet and found them cold.

'Madam, shall I send for a doctor?'

'No need to do that, Rangan. When Bhagwan is with us, why do we need a doctor?'

'Your hands and feet feel icy cold, madam.'

'Our home remedy will cure that.'

'One more, stiff one?'

'Yes, Rangan.'

After swallowing the next shot of brandy, Surekha started speaking animatedly. 'There's nothing wrong with me. I didn't sleep properly yesterday. And so, I'm a little tired. I'm much better now. The VIP visitors will come soon, won't they? If I'm not in the prayer hall, things won't be all right. Let's go there. What will the Baba think when he finds me missing?'

Suddenly she caught hold of Rangarajan's hand and started

crying like a child. Even as she wept she was speaking, in broken words and phrases, 'Rangan, what will the Baba think? What could the Baba think about me? Why should I imagine I'm in his thoughts? I'm a fool. I'm not Yogini Mata, just a fool of a madwoman called Surekha. Isn't it foolish to think that I have a place in the heart of Bhagwan who cares about the griefs of the whole world?'

'Madam, calm down, calm down.'

'I don't think I can, Rangan. I'm growing old. Who has any need for me now? I don't have the power to bind anyone to me, anything to me.'

Surekha lay face down on the bed hugging the satin pillows tight and wept again.

Rangarajan withdrew from the room. Let her cry. Let the tears flow till they end.

He walked to the prayer hall.

The Baba was talking to a group of VIPs. His conversation was attractive, a mixture of grave advice and drawing room jokes.

Surekha was not present at lunch either. Rangarajan did not say anything. The Baba had been cracking jokes with Nina. Suddenly he asked Rangan, 'Where is Yogini Mata?'

'I think she's not too well. She's lying down,' Rangan said.

Baba did not ask anything further about Surekha. His attention was focused on Nina, 'Nina, when does our Divine Dialling Service start functioning?'

Nina smiled as she replied, 'Advertisements are appearing in the newspapers. The headline is "Dial-a-god". I've asked Mark to send the cuttings. As soon as we complete the recording of your message, we can go on stream.'

'What you're saying is that we should spend even more time together, right?'

After lunch, Vedan Baba and Nina walked to the meditation centre – for another recording session.

Rangarajan went to Surekha's room. She was sitting on the bed, looking miserable, looking like she had lost everything.

'Madam, I believe I have the old freedom still. With that freedom, I'd like to say something. I know what caused your illness. I've spoken of this before.'

'You're about to say that it is caused by my jealousy.'

'Yes, madam!'

'It's not jealousy; it's anger. Sheer anger. Today, in the early hours of the morning...No, I won't speak of it. Can I ask you something, Rangan? Hasn't Baba started showing more interest in that White woman recently?'

'There's a reason for that.'

'What?'

'They're busy giving the finishing touches to the Divine Dialling Service.'

'Divine dialling, my foot! I'm not an ordinary jealous woman, I'm not prey to sexual jealousy. I've been thinking about practical matters. As I think about the future, my mind fails me at times. Actually, we, you and I, run the ashram. There is something other than spirituality in this ashram. It may appear very profane to say so, but I'm talking about the wealth of the ashram. The collection of funds is important. After the election in June, the picture will be even more beautiful. Our bank deposits will cross fifty crore rupees by the end of the year. Do you have any doubt about it?'

'Not at all, madam.'

'Isn't it our duty to use this money for the propagation of Bhagwan's messages?'

'Of course.'

'Let me be frank, Rangan. Nina Hyde is not a devotee of the Baba; she's a devotee of the wealth of this ashram. I strongly suspect her of having ulterior motives. If we don't stop her, everything that we've worked hard to build will be lost for ever.'

Rangarajan did not know what to say. It was possible that Nina was not avaricious, but a true devotee of the Baba. However, it was not possible to dismiss Surekha's accusation off hand. Anyway, he was bound to support Surekha whom he had known for years against Nina who was a newcomer. He stood and listened intently to what Surekha had to say.

'Rangan, if I'm Yogini Mata, I have to start acting. I'm not jealous; I'm angry. This anger comes from my commitment to our goals. Tell me, will you stand by me, firmly, strong as a rock?'

Rangarajan said, 'Madam, no, Yogini Mata, you need have no doubts about that. I'm with you.'

Surekha was effervescent. She made herself up with greater care than usual. Instead of wearing the usual clothes of Yogini Mata, she chose a sleeveless blouse and a thin sari that revealed the beauty of her body. As she stood before the full-length mirror and examined her reflection critically, Nina entered the room.

She said, 'Oh lovely! You are dressed to kill today.'

Though she could feel the flames of anger rising, Surekha responded pleasantly. 'Nina, it's a special occasion. Besides... I feel rather guilty. I did not take part in the morning function or even join you all for lunch. Bhagwan must be angry with me.'

'Never! Even Bhagwan will not dare to be angry with the Yogini Mata.'

Surekha examined the special flower arrangement in the prayer hall. It was fine. She called Rangarajan to her, 'Rangan, you must tell Minnal Babu that today's bhajan performance should be extraordinary. There must be guitar and drums among the instruments. I might sing today – English hymns. The kitchen staff should be ready to serve dinner at exactly 8 o'clock.'

'Madam, leave everything to me. All will be perfect!'

It was evening.

Arunagiri, Chinnappa, Madhavan Nair and the Karnataka chief minister reached the ashram together. Nina and Major Chandrasenan welcomed them. Surekha was with Vedan Baba. She did not want to leave the important ritual of leading him to the prayer hall to anyone else. Rangarajan stood with her like a shadow.

When Surekha led Vedan Baba to the lotus mandap, everyone got up and bowed before him. The Baba blessed everyone by waving his hand. He called the Karnataka chief minister by name, 'Come closer, Mahabala Rao!'

When Rao moved closer to the mandap humbly, the Baba laughed, 'Rao, come and sit next to me. I invite the future chief minister of Tamil Nadu, too.'

Arunagiri moved close to Rao.

'Please come up, both of you! Take your seats on either side of me.'

When Arunagiri and Mahabala Rao stepped on to the mandap, the Baba himself seated Arunagiri on his right and Mahabala Rao on his left. Lifting his hand with its glowing finger, the Baba said, 'This is a special occasion. There are very few people here today. I'd decided that it was to be so. The number of people is not important. I bless everyone. Arunagiri and Rao have my special blessings. At the end of June, Tamil Nadu will get a new life under Arunagiri's leadership. This is just a repetition of my earlier prophecy. Now a new prophecy – Mahabala Rao is going to the Centre, before the end of the year. I have already sown the seeds of this idea in the mind of the Northern emperor. Rao need have no worries about the change. And don't think that the position of a Central minister does not have the glory of that of a chief minister. You will reach the Centre not as just another central minister, but as the right hand man of the emperor. Now... (looking at Surekha, he continued) Yogini Mata, let the bhajans start.'

The singers and the orchestra appeared under the leadership of Minnal Babu. As songs of devotion rose, one after the other, the Baba started swaying as if he was experiencing bliss.

When the singers paused for a break, Surekha stood up. She sang an English psalm, moving in rhythm with it. It had a Latin rhythm. When the song filled the hall, backed by guitar and drums, everyone including the Baba started clapping.

When Surekha stopped, there was a round of deafening applause. The Baba said loudly, 'Yogini Mata, that was a beautiful performance! Shall we lead our guests to the dinner table?'

Surekha and Nina led the way to the dining hall. The others followed them. That was when Rangarajan touched Chinnappa's arm and whispered, 'I have something to tell you, Boss.'

'What is it?'

'We must send Nina to England as quickly as possible. If not, there'll be a crisis at the ashram…'

'What are you saying? Explain, Rangan!'

'This is not the right time, Boss.'

'You can't evade the question like this after making me curious…'

'Let the dinner be over.'

As the dinner went on with pleasant conversation, Chinnappa asked Nina, 'Nina, when do you plan to go to England? Murugappan keeps asking me. What shall I tell him?'

'I'll talk it over with Mark when we speak next.'

Chinnappa did not like that reply. He looked at Rangarajan and Rangarajan looked at Surekha. She was wondering why Chinnappa had aimed such a question at Nina. There hadn't been an opportunity for Rangarajan to speak privately with Chinnappa.

And yet…

The conversation took an unexpected direction after that.

Arunagiri spoke, 'Nina is the person to decide when she should return. But I think she should not delay too much. Bhagwan's message has to be disseminated in the UK and America. That duty had been taken up by Nina and Murugappan. At least, that was my understanding.'

'Yes, sir. You are right,' Rangarajan said.

'Let Bhagwan decide,' Nina's face was gloomy.

'What's the hurry about going to England?' Surekha asked innocently.

At this point the Baba intervened, 'Who said there's a hurry? But you can't say there is absolutely no hurry either. Nina has to be in London to kick-start the Divine Dialling Service. Let me think about it.'

The dinner got over and the guests departed. Nina and Surekha went to their respective bedrooms.

The Baba could not sleep. He drank a little from the locker in the meditation centre and walked out of the building. He walked to the Japanese garden.

Lying on his back on the sand, the Baba looked at the stars.

It was pleasant to be Bhagwan. But danger was a companion to this pleasure.

Who had said that?

The Baba felt like laughing. It was a day when all sorts of unwanted thoughts were invading his mind. Who was so concerned about sending Nina away? Clouds were gathering somewhere. Even an uruli thief like him could not understand the currents.

Time passed.

He felt there was someone standing next to him. When he looked up, it was Surekha. Why was she crying?

The Baba sat up.

'Why are you crying, Sura?'

The weeping became more violent.

'Tell me, Sura!'

'I'm beginning to feel that there's no place for me in your mind...'

'That's a joke. Why did you suddenly feel that?'

'I was ill today and you did not enquire about me at all.'

'I heard that you were not well at lunch time. But when I saw you in the evening I forgot all about it. You were so lively. Do you know how beautiful you looked today? When you were singing...'

'Bhagwan, stop laughing at me.'

The Baba pulled her close to him and said, 'Sura!'

'My pet! My darling!'

'You are worried about something, I know.'

'I'm the Yogini Mata. Why should I worry about anything?'

'Just now, you are Surekha and I'm Vedaraman. There's some

problem between you and Nina. What is it? Tell me frankly.'

'There is no problem.'

'Nina is nothing to me. Do you understand?'

Though the image of the Baba clad in only a towel standing close to Nina and laughing aloud came to her mind, Surekha spoke in a satisfied tone, 'I understand. Nina is nothing to my Bhagwan.'

'That's right. Also, I've decided to send her back to England by the end of this month.'

'For my sake?'

'No, for my sake.'

Forty

Surekha behaved like an accomplished actress with Nina. She hid the jealousy and anger she felt. She went to Nina's room before dawn. Nina's eyes were red and swollen. She had definitely not slept at all. Had she developed a cold from crying?

Surekha said, 'My dear girl, I think you have a running cold setting in. The tip of your nose is swollen. I won't allow you to fly to England carrying a cold from India. Wash your face and change your clothes. Let's walk a little outside. Cheer up! You should show a smiling face to the people who send you off.'

When Surekha spoke sweetly, her words filled with love and sympathy. Nina hugged her and wept.

'Silly girl, why do you weep?'

'Didi, what can I do but weep when I leave this sacred land?'

'You should be happy. You came here seeking truth. You found that... in Vedan Baba, our Bhagwan. You are a lucky woman – you're going to England in accordance with his command, to spread his gospel. You should not show this weakness before Bhagwan. Give me your word.'

They walked out of the ashram building and walked to the Japanese garden.

'Didi, Yogini Mata, is what you said true? I should be courageous, I should be happy. This ashram is almost complete. I should be able to build versions of this in England and America, you think? May I gain in confidence. Please pray for me.'

'Nina, my prayers are always with you. And you have Baba's

blessings. You will be the strength of this movement in the future. Let's meditate for a while and sing bhajans. And then when Bhagwan awakens, let's look after him as we always do.'

They turned to the brightening sky and started singing bhajans.

❖

After breakfast Surekha and Nina reached the drawing room with the Baba. Rangarajan, Major Chandrasenan and some of the ashram staff awaited them there.

The car was ready in the porch.

Rangarajan and the Major presented bouquets of flowers to Nina. When Surekha gestured to one of the servants, he brought a carton that had been gift-wrapped. She took it from him and spoke to the Baba. 'This is a gift to Nina from me. Let me tell you what the carton contains. There is a coral necklace, a white silk gown that had been presented to me by my Margarita Aunty, a new kanchipuram sari, a Nataraja statue, and then there is the most important thing, something that is priceless – a small casket containing sand from the paths trodden by Bhagwan, collected by me.'

Nina's eyes grew moist when Surekha handed over her gift.

The Baba lifted his hands to bless her. The sixth finger glowed. He held her close and caressed her cheeks, kissed her on the head.

The Baba said, 'I was expecting to see Chinnappa, Arunagiri and Madhavan Nair here. Does their absence trouble me? Not at all. I know they'll be at the airport. Let them wish Nina a happy journey there. Nina, daughter, I wish you all that is good. May you be showered with glories. The mission you've undertaken is a huge one. You are going to fly around the skies of the West like a bird, spreading our gospel. It will all end well. Within a year we shall come there with the Yogini Mata – to see the ashrams set up by our Nina. Don't delay now. Nina, my daughter, go to come back.'

Nina touched Bhagwan's feet.

Surekha touched her gently and said, 'Come.'

Nina went out with Surekha.

Major Chandrasenan stood with the car door open. Nina and Surekha got into the back seat.

As the car moved off, Baba, Rangarajan, Major Chandrasenan and the ashram staff waved farewell to Nina.

What the Baba had said turned out to be true. Arunagiri, Chinnappa and Madhavan Nair were waiting at the airport.

Surekha whispered to Madhavan Nair, 'Come with me to the ashram. Some things need to be discussed.'

Madhavan Nair stayed the night at the ashram. After dinner the Baba invited Madhavan Nair and Surekha to sit with him. They continued to stand respectfully.

'I told you to sit down,' the Baba said.

'To sit before you…' Madhavan Nair stopped mid-sentence. The Baba started laughing aloud like a little child.

Then he started speaking. The words were unexpected. 'I declare that I'm not a god. I'm not a god, nor am I the devil. In Madhavan Nair, I see my Uncle. I see the beautiful Surekha in this sacred persona of the Yogini Mata.'

'Bhagwan, what are you saying?' Surekha asked touching Baba's feet.

'Sit down!' the Baba said.

Madhavan Nair and Surekha obeyed.

'I may be a god. I may not be one. One thing is sure though. I am a messenger of god. In truth anyone who finds himself is a messenger of god. Surekha, it is all a fantasy. Life is a perfect circle. Or is it a vicious circle? I sometimes feel that we are all acting in a play that does not have a last scene.'

Vedan Baba shut his eyes and then spoke in a soft voice, 'Sura I wish to hear you sing.'

She sang and the Baba sang with her.

Suddenly opening his eyes, the Baba said, 'I feel a sense of loss. Why is that? Is it because Nina has left the ashram? It is getting late, isn't it? I'm going to the meditation centre. Both of you take rest.'

Surekha and Madhavan Nair got up to leave. After touching them with his sixth finger in blessing, the Baba went to the meditation centre.

Surekha whispered to Madhavan Nair, 'Come, come to my room.'

When they reached the room, Madhavan Nair asked, 'Why do you look sad?'

'I've some things to tell you. Some important things. I'm not sad, I'm anxious. Anxiety...a kind of fear...If you don't agree with what I'm saying, you must forget it all. Promise me.'

'I promise.'

'What do you think about Vedan Baba?'

'What sort of a question is this?'

'Is Baba a living god?'

Madhavan Nair smiled a little. Looking into Surekha's eyes, he said, 'How is the answer to this question relevant? Can Vedan Baba become Vedaraman again? We have made Vedan a Bhagwan. Even the prime minister of India accepts the Baba as a living god.'

Surekha clasped Madhavan Nair's hand and said, 'Uncle, you think like me. I am happy. I can speak openly now. Vedan Baba can never become Vedaraman now. Though we created Vedan Baba we can never cut him down to the size of a human. So, now, since she's gone from here...'

'She? Are you speaking of Nina?'

'Yes, she's a devil. She wanted to own Baba's body and soul. She was trying to get rid of me. She inflamed the sleeping libido in the Baba. She is prettier than me, much younger too. What did the Baba say a little while ago? A sense of loss! She has influenced the Baba so much. Anyway, now that she's gone...I have total control.'

'Why did you stop? Say whatever you want to say. I'm listening.'

'From now on, the ashram trust will effectively be run by me. Do you have any objection?'

'Objection? Chinnappa and I shall agree to whatever you do. And now, once we get caught up in the preparations for the elections, we won't have time to look at this place.'

'You'll be even busier once the elections are over. When Arunagiri becomes the chief minister, Chinnappa and you will be among the top personalities in industry. When you conquer new lands, I, Yogini Mata will be the empress of this ashram. Even now, the trust has wealth to the tune of crores. More crores will flow in. Uncle, I'll appoint expert accountants. The security staff will have to be expanded. I plan to control even the Baba. I shall change the present system. Why should Bhagwan give darshan to the devotees every day? He should keep a distance; he should be difficult to reach. He should give darshan to ordinary devotees only once a week. Then the mystery and the mystique will increase. Foreigners, top people from all fields in this country – I shall reserve Baba's time for them. Even they should come by special appointment. Uncle, shall I get you a drink?'

'Sura, I was about to ask you for one.'

Surekha brought the drinks.

'Sura, you look ravishing today.'

Surekha smiled saying, 'I shall make someone else say "ravishing" and "lovely".'

'You're saying you'll make the Baba say that?'

'Yes. I don't want to hide anything from you. I want Baba's body. That body is my property.'

'Is that all? This is not something new. I know that you slept with him when the Baba was just ordinary Vedaraman.'

'You don't mind?'

'Why should I mind? I know about your affair with that Central minister too.'

'I've given that up now.'

'Surekha, I'm an old man. But you seem to have woken me up with your nonsense.'

Surekha kissed Madhavan Nair, 'You want me? You desire me?'

'Yes.'

'Suppose, I don't yield to you?'

'I'll lie down in the ashram yard, weeping.'

'You needn't make fun of me. You'll weep if you can't sleep with me, if you please!'

'You sweet bitch! I'll rape you if you don't yield. Enough of your teasing!'

'Uncle, it's been a long time. I'll sleep with you, just this once. With a small sense of guilt.'

'A sense of guilt? Why?'

'I'm cheating on the Baba. When I think of that…'

Madhavan Nair embraced Surekha and laid her down on the bed. He said, 'You bitch, we shall sing bhajans now.'

Forty-one

Elections in Tamil Nadu took place in the third week of June. Though Baba's predictions had been favourable, Arunagiri had only expected that his party would be the largest one in the legislative assembly. If so, he would have to seek the support of the legislators of the prime minister's party. Taking into account the attitude of the prime minister, such support was certain. Still, that would make the picture less attractive. It was the prime minister's party that had propped up Nachimuthu's government. So, wouldn't that make his government a copy of Nachimuthu's government? The thought was not a pleasant one.

The election results were declared. They surprised Arunagiri more than anyone else. His victory was so overwhelming that one had to wonder whether such a thing as an opposition existed. A landslide victory, indeed.

Nachimuthu lost. Only five candidates from his party retained their seats. The prime minister's party also suffered losses. They were able to retain only half the seats they had in the previous legislature.

Arunagiri felt grateful to Vedan Baba. He even started feeling a sense of devotion. When the noise and colour of the victory celebrations had quietened a little, Arunagiri reached the ashram at Thiruvanmiyur with Chinnappa and Madhavan Nair.

Arunagiri was particular that his visit should not attract the attention of the media. He did not want to give anyone the chance to say that he was the sort to prostrate himself before gurus and human gods. He had to retain the image of the old revolutionary even as chief minister.

At the very minimum it had to be a neutral image. I don't prostrate myself before babas. But I have no objection to others doing so. I have great respect for the mathas and temples which contribute in the fields of education and healthcare. And yet, I do oppose some of their other activities. An image like that – realistic, fair, neutral.

Atheism had been the cornerstone of the party's policies. The past story of the party was of capturing the imagination and devotion of the people by tearing up the palm leaves of sanatana dharma, of calling the Ramayana, 'Kimayana'. Though a lot had happened and the party had even split, a special identity was always necessary for his party. That identity was a compound of Tamil greatness, Dravidian self-respect, atheism, and antipathy towards brahmins. He could not forget that. His party men should not hear that 'Ezhaithozhan Arunagiri' had gone to some baba's ashram to seek his blessings before he took over the government. That was why he had come to the ashram at midnight without any escort or noise.

Since there had been a telephone call earlier, the ashram was well prepared to receive the would-be chief minister. Surekha, Rangarajan and Major Chandrasenan stood in the drawing room with huge rose garlands. Arunagiri got down from the car with a smile. With him were Chinnappa and Madhavan Nair.

'Greetings, Puratchi Talaivare, Mutalamaichare!' said Surekha as she garlanded him. Rangarajan also garlanded him. There was one more rose garland. Surekha had an idea. She said, 'Vanakkam, Boss', and put it round Chinnappa's neck.

Arunagiri commented, 'Look at that, Chinnu. Look at Surekha's eternal loyalty to you.'

Chinnappa was pleased. He asked, 'Sura, where is the Baba?'

Surekha said, 'Come, let us go to the prayer hall. I'll bring Baba there.'

They entered the prayer hall.

'Please be seated, I'll go and call the Baba.'

Surekha knocked on the door of the meditation centre. The Baba himself came and opened the door. His eyes were red.

'Bhagwan, important guests have come.'

'Let them rest there for a while. Sura, today...why do I say "today"? I should say "recently"...my mind wavers so much that it frightens me. Pour me a drink!'

Surekha took out the whisky and decanter from the locker in the chamber.

'Baba, don't misunderstand me. A small one will do.'

Vedan Baba touched her cheek with his sixth finger, 'Sura, my sweet one, it is as you wish. Have I ever gone against your wishes?'

He had the drink poured out by Surekha. He then put his hand in the pocket of the silk kurta he was wearing, as though he was examining something.

'Come Sura, let's go and meet them.'

Surekha led the way and the Baba followed her to the prayer hall.

Arunagiri and the others stood up when they saw the Baba. The Baba walked to the lotus mandap and sat there with a smile. He raised his hands and blessed everyone.

Then, with a laugh like ringing bells, he called Arunagiri towards him, 'Come, chief minister!'

Arunagiri approached him respectfully.

'Thick rose garlands on the floor! The inmates of the ashram have welcomed the chief minister properly. I am very happy. Let me give you a small gift now.' The Baba took out a pearl necklace of three strands from his kurta pocket. 'Arunagiri, sit here next to me. Bend your head. Let me put this pearl string around your neck.'

Arunagiri bent his head. When the Baba put the pearl necklace around his neck Arunagiri struggled to find words to express his gratitude. His voice broke. The chief minister of Tamil Nadu somehow managed to say, 'It's all your blessings, Bhagwan.'

The Baba clapped his hands and laughed with the innocence of a child. He said, 'Arunagiri, you are an ace politician. I admit that. That is the way you should be, too. I can read your mind like an open book. Please understand that I shall never be offended. In the days to come, perhaps because of the old principles of the party, perhaps because you are too busy, you may not come here to visit me. It does not matter. Madhavan Nair and Chinnappa will also be very busy people from now on. Their visits too might become infrequent. That too does not really matter! What does matter? You want my blessings. Those shall always be with you. This moment is a precious one. Not just for you, but for me too. Aruna you must always wear the pearl string I gave you. Pearls are available in the market. But these were strung by me. The chief minister need not come and prostrate himself before me. After all, I am always with him, in the form of a string of pearls.'

Arunagiri fell at Baba's feet.

'Get up, Aruna. We shall all sit together on the floor. We can listen to a bhajan sung by the Yogini Mata. And then I shall distribute sacred water to all,' Bhagwan got up.

The Baba came down from the mandap and sat on the carpeted floor. The others sat around in a semicircle.

When Surekha started singing an English song, the Baba stopped her, 'Yogini Mata, sing something in Tamil.'

Surekha sang a bhajan in Tamil.

When it ended the Baba looked at Rangarajan and said, 'Rangan, bring the sacred water.'

Surekha went along to help Rangarajan. They brought the liquor and the goblets.

The Baba looked at Arunagiri and winked. 'Aruna, don't think of this as alcohol. Just consider it thirtha, sacred water, with my blessings in it.'

'Yes, Bhagwan.'

There was silence for a while. The small audience expected the Baba to say something and decided to wait.

The Baba said, 'None of you are saying anything.'

'You, Bhagwan, are the one who should say something. We are only to obey,' Chinnappa replied.

'I did say a few things. I shall explain if you like. I am rather disturbed. Who is responsible for the day-to-day running of the ashram?'

'The trust,' Madhavan Nair said.

'Yes, theoretically. But, in effect? Especially under the new circumstances, when the three of you, Arunagiri, Chinnappa and Madhavan Nair, will not be able to come here as frequently as before...'

'Baba, the Yogini Mata is here to take care of everything,' Rangarajan said.

'That's right! All of you are agreeable to that, aren't you?'

'Yes, Bhagwan!' The reply was a chorus.

'Our mind wanders on the spiritual plane. At the same time, we understand that the ashram has an existence at the material level and things will become more complicated from now on. The money that has started flowing in, the increasing fame – all these might cause problems.'

Surekha intervened, 'With Bhagwan's blessings and with the full cooperation of the trust members, I shall be able to manage the affairs of the ashram efficiently.'

'Yes, we are all confident of that, Yogini Mata. Do you know Chinnappa, Yogini Mata has plans to introduce a number of new measures. There are only two cars at present. Yogini Mata says that we need at least a fleet of fifteen cars. It doesn't stop there. At least four or five of them should be Rolls Royces, according to her. What do you think of her ambitious plans?' the Baba asked.

'They are not over-ambitious. The ashram has plenty of money. More money will come. There will be no problem about buying the cars through the State Trading Corporation,' Arunagiri said.

'Why should we buy any? They'll come as gifts from abroad,' Surekha said proudly.

The Baba laughed, 'Oh yes, that's true. Nina and Murugappan

have started spreading our cult there. Rolls Royces and Bentleys will definitely roll in. Let me ask you something Chinnappa. Aren't Murugappan and Nina coming to congratulate Arunagiri in person?'

'They'll come Bhagwan! I shall ask them to come.'

'Good, Chinnappa! Nina completed most of the recording. Some tapes have been prepared by the Yogini Mata as well. Let's not delay the inauguration of the Divine Dialling Service. Let our message travel all over the world through the dialling service. As for some of Yogini Mata's other ideas...we shall talk about all that on some other occasion. Or perhaps Mata herself had better explain them to you. Anyway, I shall give an indication. Yogini Mata's direct and energetic administration will affect the life of the ashram. It will change a lot of things. You should not be surprised if she effects some controls on my routine as well. It is all for the good. What more shall I say? Let there be one more song from the Yogini Mata and one more round of drinks. I shall go to the meditation centre after that. All of you, relax. I wish to be alone. I shall pray for you.'

Bhagwan lifted his glass. Surekha sang another bhajan.

Bhagwan got up and started moving towards the meditation centre without another word. When Surekha got up to accompany him, he stopped her with a gesture.

After the Baba had departed, Arunagiri asked the others, 'Shall we go now too?'

Madhavan Nair agreed, 'Let's go.'

Surekha turned into a pleasant hostess, 'No, no. I shall arrange for a quick supper. We'll break up after that.'

Arunagiri spoke laughing, 'I listen and I obey. We have to obey the Yogini Mata whom even the Baba obeys unquestioningly.'

Surekha said with an excess of humility, smiling her attractive smile, 'Thank you, chief minister!'

She turned to Rangarajan, 'Rangan, you and the Major alert the kitchen staff.'

Rangarajan and Chandrasenan walked towards the kitchen.

Surekha touched Madhavan Nair's shoulder and said, 'Uncle, could you entertain the chief minister for a while. I need to talk to Boss privately.'

Chinnappa pretended to be surprised, 'A secret? With me?'

'Yes, it's about the ashram. I shall tell you, and you can tell the others later.'

Arunagiri said, 'Go along, Chinnu. Call it a sub-committee meeting.'

Surekha walked towards a corner of the prayer hall with Chinnappa and said, 'Boss, please listen carefully to what I'm saying...'

'I know what you're going to say. It's about Nina, isn't it?'

'Yes, but how do you know?'

'Do you remember that dinner held here? I guessed some of it then. Later Rangarajan had come to see me. He gave me the total picture.'

'Nina should not come here again. You must ensure that. Tell Murugappan about it.'

'Surekha, I'm older than you. I'm also more experienced. I'm not willing to issue a prohibitory order. I fully understand your fears. But there's something, something important... are you listening?'

'Yes, Boss.'

'It is not a good idea to invite a confrontation. In any case, Nina plays a big role in our plans. We have appointed her as our ambassador in foreign countries. If Nina comes here with Murugappan, do you think we can throw her out? Be realistic! Be civilized! Nina comes... and goes. I shall manage everything. Baba will not go against your wishes. He has placed you on a high pedestal. What Rangan said is true. You are jealous, totally jealous. Let me ask you something, you woman? What does it matter if Baba sleeps with Nina one night? Is our movement so small that it should be limited to a bed and a night?'

'Boss, you don't understand.'

'I do. I understand everything. Only the lower part of my body is showing signs of age. My brain is still young and active.'

'Boss, Nina's eyes are on the wealth that is piling up in the ashram.'

'Don't be silly. It's my eyes that are fixed there. All the cases will be withdrawn immediately. Bengal Bay is going to grow wings and fly high. The automobile factory that I've been dreaming of must take shape. Don't we need funds for all that? You can run the ashram as you please. All of us are with you. Enough of this discussion...or rather, sub-committee work. Let's join Aruna and Nair.'

Forty-two

Even as Arunagiri's ministry was changing the horoscope of Tamil Nadu, the winds of change started blowing in the ashram at Thiruvanmiyur.

The Yogini Mata introduced new restrictions. The Baba gave in to all those new rules without any protest.

When Surekha kept insisting that Baba's mystique would be dulled by giving daily darshan to all and sundry, the Baba gave up appearing before the public every day.

'We had decided that you should take care of everything. All right. I will not appear before people every day. What else? Tell me.' Baba sought instructions from Surekha.

And so new rules and regulations appeared. Big changes.

People could come on Sundays without appointment. The Baba would give darshan.

On Mondays, Tuesdays and Wednesdays – the orchestra under Minnal Babu would sing bhajans from eight in the morning till noon on the platform outside. After that, there would be 'feeding the poor'. The Yogini Mata would be in charge of this food distribution. On Thursdays and Fridays there would be meetings with representatives of all religions who would give talks in the front yard. Once again, there would be distribution of food.

On Saturdays, songs about the Baba would be sung from morning till evening. Famous singers would take part in this. Before the concert ended the Baba would appear among the artists and request everyone to sing together. He might sing along too.

All evenings (except Saturdays) were reserved for meetings with VIP visitors.

The important internal meeting would take place on Saturday night. The Baba would preside over the meeting to evaluate the working of the ashram. Yogini Mata, Rangarajan and Major Chandrasenan would participate in this meeting. Arunagiri, Chinnappa and Madhavan Nair could take part in the meeting according to their convenience.

Surekha also took steps to further beautify the exterior of the ashram.

There were seventeen cars in the ashram fleet now. The landscaping was over. The Japanese garden had been made larger. All the construction and other activities according to the original plan had been completed satisfactorily by the architect.

The next stage of expansion and development had to be planned.

After three or four meetings that took place on Saturdays, the Yogini Mata managed to ensure that she had a right to some private hours with Baba. On those occasions she would become the beautiful woman named Surekha and she would transform Vedan Baba into the strong young man called Vedaraman.

Months passed. The ashram's bank balance was now over forty-five crores.

At one of the review meetings, Chinnappa talked at length about the financial position of the ashram. He asked the Baba, 'Do you have any instructions about the deployment of the funds now available with the ashram?'

The Baba laughed. 'Wealth! Crores! What do I know about the use of money? You and Yogini Mata can deal with it. The wealth I seek is at a different level.'

'I know, Bhagwan, I know. I wish to say some things now. All of you please listen carefully, especially the Yogini Mata.'

'Speak, Chinnappa!'

'Arunagiri wishes to give the ashram some land in Ooty. If Bhagwan permits...'

'Chinnappa, why would I refuse a dakshina, an offering made by the chief minister?'

'We shall create a mini ashram there. A retreat for Bhagwan, a place to stay in once in a while.'

'Very good,' the Baba said.

'I plan to allocate one crore for that. What do you say, Yogini Mata?'

'It's your wish, Boss.'

'Bhagwan, what I'm about to say is even more important. I'm seeking your blessing for a concept, an idea about investment.'

'Chinnappa, all your activities have our blessing.'

'I do know that, Bhagwan. Officially, the administration of the ashram is the responsibility of the trust. So, the trust should know of all the decisions, don't you agree?'

'Chinnappa, you know I'm not interested in all these matters. As long as it is not against dharma, you can do anything you like.'

'What I'm saying is...'

'Go ahead.'

'Arunagiri and Madhavan Nair should have been here today. Never mind, I'll let them know. I understand that we have more than forty crore rupees in hand.'

'Forty-five,' Yogini Mata corrected Chinnappa.

'All right, forty-five. What is the point if this money lying idle? It does earn interest, that's true. But that's not much. I feel that the money should be invested in industries when the opportunity presents itself. Only in industries that have an assured profit. From the large profits that are earned, without touching the capital, we can start educational institutions and hospitals in Bhagwan's name, start social welfare programmes.'

'Very good! I don't think anyone will have objections to these plans. Just keep one thing in mind. None of this should affect my meditation, my seeking. All of you are wise, serve as trustees of the good deeds!'

The Baba ended the meeting and was about to go to the meditation centre when Surekha sought his permission to stay back, saying, 'Bhagwan, I shall come there after seeing off Chinnappa.'

The Baba walked away, smiling. Rangarajan and Chandrasenan bid farewell to Chinnappa.

When they were alone, Chinnappa asked the Yogini Mata, 'Do you know why I came here today?'

'To speak of investments.'

'No, I could have done that another Saturday as well. I came to give you a warning. I could have let you know of this through a messenger or even a telephone call. I decided that it was too important for that. You have to make a promise.'

'What is it about?'

'I'll tell you. But I want your promise before that.'

'Boss, what do you want me to promise?'

'Normal behaviour. Even if someone throws a stone into the placid lake, you should be normal. You must behave sensibly.'

'I don't understand. Whatever you say, I shall obey you, I promise.'

'That's good. Nina and Murugappan are in Madras. It has been two days since they came. They're staying at the Taj. They had come to my bungalow. I think they are having some problems. Anyway, tomorrow, when Baba's darshan is over, they will come here. They'll be staying here. Murugappan will return. Nina might say that she plans to stay here permanently.'

Surekha's voice faltered as she said, 'Let her look after everything. Let her reign here as the Yogini Mata. I'll go away.'

'Che! It looks like you'll ruin everything. I'm giving you a final warning. If there is any problem in the running of the ashram because of your behaviour, if the Baba is disturbed in any way, I shall not forgive you. Do you understand, you silly woman!'

When Surekha started weeping, Chinnappa changed his tactics. He spoke in a soft voice, 'Sura, sorry. I was not threatening you. Baba, the ashram...these should not receive even a scratch from our actions. You know that. Do we have a future if there is no Baba and ashram?'

Chinnappa patted her cheek, 'Sura, perhaps a final solution is possible. Let me find out what Murugappan's plans are.'

After seeing Chinnappa off, the Yogini Mata reached the meditation centre. Baba was sitting in the padmasana pose with his eyes shut. The Yogini Mata waited.

Finally Baba opened his eyes. He stretched out his hands as though he were helpless. 'Mata, come closer, give me courage.'

The Yogini Mata bowed and touched his feet with her head.

'Mata, why am I so disturbed? What am I afraid of? Am I afraid of myself? Is my past coming to haunt me?'

'Bhagwan! If you are disturbed like this without any reason, how can I hold on?'

'Bhagwan! Am I a Bhagwan? I'm a child, just a child. You are my mother.'

'That's right Bhagwan, come and lie in my lap.'

Bhagwan obeyed.

He said, 'Mata, stay with me till dawn.'

❖

It was Sunday.

The Baba reached the prayer hall after giving darshan to the people. Rangarajan and Chandrasenan went to take care of their usual duties. A sea of anxiety was roaring in Surekha's mind. When would Nina come? Murugappan would be with her. But he would go. What could she do if Nina decided to stay here for an indefinite period?

'What is it, Yogini Mata? You are unusually serious. What happened? I spoke my mind yesterday. Forget about it. My mind is disturbed by doubts. Who else can I express these doubts to? Are you thinking of me? Or is there some other black cloud enveloping you?' The Baba wrote 'Om' with his sixth finger on Yogini Mata's forehead.

Surekha touched his feet and touched her fingers to her eyes. 'Bhagwan, my mind is peaceful. There is no black cloud there. A sort of – what shall I say – an indescribable happiness fills my heart now. I don't know how to make prophecies. Still let me say. Something that gives all of us immense pleasure is going to happen. Today.'

'Is that so? Let's wait then.'

Rangarajan reached there in a rush. He said, 'Bhagwan, we have visitors. From England.'

'It must be Nina,' Surekha pretended to be very pleased and got up. 'Baba, let me welcome her and bring her here.'

Vedan Baba's reaction surprised Surekha. He said in a serious voice, 'Yogini Mata, you forget yourself and your position. Sit down. I said, sit down. Those who are coming, will come here.'

Surekha sat.

Within moments Murugappan and Nina entered the prayer hall.

'Jai Bhagwan!' Nina folded her hands and greeted him.

'Vanakkam, Bhagwan!' Murugappan too folded his hands.

Surekha got up. Baba did not stop her. She embraced Nina and shook hands with Murugappan.

She pulled them towards the Baba saying, 'Come Nina, come Murugappan. This is a pleasant surprise.'

Baba lifted both his hands and blessed them. Both of them fell at his feet.

'I was expecting the two of you. But I did not foresee that you would reach today. The credit for foreseeing that is Yogini Mata's.' Vedan Baba was smiling as he spoke.

'Bhagwan, what are you giving me credit for?' Surekha asked.

'A little while ago, you said that something that would give us all immense pleasure was going to happen. Nina and Murugappan have reached. What could give us more happiness?'

As Nina gazed at him gratefully, the Baba said lightly, 'Nina and Murugappan would have come after conquering England for me.'

'Please don't think the Baba is making fun of you,' Surekha said.

'Look at that, Nina and Murugappan. The Yogini Mata is making fun of me now!' the Baba laughed aloud.

Surekha, Nina and Murugappan laughed along with him. The Baba made his sixth finger glow and said, 'I'm not Bhagwan. I'm soft-hearted, my mind is disturbed. When did my Nina leave me and go away? Was it years ago? Or was it just weeks back? The Yogini Mata might know. At least, Nina might know.'

Whatever the meaning of Baba's words, Surekha thought that the direction of the conversation had to be changed. She told Nina and Murugappan, 'It looks like Bhagwan is in a mischievous mood today. Mischievous and humorous.'

'Is that so? If you people insist that I should always be the Bhagwan, completely serious, I shall be in trouble. All right, I'm going to be serious now. Come, let us go to the drawing room. Once we reach there I shall ask Nina and Murugappan with all the seriousness of a schoolmaster about the happenings in the western countries. Yogini Mata, let us get Rangarajan to join us.' The Baba got up.

They sat together in the drawing room. When Surekha pressed the buzzer, a uniformed security guard appeared.

'Ask Rangarajan to join us here,' Surekha gave the order in a manner suitable to the stature of the Yogini Mata.

'All right, children. Now let me ask in my schoolmaster role. What have you done to spread my teachings in England? Ah, Rangan has come in. Rangan, the question I've asked is, what have Nina and Murugappan done on my behalf?'

'We have spread your teachings. That is, we have made a good beginning. Nina can explain better than me,' Murugappan said.

'Baba, I'll tell you – about Kevin Bird, about Praveen Deshmukh, about Alfred Chlore, about Anthony Marcus,' Nina started with the stories of four people.

'Kevin Bird was a mechanic in an aircraft company. He is a devotee of Vedan Baba. I, this humble devotee, showed him Baba's light. There is a group of twelve Baba devotees in that aircraft company now.

'Praveen Deshmukh, who runs a restaurant in Southall, holds Baba bhajans every Sunday in his flat. Here, Mark was the proselytizer. I mean Murugappan.

'Bhagwan, let me tell you about some of the big guns, about millionaires who have become devotees of Baba.

'Alfred Chlore keeps a picture of Baba in his flat and offers puja every day. He wishes to donate a large sum to the ashram. Anthony Marcus who holds a major portion of the shares of Marks and Spencer is a devotee of the Baba.'

The Baba lifted his right hand, 'Enough, Nina. I don't want to hear the full list. I'm happy. I congratulate you, and Murugappan.'

The Baba looked at Surekha and asked, 'What do you think, Yogini Mata? Haven't I congratulated Nina enough?'

Surekha caressed Nina affectionately and said, 'Nina, my dear. Do you and I need congratulations? We only want Bhagwan's blessings and his nearness.'

Nina said, 'Yes, that's all we want. I would like to stay here for a while if Bhagwan permits.'

The Baba smiled and looked at Surekha and Murugappan in turn. He said, 'Very good. I'm only happy to permit it. What do you say, Yogini Mata?'

Surekha managed to say without showing any displeasure, 'True, Bhagwan. It is a good thing if Nina and Murugappan can stay here with us for a while.'

Murugappan shook his head, 'Bhagwan, I hope you will understand what I'm saying. It is better for the growth of the movement if Nina and I stay in London permanently. In this jet age, it will take us only hours to reach here if we need to.'

Rangarajan said, 'I agree with Murugappan.'

Surekha asked in a light tone, 'Murugappan, do you know just logic? Don't you know about emotions?'

'I don't understand your question, Yogini Mata?'

'Murugappan, your viewpoint is correct. But Nina's desire to be here is an emotional one. She wishes to sit at Baba's lotus feet for a while. What's wrong with that?'

'There's nothing wrong with that. But I have to fulfil my duties. I have made some American contacts. I need to start preliminary work to establish Baba's ashrams in Washington, Dallas in Texas immediately. Nina can stay here. But I have to go.'

Nina's voice rose, 'Mark, you are trying to make me look small before Baba.'

The Baba now behaved like a mischievous child. He clapped his hands and laughed aloud. 'I think today is going to be fun. Murugappan and Nina are going to provide us with a big fight while the rest of us watch as neutral observers from the sidelines.'

Murugappan said humbly, 'I'm not up to any fight, Bhagwan!'

'So, what you're saying is that I'm the quarrelsome one, the unreasonable one?' Nina's voice was harsh.

'I was the one who spoke about fighting, Nina!' The Baba pointed out.

'So...Bhagwan...you too are deserting me. You are blaming me too...' Nina started crying.

The Yogini Mata turned into a capable administrator at that moment.

'Bhagwan, may I say something as the Yogini Mata. I request that what I say be followed.'

'Tell us. I leave the management of this moment to you.'

'Baba, please console Nina. I think there are waves of trouble disturbing her mind. All of us will stay apart. Let Nina open the inner reaches of her heart before Bhagwan. Let her talk without any inhibition. Like confession in the Catholic church.'

'All right, Yogini Mata,' Baba said.

❖

When they reached Surekha's room, Murugappan said, 'I have a confession to make as well. I'll make it before the Yogini Mata.'

'That's interesting. I'm waiting to hear it.'

'Is my presence a problem?' Rangarajan asked.

'A problem? Never. You and I have known each other for so many years,' Murugappan said.

'That's true. Madam, a suggestion. Before the confession starts...'

'I understand. Gangajal, right? Good idea. What's your drink, Murugappan?'

'Surekha, I'll drink any poison you give me.'

The glasses rose in the air and Murugappan said, 'Cheers.'

'Surekha, what is my reputation? What do people say about me as a man?'

'Philanderer, a big flirt.'

'Yes. But actually that label is not strictly accurate. I have never hunted anyone. I have only accepted whatever came my way. Beautiful women have cornered me and I have surrendered to their charms. But believe me, I've never wished to make any woman my own. Marriage was not even a word in the dictionary to me. Let me correct myself by adding the phrase – till recently.'

Surekha patted Murugappan on his thigh and said, 'Let me fill in the rest. You wish to marry Nina.'

'Yes, that, in brief, is my confession. But, my dear Sura, please let me elaborate a little here. When I came here with Nina for the first time...I mean when I came here the last time, she was nothing to me. I had not wanted her to come with me. Still, she came with me. That was because she insisted and I thought I would not stand against her wishes. Sura, I am a gentleman. I have never hurt any woman I slept with. I have got rid of women I was in relationships with. But in such a way that they did not get hurt. That is another matter. My point is that Nina was just an episode in my love life. Just a fleeting episode.'

Murugappan paused for a moment, poured himself another drink and started talking again. He talked haltingly, as if he was choosing each word carefully.

'That is the old story. Today, I love Nina deeply and I wish to make her my wife. Why do I, philanderer and flirt, suddenly feel this way? Not just feel, desire that so much that it has become a madness and an obsession? Why has this happened? Can you explain, Sura?'

Surekha did not reply.

'Not just you, no one would be able to explain such madness.'

'Go ahead, Murugappan, get married to Nina,' Rangarajan said.

Murugappan spoke with a half-smile that was full of contempt for himself, 'Such a simple solution! But it won't happen. Nina does not agree.'

'But why?' Surekha could not hide her surprise.

'Let me speak frankly. Nina, who has been sharing my bed for months, says we can live together. But she'll not marry me. How is that?'

'And the reason?'

'Surekha, Yogini Mata! Rangan! There is a reason, the reason she gave me. I am afraid to reveal it.'

'Afraid? Of what? Of whom?'

Murugappan sat silent for a long while. He also drank some more.

After a while he threw a question at them, 'Is Vedan Baba really divine? Is he a living god?'

'He is. It is something that all of us have accepted,' Surekha replied.

'If I speak frankly, will you take it as a criticism of the Baba?'

Surekha and Rangarajan did not reply to that.

Murugappan laughed aloud, 'What happened? Cat got your tongues? I know. You will not support me. Never mind. Either way, I have untied my bundle, said a few things. To hell with it. I don't plan to hide anything. You want to know why Nina refuses to marry me, right? She's going to marry Vedan Baba!'

Forty-three

Surekha's heart stopped beating for a moment. She did not know what to say to Murugappan. He did not seem to require a reply. His attention was on the drink he was pouring.

Suddenly, he put his head down and started crying. He seemed to have lost the maturity of his age and the equanimity that his knowledge of the world had given him.

Surekha could not bear to see him cry. She spoke in an aside to Rangarajan and said, 'Rangan, look after Murugappan. I'm going out for a while.'

Surekha reached the main entrance of the ashram. She could feel anger flaming in her at the sight that met her eyes there.

The Baba was wandering in the Japanese garden with Nina. Were their fingers entwined? Were they laughing at jokes?

'Baba, you needn't think you can trick me that easily. Are you an innocent person who has fallen into the trap of the seductive Nina? Or, are you also plotting against me in your heart of hearts? You and Nina are joining together to trick me, aren't you? You think you can beat me?'

Surekha did not realize that Rangarajan had reached the place.

'Madam!'

Surekha turned around with a start.

'Madam, I can't sit and watch a man break down like that. And now...' When his eyes fell on the scene in the Japanese garden, he stopped mid-sentence.

'Rangan, I told you from the beginning. You didn't believe me then. What do you say now?'

'Madam, I'm convinced now. Don't worry about anything. I'm with you.'

'Rangan, I'm going to Poes Garden now. I need Boss's advice.'

'Shall I telephone Boss?'

'No, just be with Murugappan till I return.'

'Madam, please come back by lunch time.'

'I don't think that will be possible. You'll have to manage till I come back.'

'If the Baba asks where you are...'

'You can tell him that Chinnappa sir had rung up and I had to go in a hurry. Something to the effect.'

When Surekha reached Poes Garden, Chinnappa asked in surprise, 'What happened? Why have you come? Any problem?'

She explained the situation to him.

Chinnappa frowned. He then leaned back in the sofa and started laughing aloud. 'What happened to Murugappan? Couldn't he find any other girl to make his wife? Never mind... I'll arrange everything.'

'What do you mean, Boss?'

'I'm going to become a marriage broker. Murugappan will marry Nina within two days with Baba's blessings. Will that satisfy you?'

'That...'

'Um? Are you trying to tell me that is impossible? Wait and see. Murugappan said Nina is going to marry Baba, didn't he? Did Baba say anything of the sort? Sura, this ashram, this movement has to go forward. I need it to. Looking at it from one viewpoint, I'm being frank with you, who is this Baba? He's our creation. He's a product launched by us in the market of devotion. Who is going to manipulate whom? I'll show you. The Baba may have divine powers and be a Bhagwan. Yes, but... I'm not saying anything further just now.'

That afternoon Baba had VIP visitors, as on every other day.

Chinnappa and Surekha reached the ashram when the visitors were going away. One of the them recognized Chinnappa. He said, 'Mr Chinnappa, I don't know if you remember me. I'm Thompson, we met at the Rotary convention two years ago...'

'Of course, Thompson. How is the tie-up with Holiday International? Do you know, I have also bought your shares?'

'I'm flattered, Chinnappa. All goes well. The plan is to start a few resorts on time-share basis. My new venture. I came here to seek Bhagwan's blessings.'

'You can start anything with confidence. Bhagwan's blessings are always with you.'

Thompson's eyes were sparkling as he said, 'Yes, I know it. Bhagwan has given me his blessings.'

'I too came here to seek blessings. Bye Thompson!'

Chinnappa entered the ashram. He said, 'Sura, let's go to your room. I need to ask Murugappan a few questions. Let's also call Rangan.'

'And when do you plan to see the Baba...'

'Later.'

Murugappan stood up when he saw Chinnappa. Like someone who had been caught committing a crime. A picture of regret.

When he started to speak, Chinnappa stopped him and said, 'I know everything. I'm taking command. Sura, where's Rangan?'

'I'll call him.'

She went out of the room in search of Rangarajan. He was coming towards her, panting.

'Boss has come? Chandrasenan told me...'

'What did you tell the Baba when he asked for me at lunch?'

'He did not ask for you.'

Surekha's face fell.

'Come, Rangan, Boss is waiting for you. Where are Baba and Nina?'

'They are in the meditation centre. The door is shut.'

Rangarajan told all of them in Surekha's room, 'Lunch was rather peculiar today. The Baba did not call for me or the Major.

He did not ask for madam. There was only one person in Baba's world today – Nina. As soon as the visitors left, the Baba went with Nina to the meditation centre.'

'So, you want to marry Nina. I'm rather surprised. But it is now my need as well. It will happen. I'll make it happen.' Chinnappa patted Murugappan on the back.

'Boss, shall I call the Baba?'

'No, Sura. The Baba is Bhagwan. I'm just a devotee. I'll wait for him. But I must have private audience with him sometime today. I must meet him alone. I'll rest for a while. Call me when Bhagwan comes out.'

'Yes, Boss!'

❖

The Baba came out of the meditation centre late in the evening. Nina looked happy. She was holding on tight to Baba's arm. There was a soft smile on Baba's lips. They looked like lovers who had come for an evening's outing.

They did not seem to be looking for anyone as they moved towards the main entrance of the ashram through the drawing room. That was when Chinnappa, who had been waiting in a corner of the room, said, 'Vanakkam, Bhagwan!'

The Baba turned around and looked with the obvious displeasure of someone whose journey had been checked by an inauspicious call from behind. When he recognized the source of the call, he smiled beatifically.

'Who is it? Chinnappa? We had not expected you today. Today is a day when I am getting unexpected treats. Nina came. And now you have. Come, come with me.'

'I'll wait here, Baba! Don't disappoint Nina. I should not steal the time allowed by you to her.'

'Are you sure you are not in a hurry?'

'I'm not in a hurry. I'm even willing to stay here tonight. You have to grant me a boon though. You must allow me a private audience tonight. There is a problem.'

'We'll find a solution, Chinnappa! Let me show Nina around

the ashram now – a conducted tour. What do you say?'

❖

Vedan Baba and Chinnappa entered the meditation centre.

'Chinnappa, close the door. What is the problem? Speak openly.'

'Baba, Bhagwan! Isn't it necessary for the growth of our movement that Murugappan and Nina should move together?'

'Of course! They are together now.'

'No, Bhagwan! They're fighting with each other.'

'Oh that! That's just a silly fight. Murugappan wants to go to London. Nina wants to stay here. Isn't that what the fight is about? They were arguing before me too, like small children. They'll be all right after a couple of days.'

'I don't think the problem is as simple as that. Some unexpected developments have taken place. You know, Bhagwan, what the relationship between Nina and Murugappan is.'

'Friends...Lovers...'

'Yes, they live together. It is a long-time affair. If it had continued like that there would have been no problem. But things have changed now.'

The Baba laughed, 'You mean that Murugappan wishes to marry Nina? And Nina does not agree. I've seen it with my inner eye.'

Chinnappa's eyes opened in wonder. The Baba knew everything. He did not have to tell him anything. The Baba might even have decided on what to do. There, the Baba was shutting his eyes.

'Chinnappa, I'll tell you something else. Nina has taken me as her husband – in her imagination. What's wrong with that?'

'I...What shall I...Bhagwan, I can't find words to express myself.'

'Chinnappa, I don't know whether I'm a Bhagwan or not. You people say I am Bhagwan. You have given me a role. I act it out. That might be the truth. Or else, I might be Bhagwan. Anyway, you have your doubts about me. That might be the truth as well.'

Chinnappa's confidence and pride ebbed away.

'Baba, you are Bhagwan. You know everything. You must have thought of a solution as well.

Baba opened his eyes. The sixth finger started glowing.

'Chinnappa, what am I who call myself "we"? I am pure love. I love this whole world. I love you and Arunagiri and Madhavan Nair, Rangan, Senan and all the inmates of this ashram. I love the thousands of people who come here to see me. I love the Yogini Mata and Nina. May my empire of love grow. My language, my definitions may seem obscure to you, you may not understand them. I know that Nina loves me in the bodily sense. Her age, the western culture she grew up in – all these are the reasons. My love is spiritual. I was making her understand that today. Isn't it a welcome change that she has understood my viewpoint? I cannot object if she sees me as the love of her heart. But my love is not of this world. Do you know what I propose to do? I'm going to give you the boon you crave. I've decided to conduct Murugappan and Nina's wedding as soon as possible, at the ashram. Are you satisfied now?'

Chinnappa fell at Baba's feet. 'Please forgive me, Bhagwan.'

'Get up. I need to talk to three people now. Nina, Murugappan and the Yogini Mata. Please go and send Nina to me.'

After Chinnappa had gone out of the room, the Baba took out a cigarette from the box that Nina had given him and started smoking.

Nina's form appeared through the transparent blue curtains of smoke.

'Nina, come here. Embrace me.'

Nina came forward and lost herself in Baba's arms.

'When we were in the Japanese garden I told you about some doubts I had. It is now clear that my fears were not unfounded. I love you. And because of that I know that you'll obey me.'

'Bhagwan, tell me! I am ready to obey any order of yours.'

'Nina, you must marry Murugappan.'

Nina was startled.

'You must understand what I say. I'm saying this for your sake. You have been sleeping with Murugappan for years. If you allow Murugappan to put a mangalsutra, handed over to you by me, around your neck before a small crowd, it will satisfy everyone. The ashram will go forward without any disturbance. There will be no change in our relationship.'

Nina hugged him closer, 'Yes, Bhagwan.'

'I'm going to announce your wedding with Mark at the dinner table. Let's not delay things. Ask Surekha and Mark to come here.'

Nina got up.

The Baba continued smoking. He felt that he was speaking to himself. You uruli thief – play the game, intelligently. Who is keeping whom in prison now? This cigarette is good. I, or we, is rising right up to the sky. There were so many moons and stars all around. Why didn't he catch the tip of the meteor that was approaching him?

'Bhagwan!'

Who was calling him? What were those small dots that he could see down below?

The Baba came back to the earth.

'Oh, Yogini Mata and Murugappan! Come, we wish to give you some good news. You would have guessed. Chinnappa must have given you a hint. Murugappan, you wish to marry Nina, do you? Very good. Yogini Mata, good things should happen without delay. What do you say? Whose responsibility is it to see to all the preparations, to see that everything goes smoothly?'

'It is my responsibility as the Yogini Mata, Bhagwan.'

'Sura, I am sure everything will work as it should when you are in charge. Murugappan, why are you standing there, looking stunned?'

Murugappan fell at Baba's feet without a word.

The Baba lifted him up and said, 'May all good things come to you and Nina.'

The Baba led them all to the dining table in high spirits. He said, 'Sura, call everyone.' Surekha called Chinnappa, Nina and Rangarajan.

'Where is the Major? Call him too. Rangan, please ask Madhavan Nair to come too. He should be able to get here before we break up.'

Rangarajan brought Major Chandrasenan. He came back to the dining table after telephoning Madhavan Nair.

The Baba looked at everyone as they sat around and started speaking, 'My devotees, let me first congratulate Murugappan and Nina who have given me this chance to make a happy announcement. The duty of joining them together, in the Indian fashion, this couple who are in love, has fallen to us. Nina and Murugappan are getting married, the day after tomorrow. Here! When those present here today, Arunagiri, Madhavan Nair and the ashram staff shower them with blessings, Murugappan will tie the mangalsutra around my Nina's neck. After marriage they will be the propagators of our movement in the West with even more vigour. Now, let me ask like the priest in the church, "Murugappan, are you ready to accept Nina as your wife?"'

'I am, Bhagwan.'

'Nina, are you ready to accept this Mark, otherwise known as Murugappan, as your husband?'

'I am ready, Bhagwan.'

Rangarajan clapped his hands. Everyone else including Bhagwan followed suit.

Rangan sang, 'Lakshmi Kalyana Vaibhogame...'

The Yogini Mata sang, 'Sita Kalyana Vaibhogame...'

'Dinner now, Bhagwan?' Major Chandrasenan asked.

'What do you say, Yogini Mata?' Bhagwan asked.

'Before dinner... if we had planned it earlier, we could have opened a champagne bottle,' Surekha said.

'That's no problem. There is champagne in my bungalow. We can send someone over to get it,' Chinnappa said.

'Chinnappa, don't bother. The sacred water we have here shall do.' Baba smiled.

The sacred water came.

Dinner followed.

Madhavan Nair arrived before dinner was over.

'Uncle, there's to be a wedding here the day after tomorrow. Murugappan and Nina are entering grihasthashrama officially,' Surekha said.

Madhavan Nair folded his hands and said, 'It is all Bhagwan's blessings. Murugappan, Nina, congratulations.'

'Madhavan Nair, Chinnappa...I declare that any time the day after tomorrow is a good muhurtam, an auspicious time. Arunagiri should be here. Whenever he can reach here, that becomes our wedding muhurtam. Let's break up now. We shouldn't keep Murugappan and Nina here and bore them. Murugappan, make Nina happy,' the Baba got up.

Murugappan walked towards Nina's room, caressing her.

Chinnappa and Madhavan Nair said goodbye to Surekha and went away.

'Rangan, Major, good night to you too.' Surekha was in a hurry to find the Baba.

As he lay stretched out on the bed in the meditation centre, 'You terrible woman, you have defeated me.'

The lights dimmed.

He could feel a weight on his body. What was it?

'Vedan, my pet!'

'Oh! It's you, Kozhukatta Paru!'

Surekha did not understand what the Baba had said.

Forty-four

The ceremony that took place in the prayer room was a simple one. Arunagiri, Chinnappa, Madhavan Nair, Surekha, Rangarajan and Major Chandrasenan were present.

The lamp with seven wicks placed on the lotus mandap bathed the surroundings in a sacred glow. The electric bulbs in the hall had not been switched on.

The Yogini Mata led the bride and groom to the hall. Nina wore a light blue sari with a dark blue blouse. Murugappan wore a cream kurta and a dhoti with golden lace. The garlands of flowers rested on a low table. Piped wedding music floated in from somewhere.

The Baba appeared. He was not wearing his official costume, but a red silk dhoti. His upper body was covered with an angavastra, a smaller dhoti of the same colour.

Everyone present folded their hands and greeted the Baba. Murugappan and Nina fell at his feet.

'Get up!' the Baba said, with his sixth finger glowing.

Murugappan and Nina obeyed.

The Baba lifted both hands and blessed everyone. 'We wish Murugappan and Nina all the good things of life. May they be as Vishnu and Rema, Uma and Hara, the moon and the night. Let them possess the purushartha called kama in all its strength.'

The Baba gestured to the Yogini Mata. Surekha and Rangan brought the garlands from the table. The Baba gave one garland to Murugappan and one to Nina. He announced in a resounding voice, 'I now pronounce you man and wife.'

Nina and Murugappan exchanged garlands. The Baba took out a mangalsutra made of gold with diamonds set in it and said, 'Murugappan, tie this around Nina's neck.'

When everyone clapped their hands and the music grew louder, Murugappan tied the mangalsutra around Nina's neck.

Surekha embraced Nina, who stood with the humility of an Indian bride. Arunagiri, Chinnappa and Madhavan Nair came forward with expensive gifts.

Rangarajan tried to crack a joke, 'Bhagwan, I've heard that friends and well-wishers have the right to kiss the bride. I don't know if it's true.'

Everyone laughed. It was Nina who laughed the most.

'Come, Rangan! You are the best man!' Murugappan encouraged Rangarajan.

Rangan kissed Nina on her cheek.

Murugappan and Nina returned to London. The ashram went back to running on the rails of the old routine. Surekha was very happy. Now, everything would work out as she wished. She had been able to gain control, to get rid of Nina who was threatening to be a rival.

But the Yogini Mata was disturbed every now and then – when Nina rang Baba up from London or when she wrote letters to the Baba.

Surekha could have tapped the telephone if she wished. She could have steamed open the letters, read them and stuck them again so that no one would know that they had been opened. She did not do any of those things. She remembered what Chinnappa had said. What did it matter if the Baba did sleep with Nina on one occasion or two. Is our new Bhakti movement something that ends in one night or one bed?

Probably not! Not at all! Why should she be afraid of Nina, who was thousands of miles away? She had to be afraid of something else – her age, which was advancing fast, of those lines that were being drawn under her eyes, and of the grey hair that she had seen when she examined herself before the mirror the other day.

No, she would not be afraid of even them. She could dye her hair and her skin could look rejuvenated with good foundation creams. She could even get a facelift. Dr Jayabhaskar of the Jupiter Hospital was an excellent cosmetic surgeon.

Surekha became confident as days passed that Nina's absence had not affected the Baba at all. She was able to rock the Baba in the waves of love-making in the meditation centre at night.

Everything was going smoothly. Everything was moving according to her wishes.

The rush of VIPs was ever-increasing. Recent visitors included the American consul, the Italian prime minister, the pop singer Dean Pollock, the Nobel laureate John Williams and the sex symbol Brigitte.

The Baba's predictions were coming true.

Mahabala Rao, the erstwhile chief minister of Karnataka, had become the Home Minister in the Central ministry. It was not just Arunagiri who had issued orders to withdraw the cases against Chinnappa, the cases framed under Central laws were also being withdrawn.

As many crores from the ashram funds had flowed into his coffers, Chinnappa would be able to realize his old dream. The prime minister would come for the inauguration of Mercury Automobiles.

The order detailing the grant of land to the ashram at Ooty had been brought in person by the chief secretary of Tamil Nadu, Gopikrishnan.

Yes Bhagwan, I, Yogini Mata, feel proud of myself. My confidence has grown. Let's stay together and realize new dreams.

❖

Months passed – months when no one knew that Vedan Baba's mind was being disturbed by great churnings.

The Baba knew about the conspiracy that had served to drive

his darling Nina away from him. He also knew that Surekha had initiated everything. But he did not dare show her his displeasure. This ashram was a large puppet theatre. He was only the puppet. The strings that controlled him were with the puppet master, Surekha. He did not dare disobey her.

He felt like spending more time in the Japanese garden.

When he lay on his back and gazed at the sky, Kozhukatta Paru's face would appear before him. His body seemed to have no weight at all. He was rising higher and higher. He was shooting through the sky and going up. Perfumed clouds enveloped him. As he stepped on them and went further upwards, he could hear terrible roars. What did he see? He saw corpses that danced, vultures that came to pluck at them. He trembled with fear. 'Amma!' he cried out aloud. And a beautiful arm wearing bangles came down from the heights. It guided him to a beautiful garden. He wondered whose hand it could be.

He did not know.

The arm vanished.

There was a pathway through the garden with gem-encrusted pillars on either side. He walked further.

Young and beautiful girls came flowing from behind the pillars and surrounded him. They laughed aloud as they led him forward into a dazzling bedroom. There on the soft bed sat Kozhukatta Paru covered by a thin veil.

Paru hissed, and the young beauties became swirls of mist and vanished into the air.

When she removed the veil and started dancing, Kozhukatta Paru became the Yogini Mata.

She came forward naked and locked him in an embrace.

'Vedan, my pet! Vedan, my darling!' Yogini Mata panted.

'Let me go!' he tried to struggle out of her arms.

The Yogini Mata sucked at his lips and all the blood flowed from his body to hers.

'Let me go!'

'Let you go? You are Bhagwan, aren't you? Can you perform a

miracle and escape from me? Try to if you dare.'

'I'm not Bhagwan. I'm only Ramankutty, the uruli thief.'

'Don't speak nonsense, Baba. We have made you a prisoner. You are in eternal and sacred imprisonment.'

'I'm not Bhagwan, I'm a man.'

'Don't be crazy. You are god.'

'Surekha, I'm not god. There is no god who creates and looks after the world.'

'Bhagwan, you once told me: matha kamniya sevyah!'

'Um, it means: consort with women who are intoxicating.'

'So, why do you try to control your instincts? Why won't you come with me?

'Are you planning to be the yajamanapatni of the Aswamedha yagna, the mistress of the horse sacrifice...?'

'Baba, you are my prisoner. I won't let you go.'

'Amma, please save me from this demoness.'

There, the beautiful arm with its bangles appeared. First the hand appeared, and then the whole body.

'Who are you?' Surekha screamed.

'I am Gopika. I'm the lover in my beloved Vedan's dreams. Let my Vedan go, you demoness.'

'I won't let him go, I won't let him go,' Surekha shouted.

'Demoness, may you become an anthill,' Gopika cursed.

Surekha became an anthill.

A strong wind blew. The anthill collapsed. Dust from it rose to the skies.

Vedaraman woke up with a start.

He was in the Japanese garden. Before him stood the Yogini Mata.

'Baba, who did you call in your sleep? Who's this Gopika?'

'I didn't call anyone.'

'You called out many times. Who's this Gopika?'

'Yogini Mata, let's return to the ashram.'

'Tell me, who's this Gopika?'

'I don't know.'

'Is there a woman like that?'

'There might be.'

'Really...?'

'Sura, what is the truth? What is illusion? Who can really say? I won't hide anything from you. I saw an arm in my dreams, an arm with bangles. It was the arm of a beautiful woman. That beautiful woman is Gopika.'

'Let us hope that she does not break the cage of dreams and come out.'

'Sura, are you jealous?'

'No, no. Let's go to the meditation centre. I have to tell you something.'

When they reached the meditation centre, Surekha shut the door. She said, 'I'm planning to go to Ooty with the architect. We have to start work on the ashram there, don't we?'

'Good, a retreat at Ooty! A hermitage! If Gopika ever becomes a reality, we can entrust the responsibility of the new ashram to her.'

'Vedan, are you joking? Why do you speak to me like this? I am your mother and your lover, isn't that so?'

Vedaraman did not reply.

'Tell me. Tell me I am everything.'

'You are just one thing – my jailer.'

She laughed aloud. 'Maybe. So come to my prison.'

She embraced Vedan. Vedan pushed her away.

Surekha was now aroused and ran her fingers over Vedan's body.

Vedan Baba hung his head, 'However much you try, I don't think I'll awaken today. Please leave me alone.'

Forty-five

What had happened to Vedaraman? What was persuading the Baba to spend his nights in the meditation centre? Why did he refuse to sleep on the peacock bed in his room? Many such questions troubled Surekha's mind. Questions to which she could not find any answer.

Surekha felt that the Baba was keeping her at a distance. He had changed a lot.

When she thought of the night he had pushed her away, her heart sank.

Rangarajan had asked once, 'What's the matter, madam? What's happened to the Baba? What's happened to you? Who's keeping a distance from whom?'

She had laughed and evaded the question, 'Rangan you are allowing your imagination to run wild. Everything is as before...'

She had decided then: I, as Yogini Mata, should be careful. No one should believe that there's been a rift between Bhagwan and myself. I need to be extremely patient. The growth and working of the ashram should not be at risk in any way. I'll have to cultivate patience. I have to forget the rejection and insult of that night. After all, I still have the beauty and shape to excite any man. Vedan, I accept that rejection for the time being. But I've been hurt badly. There's only one thing in my favour. Only I know that Bhagwan turned away from my advances that night when I approached him. Therefore, my dear Bhagwan, I can save face. Only I need to know the injury that I suffered. So, I work hard to maintain the impression that everything is going on as before. I still come to the meditation centre. Even when you turn your face away and are silent, I keep coming. When I reach my bedroom alone, the satin pillows get soaked in tears. Let that remain my secret sorrow. In the mornings, I come to the meditation centre again and lead you to the bathroom. I become crazy when I bathe you. Still, I keep control over myself.

Yes, what is needed now is patience.

Let weeks pass. Or months. If I behave sensibly, Bhagwan, I will bring you around. Everything will be as before. It has to be. No, everything should be better. We shall need larger amounts now. Chinnappa will ask for more crores. Mercury Automobiles is like the legendary Bakasur who always had his mouth open for more. Chinnappa's prestige project was awaiting the arrival of the prime minister. Vedan Baba, I shall see to it that you remain the living god.

We have to achieve our aims.

Even as she consoled herself with these thoughts, there was a small worm creeping in her heart – a worm called Gopika.

Bhagwan speaks frequently of Gopika now, without any care for the time or occasion, before anyone. It is always in a way that surprises the listeners, and raises doubts in their minds.

'Who is this woman, this Gopika?'

Even Rangarajan had started asking, 'Who's Gopika? Is there a woman like that?'

Rangan was not a liar. Nor did he exaggerate or add frills when he spoke. So some of the things that he said were upsetting. She had to admit that.

The Baba had described Gopika to Rangan – she was beautiful with long slim arms with bangles on them. When the Baba lay on his back in the Japanese garden and meditated, he could see her.

The Baba had asked Rangarajan to write a song about Gopika. Rangan had entrusted the job to Minnal Babu. Rangan said that the Baba kept scribbling when he sat alone in the meditation centre. He wrote and then tore it all up. Major Chandrasenan said that some bits of paper had been recovered when the meditation centre was cleaned. All of them had one word written repeatedly – Gopika…Gopika…Gopika…

Though it was not possible to be fully open with Rangarajan, Surekha was beginning to feel that she should share some of her misgivings with him. As she waited for a suitable moment, Rangan informed her one Saturday, 'Madam, Boss had rung up. He wants to conduct an internal meeting this evening.'

The internal meeting or review meeting that took place on Saturdays had been discontinued for some time. There had been no meeting since Nina left.

Now, suddenly…?

'Rangan, is there anything special to be discussed? Did Boss hint at anything?'

'No, madam.'

'Shouldn't we inform Baba?'

'We'll tell him at lunch time. He is meditating in the Japanese garden.'

'Rangan, I think one of the points of discussion at today's meeting will be the hermitage at Ooty. It is quite some time since Gopikrishnan handed over the government order.'

'Yes, madam. There has been delay in the matter of the hermitage, we have to admit that. Boss might point that out.'

'I admit I'm guilty. That architect gave me dates more than once. I kept cancelling the programme at the last moment. Would the architect have complained to our Boss? He is a busy man.'

'No, no. He wouldn't dare complain or anything of that sort. Would he risk his ten per cent? Our outlay is more than a crore. But, madam, if Boss brings up the topic we have to admit that we have delayed.'

'I shall, Rangan. Do you know why I keep postponing the Ooty trip, Rangan? I would have to stay there for a few days. If I stay away for some days, what will happen here…?'

Rangan laughed. 'I'm here to look after things. That's not the problem. I know what the real matter is. You think that it will be unwise to leave the Baba alone even for a very short period.'

'That's true, Rangan.'

'Why are you scared, madam? Your rival is far away, in London.'

'Nina is not a rival at all now, Rangan! She's Murugappan's wife. I'm not afraid of Nina any longer. In any case, Nina has a well-defined form. She's a known danger. Once you know who your opponent is, you can plan your strategy. But that is not the situation here.'

'Oh, you're talking about Gopika?'

'That's right, Rangan. Who's this Gopika?'

When Chinnappa came for the internal meeting, he prostrated himself before Bhagwan.

'Get up. Come and sit beside me,' the Baba spoke. His sixth finger glowed as he continued, 'I desire that everyone should be with me always. Only the three of you are here now. Let me say something. All of you are drifting away from me. Once the purpose of my incarnation is complete, who am I? What purpose do I serve? Who are you? And why do I need you? When I set out on my return journey, will there be anyone with me? A stupid question, isn't it? I dream. I turn creator in my dreams. Am I god? A magician? I see long slim fair hands and bangles that make them beautiful. When I speak of all that, the world may pelt me with stones. I shall not throw stones in return. Instead I shall pick up the stones that are thrown at me. They will become diamonds and rubies and emeralds. Chinnappa, give me your hand. Let your hand clasp mine. Shut your eyes everyone, and meditate!'

Chinnappa, Surekha and Rangarajan shut their eyes.

'Did you see her? Did you see my Gopika? Don't her hands touch you? Doesn't her love envelope you?'

No one said anything in reply.

'You might feel that this "We or I" am speaking in riddles. I'm not blaming any of you. The magnetism of my vibrations does not touch your hearts now. The cobwebs of ignorance have covered your brains. Never mind. Open your eyes now. At least your outer eyes.'

Chinnappa, Surekha and Rangarajan opened their eyes.

'Chinnappa, I know that these are busy days for all of you. Arunagiri has the problems of governing. Madhavan Nair is in the throes of conquering new heights of success. So, they do not have the time to come here. Chinnappa, even you have learnt to stay away.'

Chinnappa folded his hands and said, 'Bhagwan, please don't misunderstand me. Since the Yogini Mata was taking care of everything here, I...'

The Baba laughed aloud. 'Good logic! Since the Yogini Mata was taking care of everything, I, known as Chinnappa, had no reason to come here. Is that it?'

Chinnappa did not say anything, but bent his head as someone who had been caught red-handed.

'I have a question for the Yogini Mata.'

'Please ask me, Bhagwan?'

'There has been much delay in the construction of our hermitage at Ooty. Why?'

'Bhagwan, I beg your forgiveness. I also admit that I am at fault. Within two days, I shall go to Ooty with the architect.'

'You must see to it that there's a Japanese garden just like the one here.'

'Yes, Bhagwan.'

'Chinnappa, I shall now speak of the subject that interests you most. You have come here to talk about the inauguration of Mercury Automobiles, isn't it?'

'Yes, Bhagwan! You know everything.'

'The letter you sent to the emperor of the North is now...'

Vedan Baba stared at the ceiling. The words that came from Baba's mouth after that had a special resonance to them.

'The emperor of the North is reading the letter now. Within five weeks he will let you know the date for the inauguration. The inauguration will be a great success. You are getting five weeks to prepare for it. Count that as a blessing from me. I will not go into the details. You have got involved in some financial problems as well. The knots will be unravelled in three weeks. Yogini Mata, release more funds.'

'Yes, Bhagwan.'

'Shall we break up now? My Gopika has come and is waiting for me.'

The Baba got up.

Surekha and Rangarajan came out of the ashram to see off Chinnappa.

Chinnappa was immersed in thought. He said, 'Surekha, Bhagwan has understood my problems. I need eighteen crores immediately for the Mercury project.'

'Boss, the money is available!'

'I feel rather bad. Was Bhagwan displeased today? Did he hint that all of us have forgotten him and become selfish?'

'You are imagining things, Boss. Bhagwan has only affection for us.'

'What do you say, Rangan?'

'I agree with madam. Bhagwan has only affection for us, Boss.'

'Let that remain true. Still, I do feel guilty. Nair and I are not like Aruna. Aruna's problem is not just that he's busy with the government. There is also the problem of his image. If he appears to be worshipping at the feet of sages and living gods, the old foxes in his party will criticize him. He had told us that right at the beginning. But what justification do Nair and I have for staying away from the ashram? Forget it! Surekha, don't delay any further. Go to Ooty immediately. By the way, who's this Gopika?'

Forty-six

It was Saturday morning. As she returned with the Baba from the bathroom, Surekha asked, 'Bhagwan, why is my mind so disturbed? Why am I losing all my confidence?'

The Baba said, 'You have filled your mind with darkness. You spend too much time thinking about me. That is why this unnecessary fear has you in its grip.'

'Shall I postpone my trip? My mind does not permit me to leave you alone and go away.'

'Surekha, you are not going to Ooty to stay there permanently. You should be back in four or five days. This trip is good – for you and for me.'

'You said that so easily. Just four or five days! They'll be as long as yugas, Bhagwan. I can't bear to be away from you.'

'Sura, it is good to be apart. When you are with me, when you imprison me, the cobwebs of avidya, ignorance, cover you. You turn away from the truth. You become the slave of raga and dwesha, desire and anger. If we separate, if we stay away from each other, even if it is for a few days – we may gain new perspectives. I may be able to judge you truthfully, and you may be able to judge me truly. You may realize that I am not Bhagwan.'

'Don't say that, Baba! You are Bhagwan. A living god.'

'Go now. The architect is waiting for you.'

'Let me dress you as I usually do. When the stars of the music world line up today...When the concert of devotional music takes place...'

Vedaraman smiled, 'Yogini Mata, I shall dress on my own. I shall not appear at the concert naked.'

❖

'Rangan, I may need to stay in Ooty for three or four days.'

'Madam, take your time. You should stay there till the architect finishes his preliminary survey.'

'Rangan, I'm going to be away from the ashram for a few days for the first time. In my absence...'

'I'm here, madam. There'll be no problem.'

'Yes. I do feel reassured when I tell myself that you'll be here, Rangan. Look after the Baba properly. Be with him always.'

'Don't worry, madam.'

'Can I ask you something?'

'Yes, madam.'

'I'm a little worried. Do you feel that Baba has changed a lot recently, Rangan?'

'He is a little moody.'

'Has he become a little indifferent towards me? What's your assessment?'

'I have a feeling that the Baba is no longer as cheerful as he used to be since Nina left. Then...there's that Gopika angle. That might be what's upsetting you. But that's only Baba's imagination.'

'I'll try to reassure myself with that. Still, we have to be careful. Imagination running wild can become a problem. Okay, is our Major Chandrasenan reliable?'

'Certainly! Why do you ask?'

'Just a thought. Forget about it. I'll leave now.'

'Breakfast?'

'It's packed and kept in the car.'

When the car bearing Surekha and the architect drove off, Vedan Baba's voice was heard calling out, 'Rangan!'

Rangan came running. Vedan Baba was standing in the corridor in front of the meditation centre, clad in a dressing gown. He was laughing aloud.

'There has to be a reason for me to be laughing aloud like this. Tell me, what is it?'

'You tell me, Bhagwan.'

'The mischievous boy feels like laughing aloud when the headmistress has left the school. Do you know, Rangan, I'm afraid of the Yogini Mata.'

'Bhagwan, this is a good joke.'

'It's not a joke, Rangan. I'm telling the truth. Remember one thing. I'm not Bhagwan. At least for today. I want total relaxation today. I wish to be myself till the Yogini Mata returns.'

'As you wish, Bhagwan.'

'You continue to call me that. Never mind. Let's go to the breakfast table. Where's our Major? Call him too.'

As they sat at breakfast, Vedan Baba told Chandrasenan, 'Major, you consider me Bhagwan. Why is that? When you saw me for the first time, I was already Bhagwan. But Rangan has seen me before I became a Bhagwan. Do you remember, Rangan?'

Rangarajan was silent.

'Major, Rangan is a scholar. When he saw me for the first time at Chinnappa's bungalow, he told me so many things. About the shad-darshanas – nyaya, vaisheshika, yoga, mimamsa, vedanta . . . Do you know Major, to begin with these shad-darshanas, the six streams of philosophical thought, did not recognize the existence of god. If I go on like this, you'll not be able to enjoy your breakfast.'

For some time there was only the sound of cutlery knocking against the plates.

Suddenly Vedan Baba asked, 'Has Minnal Babu written the song about Gopika? I would like to hear it in the concert of devotional songs this evening.'

'I'll ask Minnal, Baba!'

Breakfast ended.

'Shouldn't you get dressed, Bhagwan?' Rangarajan asked.

'Oh! Turban, silk shervani, waistband, what else? No, Rangan. We are not ready to wear the uniform of Bhagwan today. I'm not coming out today. I told you earlier. I'm a naughty boy today. A small child.'

The Baba got up.

He wandered around, humming something under his breath.

Gopika, my beautiful one.

The nymph of my dreams.

Come, come close.

Capture me in your slim arms adorned with bangles.

Let my body and senses be satiated with the desires of this world.

Rangarajan and Major left with Baba's permission. There was not much time before the concert of devotional songs started.

Famous singers with value at box-office took part in the concert. Minnal Babu stood near the orchestra pit as if he were in control of everything.

Rangarajan told the Major, 'Senan, you oversee everything. Let me go and see what the Baba is doing.'

Rangan went in search of the Baba. He was lying on the peacock bed. He was speaking to himself as if he were reciting poetry.

My mind, don't be a monkey.

Stay fixed in one place, tied by just one leash.

Come Gopika, this potter shall do the impossible.

He'll mix the mud of his mind and build a golden pot.

Rangarajan coughed to attract Baba's attention.

'Rangan, it's you. I don't have the least bit of poetic sensibility and yet I was trying to hum a few lines. I'm celebrating my day of independence after all. Rangan, you'll be with me, won't you? You'll obey me?'

'I'm always with you, Bhagwan. I'm ready to obey any of Bhagwan's instructions.'

'Very good. Hear the first instruction. You shall not call me Bhagwan.'

'Bhagwan, I find it difficult to obey that order.'

'You can't change your habit, can you? All right. I'll ask you to do some easier things. These won't be difficult to obey. I want some clay – to make a golden pot.'

'I did not understand, Bhagwan.'

'I'll explain. Shall we have some gangajal before that?'

Rangarajan brought the drinks.

'Rangan, shall we call the Major and Minnal Babu?'

'We could call the Major. Wouldn't it be better to keep some distance from Minnal? He's a blabbermouth. I think it would be better to avoid having him here.'

'All of us are blabbermouths. And I'm the king of them. Let's feel free...If the concert is over, ask them to come here.

Rangarajan brought Major Chandrasenan and Minnal Babu. The Baba was sitting with his eyes closed when they came. His sixth finger was glowing. As they stood waiting, the Baba opened his eyes and smiled. He said, 'Sit down. I'm coming too. Let's make a magic circle.'

The Baba sat on the floor. Rangan, Major and Minnal sat before him.

'Rangan, give everyone the sacred water,' Baba ordered.

When Minnal was reluctant to accept the glass, the Baba told him, 'Have it, think of it as prasad given by me.'

All of them drank.

'Minnal, I'm a little angry with you.'

When Baba said this with a little smile and a wink, Rangarajan nudged Minnal Babu and whispered, 'That song about Gopika. That's what Baba is talking about.'

'Bhagwan, I'll write that song immediately,' Minnal said, folding his hands together.

Vedan Baba lifted his right hand – as if to stop something.

'Let me repeat what I've already told Rangan today. Today, at least today, no one should call me Bhagwan. I am not Bhagwan.'

Minnal Babu's voice broke as he protested, 'Today and every day, you are Bhagwan. You are a divine incarnation who has come to earth to rescue us sinners.'

'Minnal you are an ignorant man. I won't argue with you. But Rangan is wise. Let me ask Rangan. Is there a god who creates everything and ensures that we experience the consequences of our deeds? Give me an answer.'

Rangarajan did not open his mouth.

The Baba continued, 'Space, time, direction, soul, mind – all these are said to be eternal. How can you create something that is eternal? The atoms of earth, water, fire and air are also eternal. They too cannot be created. As for karma – we think that each karma, each deed has an allocated consequence. So, for someone who has done bad deeds the consequences can never be good. Then, how can there be a god who will serve as a middleman to give a sinner a good life? There cannot be. So there's no god, no Bhagwan. How can a god who does not exist have a representative in this world? I'm talking wildly. Let's get to the matter at hand. Let's try to create a golden pot from clay.'

Rangan, Major and Minnal exchanged glances without following what the Baba was saying.

The Baba laughed, 'I'll come down to the earth. I shall ask an earthy question. Who knows how to make a statue from clay?'

'Lots of people know, Bhagwan,' Minnal said.

'Tell me the name of one person who does.'

'Muniswami who does the sets in Vijayavahini Studio. He's a friend of mine.'

'Minnal, ask him to come here. I want him to make a statue according to my instructions.'

Muniswami came to the ashram before lunch time. Baba was seated on the lotus mandap in the prayer hall.

When Muniswami was brought before the Baba by Rangan and the others, he put aside the big bag he had brought on the floor and fell at Baba's feet.

'Muniswami, Minnal tells me you are a very good sculptor. You are the creator. You must make me the statue of a beautiful woman,' Baba said.

'I'll try Bhagwan,' Muniswami stood with folded hands.

'You can start.'

'Bhagwan, I work in a cinema studio. Sometimes there are models there. Sometimes I look at calendar pictures and make statues. Lakshmi, Saraswati, Krishna, salabhanjika or the guard at the door, I do all these. What should I make here?'

'The statue of a beautiful woman. I'll describe her. Shall we start?'

'How big?'

'You decide.'

'Bhagwan, I'll make one of one foot height. If you are satisfied, I'll make it full size.'

'Very good, Muniswami.'

Muniswami sat on the floor. He opened his bag and took out a wooden plank, followed by wet clay, wire mesh, plaster of paris, the implements of his trade...

Using the wire mesh, Muniswami prepared a one-foot high skeleton. Preparing to cover it with clay, he looked at the Baba with devotion in his eyes.

The Baba started explaining.

'Muniswami, she has long arms, beautifully rounded arms. She wears bangles. She does not have big breasts. Nor is she narrow chested. Can the navel look like a dimple? If so, that is the kind of navel she has. A narrow waist and flaring hips...' Muniswami's fingers moved fast. A beautiful woman's form grew clearer.

'Bhagwan, tell me about the face,' Muniswami requested humbly.

Vedan Baba looked at Rangan and gestured. Rangan understood. The Baba wanted more gangajal. After a stiff drink, the Baba said, 'Muniswami! I've not seen that face. So, what can I say? You are an artist. Shape the face as you think it should be. It may become Gopika...

Muniswami was sweating as he carved out the face of the statue with his flat steel instrument.

Finally, when he had used all his skill to finish the beautiful statue, Muniswami withdrew his eyes from the eyes of his creation and sighed. He looked around for approval.

Rangan and the Major knelt on the floor and examined the statue.

'Marvellous!' Rangan commented.

'Bring it here!' The Baba said. Muniswami took the statue on the plank to the Baba. For a long time the Baba sat and gazed at the statue. He ran a finger over it so lightly that he barely touched it.

Everyone waited for Baba's opinion. Muniswami was most anxious.

The Baba spoke haltingly, 'I like this statue as a work of art. It's really beautiful, Muniswami. But it's not Gopika. So, I'm going to destroy it.'

The Baba's right hand fell on the statue like a big chisel. It became a deformed mass of clay and wire mesh.

The Baba got up.

'Rangan, I don't want any lunch today. Muniswami should go only after having lunch. Minnal, please make Muniswami understand. The statue was beautiful. That it did not become Gopika was my fault. I have never seen Gopika's face. How can any sculptor copy something that I have not seen? Thank you, Muniswami. Rangan please pay him a thousand rupees.'

The Baba went to his bedroom.

He shut the door, and drank.

He kept muttering.

'Sura, Kozhukatta Paru, my jailor. Be damned. I'll defeat you. I'll escape. I'll become Vedaraman again.'

Forty-seven

Vedan Baba went to the meditation centre in the evening. Since he had not had lunch, Rangan had thought that he would come out in the night and take some food. But he was mistaken. Rangan felt concerned when it was past 8 o'clock in the night. He went in search of Chandrasenan. What should they do now?

'Go and call him. If he does not want to come to the dining hall, never mind. We could serve him dinner in the meditation centre,' Senan advised him.

The door to the meditation centre stayed shut.

The Baba opened the door only after Rangan knocked a number of times. His eyes were bloodshot.

'It's time for dinner, Bhagwan.'

'I don't want anything.'

'Take something, at least for my sake. Some fruit... a little milk...'

'I don't want anything, Rangan.'

'Bhagwan, you are putting me through a terrible test. If you sit here, alone like this...'

'What's wrong with my sitting alone? All of you worship me too much. Sitting alone, meditating, collecting and arranging scattered thoughts... aren't these good things to do? Another thing, I'm not alone here. Gopika is with me. Leave me to myself!'

Rangan withdrew helplessly.

He spoke to Chandrasenan, 'Baba's behaviour is upsetting

me. He says he does not want anything. He does not want any of us. He only wants Gopika!'

It was very late at night. All the inmates of the ashram were asleep. Vedan Baba got out of the meditation centre and staggered to the Japanese garden.

The Baba stood for a while looking at the sky. Was the crescent moon spinning like a top? Were the stars dancing?

The Baba lay on his back on the sand in the garden. He felt as if a dark cloud were descending from the sky. It became a black horse. If he could climb on that he could rush away. Where to? The Baba lifted a leg. Had he climbed the horse? It started galloping, through the paths of memory.

Sreedhara Menon lay dead.

Koman Nair had killed him.

Good thing. Sreedhara Menon should have died; should have been killed.

Mulamkunnam Yajamanan, why did you kick my mother to death?

Was that singer Swami the cause of my birth?

Hey Sreedhara Menon, did you kill my mother because I had six fingers like that singer?

What were the Big Man and Cherian Munshi talking about? Were they saying that, according to numerology, a sixth finger denoted prosperity and good fortune?

Why did Kozhukatta Paru come in between? She was screaming, 'Ramankutty, you'll never know what love is, you'll never experience it. You'll never be able to keep a young woman with you. You were born to embrace anthills.'

You rotten woman, you forget that Nina loved me. I too loved her.

'Oh Nina! The famous prostitute from London! Anyway, you weren't able to make her your own. The older prostitute Surekha defeated you cleverly. Still, you shameless fellow, you call her mother! Mother...Yogini Mata. Who's your mother? I'm your mother. I gave you milk.'

Che! You gave me milk for your pleasure. Do you know my elder brother Sankaran, who is a typist in Bombay? Do you know my other brother Narayanan who's a peon in Fort St George here? They escaped. You weren't able to grab them...

Kozhukatta Paru became silent.

My dear brothers, do you know – your younger brother Ramankutty is now Bhagwan! That's what people say.

Let that be.

My dear brothers, I hope both of you are married and that your wives are good women and that you have lots of children. I believe that you live an ordinary contented life. You are the people who escaped. Even Kuttisankaran escaped. Some woman waited for him in Kothakurissi.

Brother Narayanan, can I escape from here? Maybe I can. I must. If I can find Gopika, I shall be able to escape. Who's this Gopika? A girl has been born somewhere, a girl destined to be my bride. A girl who wears bangles. She's Gopika. I must look for her, find her. She'll give me happiness and peace.

Brother Narayanan, why should I speak to you now? I'm a useless fellow, a thief, a fraud. You are a peon. You know your chief minister, Arunagiri. He's my devotee. He falls at my feet. I'll tell him, 'Hey, Arunagiri, make my brother a government secretary, or the managing director of a company!' Narayanan, you think it won't work. It will. It will work easily. Why do you laugh at me? Are you asking me why I did not do this earlier if it were so easy? I'll get it done. Just help me. Help me find my Gopika. I shall stay in our compound with the stone quarry and the pond with its water snakes. I'm sure I'll be at peace there. Achuettan is there, Koman Nair is there, Unneera is there, there are lots of people there. None of them will cheat me, calling me Bhagwan. I shall also not cheat them. Mukundan must have got out from Viyyur jail. I'll accept him again as a friend. Everyone cheats me in Madras. I too cheat them. I'm not a god. I'm tired, my dear brother.

❖

It was Sunday. Rangarajan woke up with a start at dawn. Today was a busy day. The day when tens of thousands of people came for Baba's darshan.

Rangarajan went to see the Baba. He did not find him.

The doors of the bedroom and the meditation centre were open. The pillows and sheets of the peacock bed were not rumpled at all. Where was the Baba? Where had he slept?

Rangarajan woke Chandrasenan in a bit of a flap, 'I can't find the Baba.'

'Let's see if he's somewhere outside.'

They found the Baba in the Japanese garden. He was lying down, but not asleep.

'Baba…here…?'

'I felt like coming and sleeping here. That's all.'

'Please come, Bhagwan, today is the day for public darshan.'

'I'll come. But you won't get me to do anything today. Don't trouble me today.'

Rangan and Senan led the Baba to the bedroom without saying anything.

By 9 o'clock, devotees started gathering in the yard of the ashram in small groups. By ten, the yard was full. People of different ages, different types, people who were ill and people who were healthy, men and women.

Shouts resounded.

Jai Bhagwan!

Baba nidhuzhi vazhga! May Baba live long!

When minutes lengthened to hours they became impatient. They started asking each other: Why doesn't Baba appear?

This question became a huge roar, a roar that rose to the sky. The disappointed devotees started moving forward in small waves.

There were shouts – from individual throats and in groups: 'Give us darshan, Bhagwan! We have come a long way, bless us, Swami!'

Rangarajan reached Baba's bedroom. He was sleeping an exhausted sleep on the peacock bed. Rangarajan hesitated to shake him awake. Finally, he gathered courage and did so. If the Baba did not appear before the crowd at least for a moment, the situation could become ugly. The roars that could be heard now had traces of anger.

Where's Bhagwan?

Why has Bhagwan not come?

Oye you frauds, let out Bhagwan and let him come.

Rangarajan could not wake the Baba up. Chandrasenan came panting before Rangarajan as he stood there wondering what to do.

'The crowd is getting out of control. It is going mad. Shall I tell the security staff to use force?'

'No, Senan. I'll face the crowd. Bring some vibhuti, sacred ash, immediately.'

Rangarajan came out of the building, calling on all the gods.

The crowd came roaring forward. Rangarajan jumped on to the platform that was normally used by the choir.

'Thaimarkale, Thozharkale, Bhagwane vananka vanthirikkum podumakkale amaithi...Mothers, friends, devotees who have come to bow before Bhagwan, please be patient. This is not just my request, it is Bhagwan's message. Bhagwan is on a vow of silence today. He prays for all of us in silence today. His blessings are with everyone. We shall be distributing vibhuti created by Bhagwan from emptiness. None of you should go away before the daridranarayana puja. There will also be a dakshina, a gift of money, after the food today.'

The crowd cooled down. There was applause from here and there. A number of people shouted, 'Jai Bhagwan!'

When everything was over, Rangarajan sipped a stiff whisky and said, 'Senan, that was a close call. We were lucky. We have this headache for another couple of days. The Yogini Mata should be here before Wednesday.'

The Baba did not come out of the ashram on Tuesday and

Wednesday. He was not even willing to greet VIP visitors. He spent his time divided between the bedroom and the meditation centre.

The only thing that gave some consolation to Rangarajan was that the Baba took some food at least.

What would Surekha think when she saw the Baba? That question troubled Rangarajan's mind.

Baba had not bathed or changed his clothes. There was stubble on his cheeks. Would Surekha say accusingly, 'Rangan, you have neglected Bhagwan!'

Surekha returned by Wednesday afternoon. As soon as she came in she asked for a detailed report of what had happened in her absence. Rangarajan did not hide anything.

'The Yogini Mata has returned. I'm relieved. There will be no problem now.' He ended with that.

Surekha's eyes were damp when she went to the bedroom and saw Vedan who was lying there in a half-conscious state.

She touched Vedan and asked, 'Bhagwan, what happened?'

Vedaraman muttered, 'Oh Yogini Mata! My jailer!'

'I know everything. You can't hide in a hole like this, Bhagwan. What'll your devotees think?'

'How many times must I tell all of you that I'm not Bhagwan.'

'However many times you say that, we shan't agree. You are Bhagwan. None of us have any doubts. Sit up. I'll tell you about my Ooty trip.'

'Ooty! My second jail. Sura, I need to escape. I have to go somewhere, anywhere. I want to enter the reality of the world.'

Surekha smiled, 'I understand now. You need a change, that's it. An outing? I'll take you.'

'Really? That's a good idea. I get confused when I dress up and sit here as god. Take me somewhere else.'

'We'll wander around the city, okay? Before that, you've got to be made presentable. I'll bring the razor.' Surekha caressed Vedaraman's cheek.

Surekha shaved him. As the razor ran over his cheeks, she could not control herself and kissed him on the lips. The razor slipped and blood showed on Vedan's cheeks. She put her lips to that blood as well.

'Darling, to the bathroom now. I'll bathe you.'

It was dusk. Rangarajan and Chandrasenan watched in surprise as Surekha led Vedan dressed in trousers and a shirt into the car.

Where could they be going?

Forty-eight

The car ran through the main streets. The city was flooded with light. Multi-coloured neon and halogen advertisements spread brightness in shopping areas. Vedaraman sat on the left side of the back seat. Surekha sat next to him and spoke with the fluency of a guide about the streets they passed through, the landmarks that flowed past. She felt that Vedan, who sat and looked at the sights through the window, had the expression of a child who had been taken to a carnival. Vedan did not say anything. He would laugh once in a while, move his fingers on the handle of the door. Surekha felt that the sights were entertaining Bhagwan. She asked, 'Enjoying yourself, my pet?'

Vedaraman grunted in reply.

'Where shall I go next, madam?' driver Kuppan asked.

'Let the car run, Kuppan. There's no special destination. This is just a run around the city for fun.'

It was a busy road with four-lane traffic.

When the lights turned red, the cars stopped one by one. The engines continued to roar, waiting for the moment when the lights would turn green. Autorickshaws and two-wheelers squeezed in between, leading to a traffic jam.

That was when it happened. Vedaraman opened the door of the car and jumped out. He disappeared into the crowd. Kuppan, who was watching the lights, was unaware of this. Surekha was so stunned she could not even shout. She thought of jumping out through the open door. But by then the lights changed and

Kuppan drove the car forward. It followed the cars in front.

A low shriek issued from Surekha's throat. Kuppan turned around. His eyes opened wide in surprise. Where was Bhagwan?

But he did not dare ask anything. He put out his hand and shut the door that was open and swinging.

Surekha screamed, 'Stop, Kuppan, stop!'

Kuppan moved out of the flow of traffic and stopped the car near the footpath.

Surekha somehow said, 'Back...to the ashram.'

The Yogini Mata was weeping uncontrollably. Rangan and Chandrasenan stood silently before her, unable to think of anything to say.

They were all in the grip of a terrible anxiety. What should they do now? The world could not be allowed to know that Bhagwan had vanished. They couldn't even think of the repercussions if such a piece of news leaked out. There were many questions that frightened them. Surekha tried to articulate the most fearsome one.

What would Chinnappa's reaction be?

What could she say if Boss asked why she had gone out in the car for a drive with the Baba? Chinnappa's politeness and pleasant behaviour were only skin deep. He carried many daggers hidden in his heart. When he was angry he could become a devil. The Baba had vanished at a terrible juncture. Within weeks the prime minister would arrive, for the inauguration of Mercury Automobiles. It was the moment of Chinnappa's greatest triumph. The prime minister might wish to see Vedan Baba. Would they be able to find Bhagwan before the Northern emperor landed?

Finally Rangan said, 'There's no point being afraid and nervous. This is not a problem that anyone can solve. There's only one thing to be done. Let the Boss know what has happened. You must go immediately to Poes Garden.'

'Me alone?'

'I'll come with you. The Major can stay here.'

Surekha told the Major, 'See that this does not become a topic of discussion here.'

'It's a tall order, madam. I'll try my best. I'm afraid of Kuppan's tongue. He saw the Baba escape, I mean, he is aware of it,' Senan said.

'We'll take Kuppan with us, Major.'

Chinnappa and Madhavan Nair were in a good mood. Arunagiri had given them the news only a little while ago.

'Chinnu, the PM comes much earlier than expected. Today is the 19th. He arrives on the 26th. I got Maniappan's message this afternoon, and an hour back the chief secretary confirmed it. Get busy!'

Sipping whisky, Chinnappa said, 'It's all Vedan Baba's blessings.'

A time of contentment.

As Surekha and Rangarajan entered, Chinnappa welcomed them happily, 'Come. You've come at a good moment. Do you know, the PM's coming on the 26th? It's all Bhagwan's blessings.'

Surekha clutched Rangan's hand, and then fell down unconscious.

Rangarajan muttered, 'Boss, something terrible has happened.'

'What?'

'Baba has disappeared. He's missing. Escaped.'

Chinnappa roared, 'What are you saying?'

After he had heard the whole story, Chinnappa showed extraordinary patience and sense. He consoled Surekha, 'What has happened has happened. I'll get in touch with Arunagiri. We have just one thing to do now. Damage control.'

Chinnappa started speaking clearly, 'The Baba is missing, Baba ran away... these rumours should not reach the people. Where could the Baba have gone? No one knows. That area where he jumped out of the car can be searched. But should we allow such a search when Baba is involved? There should be no publicity at all. If there is to be a search, it should be very discreet. There's time to think of all that. Perhaps we might have to extend the search to the Kochi area as well. If the Baba goes away from this city, it is likely to be to his own village. Let that be, let's stop guessing. What can we do now? I see just one way to keep a lid on everything. The Baba is now in Ooty. That's our story. He went to see the site with the architect. He decided that he would spend some time meditating in that quiet atmosphere. You understand the line we are taking? Somehow, I think the Baba will come back. Perhaps even this running away we speak of may have a purpose...a spiritual purpose. Bhagwan sees with his inner eye much more than we can see. That's our experience till date. Only one thing makes me anxious. If Bhagwan does not return before the 26th, if the prime minister insists on seeing Bhagwan...Arunagiri should be able to find a solution to that problem. Get back. Go. Behave as if everything is normal. There are no activities, that is all. Remember this. Bhagwan is in Ooty.'

Rangan said, 'Boss, driver Kuppan knows what happened. We've come here with him. He has to be kept quiet.'

Chinnappa looked at Madhavan Nair, 'Nair, Rangan has brains. Let Kuppan stay here. We'll keep him under wraps.'

'Wouldn't it be better to let the ashram staff go for some time?' Madhavan Nair asked.

'I'll arrange that. I'll also see Aruna immediately. We'll remove the security staff and kitchen staff from the ashram. The police can take over. Rangan, Sura, you both and Senan must see that this show succeeds. No further mistakes should be made.'

The ashram lay asleep.

Surekha kept to her room.

Devotees who tried to come in were prevented from doing so by the new security staff. They spoke politely and explained, 'Devotees, Bhagwan is in Ooty.'

Telephone calls got a recorded reply, 'Bhagwan is in Ooty. He cannot be disturbed for one month.'

On the 24th night Surekha was woken up by Rangan and the Major.

Bhagwan had returned.

As they patrolled the ashram yard, policemen had heard a groan from the Japanese garden. They found a young man wearing torn trousers and shirt. He was laughing like a madman.

Surekha prevented Rangan from elaborating further. She screamed, 'Where's Baba?'

Rangan and Senan led Surekha to Baba's bedroom. A bedraggled form lay on the peacock bed. His clothes were stinking. His face was covered with stubble and there was liquid oozing from the cuts on his legs.

Vedan laughed aloud when he saw Surekha, 'Will you still say that I am Bhagwan?'

'I shall say so. You are Bhagwan...a living god! Rangan, Senan, go and prepare the bathroom.'

When they had left, Surekha caressed Vedaraman and said, 'Bhagwan, my pet!'

'How many times do I have to tell you I'm not a Bhagwan? I wandered around these past few days. I saw a lot of people. Not a crowd, but people. None of them called me Bhagwan. They surrounded me, hooted at me, pelted me with stones. In their eyes I was a madman. They beat me up. Do you want to see my wounds? Do you want to see the pus that oozes from them? Why did I come back? Because I received enlightenment. I realized that this was not a jail and that you were not my jailer. Do you know... I've found my actual jailer.'

'Baba, shall I bring you a drink?'

'To steady me?'

'Why do you trouble me like this, Bhagwan?'

'All right. Get me a drink.'

'After that, you must have a bath and get ready. Chinnappa and Madhavan Nair and the chief minister are likely to come here.'

'Are you going to ring them up?'

'I have to let them know, don't I? Your vanishing like that has upset all of them so much...'

'Vanishing? Call it an escape. In a way, it was not an escape, but just an excursion. A trip to reality. Sura, Mata, where's my drink? Make it a stiff one. I have a lot to say. I have an idea. Let's go to the bathroom, with a bottle. Oh yes, don't forget the razor. All this has to be removed and what lies below, polished,' Vedaraman ran his fingers over his cheek.

Lying in the rich foam in the bathtub, Vedaraman asked Surekha, 'Who am I? Why do you love me still? I don't know. You don't know either. Have I drunk a lot? Am I speaking sense?'

'My darling!' Surekha caressed him. 'I'm lucky, Bhagwan.'

'I'm not Bhagwan. I'm saying this finally...I'm not Bhagwan...I'm not even an enlightened being. I'm a criminal, a wastrel. In a way, all of us are criminals. Look at this sixth finger. This is a big fraud, Sura! We've built such an edifice around it. I remember you had an aunty, didn't you? Margarita Aunty. When Murugappan married Nina...or was it earlier when you first exiled her...you had given her a gift. A gown that belonged to Margarita Aunty. You told me about this aunt one night. She had unusual powers, didn't she?'

'She knew psychometry. The past...and sometimes the future...were like an open book to aunty.'

'Lucky woman! In spite of that no one made her the incarnation of Virgin Mary. You made me play this role. You made me a god. I'm not complaining. I too participated willingly. You will go on taking me around like this, as a Bhagwan. I wish to escape, mother. This drama has to end. I'm going to disobey my jailer. I'm going to escape. My final escape!'

'Jailer? Who's your jailer?'

Vedaraman lifted his left hand and showed his sixth finger. The glow from that had grown into a flame.

Someone knocked on the bathroom door that was shut.

'I think they've come, Sura.'

They could hear voices from outside, 'Madam, madam!'

Surekha opened the bathroom door a little and went outside. It was Rangarajan.

'Madam, Boss, Madhavan Nair and Arunagiri have come. I didn't inform them. It was the policemen.'

'Rangan, the Baba is not ready.'

Vedaraman spoke from the bathtub, 'Go along, Sura. I'll come soon.'

'Darling, I'll be back in a minute.'

Surekha covered herself with a robe and rushed out. Vedaraman jumped out of the bathtub, shut the door and returned to the bathtub.

He took the razor.

The razor moved over the sixth finger.

The sixth finger that had been detached floated in the water and foam like an incandescent worm.

His strength was draining away. Vedaraman's head hung down.

Had his life been in this dirty finger?

The palm trees were growing. They changed into demons. The demons jumped into the water.

Bhlum...bhlum...bhlum!

His ancestors were swimming across the river.

What was the raga being sung by the singer Swami?

What was coming down from the ceiling?

Were they the sharp nails of Kozhukatta Paru?

Were they the slender arms of Gopika with the bangles?

Bhagwan was interred in the Japanese garden. A carved marble slab said: Vedan Baba was not born. Vedan Baba does not die.

The sixth finger still glows. The sacred relic rests in a glass casket on the lotus mandap.

It is heavily protected.

The flow of devotees increases day by day.

The Yogini Mata runs her hand through her silver hair and murmurs, 'Come, I'll tell you Bhagwan's story.'

Some other titles from the
RATNA TRANSLATION SERIES

—✎—

After Yesterday and other stories
by APPADURAI MUTTULINGAM
Translated from Tamil by Padma Narayanan

A Faceless Evening and other stories
by GANGADHAR GADGIL
Translated from Marathi by Keerti Ramachandra

If A River and other stories by KULA SAIKIA
Translated from Asamiya

On A River's Bank by A. MADHAVAN
Translated from Tamil by M. Vijayalakshmi

Havan by MALLIKARJUN HIREMATH
Translated from Kannada by S. Mohanraj

Echoes of the Veena by R. CHUDAMANI
Translated from Tamil by Prabha Sridevan

Here am I and other stories by P. SATHYAVATHI
Translated from Telugu

Sripantha's Kolkata
Translated from Bangla by Anita Kar

—✎—

www.ratnabooks.in